The Venetian Contract

The Venetian Contract

MARINA FIORATO

JOHN MURRAY

First published in Great Britain in 2012 by John Murray (Publishers)
An Hachette UK Company

1

Text and illustrations © Marina Fiorato 2012

A CIP catalogue record for this title is available from the British Library

ISBN 978-1-84854-565-6
Ebook ISBN 978-1-84854-566-3

Typeset in Dante by Servis Filmsetting Ltd, Stockport, Cheshire

Printed and bound in Australia by Griffin Press

The paper this book is printed on is certified against the
Forest Stewardship Council® Standards. Griffin Press holds
FSC chain of custody certification SGS-COC-005088. FSC
promotes environmentally responsible, socially beneficial and
economically viable management of the world's forests.

John Murray (Publishers)
338 Euston Road
London NW1 3BH

www.johnmurray.co.uk

To Ileen Maisel,
who first suggested that I write about Palladio

When the Lamb opened the fourth seal, I heard the voice of the fourth living creature say, 'Come and see!' I looked and there before me was a pale horse! Its rider was named Death, and Hades was following close behind him. They were given power over a fourth of the earth to kill by sword, famine and plague, and by the wild beasts of the earth.

REVELATION 6:7–8

PART I

The Black Horse

PROLOGUE

Venice

Christian Year 1576

S ebastiano Venier, Doge of Venice, gazed from the stone quatrefoil window, with eyes that were as troubled as the ocean.

His weather-eye, sharpened by many years at sea, had seen the storm approaching for three days, clotting and clouding on the horizon and rolling in across the sickly amethyst waves. Now the maelstrom was here, and it had brought with it something more malign than ill weather.

With his flowing white beard and noble countenance, the Doge had been immortalized by Tintoretto and been compared to Neptune who also ruled a seabound kingdom. He had even, in hushed tones, been compared to the Almighty. A profoundly devout man, the Doge would have been deeply troubled, for different reasons, by each comparison; but today he would have given anything to have the omnipotence to save Venice from her darkest hour.

He watched as six figures, huddled together against the elements, hurried along a dock already glazed with water at every flow of the tide, the ebb tugging at the hems of their black robes. The cloaks and cowls gave them a monastic look, but these six men were men of science, not religion. They dealt in life and death. They were doctors.

As they drew closer he could see their masks clearly;

bone-white beaks curving in a predatory hook from the dark cowls. The masks were frightening enough, but the reason for them even more ominous.

They were his *Medico delle Peste*. Plague doctors.

They were six scholars, men of letters from good families, all schooled at the best medical academies, one for each of the six *sestieri* of Venice. To see the Doctors together was an ill omen. Doge Sebastiano Venier doubted that they had ever even met together before; and they seemed to him to swoop like a murder of crows at a graveside. Perhaps his own. His shoulders dropped for an instant; he felt very old.

He watched the doctors wade along the peerless Riva degli Schiavoni, one of the most wondrous streets in the world, and knew that any minute now they would enter his great white palace. The Doge's skin chilled as if sea-spray had doused him. He leaned his head against the cool quarrels of glass, and shut his eyes for one blessed instant. If he hadn't done so, he might have seen a Venetian galleass sailing swiftly away on the dark and swelling waters; but he did close his eyes for a couple of heartbeats, just to be still and breathe in the salt ether.

The smell of Venice.

Sebastiano Venier straightened up, reminding himself who he was, where he was. He looked at the delicate stonework of his windows, the finest Venetian glazing keeping the thunder of the sea from his ears. He looked up, tilting his noble head to the ceiling and the peerless frescoes of red and gold painted over hundreds of years by the finest Venetian artists, covering the cavernous, glorious space above. And yet, all the riches and the glory could not keep the Pestilence from his door.

The Doge settled in his great chair and waited for the

doctors to be announced. They filed in, dripping, and semi-circled him like vultures, the red crystal eyepieces set into their masks glittering hungrily, as if ready to peck the very flesh of him. But the moment they began to speak, the Doge ceased to be afraid of them.

'We had expected it, my lord,' said one. 'In the botanical gardens of the *Jesuiti*, there have been of late unusual numbers of butterflies – hundreds upon thousands of them.'

The Doge raised a single, winter-white brow. 'Butterflies?'

The doctor, failing to register the steel in the Doge's tone, prattled on. 'Why, Doge, butterflies are well known to be harbingers of pestilence.'

'It is true,' chimed in another. 'There have been other signs too. There is a bakery in the Arsenale, and when you tear the loaves in twain, the bread itself begins to bleed.'

The Doge rapped his fingertips on the arm of his chair. 'The fact that the pestilence has arrived in Venice is not a matter for debate. The *question* is, how to best treat the Plague.'

It was no use. One physician wanted to combat the pestilence by advising his patients to wear a dead toad around the neck. The next advised backing a live pigeon into the patients' swollen buboes in the groin and armpit, so that the tail feathers could draw out the poison. They began to talk over one another, their beaks almost clashing, the masks now ridiculous; the doctors' learned, mellow voices raised in pitch until they were quacking like so many ducks.

The Doge, irritated, found his attention wandering. These physicians were charlatans, buffoons, each one more self-important than the next. His eyes drifted to the shadow of an arras, where a man, an old man like himself, stood listening; waiting for the moment when the Doge would call him forth, and tell him why he had been summoned.

The old man in the shadows – who happened to be an architect – was not really listening either. Always more interested in buildings than people, he was admiring how the stone cross ribs above his head described the curve of the ceiling, and how the proportions of the pilasters complemented the great panels of the frescoes.

Like the Doge, he had felt an initial jag of fear when he had seen the doctors enter the room. Everyone, from the Doge to the meanest beggar, knew what the masks meant. The Plague was in the city. But the architect was not overly concerned. There had been a minor outbreak of Plague two years ago, and he would do now what he'd done then. He would leave the city and go into the Veneto; perhaps back to his old home, Vicenza. There, in the hills, he would wait and plan and draw. He would sip wine while he waited for the Plague to slake its own thirst. With a fast boat to Mestre and a faster horse to Treviso, he could be at Maser by sunset, at the house of his good friends the Barbaro brothers. There would be room at their house, he knew it; after all, he had built it. As soon as he had found out what the Doge willed he would be gone.

The Doge had heard enough. These doctors could not help Venice. They would dispense their potions and remedies, make gold along the way, and some citizens would live and some would die. He grasped his chair until his knuckles whitened and as he looked down in despair. His own hands depressed him – gnarled and veined and liverspotted. How could an old man hold back the Plague?

He cleared his throat. He must act. He could not let his legacy be to allow this jewel of a city to be blasted by pestilence. The Doge's old heart quickened. He got to his feet, his blood rushing to his head. 'You are dismissed,' he said to the doctors, slightly too loudly. 'Get out.' He flapped his arms as if to scare them away like the crows they were. He waited till the doors had closed behind them. 'Andrea Palladio,' the Doge said, his tones ringing out in the great chamber, 'come forth.'

Palladio stepped from the shadows, and walked to stand before the Doge's great chair. The wind rattled at the casements, bidding to be let in, bringing its passenger the pestilence with it. Palladio fidgeted, anxious, now, to be gone; but the Doge, his anger spent, had taken his seat again, and seemed in a reflective mood.

'Have you heard of the miracle of Saint Sebastian of Giudecca?'

Palladio frowned slightly. Although he had never met the Doge before, he knew of him by repute; a sea lord of forty years standing, deeply devout, respected, and intelligent enough to have avoided the Republic's dreadful prisons through many successive councils of The Ten. Had Sebastiano Venier come to the greatest office too late? Was his mind now addled? Through the windows he could see the island of Giudecca, battered by rain, but still one of the most beautiful *sestieri* of Venice, curving round the back of the old city like a spine. 'Yes, of course.' He answered slowly, wondering where the question tended. The Doge began to speak again, as if telling a tale or preaching a parable.

'In the grip of the last great Plague in 1464, a young soldier came to the gates of the monastery of Santa Croce on Giudecca and called out for water. The sisters were all within, the Lady Abbess herself suffering from the pestilence. The *portonera*, one Sister Scholastica, came to the gate. When she cast her eyes on the young man she saw he had armour of shining silver, hair of golden fire and eyes of sapphire blue. Awed, she passed him a cup of water on the convent's wheel, and he drank. The vision thanked Scholastica and instructed her and all her sisters to pray to Saint Sebastian day and night, and drink of the water of the well. If they did this, the convent would be spared of the Plague. Then he struck his sword to the ground and departed from her, as if no more than a wisp.'

Palladio, who had been wondering how fast he could get to Mestre once the Doge was done, felt prompted by the sudden silence. 'What happened?' he asked.

'The Lady Abbess recovered that night, as did every other nun who was ill. None of the other sisters was touched by the Plague, and all those who drank of the well were saved.' The Doge rose and stepped off his dais. He walked to Palladio and faced him, looking down from his greater height. 'The monastery was a place of pilgrimage for many years, and the people took the waters from the well for the Plague, and later, other ailments. When I was born, four doors away from Santa Croce in the Venier Palace, I was named Sebastiano after this miracle. But now the convent is a ruin.' He fell quiet.

The wind whistled into the silence. Palladio thought he knew, now, what was required of him, and his heart sank. For years he'd wanted to build on Giudecca, an island with good ground of solid rock and some of the best vistas on to the lagoon. For years he'd petitioned the Council of Ten for a site there, to no avail. But now, when all he wanted to do was quit the city, the very thing he wanted most was to be presented to him. Palladio's thin mouth twisted in half a smile. Sometimes he thought that the Almighty had a rich sense of irony. 'And you want me to rebuild the monastery of Santa Croce?'

'No, not precisely that.' The Doge crossed to the window once again. 'Look at them, Andrea.' With a sweep of his gnarled hand he invited Palladio to look down on to the wondrous expanse of Saint Mark's Square. Two prostitutes strolled below the window in their traditional yellow and red, and despite the lashing rain, their breasts were bare and swinging freely as they walked.

Palladio, too old to be moved by such sights, spotted one who was not; a man watched them from the arches of the Procuratie Vecchie, his hand revoltingly busy in his crotch. The watcher beckoned the women into the arch with him, and, as soon as a coin had changed hands he pushed one against one of the noble pillars of the loggia, rutting and thrusting below her bunched skirts. The other woman pushed her hand down the back of his breeches to assist her client's pleasure. 'In the *street*, Andrea,' said the Doge, turning away. 'In the very *street*. That magnificent pillar, constructed by your brother-architect Sansovino to make this square the most beautiful in the world, is now a polly-pole.' He sighed in counterpoint with the wind. 'The licentiousness, the decadence, it is getting worse. Such behaviour used only to manifest itself at Carnevale, for two short weeks of the year. Now such sights are commonplace. We are known for it abroad. Derided. They do not speak of Sansovino's pillars, nor your own villas and churches. They speak of the whores that ply their trade in the streets.' The Doge placed his hand on the window catch, trying it, as if to make sure the miasma was kept out. 'And once word spreads about the city that the Plague is with us, it will be worse. The shadow of death does strange things to a man – he becomes lawless, and he feels he must rut and steal and lie and make coin while he may.'

Palladio was trying to connect the fractured tracks of the Doge's discourse, the miracles and the harlots.

'Only one man can save these wanton, wonderful people from the Plague, and from themselves, and it is not I.'

Palladio thought of the six doctors of the *sestieri*, none of whom seemed to be worthy of the mantle of saviour. Then he realized that the Doge was speaking of Christ, and he arranged his features into an expression of piety. The Doge turned his watery blue eyes upon him. Pale and rheumy, the orbs looked old and defeated. '*You* are that man.'

Palladio's expression of reverence dropped with his jaw.

'Don't you see? God is punishing Venice. We need an offering, a gift so great that we will turn the edge of the divine anger and stay His hand from smiting our city. If medicine cannot help us, then we must turn to prayer. You, Andrea, you will build a church, on the ruins of the convent of Santa Croce. You will work in the footsteps of Saint Sebastian and build a church so wonderful, so pleasing to the glory of God, that it rivals His creation. And when you are done, the people will come, in their hundreds and thousands, and turn to God; they will praise Him with their voices and thank Him upon their knees. The power of prayer will redeem us all.'

Palladio blustered his reluctance. 'But . . . I'd thought,

of course I'd be honoured, but perhaps I could direct operations from Vicenza or maybe Treviso . . .'

The sentence died under the Doge's eye, and the wind whistled in mockery. The Doge let a moment pass before speaking. 'Andrea. We are old men. The time left to us is short. You will stay in Venice, as will I. There is no greater service you can render your city than this. Don't you see?' He took Palladio's shoulders in his hands, with a surprisingly strong grip. 'You are entering into a contract with God himself.'

Palladio remembered that as a young mason he always used to find fossils in the stone that he worked. No day would pass without him finding at least one nautilus, fossilized in its perfect Vitruvian spiral, compressed and entombed for thousands of years in the Carrera marble. And now he was equally trapped: his appointment held him; he was imprisoned, literally, in stone.

He recognized the devotion in the Doge's eyes and knew that Sebastiano Venier would not be gainsaid. How could he ever have thought the Doge's eyes were those of an old man? They blazed now with the blue fire of the zealot, the fire of Saint Sebastian. Even if he'd had the courage to refuse, the proximity of the prisons settled the matter. Palladio bowed his head in silent acquiescence.

The Doge, who had not been anticipating a refusal, called for his chamberlain. '*Camerlengo*, take Signor Palladio to his house – he is to have everything he needs. And, *Camerlengo*,' he called as the chamberlain was about to follow Palladio through the great doors, 'now find me a *real* Doctor.'

Chapter 1

Constantinople, Ottoman Year 983
One Month Earlier

Feyra Adalet bint Timurhan Murad took extra care with her appearance that morning.

Her father had already left the house, so she could not – as she often did – put on *his* clothes. It was common in Constantinople, among the poorer families, for women and men to wear the same; male and female clothing was so similar anyway, and there was often only enough money for one good suit of clothes; for one good pair of shoes. Feyra and her father were not badly off, as Timurhan bin Yunus Murad was a sea captain of good rank and standing, but Feyra still approved of the tradition: it helped her to hide.

Today, her father must have had an appointment of some consequence, and an early one at that; for when Feyra opened the carved lattice shutters of her window she could see that the sun had barely risen over the city. The domes and the minarets that she loved were still only silhouettes, describing a perfect negative contour of darkness bitten out of the coral sky. Feyra breathed in the salt of the ether.

The smell of Constantinople.

She looked out to sea, barely yet a silver line in the dawn light, wondering what lay beyond it. For an instant she felt a yearning for another land, for those places that lived for her only in the stories of a seafaring father.

But Feyra's reverie had cost her time. Turning away from the view, she faced, instead, the rectangle of silver that hung on the wall, edged in enamel and polished to almost perfect reflection, distorted only slightly by the dents of the metal. It had been brought back for her by her father from some Eastern land over some Eastern sea and had hung in her room since she was a baby. As a child the mirror had been a curiosity; it had shown her what colour her eyes were, what her face looked like as she pulled it into odd shapes, how far her tongue could reach when she stuck it out. Now that Feyra was a woman, the mirror was her best friend.

Feyra looked carefully at her reflected self, trying to see what the men saw. When she'd first noticed men staring at her in the street, she had begun to cover her hair. Then they stared at her mouth, so she took to wearing the half-face veil, the *yashmak*. She had even chosen one with sequins at the hem, so that the gold would draw their eyes away from hers. But still they stared, so she switched to the *ormisi,* a thin veil about a hand span in width that was worn over the eyes. When this didn't work she surmised that her body must be attracting the male gaze. She began to bind her budding breasts so tightly that they hurt, and yet still they stared. *Why* did they stare?

Feyra had read enough sonnets and odes of the lovesick to know that she did not confirm to the ideals of the Ottoman poets. Nor did she even resemble the maidens who featured in the bawdy macaroons her father's sailor friends sang; she overheard them, sometimes, when she was in bed and they were downstairs at dinner and had had too much to drink.

Feyra did not consider her amber eyes, large but slightly slanted like a cat's, round and dark enough to be praised in song. Her small, neat nose was too upturned for beauty. Her skin was the colour of coffee, not dusky enough for men to write poems about. Her hair, falling in thick swags and ringlets to her shoulder blades, was not silken and straight enough for the poets, and the colour was wrong too: every shade of tawny brown, not one of them dark enough to be compared to a raven's wing. And her wide, ruddy mouth, strangest of all, with the top lip bigger than the bottom, was a generous shape that could not, in even the most heroic couplet, be compared to a rosebud.

To her, her features – taken separately, taken as a whole – were unremarkable, even odd. But they seemed to have some strange power that she didn't understand, and certainly didn't welcome. Even her disguises had limited efficacy. If she covered her eyes, men looked at her mouth. If she covered her mouth, they stared at her eyes. If she covered her hair, they looked at her figure. But she still had to try, for the inconveniences of her daily disguise were nothing to the consequences of revealing herself.

The Feyra in the looking-glass raised her chin a fraction and the reflection encouraged her. Today she must wear feminine garb; very well, she would make the best of it. She began her ritual.

Wearing only her wide billowing breeches made of transparent silk, Feyra took a long, cream bandage and tucked one end into her armpit. She pulled the material tight to her flesh, round and round her ample chest. When her breasts pained her and her breath felt short, she was grimly happy.

Now it was time for the gown. Feyra's father had brought her gowns of gold and silver satin, brocade, bales of samite and Damascene silk from the four corners of the world. But they lay untouched in a sea chest below the window. Instead she had bought a plain shift dress, a *barami*, in the Bedestan market. The dress fell without folds to the ground, disguising her shape. Next she added the upper gown, the *ferace*, bodice buttoned to the waist after which it was left open.

Then she combed and plaited her hair, coiling it around the top of her head like a crown. She struggled with the curls that crept from her veil by the day's end however hard she tucked them back. Every day she tried to tame them. She placed and tied a veil of thin taminy over her hair, and tied it around the forehead with a braided thread. Then she damped the tendrils around her face with rosewater and pushed them viciously back until not a single strand could be seen.

Over it all she crammed a four-cornered *hotoz* cap, which buttoned under the chin, and a square *yemine* veil to cover her whole face. Then she took a length of plain tulle and wound it around her neck several times. She looked in the mirror again. Effectively swaddled, she was unrecognizable. Her clothes were the hue of sand and cinnamon, designed to blend in to the city and offer her camouflage. The only flare of colour were the yellow slippers of her faith – leather slippers with upturned toes that were fastened over the instep, practical and proof to water and the other more noxious fluids she was wont to encounter in her job.

Dressed at last, she added no ornaments to her apparel. Feyra had gold enough – she had as many trinkets as an indulgent father could provide, but bangles and baubles would draw attention to her – and what was more, interfere with her work.

Feyra's finishing touch was born of utility, not fashion

nor status: a belt, bulky and ugly, an invention of her own. It held a series of little glass bottles and vials, each in an individual leather capsa, all strung together on a broad leather band with a large brass buckle. She strapped the thing beneath her *ferace*, so it was completely hidden at her waist while at the same time making her dumpy in the middle and giving her the silhouette of a woman twice her age.

By the time she was finished, the sun was fully up and the sky had bleached to a birds-egg blue. She allowed herself one more glance at the city she loved, now described in every daylit detail. The heartbreaking curve of the glittering bay, the houses and temples lying like a jewelled collar upon this matchless curve of coastline. Crouching like a sentinel of the Bosphorus was the great temple of the Hagia Sophia, where the Sultan's hawks rose on the thermals from the sunbeaten golden dome. Feyra forgot her moment of yearning; she no longer wanted to know where the sea went. She vowed, instead, that she would never leave this city.

The wailing song of the *muezzin-basi* floated in a sweet, mournful thread from the towers of the Sophia to her ear. *Sabah*, sunrise prayer. Feyra turned and ran, clattering down the stairs.

She was very, very, late.

Chapter 2

In the street it was still cold, the shadows untouched by the sun.

In the normal way this would be Feyra's favourite part of the day – it pleased her to dawdle, greeting the laundry-women carrying their baskets of washing to the bay, or buying a breakfast of *simit* and *salep*, cinnamon bread and root tea, from one of the blue and gold carts that seemed to be on every corner. It pleased her too, to pay with her own coin, for she was a professional, a working woman. Today she had to ignore the growling of her stomach, as she hurried on.

Now and again, as she climbed the hill from Sultanamet to Seraglio point, she would see the brief blue glances of the sea. Today she did not turn, as she did every other morning, to drink her fill of the view. Consequently, she did not notice a Genoese galleass which she would have had no trouble identifying due to her father's schooling, sailing away, cleaving the cobalt waters of the mouth of the Bosphorus.

Feyra kept her eyes front, walked to the top of Mese Avenue and the Topkapi Palace. Set upon the perfect peninsula that was the Seraglio point, jutting out into the ocean where the Golden Horn, the Sea of Marmara and the

Bosphorus met, Topkapi was a small city of itself. The Imperial Gate, as the first point of entry for the visitor, was a powerful architectural assertion of importance, and a hint at the glories within. Between the twin conical towers of the gatehouse, below the golden inscription of past Sultans' wisdom on the architrave (for the new Sultan, Feyra understood, had little wisdom to speak of, let alone inscribe in gold) stood a guard bearing a scroll, the first of many layers of security within the palace.

She didn't know the man and didn't expect to. He would have been drawn by lot this morning in the guard room, for there was a pool of three hundred and fifty-four sentinels of the Sultan, one for every day of the year in the Hicri Takvim calendar. No man could serve twice in a year, and no man knew which his day would be, so that he may not be bribed or coerced to let in an interloper.

'Name?'

'Feyra Adalet bint Timurhan Murad.'

'And what do you do here?'

'I am *Kira* to Nur Banu, the Valide Sultan.' She took a breath. 'And Harem Doctor.'

She watched him, and he behaved exactly as she predicted. He had barely looked up from his vellum when she told him she was a *Kira*, a go-between for the women of the Harem and the outside world. Sometimes the guard of the day would make a moue with their mouth, or raise an eyebrow, when she mentioned the name of Nur Banu, the Valide Sultan, mother of the Sultan and as such the most powerful woman in the palace, in Constantinople and in the Ottoman world. But all of them, without exception, reacted with surprise when she told them she was a doctor.

Only twenty-one, she had been distributing medicine and

performing minor operations for years. She had begun, at the age of thirteen, carrying medicines from the palace doctor from the main part of the palace to the Harem. She would meet the physician in the Hall of the Ablution Fountain, a beautiful courtyard which marked the limit of how far a man could pass into the Harem complex. At that age her task was merely to listen carefully to his directions resounding in the mosaicked atrium, parrot them back to him in competition with the echo, bow and walk down the Hall of the Concubines to the Harem proper.

As she became older Feyra was sent out of the palace to the market to buy herbs and compounds from the Grand Bazaar. There she would wander the crowded alleys, feeling the acrid, sweet and spicy smells gather in her nose as she bought the alien bottles and packages back to Topkapi. She began to pay attention and quickly learned to appreciate the workings of the medicines. As the years passed and as the doctor passed his prime and Feyra approached hers, their relationship subtly changed and she would begin to adjust the amounts he had directed. Sometimes she would substitute different herbs; some medicines the doctor prescribed never reached their patients. The ladies of the Harem had never been healthier. By now, Feyra knew precisely how to treat the women, but she still made her daily walk to the middle court, as a matter of courtesy. The doctor, now well into his dotage, concerned himself with the main palace and the Sultan himself; he trusted Feyra to take care of most of the ailments of the two hundred or more women in the Harem. He had even, two years before and with the blessing of the old Sultan, conferred upon her the title she now used with pride. The doctor barely came to the middle court any more, so she was surprised once she'd finally reached the Hall of the Ablution Fountain, to find him waiting for her.

He seemed agitated and was wringing his hands. He looked old and small in this incredible setting, where once he would have stood tall. His name was Haji Musa, and he had once been respected for his surgical methods and medical writings throughout the world. Now the vast archway diminished him; the fine Kütahya tiles in watery greens and blues and whites gave his flesh a sickly hue, and the spouting fountain drowned his quavering voice so that Feyra had to ask him to repeat himself.

'I beg your pardon, Teacher?'

'Nur Banu Sultan,' he said, his querulous tones rising above the fountain. 'She is ill. So ill that they called me from the Second Court.' He raised a shaking forefinger and waved it before her veil. 'Listen to me, Feyra, never forget that Nur Banu is the Sultan's mother. You will never treat a more exalted patient.'

Feyra felt impatient. She was already late. She didn't see why Haji Musa was so agitated; after all, she had treated her mistress many times before. She bowed, as she had done that first time before him as a thirteen-year-old girl. Then she had been showing obedience. Now she was showing him that she wished to go.

He saw it at once. 'Report to me. I'll be waiting. Blessings be upon the Sultan.'

Feyra straightened. 'For he is the light of my eyes and the delight of my heart.'

As she uttered the automatic rejoinder she was already turning to the women's quarters. As she hurried away she was aware of the doctor patting and adjusting his turban as if the traditional blessing upon the Sultan had rattled him.

The reputation of the new Sultan was frightening enough in the ordinary way – if something was to befall his mother, his rage would be incendiary. She knew that Haji Musa was afraid for his head, and hoped that it would still be upon his shoulders at sundown.

Feyra hurried to the inner court and through the gates of the Harem. Here there was no interrogation – two of the black eunuchs opened the doors for her and she barely acknowledged them. She walked the Golden Way, where concubines were once showered with coins, straight to the quarters of Nur Banu and opened another door to the inner chamber. The large airy room, lined with incredible blue *Iznik* mosaic, had a small open court with a fountain, and a dais with a bed upon it. From the threshold Feyra could already hear cries.

She was met at the door by the Kelebek, Nur Banu's *Gedik*, her lady-in-waiting. 'Blessings be upon the Sultan, Feyra.'

Kelebek, a plain woman among all this beauty, was clearly agitated, but still observed protocol. Feyra was too flustered to reply formally. She was not, yet, truly worried about Nur Banu's condition – the Valide Sultan suffered occasionally with a malady of the stomach which gave her much bloating and pain, but an emetic of Feyra's own making usually settled matters within the hour. Feyra was more concerned that her tardiness had bought her trouble. She saw a silver dish on the nightstand, piled high with iced fruit, and her own stomach grumbled, reminding her that she had not eaten. The grapes, tumbling down from the dish, tempted her with their green globes. She reached out to pluck one, but another moan sounded from the bed and she pulled her hand back. 'Has she been asking for me?'

'No. She asks for Cecilia Baffo.'

'Who is Cecilia Baffo?'

'We don't know. None of us know.' Kelebek swept her hand to indicate the Odalisques, the concubines-in-training for the Sultan's bed. Five young women, all beautiful, all dressed in white shifts, all of them biting their lips or looking at the floor. Unschooled and unlettered as they were, they knew there was something wrong.

Feeling a sickly foreboding Feyra climbed the steps of the dais and drew back the fine embroidered muslin curtains of the Valide Sultan's bed.

The Sultan's mother lay twisted on the bed, her eyes half closed, her skin an unnatural hue, somewhere between the colour of bone and bile. Her veins stood out knotted on her throat, black and blue as if a mandrake was grown about her neck. Her cheeks, normally plump and pink, were drawn in dark hollows, and her eyes seemed painted beneath with violet shadows. The blonde hair was damp and lank, dark with sweat and plastered to her forehead. Nur Banu was a woman of perhaps fifty, and pleasantly fleshy, her skin usually pale as a foreigner's, but now her skin beneath her jewelled shift looked pouchy, livid and mottled, and instead of being pleasantly rounded the flesh was sunken and loose, as if a bladder had been popped and deflated. The cries had ceased and Nur Banu was, it seemed, asleep.

Feyra took the Valide Sultan's wrist where the blood passed and her mistress, at the pressure, moved, moaned and spoke, calling out, in the accents of another tongue, 'Cecilia Baffo. Cecilia Baffo.'

Nur Banu's voice, usually low and musical, was now the rasp of a crow. Her eyes flew open, shot with blood and milky. But she seemed to recognize Feyra. She said the girl's name, clasped her close, and spoke in a language that only Feyra knew – Nur Banu's own language, a language that lilted and bounced as if it had hoofbeats, a language where every word seemed to end in in an *a* or an *o*. The Valide Sultan had taught this language – Phoenician, she called it – to Feyra since she was a little girl visiting the palace with her father. It had become a language of secrets between them, used for the Valide Sultan's most private business, and she used it now. 'You must tell him. Tell him, Feyra, you and only you.'

Feyra thought she understood. She turned to Kelebek, now afraid. 'We must tell the doctor and get word to the Sultan.'

'No!' The Valide Sultan sat up, suddenly wide awake and fearful. 'Cecilia Baffo. Cecilia Baffo. Four Horsemen; riding, riding. *Come and see.*' Nur Banu's breath was foul, and a thread of bile-coloured spittle dropped from her chin. Feyra soothed her, shushing her and stroking her cheek like a child until her mistress seemed to sleep fitfully once more.

Feyra retreated through the curtain and closed it behind her, beckoning Kelebek to her. 'Cecilia Baffo,' Feyra murmured. 'Who is she? And who are the Four Horsemen?'

Kelebek shrugged. 'My lady was brought here many years ago, by corsairs who captured her. Could there have been four of them?'

'Perhaps. But what of the name? Who is Cecilia Baffo?'

'I don't know!' Kelebek's voice was shrill with anxiety.

Feyra thought. 'Describe to me my lady's day, precisely, from sun-up.'

Kelebek knitted her fingers together. 'She woke and directed that we dress her in her jewelled bedgown, for she was to have company.'

Feyra narrowed her eyes. It was not against protocol for the Valide Sultan, a widow after all, to take a lover, but Feyra had not known her mistress lie with a man since the death of her husband Selim Sultan, two years ago. 'Who? A man?'

'No. She said she was to break her fast with the Dogaressa of Genoa, before the Genoese ship sailed on the morning tide.'

'Has the ship now sailed?'

'Moments ago.'

'Cecilia Baffo.' Feyra mused aloud. 'It is a foreign-sounding name. Could be Genoese. What is the Genoese Dogaressa called? Can someone find out?'

'How, Feyra?' Capable enough in the ordinary way, Kelebek reverted, in crisis, to her village girl origins.

Feyra was suddenly impatient with her peasant ways. '*Ask* someone,' she snapped. 'The Kizlar Agha.'

Kelebek's eyes widened in fear – the Kizlar Agha, master of the girls and chief of the Black Eunuchs, was the Sultan's deputy in the Harem who administered justice in these walls. This current Agha, Beyazid, was a fearsome basilisk of a man; seven feet tall with ebony skin. If a girl displeased the Sultan, if perhaps she found the Sultan's tastes too adventurous, she was sewn into a sack and Beyazid person-ally threw her from the ramparts of the Tower of Justice into the Bosphorus. The girls were forced to gather and watch as the sack darkened with water and sank below the surface, to listen to the screams of the victim, to witness the consequences of disobedience. At the sound of the Kizlar Agha's name, Kelebek took a pace backward. 'I cannot ask him, Feyra.'

Feyra sighed testily. She feared the Agha as much as

Kelebek did, but she feared what might be happening to her mistress more. She left the room and crossed the Courtyard of the Concubines. The sun was fully up, and as she turned right into the Courtyard of the Black Eunuchs the shadows under the marble columns were deep and dark, and the sun's rays refracted through the wrought iron lamps hanging above, splitting them into diamonds, dazzling her. When she knocked and entered the Kizlar Agha's chamber, she briefly could not see at all.

Slowly Feyra's eyes began to adjust. She was in a long room with two streams of water running in marble channels set into the floor. The little light that silvered the streams came from stars cut into the stone ceiling, so that shafts of bleached sun fell in geometric shapes on the floor like paper cutouts. Feyra stepped between the shafts, as if it were a trial by light. She could almost have been alone in the room; Beyazid's skin was polished ebony, black as the chair he sat in, but he smoked a hookah pipe that issued baby clouds as he spoke. The smoke gathered about his head and was illuminated in the star shafts.

'Feyra, Timurhan's daughter? What do you want of me?

Beyazid, it seemed, had no trouble seeing her. 'O Kizlar Agha, what is the name of the Genoese Dogaressa who broke her fast with my lady Nur Banu Sultan?'

Now Feyra could make out his form, massive even in repose, his arm muscles bulging and shortening beneath their gold bands as he carried the hookah to his mouth, the false starlight silvering his bald head. 'Her name is Prospera Centurione Fattinanti.' His tones, for a man of such bulk, were high and clear like a boy's; for he had been unmanned before adulthood. The strange contradiction of voice and physique did not make him any less threatening. He breathed out another cloud. 'Is that all?'

'Yes, Kizlar Agha.' Feyra turned, then turned back with a courage she did not know she had. 'That is, no. Who is Cecilia Baffo?'

She saw two crescents of white as his eyes opened a fraction in what seemed an involuntary impulse of recognition. For a moment, she was afraid. But the eyes closed again. 'I know not. Now leave me. Blessings be upon the Sultan.'

'For he is the light of my eyes and the delight of my heart.'

Feyra left the darkness and walked back through the bright courtyard, reluctant to return to what she would find. But in the Valide Sultan's chamber it was as if the sun had risen there too. Kelebek was smiling, the Odalisques were twittering like so many white doves, and the mood had noticeably lightened. *Come and see,* invited Kelebek.

Feyra pulled the muslin curtains of the bed aside once again. Nur Banu sat up against her pillows, the knotted venous cords gone from her throat, her eyes bright, her cheeks ruddy. Her eyes were shadowed with no more than the liner that she always wore, painted on daily with a brush no bigger than a gilder's tip. She greeted Feyra, and Feyra was suffused with relief. She sat on the bed beside the Valide Sultan with a familiarity afforded to only her, and took Nur Banu's wrist once again. This time the pulse beat strong and regular, and Feyra moved her fingers up to clasp her mistress's hand. Nur Banu smiled at her. 'Feyra? What's amiss?'

'Mistress, how are you?'

Nur Banu laughed, a genuine spurt of mirth. Usually Feyra loved the sound, but today it sounded wrong, like a discord on a zither. 'Me? I have never been better. Bring my writing materials, Feyra. Then call for my breakfast and tell the Eunuchs to ready my barge – shall we sail to Pera today? The day is fair. Can you spare time from your doctoring?'

Feyra bowed in acquiescence but was troubled. The change in Nur Banu was so complete that Feyra began to believe that she had imagined that brief, dreadful illness. But Kelebek had been here too, and the Odalisques. She hesitated. 'Mistress, when I came here, not one hour ago, you were insensible, your looks were dire, you were sleeping and waking fitfully and crying out.'

Nur Banu's plump, kind face looked at her quizzically. 'Feyra, what are you talking about?'

'You do not recall?'

Feyra's dread returned as she examined her mistress closely. The bright eyes, sparkling like brilliants. The bloom of too-livid colour on the cheeks. The blonde hair now curling damply around the face like a halo. The complete absence of memory of the episode that had gone before.

Feyra turned and looked about her. She walked down the dais again and her eyes lighted on the iced fruit sitting innocently on the marquetry table. She drew the *Gedik* to her. 'Kelebek,' she hissed sharply in the girl's ear. 'Did my lady take any food or drink this morning?'

'Not yet. But it is still early . . . She has eaten nothing but a little fruit that the Dogaressa brought her.'

'Did anyone taste it first?'

Kelebek's eyes were as round and green as the grapes. 'Why, no, Feyra; you were not here. But I thought it would be all right; it was a gift from the Dogaressa, she is a friend of my mistress's heart – a beautiful lady!'

Feyra approached the abundant bowl of fruit, her feet heavy with dread. The ice pooling in the silver bowl crackled slightly in protest as it melted. Her eye was captured once again by the grapes. They looked delicious, tumbling over the edge of the bowl: round, and glittering with a bloom of dew. For the second time in as many moments Feyra thought that something had too much colour in it.

She picked a grape from its stalk and broke it open with her fingernail. She walked to the window and held the ruptured fruit to the sun. There, nestling in the jade heart of the grape, was a dark clot where the seed should have been. She gouged out the clot and spread it on a white tessera of mosaic on the windowsill. Then she reached for her medicine belt and pulled out an eye-glass with a brass surround which she fitted in her eye. She peered and poked at the black smear. She could see, once the clot was spread, a collection of tiny seeds, each one the shape of a star anise. Her stomach plunged.

Poison.

Not just any poison but the like of which she had seen only once before. Haji Musa had once intercepted an attempt on the old Sultan's life, poison found in a gift of a jug of English ale. The doctor had shown her the star-shaped spores, taken from the fruit of the Bartholomew tree found in the hills around Damascus, and told her to take care; for the spores were one of the deadliest poisons known to man, tasteless, odourless, and with no antidote. The victim would feel the ill effects for half of one hour, then recover once as if healthful again, and after this would deteriorate rapidly as the spores multiplied in the organs, crowding the liver and lights, pulping the innards to mulch.

Fascinated by such a powerful poison, Feyra had begged a lame merlin from the Sultan's falconers and fed the hawk some of the spores. He greedily pecked them down. Then Feyra sat on the stone floor of the Topkapi mews and watched him. For half an hour he had fallen to the floor and rolled and flapped, squawking in distress. Feyra watched, dispassionately, then the bird had miraculously recovered. For the following hour the merlin had been well, and lively; even his foot seemed no longer lame. But before Feyra's legs had stiffened on the stone floor he had fallen over once again and turned black, glass-eyed and gasping until she had picked him up and wrung his neck. He lay in her hand, warm and surprisingly light, his head dangling. For a moment Feyra had felt a misgiving; this hawk would never rise above the dome of the Sophia again. Then she had hardened her heart and sliced him open, there and then on the pavings with a scalpel from her belt to discover his innards black with spores, his organs riven and pulped, indistinguishable from each other, the viscera as one.

Feyra thought quickly, running in her mind through all the remedies she knew, everything she carried in her belt. Nothing would help. If she'd been here, God above, if she'd only been here when the grapes had been eaten there might have been something. She had some tallow beads in one of the little glass vials, which, if chewed, would induce instant, violent vomiting above and purging below. But even then, by the time the symptoms manifested themselves, by that first initial illness, it was already too late. And besides, Feyra thought grimly, as Kelebek had reminded her; if she *had* been here, as Nur Banu's *Kira*, she would have tasted the grapes and would now be waiting for her own death too.

Feyra thought for a moment. It was too late for her mistress – now it was all about who she could save. The Odalisques were all beauties, all virgins, they all had material value to the Sultan. The Odalisques would be left alone. 'Leave us, all of you,' she snapped to them, and watched them exit.

Kelebek remained, Kelebek who was plain and five-and-twenty. Feyra saw in her mind's eye a sack darkening with water, being pulled down until Kelebek's screams were silenced in a bubbling final cry. Feyra strode to the window where a gold filigree box caught at the filaments of the morning sun. She snatched off her headscarf and wrapped the box around and around, till there was not one telltale glimmer. She thrust it in the girl's hands. 'Kelebek, take this box and –' she rummaged in her breeches '– three *dirham*. Take a boat to Pera. Where is your father's house?'

'Edirne.'

'Sell the box at Pera and buy a mule and ride it there. Ride all the way to Edirne, and don't stop. Then have your father find you a nice man from the village and marry him. Your time at Topkapi is over.'

'What do you mean?'

'The Valide Sultan is going to die, and you gave her poisoned fruit.'

Kelebek began to tremble. 'How . . . but I didn't . . . I didn't *know* . . .' Her head weaved from side to side, and she moaned, as she struggled with this information. 'Can you not . . . there must be . . . have you nothing in your medicine belt to aid her?' For Kelebek, and the concubines too, Feyra's belt was nothing short of miraculous, a panacea for all illnesses, cures brought forth from each little stoppered bottle. Feyra looked the girl in the eyes and shook her head.

It was enough. Kelebek took the box and hurried away.

Feyra leapt back up the stairs to the bed and tore back the

curtain. Fear made her strident. 'Who is Cecilia Baffo?' she demanded.

Nur Banu Sultan, relaxed on her embroidered pillows, laughed again; but this time it was a nervous, false trill. 'I've really no idea, Feyra. Now, please get my writing materials.' But Feyra did not budge. Her mistress had not known that she had been ill, had not remembered those dreadful few minutes when she twisted and writhed in her coverlet, but she knew very well who Cecilia Baffo was.

Feyra sat down on the bed, unbidden, and looked Nur Banu Sultan full in the eyes. She spoke very clearly, and a little loudly. 'Listen to me, mistress. The grapes the Dogaressa left you were poisoned with the spores of the Bartholomew tree. When you first ingest the spores, for half of an hour, you feel dreadfully sick, as if death is at your door. Then, very quickly, you feel better. Your skin has a bloom on it, your eyes sparkle. You have no memory of what has happened to you. Your body is fighting the spores, and your humours even find some benefit in them from the opiates within the poison. You will feel, for an hour or so, better that you have ever felt. I will order you some goat's milk and some hard tack bread to slow the absorption. But soon, very soon, you will feel worse again, much worse, and soon after that you will not be able to speak. Knowing this now, is there anything you wish to say? Something you want to tell me? Do you have any messages for your son, bequests to your family, directions for your interment? Or,' she said with significance, 'the identity of Cecilia Baffo?'

The Valide Sultan drew herself up on her pillows, her eyes flashing. 'I will say that goat's milk and hard tack be damned. What nonsense, to speak of death on such a golden day! I will have my breakfast, Feyra. And the

Genoese Dogaressa is my friend. I will hear no more of this nonsense.'

Feyra nodded. 'I know at present you do not believe me, and I understand you. Your spirits feel well, your body tingles with health. But it will not last and there is no antidote. The poison is tasteless and takes some time to work, so even your taster, had she been on time –' here she mumbled shamefacedly, '– would not have saved you. As a judicial poison it cannot be rivalled. And that is why, I suppose, the Genoese favour it so. I must leave you now, and wait for your body to tell you what I cannot.'

Nur Banu Sultan opened her mouth to shout but Feyra stood her ground braced for battering. The Valide Sultan's anger could be great, and she could be as fearsome as she was kind. Feyra had never, in all her years of service, had the rough side of the Sultana's tongue, but she understood. No one wanted to accept that they were dying.

She had seen all the reactions in her years as a Harem doctor; denial, anger, dread. Some broke down at once and pleaded for a cure. She had had to tell women with a canker on the breast or the womb that death was coming for them, but that it could take weeks or months or years. But her mistress would be dead by noon, and that was something it was impossible to comprehend. Bracing herself for a blast of recrimination, she knew that it was futile to stay. The Valide Sultan had to come to terms with the truth and then put her affairs in order in the short time she had left. At last Feyra thought of something to say. Feeling as if she were throwing a stone into a storm, she said quietly, when Nur Banu paused for breath, 'Cecilia Baffo.' At the sound of the name, Nur Banu fell silent, breathing heavily. 'When you were in your greatest suffering, and did not know what you said, you asked not for your son, nor for me, but for Cecilia Baffo. She is clearly very important to you.' Feyra knelt by the bed. 'Time is short, mistress. If you want me to find her, or get a message to her, tell me now.' She got to her feet again. 'Only think of this. I have *never* lied to you. But *you* have lied to *me*. You know who Cecilia Baffo is.' Feyra spoke with utter certainty. 'And when you are ready to tell me, I will be in the Samahane.'

She hurried down the steps from the dais, tore open the door and found the five Odalisques crowded eavesdropping at the keyhole. 'Attend your mistress,' she snapped, and she walked out of the room and away, on swift slippers, until she could no longer hear Nur Banu's angry calls.

Feyra walked through the quiet courts to the Samahane, the ritual hall. She entered and climbed to the mezzanine, for women were forbidden to attend the rituals. She seated herself beneath one of the ornamental arches and drew the silken curtain behind her. She needed time and space to think.

She peered down over the balustrade. The Mevlevi order – the Dervishes – were whirling. Nine of the order revolved around their priest in the centre of the group, white skirts flying out to a perfect circle, tall brown hats seemingly motionless, forming their central axis as they turned. Their feet spun almost noiselessly on the tiled floor of the Samahane, pattering gently like rain.

Feyra fell into a trance, her thoughts pattering in her head like the soft footsteps of the Dervishes as they turned. She knew the symbolism of the order's attire – their white robes were the colour of death, and their tall brown hats, like an elongated Fez, represented a tombstone. Their apparel brought them closer to the afterlife, to the other side. *White for death*, she thought, *and brown for the tomb-stone*. The Dervishes were harbingers of death. Nur Banu would soon be wrapped in a white shroud and buried in the crypt with a stone at her head.

Feyra's legs grew stiff, and her arms ached where they rested on the stone balustrade. What would become of her? Would she be pursued and imprisoned because she had been too late to taste the deadly fruit before the Valide Sultan ate it? Because she could then not cure her mistress of her malady? Should she run, like Kelebek? And what of her father? Could he intercede for her with the Sultan? Or should they run together? Would he sail her across that sea she had wondered about, only this morning?

Feyra was suddenly visited by a vivid memory, as bright and over-coloured as the fruit and her mistress had been. She saw, as clear as day, herself as a six-year-old-child, out-side her father's door, playing in the dust with her friends. One of the boys had a top, and he spun it for what seemed like infinity. Feyra had seen magic in it, as it hung there, barely moving, held by some invisible celestial force. Then, at last, the stillness broke into a tremor, then a wobble, before the white top fell into the dust to skitter away between the children's feet. Feyra captured it and spun it once, twice, until she had the trick of it; and while it spun round its still centre it held her gaze; she and the top unmoving, fascinated that something could move so much that it became still. The other children melted away in search of another game, bored, but Feyra stayed, watching; waiting with excitement and something akin to dread.

Now, fourteen years later, she understood that seed of dread. She had been waiting for the top to fall, wanting it but dreading it too, hoping with some small fibre of will that the top would spin for ever; knowing that it would not. Now she watched the Dervishes, waiting for one of them to fall, until she heard the rasp of the curtain being drawn behind her. She turned to see one of the Odalisques, and knew what she would say before the girl spoke. *'Come and see.'*

As she rose, stiff in every sinew, Feyra turned back once, to the Dervishes.

They were still spinning. It was Nur Banu who had fallen.

Chapter 3

'I am Cecilia Baffo.'
Feyra was seated on Nur Banu's bed. The Valide Sultan looked weak, and her pale skin was darker than ever, the veins mottling. The poison was gaining on her. Feyra might have thought her mistress was raving, but she was still alert and lucid. Feyra shook her head in confusion.

'What do you mean?'

The Valide Sultan tried to raise herself up a little on her pillows. 'What do you know of me?'

Feyra parroted what she had heard from Kelebek. 'You were captured by corsairs and brought here to the Sultan Selim, may he rest in the light of Paradise.' Feyra knew that Turkish horsemen were feared the world over; supreme in battle, descending from the hillsides upon their enemy ululating like banshees.

'Captured by corsairs.' Nur Banu gave a small smile. 'Yes, that is my legend. *Captured by corsairs*; but this is not the half, the quarter, no, not the slightest piece of my history.'

'I thought I knew everything,' said Feyra, bewildered, for they had shared so many secrets over the years.

'Speak to me in our tongue.'

Feyra knew her mistress meant Phoenician. If they were to speak in that tongue, she was about to hear a great secret.

Greater than the time when Nur Banu had concealed her husband Selim's death from the world for three days until their son and heir, the current Sultan, could be recalled from the provinces. Greater than the times when Feyra had helped her mistress divert money from the treasury, and take caskets of money to put in the hands of the architect Mimar Sinan who was building a mosque in Nur Banu's name. Greater than all the times when Feyra had arranged meetings between Nur Banu and her allies from various nations around the world, to oppose or attenuate her rash son's policies.

'I find Phoenician difficult.'

'Feyra. Not Phoenician: *Venetian*.'

A word misheard as a little girl was now the password that opened a map for Feyra. Her mouth opened too.

Nur Banu exhaled in a long sigh. 'Yes, I am Venetian. I have allowed everyone to forget it. I have almost forgotten it myself. But when I lived in that life, I was Cecilia Baffo, daughter of Nicolò Venier.'

'*Venier?*' Feyra uttered the name that was a curse in Constantinople.

Nur Banu caught the intonation. 'Yes. My uncle is Sebastiano Venier, Admiral of Lepanto and Doge of Venice.'

No wonder the general population had been allowed to forget this. The Venetians had been enemies to the Turks for centuries, had taken their gold, raped their women, and even desecrated the graves of their Sultans. Mehmet II's crown had been taken from his tomb by Venetian marauders with the hairs still attached. And worst of all, most reviled of these pirate conquerors, was Sebastiano Venier, the figurehead on the warship that was Venice. The Doge's reputation was trampled daily in the pamphlets sold on street corners and his image burned in the alleys. Since he had crushed the Ottoman fleet a few short years ago at the Battle of Lepanto, the Sultan and all his people breathed revenge day and night.

'Yes. You will have noticed my son holds no love for me. He thinks my policies are pro-Venetian, that I have a partiality for my old home. And he is right.' The Valide Sultan looked from the window with eyes that now saw a different view. 'Oh Feyra, have you ever seen a city that floats on the sea? Have you ever seen towers that reach like spears instead of crouching in domes; have you seen a blade that is straight and not curved? Have you ever seen glass that glows like a jewel and palaces where hard stone is rendered as delicate as lace? Now my son plots the worst of all things against Venice, and only you can prevent it.'

'*Me?*'

'Yes, Feyra, you. You are my *Kira*; you go between me and the world. But the world is bigger than this city. I'm going to send you on the hardest errand of all.'

'Why me?'

'To understand that you must know my history. I was born Cecilia Baffo, daughter of Nicholas Venier and Violante Baffo. My father was Lord of Paros, governor of the thousand small islands off the coast of Greece called the Cyclades, under the rule of the Republic of Venice. Although I lived, at that time in Venice, I was staying on the islands with my father in the summer of 1555 – 962 by our reckoning.'

Twenty-one years ago, thought Feyra. Before she herself was born. 'And it was there that you were captured?'

'In one sense, yes. There was a great Masque held at our palace at Paros, to celebrate my betrothal. I was to be given to Ridolfo Falieri, a man of great wealth, and on the night that I was given to him, I fell in love.'

'So he was a good man?'

'Not at all. He was old and cruel and crabbed with age – the match purely dynastic. No, I did not fall in love with *him*. There was a sea captain at the Masque, a young protégé of the Sultan, whose ship was moored at the island to pick up supplies. Within the space of one hour I had given myself to him. The corsairs were his crew; we took my father's horses and rode to the shore, but I went willingly. I wanted to put the sea between myself and Ridolfo, true; but I could not bear that the captain should sail away without me.'

Feyra pleated the sheets between her fingers. 'It was my father that you loved.' It was a statement, not a question.

'It was your father,' her mistress confirmed. She looked at Feyra closely. 'And by the time we reached Constantinople, I was with child.'

Feyra went still. She could see that her mistress was beginning to have difficulty speaking; she could hear the slur in the words. She barely dared breathe. She needed to hear this next part.

'Oh, Feyra, I was not careful, like you are. I see the way you dress yourself, the pains you take to hide your light. I was not chary. I walked in Sultanamet in my fine Venetian gowns, blooming with my love and with my child, my face uncovered, my hair dressed in ringlets. I was handsome then, Feyra, I had golden hair and pearly skin and sea-coloured eyes. One day as I walked back from the Bazaar a litter passed me – the Sultan Selim was within, and as the breeze blew one of his curtains opened and our eyes met for an instant. It was enough. By nightfall I was in the Harem, I was given the name Nur Banu Afife, and Cecilia Baffo was no more.'

'What did my father do?'

Cecilia gave the ghost of a smile. 'He raged and screamed. He came to the palace and broke down the doors with his bare hands, demanding the return of his lover and the child in her belly. He was taken by the guards to the Sultan and told that if the child was born a boy it would be killed, for it could not live to challenge any true heirs born to my body. The Sultan himself did not lie with me until the child was born. He waited to claim me. It was a terrible few months Feyra, to wait for my child.'

'But the child was a girl, wasn't it?'

Feyra didn't need the affirmation of Cecilia's weak nod. Suddenly all was clear: her daily visits to the Harem for as long as she could remember; that her mistress had not raised her voice to her until today; that Nur Banu herself had taught her to read and write and speak the language of her youth; that she'd encouraged her in her medical interests to garner the knowledge that other women were rarely given.

'Your father was given rank and status in return for his acquiescence; and he was given you, his daughter, to raise in peace in the city. He was given your life in return for two things: his absolute loyalty to the Sultan and all his heirs, and his promise that he would never attempt to see me again. And I have never seen him, Feyra, not once from that day to this.' Nur Banu's eyes turned to glass. 'By the time we battled the Venetians at Lepanto your father was an Admiral, the very rank my uncle the Doge held for the Venetians. I watched from this very window, Feyra, straining my eyes, imagining I could see all the way to the Straits of Patras where the two fleets met, where my lover Timurhan and my uncle Sebastiano fought each other with fire and cannon, under the orders of my husband Selim.'

Feyra had to lean in to hear her now.

'I became happy again, over time. I came to love my lord the Sultan, not with the youthful passion I had for your father, but with a growing respect and companionship. He was a good and kind man, as different to our son as night is to day. I learned how to make myself indispensable, and rose from Odalisque to Concubine, Concubine to Kadin, Kadin to Sultana. I began, slowly, to exert my influence, to promote pro-Venetian policies. But when my husband died, as you will remember, all that ended. You will well recall, Feyra, how we strived to ensure Murad's succession, and you will know, now, why I trusted you and no other to help me in that endeavour. But it had been better if I had let Murad's rivals take the throne; for my son is truly evil, and is consumed with hatred for Venice and, by association, for me.'

Feyra climbed into the bed now, and brought her ear close to her mistress's dry and cracked lips. The Valide Sultan moved one bloated arm across Feyra's body in an embrace, and smiled the ghost of a smile, as if the intimacy gave her great happiness.

'Do not pity me. I have had the private consolation, all these years, of having a child who is the light that lightens my days. He does not know, my son, who you truly are, for he was born a year later and my ladies kept the secret well. I was able to keep you close, and watch you grow. You are so clever, courageous and kind. I see Timurhan every day, in you.' The mention of her old love roused her a little, and her voice became a little louder. 'You must not tell him any of this, promise me. It is very important that you do not, for he is a player in this tragedy of my son's.' She raised a swollen hand, with a visible effort, and cupped Feyra's cheek. 'If I were to wish for one thing, I would wish you a little less beautiful. It is well that you are to leave the city.'

Feyra felt a thrill of fear. 'Why must I go?'

'My son has conceived of the most evil plot against Venice . . .' The hand that held Feyra's cheek began to shake. Feyra moved her fingers up to the wrist with concern. Anger was her mistress's enemy for it made the blood rush and the humours churn, the spores would be crowding to her organs now.

'Calmly. Say on.'

Nur Banu pulled the wrist away and began wringing her hands – but no, she was working to loosen a ring from her distended finger, the crystal band that she always wore, 'Take this,' she said, her eyes closing and her speech beginning to clot. 'Tell my uncle the Doge, tell *him*. And if you need sanctuary, there is a house with golden callipers over the door. A man named Saturday lives within. He will help you.'

Feyra took the ring, without looking at it. She had barely listened once she had heard the name of the Doge. She propped herself on her elbow, drenched with dread. 'Tell him what?'

But Nur Banu's eyes were blank and staring.

'Take the ring *where*?'

Cecilia Baffo's eyes widened before they closed. She spoke with her eyes shut. 'To Venice, of course.'

Feyra leaned down and laid her cheek to her mistress's lips. She could not yet think *Mother*. The Valide Sultan's breath was short but regular: she still lived, but Feyra knew there would be no benefit in rousing her. A shock would possibly be too much for her beleaguered heart.

Feyra looked out of the window across the sea that led to Venice. The sun was high in the sky, the boats crowding the mouth of the Bosphorus. Some alchemy had turned the lapis water to gold. Little black boats broke the light; some crossing the sound to Pera and back, some setting sail for distant shores. How heartless, thought Feyra. How can trade continue, how can people still need silk and salt and saffron while a human life ends here?

Feyra had been at the bedside of death many times, and knew that when the dying had something to say, they rarely choked out their last word cleanly and then expired, whatever the Osmanli storytellers might say. Feyra's one, faint hope was that Nur Banu would rally one more time before the poison claimed her, as her body made one more desperate effort to fight the spores of the Bartholomew tree. But she could not expect that Nur Banu would be as lucid as she had just been. Feyra was thankful that she had had the time to hear her mother's story – and her own – but now she needed to hear what her mistress would ask of her; and the meaning of the ring.

She turned the ring on her finger in the morning light. It was beautiful, the craftsmanship exquisite; the crystal band very clear, with some sort of coloured pattern on it. Now she saw that the colours were not a pattern, they were tiny horses, four of them, galloping around the band. She peered at them: they were beautifully rendered, in glass, enamelled on the clear crystal of the band with some tool that must have been the size of a pin's point. Each horse was of a different hue: one was black, one red, one white and one the greenish colour of bile. Having contemplated, not one hour ago in the Samahane, the prospect of fleeing with her father, Feyra knew now she could not quit her patient. She had to know everything. She did not have to wait long.

'Feyra, Feyra . . .' It was little more than a whisper.

Feyra wrapped her hand around the older woman's again. *Come and see.* The breath was foul now, as if death were crawling out of Nur Banu's mouth. 'They are coming!'

Who? asked Feyra.

'The Four Horsemen.'

Nur Banu's mind must have addled now. She was making some association with the ring she had given Feyra, and perhaps also the four horses that had taken her away from Paros. Feyra spoke soothingly. 'No, no they are not coming.'

'Yes, yes . . . I see them! They are bringing Death!' The sea-blue eyes were staring now.

'No, they are not coming,' Feyra attempted to assure her, 'I can see all the way across to Pera, and there are only a few boats there. There is no one in the room, no one at our door.'

'They do not come to *me*,' protested the dying woman. 'They ride to Venice! The Great Tribulation is riding to Venice. They gallop across the waves, with the white horses, yet only one of them is white, the others are of another hue.'

Feyra looked down at the ring again, at the tiny etchings. One of the horses was enamelled in white. *'Only one of them is white, the others are of another hue.'* Perhaps her mistress was not raving after all.

'What do they mean? What do the horses bring?'

'Come and see, come and see, come and see.'

Feyra moved as close as she could. 'I am here, Mistress.'

Suddenly, Nur Banu sat bolt upright and spoke with a strength that belied her beleaguered body. *'When the Lamb opened the third seal, I heard the third living creature say, "Come and see!" I looked, and there before me was a black horse! Its rider was holding a pair of scales in his hand. Then I heard what sounded like a voice among the four living creatures, saying, "A quart of wheat for a day's wages, and three quarts of barley for a day's wages, and do not damage the oil and the wine!"'*

She sank back down on to the pillows, her voice a whisper once more. 'It is written. It is written in The Book.'

Feyra became agitated. She was no wiser. The Valide Sultan was wasting words. Soon she would no longer be able to speak, and she was wasting words on cant about wine and oil?

'What book?'

'I have not read it for years. They do not let me here. The Book, the Book of Books. It tells of the Great Tribulation. *Come and see come and see come and see.'*

Her eyes were staring, and Feyra knew the Valide Sultan's time was coming to an end. She tried a different question. 'What can I do?'

'Timurhan carries the first horse, the black horse, in his ship. Go with him, prevent him. He is followed hard upon by the red. When the third horse comes, the white horse, the conqueror, Venice will be no more. Then the pale horse will be the king of all dominions; for it is he that is the most terrible, it is he that all men fear.'

'Who is the pale horse?'

'Death.'

The single syllable echoed around the quiet court. It

seemed to be an end: the final word. But then the Valide Sultan turned her head on her pillow and looked Feyra in the eyes. She spoke quite normally. 'Am *I* going to die?'

There seemed to be an obstruction in Feyra's throat, a great cold stone blocking her voice. But she had never lied to her mistress. 'Yes.'

As if she were a little girl, as if she were the daughter and Feyra was the mother, the Valide Sultan said, in a voice that was small and afraid, 'Will it hurt?'

Feyra thought of the hawk she had fed with the spores of the Bartholomew tree. Of how the bird had looked two, three hours after infection. She thought of how Nur Banu would look, in another hour, and of how her organs would feel as they were pulped as the merlin's had been. Heart breaking, the last thing she said to her mother was a lie. 'No,' she said. 'You will not feel a thing.'

In another hour, Feyra was as sure as she could be that her mistress was dead.

The Valide Sultan's eyes were open and staring, the flesh mottled as black as a bruise. Feyra closed the eyes that were as blue as the sea, this sea and the one that cradled Venice, and then she tiptoed from the room.

Feyra knew it was time to find the doctor. She stumbled back to the Hall of the Ablution Fountain. The last time she had been here her world had been the right way up. Now her entire future was uncertain and she had found and lost a mother in a brace of hours.

She sent one of the black eunuchs for the doctor and when he came he looked little better than her poor mistress. He was grey and shaking, and his turban was awry. She bowed to him. 'It seems you already know, Teacher, what it is that I would say.'

Haji Musa looked at her, as if he had taken a glimpse down the pit. 'Feyra, I must tell you, your father is in danger. Don't let him sail.'

'My *father*? But I came to tell you my –' she paused '– my mistress, she has passed away. You did not know?'

It was as if the doctor could not hear her. 'I have already said too much. Don't let him sail. His cargo is dangerous. It will kill him.'

Feyra froze. 'His cargo? What is my father's cargo?' She was shredded by loss and confusion, sick of hints and intimations; it made her strident. 'Tell me, quickly and plainly.'

Her teacher and mentor, the great Haji Musa, visibly shrunk before her. He backed away. 'I have already said too much.' His hands fluttered to his mouth. 'Did you say your mistress was dying?'

'She is already dead.'

The news seemed not to matter to him at all, a mere detail. 'Then, Feyra, go home *now*. Do not be here when she is discovered. And take your father away, *do not let him sail*.'

'Wait!'

He was already walking away. 'I have already said too much. They may take my head for just this much. If I say more, I am surely a dead man.'

Feyra watched him scuttle off and knew that she would never see him again.

Not knowing what else to do, she walked through the quiet courts in the direction of the palace gates. Her mother had told her to go with Timurhan on his voyage. Her mentor had told her on no account to let her father sail. Both of them had spoken of his cargo. Nur Banu had named it the black horse, and Haji Musa had warned her it would kill him. Feyra felt suddenly very young. All she wanted to do was climb into Timurhan's lap, pull his beard as she used to as a child, lay all before him and ask him what they should do.

As she passed the Sultan's quarters she could hear the Sultan's voice booming within. She quickened her steps, as if Murad himself might emerge from his rooms and strike her down for letting his mother die. If she'd listened more carefully, if she'd not been in quite such a hurry, she might have heard another male voice.

She might have recognized the second voice too. The Sultan was in conference with her father.

Chapter 4

S ultan Murad III had begun his reign as he had meant to go on.

On his return from the province of Manisa to claim the throne, he had ordered the strangulation of the five younger brothers his father had sired by other wives. The succession was clear; and now at nineteen, young, vigorous and unopposed, he was ready to put his life's ambition into play.

According to the Kizlar Agha, with whom he'd just had an interesting conference, his mother should be dead by now. He was at last free of the tie that had of late been squeezing him like a noose and he would no longer have to brook her interference.

Conveniently, too, he had contrived to allow the Genoese to do the deed. His hands were clean, for while his suppression of his brothers had been popular with his people, and expected in a strong ruler, the murder of his mother, a well-loved figure, would have been a step too far. To blame the Genoese, though, was a masterstroke. He would have her *Gedik* strangled for negligence and denounce the Genoese who had, in his opinion, taken over too much of his city with their quarters in the Galata tower and the surrounding ghetto. He could not only mourn his mother with all civic honours, but also whip up righteous anger against foreigners. And such hatred would only serve to strengthen this latest, greatest and most audacious piece of foreign policy to ever have been attempted.

The Sultan sat on his throne and regarded the man standing obediently before him on the marble map of the known world that covered the entire floor of this vast presence chamber. The man was, appropriately, standing in the sea.

This man had once given an oath of utter allegiance to his father Selim and all his heirs. A one-time admiral, and now, in peacetime, just an old sea captain. Well, the old fellow was about to be an admiral again. The notion made the Sultan feel magnanimous, a sensation that he enjoyed, concomitant, as it was, with power. There would be one last fight for the old sea-dog. Sultan Murad III was about to call in his debt.

As he gave his instructions to the captain he thought he could detect the exact moment, the very *second* in their discourse where Timurhan had realized that he would never be coming back. This man who had been crossing all the charted waters of the Ottoman Empire and beyond since he was a boy, was now to embark on his last voyage. Murad enjoyed the moment. It was part of the whole picture. The gold of the room, the vast marble map, and the attendant white eunuchs, all deaf and dumb, having had their eardrums pierced and their tongues torn out at his command. The cloth he was wearing, the palace walls around him, the Harem full of women that he could take at a word. And, best of all, the power to end a man's life and expect him to accept it. And the sea captain did.

Timurhan bin Yunus Murad was perfect for the task – no

one knew the waters like him, he was a veteran of Lepanto and had seen enough atrocity in that greatest of sea battles to hate Venice and its Doge. And he had only one dependant; one whose care Murad would be only too happy to assume.

'Our good doctor has played his part and found a case, from one of the temples outside the city. The white eunuchs will arrange for your cargo to be delivered to the dock tonight at midnight. You will sail in one of the Venetian ships that we captured at Lepanto. It is named *Il Cavaliere*.'

From the Sultan's voice you might have supposed that he had been there. In fact it was Timurhan who had been at the skirmish which had resulted in the capture of this very galleass. *The Corsair.* The name meant as much to him as it did to Murad. The Sultan, who was familiar with every detail of his mother's history, found the name amusing. He liked coincidences and serendipity – it made him feel that God was with him. 'You will take the ship to Venice and wait.'

He rose from his throne and walked the map noiselessly, charting the ship's route in his golden slippers. When he reached the marble rendering of Venice he walked deliberately all over the city. It pleased him to sully the place with his feet. 'When you reach the mouth of the lagoon –' he stood at the very place '– wait for a storm. Under the cover of a tempest, and in a Venetian ship, you have a good chance of slipping past the quarantine island.' He indicated a small land mass on the map with a legend beneath which read *Vigna Murada*. 'Here, they will keep you, if they catch you, for forty days, and all will be lost. The sailors are detained in almshouses and the cargo washed and smoked to be free of all contagion. I need not tell you, that if this came to pass, our venture would be at an end. Take your freight instead to San Marco's basin, right before the palace of the Doge. It is here –' he placed the point of his slipper precisely '– that you will release your payload.'

The Sultan waited long enough to be sure he would hear no demurral. The sea captain had followed him obediently, like the cur that he was. 'Then, you will proceed to the lee of this island, named Giudecca. There you will find a safe house, here at the place called Santa Croce.' The Sultan was confident that Timurhan would not understand the significance of the holy name, but swallowed the words a little, just in case. 'Here you will find those who will shelter you and give you succour, sanctuary and sustenance. Then you will be able to sail safely back to Turkey.' He delivered the lie breezily.

The sea captain, looking down at the map, was silent. The Sultan was used to silence in his presence but this one went on so long as to irritate him. Then it occurred to him that this man, who had been in his father's presence many times but never in his, was cowed by his power and person. He was pleased. His mother, God rot her, always said he was as different from his father as night was from day. *Of course* this man was afraid of him. He was not his father Selim, a weak man, kind and merciful, a sop and a sot. 'You may speak,' he said to the sea captain magnanimously.

Timurhan bin Yunus Murad was not, in fact, cowed by the Sultan. He thought him a vicious young puppy and not fit to lick the boots of his late father. He was silent because he was attempting to come to terms with this latest blow that fate had dealt him.

Timurhan was used to loss. He had found a woman he loved and loved him, and lost her to this Sultan's father. He had thrown himself into his seafaring, risen to prominence at Lepanto, and lost his fleet. The only thing he had managed to keep hold of in his life was Feyra, and now he was to lose her too. The irony was not lost upon him. When his daughter was born, he had made a pledge of allegiance to Selim and his heirs in return for being allowed to take his daughter home and raise her in peace in the city. That very pledge had brought him here, to this room, to accept the mission which would separate him from Feyra for ever. He spoke at last, asking the one question that consumed his mind.

'O light of my eyes and delight of my heart, what will happen to Feyra?'

'Ah, your clever daughter. Yes, very clever,' the Sultan said, thinking back to his illuminating conversation with the Kizlar Agha. 'She already knows that which she should not.'

Timurhan held out both his palms, as if to ward off a blow. 'Sire, I know that she has too much learning, but if you would, of your kindness, just let her remain in your mother's employ—'

The Sultan interrupted. 'My mother has chosen her side in this war, and for this, she will no longer be needing your daughter.'

'But—'

'Calm yourself. I do not deprecate your daughter's knowledge of medicine, which I can only commend. No, a clever wife is an asset. But she is also beautiful, a fact, I note, that she is at pains to disguise.'

Timurhan asked the question with dread. 'What are you saying?'

'I am saying that in recognition of your services to my empire, I will take care of her personally. I have decided to confer upon Feyra the great honour of taking her to wife in the Harem as my *Kadin.*'

Timurhan was trapped. How could he reveal to the Sultan that Feyra was his half-sister, that he, a humble sea captain, had once lain with Murad's mother? He would be cut down where he stood, and Feyra likely murdered too. Should he bow and accept the honour, go on the mission of death, and accept that Feyra would be safe and well but importuned by her brother on a daily basis?

The choice was not really a choice. He bowed.

The Sultan watched him walk to the door, smiling. Timurhan had underestimated him, as so many people did. Feyra was not the only one who knew something that she should not.

He knew that Feyra was sister to him, and he did not care.

Timurhan walked through the precincts of the Topkapi palace, aware that he was never likely to walk those courts again. As he passed the Harem, he wondered as he often did, if *she* was within. Always, the door was closed to his eyes, and the black eunuchs guarding it.

Except for today.

The outer doors were thrown open and the inner doors too. Reluctantly, as if even his male gaze were as intrusion in this place, he looked through the doors across a small courtyard to where another door lay open too. Beyond those second doors a woman was propped on her pillow. She was motionless, her flesh discoloured, and it seemed that she was dead. But as he looked she opened her eyes, eyes that were the colour of the sea.

Suddenly he was back twenty-one years, to the moment those same eyes had bewitched him at a masque at Paros. Those eyes had held his, and persuaded him to take her away, ride with her to his ship and steal her away to Constantinople. He held those eyes again now, for a last moment and then, realizing what he was witnessing – an ending, not a beginning – he turned away.

Chapter 5

Feyra could not remember, afterwards, what they had for dinner that evening.

She had prepared the various dishes, and carried them to the table, she had lit the brass lamps when the sun fell, she had laid out the knives and cups. She had carried different morsels to her lips, but tasted nothing.

While she'd prepared the food she had trodden over and over the pathways open to her. She could reveal everything to her father, and break the confidence of her dying mother. Or she could keep her counsel and say nothing at all. She had still not decided when she took her place opposite her father at the table. The one thing she was sure of was that she was not about to leave Constantinople. If her mother was gone and her father was leaving, the city was all she had.

Feyra studied Timurhan carefully. He seemed distracted. She gazed at his face, tanned and weatherbeaten by the four winds for four decades at sea – the beard, oiled to a point and now flecked with grey, the amber eyes, just like hers. He sat where he always did when he was home, at the head of their polished table, before the latticed window which pricked out his form with crosses and diamonds of light. He was silent, and he ate little more than she did.

Feyra respected her father, was obedient to him as all good daughters should be; she loved him, and, what was more, she liked him. But she was still a little afraid of him.

He was stern. He was jealous of her chastity and as such approved of her careful dressing. He beat her when she crossed him – for which she held him no grudge, for what father did not beat his daughters? – and kissed her when she pleased him. But lately, just lately, there had been a subtle, tiny change. Just now and again, when she uttered some remark at dinner, or spoke of her work, she noticed a change as imperceptible as an alteration of tide when the waters begin to turn and favour the converse direction. She'd begun to see some respect in her father's eyes, and, what was more, a modicum of fear.

Knowledge was the source of this new power of hers. Once or twice he asked her opinion on medical matters, and sometimes he would defer to her, even in the company of his crew. Only last night, when their dinner was just an evening meal, he had asked her several questions about the care of an infected person, about how to contain a serious illness when a patient was in the close company of others. But he did so grudgingly. She could see that he did not like the change, that he felt like something was lost.

Feyra decided to tell her father something that would not break her mother's trust but something that would help her decide what to do. 'My mistress is dead.'

The words dropped and rolled between him and her in the silence, like marbles cast on the table.

Her father's eyes flickered a little. 'I am sorry,' he said.

From those few words Feyra realized he already knew. And moreover, he *was* sorry, and sad and still in love. It was enough. Feyra dropped her platter with a clash and fell to her knees beside him. 'Father, what should I do? She was raving at the end, she said all manner of strange things – should I return there tomorrow?'

He cupped her face. 'Feyra. I am to go on a voyage tomorrow. And you are to return to the Harem, but as *Kadim* to the Sultan.' He could not meet her eyes.

The blood beat in Feyra's head. A thousand emotions crowded her brain and the overriding one was anger. All the effort that she had gone to, day after day since she reached adulthood, had been for nothing.

The Sultan had seen through the veils.

To repeat her mother's history would be dreadful enough, but Feyra's fate was worse: she would be wived to her brother, an offence against nature as well as woman-hood. She grasped the hand that held her cheek. 'No, Father,' she said firmly, and then softened her voice for an appeal. 'You will not let it happen, will you?'

He relaxed, and met her eyes now, as the answer was revealed to him. His fealty to the Sultan had been given in exchange for this dearest of daughters. If he was to lose Feyra anyway, what use was his fealty or his life? He would not go on this fool's errand. He would take Feyra, take the ship without its cargo, and sail away, anywhere, where the Sultan could not follow him.

Perhaps they would go to Paros, a place that would always be paradise to him. He could still smell the lemon trees as he had swept past on that warm night when he had ridden after beautiful Cecilia Baffo, down to the sea. It had thrilled him that she was faster than he. He saw her now, turning back, laughing at him, terrified and adventurous and sick with love all at once.

He looked down at the face that he now held, a matchless

face that he rarely saw uncovered. Feyra, so like her mother, yet so unlike her. On the hand that held his, he recognized Cecilia's ring. There was so much for him to ask, and so much for her to tell; but there was no time. 'I cannot let you go. Get your things. We must go *now*, before sundown.'

Feyra stood and fetched her cloak and buckled on her medicine belt. It was the work of a moment. 'Ready,' she said. There was no need to cover herself tonight, to apply those painstaking, useless disguises. She looked at her father and they shared a rare smile.

Timurhan opened the door and their smiles died.

Outside the door, blocking the dying light with his massive bulk, was the Kizlar Agha.

'Captain Yunus Murad,' he said in his strangely high voice, 'I am to escort you to your ship where your crew awaits you. Lady –' he turned to Feyra. 'Take your rest. My deputies will guard your door and take you to the Harem at dawn.'

There was nothing for Feyra to do but say her farewells, to press her cheek to her father's so hard that their tears mingled, and to wave and wave until he and the Kizlar Agha had turned the corner. She managed to stand until he was out of sight, then collapsed at the feet of the guards on to the pavings before her door.

The pavings where she'd once spun a top.

Chapter 6

Feyra lay in the dark, twisting the crystal ring.

She was no longer racked by indecision; she knew exactly what to do. She was merely waiting for her moment. She waited, and she twisted the circle on her finger, as if counting down the heartbeats until she could act.

The ring had only been hers for four hours and yet it already felt like part of her. She would twist the crystal band a quarter-turn so each time a different horse was uppermost – black horse, white horse, red horse, pale horse. She wondered if she shared the habit with her mother.

Her mother.

Nur Banu had been a mother to Feyra in all but name. She would grieve for her, yes, when the shock was past; but she had no need to place their relationship in a different perspective. There was love and respect given and received, embraces, encouragement, hours of time spent in each other's company; more than any other daughter could expect. Feyra did not torture herself with things unsaid. All needful things had been told in those last awful hours, and the rest unspoken in the twenty years before them. Feyra's one regret was that her mother had not been able to say more about the horsemen. About the black horse her father was to carry to Venice, about what she herself had to do.

The street outside fell quiet at last. It was time.

Feyra rose, quiet as a cat. She did not need to dress for she had never disrobed; she did, however, place a full veil under her hat. She was not hiding her beauty, now, but her identity.

Noiselessly she opened the casement and the filigree shutters where she had stood that morning. Kizlar Agha had not thought it necessary to post guards at the back of the house. She dropped silently down on to the roof of the outhouse where the neighbours shut up their goats at night. The wretched creatures began to bleat, and she breathed in their stink with an involuntary gasp of terror, before climbing down into the dark alley below. Creeping to the corner, she saw the street was deserted and ran as fast as she could down to the docks. There, heart beating in her throat, she saw the hundreds of crowded wooden hulls and spars and the cluster of masts standing like a rank of enemy pikes in the moonlight, preventing her escape. How would she ever know which vessel her father would take? He was given a different ship for each voyage. And what if he had already sailed?

She wandered the harbour in despair, reading the rash, bombastic names that men gave their ships, foolish boasts of certain victory. Should she stow away on a boat, any boat, and take her chances with whichever crew she had thrown in her lot with, or return home unseen, wake in her own bed and be taken in the Harem? Feyra was not ignorant of the ways of men. She knew what her fate would be, as the only woman on board a strange ship of men without her father to protect her. But was this worse than the fate that awaited her in the Harem? She would be the plaything of one man as opposed to twenty, but that man was her brother, and a monster to boot. It was hardly a choice.

Just as she was about to turn back for the last time, she spotted a name painted in gold on a ship that looked different to the rest. With its straight timber cambers and decorated forecastle it seemed foreign, and the name, painted in gold, read *Il Cavaliere*. Nur Banu had not neglected to teach her letters – this name in Venetian meant simply 'the horseman'.

Feyra hid behind a stack of barrels and watched. The gangplank was down, and a sequence of torches set into the harbour wall illuminated the comings and goings. She watched two sailors, shipmen of her father's, going back and forth to the ship with various equipment and supplies that they took from a wharfhouse on the dock. She toyed with the idea of identifying herself to them and asking to be taken to the captain's quarters, but the knowledge that he would be in the presence of the Kizlar Agha prevented her.

Instead she studied the sailors and their rhythm, back and forth, back and forth. Ships had been her playhouses since she was small, and she had explored many a hold in her time, fascinated by the barrels and boxes of freight that she found there. Usually the hold was reached from a hatch on deck, but she did not ever remember seeing one that was built quite like this. In this Venetian merchant ship, the gantry doors from the hold opened right to the air, so the cargo could be loaded directly from the dock, through double doors that closed and sealed watertight well above the waterline. A gangplank led directly into the dark doorway.

In the Harem, when Feyra had been treating the concubines, she was fond of saying that the solution to a problem was often the simplest. So it was here. She simply waited and then sneaked like a slip-shadow up the gantry and into the dark belly of the ship.

She dropped down into the cavernous, dark space, rolled herself small behind some grain sacks and settled herself to wait. Over the next hour more sacks were dropped on top of her so that she became hot and pressed. Her medicine belt, her old friend that she'd worn so long that she felt it was part of her body, dug painfully into her waist and ribs. She considered the consequences of one of the bottles cracking and the shards of glass puncturing her skin, and, what was worse, some of those compounds seeping into her flesh; compounds that, in their nature, could be curative in the right amounts; but in the wrong amounts, fatal.

Beyond this the harsh canvas crushed her face. A new fear was born: that she would suffocate, so in the short absences of the sailors she began to shift her body weight and dig herself an airhole. In the glow of a single lamp hanging from a bracket she could begin to understand that she was crushed because all of the supplies for the voyage were being piled into one side of the hold only. At the fore of the hold was a space cornered off by a muslin curtain, with yards of empty rough floor planks between the curtain and the rest of the supplies.

At length Feyra could ease the dreadful pressure on her body, and look about her. In the quarter-light she began to examine the sacks and barrels, looking for insignia, searching for the deadly cargo that her father was to carry – anything to do with a horse, anything black. There was another strange thing: the supplies that crowded around her were good firm cheeses, quarters of meat, fine white flour, quite different to the usual shipboard fare of pemmican and ship's biscuits. She extended her hand to the aft side and pushed through the sacks, the grain below the canvas whispering as she pushed her fingers through.

As she watched the sailors come and go, she stayed as silent as she could, trying to still even her breathing. But it was not, it seemed, enough; one of the loaders set down his barrel and straightened up, holding out a hand, high and fingers splayed, to quiet his fellow.

'What's amiss?' said the second, setting down his barrel likewise.

'I heard a noise,' hissed the sharp-eared one. 'From the stack.' He pointed to the barrels behind which Feyra lay. Her pulse thudded in her ears. The sweat from her finger-tips clumped the grain.

'Just a rat,' said the second. 'You're hearing things.'

'Just a rat? You should pin back your ears of cloth. Did you not hear our captain's directions? *No animals aboard –* there's not even a ship's cat. So we'll have to find it ourselves.'

'Why no animals?'

'*I* don't know. Something to do with the cargo.'

'All right. Let's look if we must, but the main payload's still for loading.'

They came so perilously close that Feyra could smell a strong aroma of goat – one of the sailors was clearly a herder by day. The second, whose eyes were evidently better than his ears, looked directly at her. 'Found it! Come 'ere, yer stowaway!'

Feyra shrunk back, but the fellow held high an enormous rat, black and slick as oil and shrieking in fright. The ship-man snapped his neck for him and all was silence. He slung the long body over his shoulder like a draftsack and carried him out to the night, followed by his sharp-eared friend.

Feyra lay back burning with relief, heart thumping fit to leap out of her chest.

Then a thump and shuffle and a curse alerted her; the sailors had one more item of cargo to load. And it was heavy. She watched as they manoeuvred their burden, four men now carrying something on their shoulders like pallbearers.

A sarcophagus.

All the pallbearers were veiled. Feyra might have thought that they were showing respect for what they carried, but for their demeanour and language. The bearers heaved and bumped the box, moaning and uttering oaths in a way that convinced her that they could not possibly be carrying a body. The sarcophagus seemed to be made of silver or pewter, some metal that gleamed low and grey. It was enamelled all over with curling designs picked out in colour, and was taken, with much groaning and shuffling and instruction and counter-instruction, to the muslin curtain. The curtain was drawn back, the burden taken beyond, and placed on the planks with a thud.

The bearers retreated in somewhat of a hurry, taking the torch with them. In their wake, there was a sudden, intense silence. Feyra could still see the white glow of the closed curtain, white as a Dervish's skirt, which had settled back into its fold.

Same as before, different than before.

For now Feyra felt the almost palpable menace emanating from the box behind it, somehow more terrifying and unsettling than anything she had witnessed that day. She looked at the drape, the colour of death, and at the rough, empty expanse of planks between her and it, and listened to the silence. It was pierced, brutally and suddenly, by the high, unmistakable voice of the Kizlar Agha as he retreated down the gangplank.

Then there was a great shove and a cry, the splash of an immense rope into the wash, and the smell of burning hemp as the ship yanked from its moorings. Feyra's stomach gave a lurch and a heave. There was no going back.

She was at sea.

Chapter 7

For the first few hours of the voyage Feyra stayed as still as she could.

She was aided in this by the pitch and roll of the ship for she was not sure she could have moved if she had wanted to. She had never been on a voyage before, never even been at sea for more than a pleasure cruise on Nur Banu's gilded barge, never left the golden basin of the Bosphorus. It was all so utterly strange, this rhythm, this rise and fall of the seas.

At the fall of the hull her body felt weightless, and at the rise her back was pressed into the sacks with such pressure that her medicine belt pained her once more. She felt unsettled and panicky, finding the movement almost unbearable, the anticipation of each rise and fall nearly intolerable. The suspension of balance at the top of each arc, just before the drop, made her queasy. Now, for the first time, Feyra understood her father's bearing when he returned from a long voyage. Little wonder that he was pale and sick for a few days after, his face the greeny-white of bone, his hands shaky, and he could not cross a room without pitching and stumbling over.

Feyra was a pragmatist. As her father had said many times, 'It takes a day and a night aboard to get my sea legs.

It takes as long ashore to rid me of them again.' She tried to regulate her breathing and in time she learned to make tiny adjustments with her body, to become used to the motion of the ship. She remembered the first time she had ridden a horse. Nur Banu's own Mistress of the Horse had taught Feyra to rise and fall with the trot so that her body could compensate to make the ride smooth. And so it was here in this alien place.

After a while she felt able to sit, and push the heavy sacks above her away from her face and to either side. Then she noiselessly proceeded to make herself a nest among the freight. Below her was a mattress of canvas; on one side of her was the aft of the ship, a rough camber of clinker-built, overlapping planks; on the other a rank of barrels. The curve of the barrel bellies made a gap though which she could clearly see the hold and the distant curtain, while at the same time completely hiding her from view. Feyra calculated from the packing of the hold that she would be safe from discovery for a number of days, perhaps weeks; for there were numerous sacks, boxes and barrels between her hiding place and the deck hatch above. The seamen would take those first for their sustenance.

Feyra knew that it was imperative that she keep her presence hidden until a very particular moment in the voyage was safely past. She had seen her father mark this point on the maps and charts that he kept rolled in their map chest at home. As a girl she would watch as her father unrolled the great parchments on their table, took out his silver callipers and marked the path of his voyage. Feyra liked watching the callipers under her father's hand, striding across the seas like a little silver manikin with pins for toes. At a certain point in his promenade the manikin would stop, one leg suspended in the air, poised like a dancer. Timurhan would then press the downward point hard into the parchment, take the callipers away and mark the place with a neat cross. 'There,' he'd say, 'the point of no return.'

The point of no return, she understood then and now, was the point at which you could not go back, but had to go forth. It was one of the most important seamarks in maritime faring; for if supplies were low, or battle broke out, or pirates gave chase, it was imperative to know if a ship could still turn about or if it were better to go forth. If Feyra could only be secret until halfway to Venice, they could not, then, turn the ship about. She would be on the voyage for better or worse, and share her father's fate, whatever it was.

Dawnlight was bleeding through the cracks of the clinkers. Feyra applied her eye to the largest crack, and the salt spray and the winds stung her gaze. But she could see nothing beyond a heaving dun mass. The waters were no longer the deep blue of lapis and sapphires but dragon grey, humped like a beast, deep and dangerous. Even the sea was changed here. She had left behind everything she had ever known. Feyra suddenly wanted her father very badly.

Tears mingled with the brine but she blinked them away with lids suddenly heavy with fatigue. Once more the doctor, she counselled herself to rest. She had been awake since that last sunrise, a day away, a world away, when she had dressed herself so carefully before her mirror. As she sank down into sleep, her last conscious thought was that in the morning she would cross the rolling hold and draw back the white curtain.

And see what malign thing crouched behind it.

When Feyra woke she was aware of a terrible thirst, but could not, at first, lift her head for it banged like a drum. She raised herself to sit with an effort, in a repeat of her struggle to rise last night. Then the sea had sickened her. Today something was amiss with her body.

Her flesh was burning, her eyes unfocused, her head bursting. She had to drink. She remembered the fragment of an image, seemingly misty and far away, of a crescent of rain-water lying on the top of a barrel. With an enormous effort of will she forced her right hand to crawl along the sack, and raised it with difficulty to the top of the barrel beside her. She curled her fingers round the cooper's band on the top into the blessed little pool. She trailed the fingers back to her lips and sucked the few precious drops of moisture.

When she took her fingers away she noted the tips were black. In the sliver of gilded morning light from the cracks in the shipboard she saw they were stained and dark, as though she had been using a quill and ink. There must have been tar in the barrel. Feyra sucked her fingertips again but the colour did not change.

It was the fingers themselves that were black as pitch.

Feyra was familiar with the symptoms of gangrene, but she had had no wound, no injury to invite the contagion in. No longer able to hold the hand before her face, she let it drop; and as she did so felt a searing pain in her armpit. With her other hand she felt above her breast in her armpit, and met a large swelling, round and swollen as a fig.

Feyra's fiery skin grew cold with horror. She examined the lump with desperate searching movements, each touch the sting of a knife. Could she have a canker, such as some of the concubines had in their breasts? No – for she had never known such a malignancy develop overnight, and besides, the peculiar menace of canker stones was that they gave no pain.

What then? Feyra knew that the pits and groin and throat swelled during illness, for the humours collected there like rainwater butts, but she had known nothing like this. She fell back, weakened by the shock, her body on fire again, her sweat running into the sacks beneath. From then on she knew little else.

She was dimly aware, in her more lucid moments over the course of the next few days, that people came and went. A lamp was brought to the hold each night to hang from a bracket so the quartermaster could see his supplies, and the lamp was gone again each morning. But soon Feyra became insensible of these changes, and lost track of how many times it happened, how many days had passed.

From time to time she heard herself crying out – talking, babbling, even singing. To begin with she was conscious of the need to be quiet when the deck hatch opened, and clamped her aching jaw closed. As time went on even this consciousness left her, and she cared not, wanting now only to be found; to be helped and cured and carried to her father, lest she die here alone and rot until the supplies grew low enough for her discovery.

Tears of self-pity ran into her ears and in time, after many lonely hours and days of vacillating between burning hot and freezing cold, she began to wish for death. She could no longer remember what it was like to feel well; health seemed another country, one she would never visit again. To will her recovery seemed far too great an effort. It was easier to die. She had finally reached the point of no return. She closed her eyes, hoping it was for the final time, and let herself drift . . .

Feyra found herself alone in a huge and airy room, mosaicked with milk white tiles smooth as an egg. In the centre of the room stood a coffin, clear as glass. She walked to it and knelt; leaning over she could see the old Sultan Selim encased in ice, dead, his eyes staring, his skin a watery blue. She placed her hands on the ice and they moistened and chilled at once. She was freezing. She had to warm her hands. She rose and crossed to the windowsill; a golden box lay there, winking at her in the sun. She took the box and was suddenly outside.

The fierce sun heated the casket in her hands until she could hardly bear to carry it further. But she climbed the hill on the Anatolian shore to Üsküdar, where the great mosque was being built above the city. She could hear herself asking for *the architect, the architect*; for she had been told to put the box only in the hands of Mimar Sinan himself.

It was imperative that she find the architect. She asked every mason, working on the fresh, sharp blocks of white stone, spinning each man around by his robe, looking into every bearded face. She was desperate. She had to get the box out of her hands, the gold was burning her. She was burning. *Where was the architect?*

At last she came to a door, with callipers carved into the architrave; the callipers were not silver like her father's but gold, and curved – the callipers of a mason. The door opened and she saw him, a kindly, bearded old man. 'Are you the man they call Saturday?' she said. He nodded, and with relief she put the box in his calloused hands, pale with stone dust. He bowed to her. 'Tell the Valide Sultan her mosque shall have a great dome,' he said. Then Feyra was running, back down the peninsula, through the Bazaar and the Beltan, running, running back to Topkapi. She ran through the inner courts and reached the Valide Sultan's chamber. She pulled back the white bed curtain but her mistress was already a corpse, bloated and staring and rotting into the coverlet. Feyra reached out to close the eyes that were the colour of the sea. As she closed her mother's eyes in the dream her own eyes, in her own dank reality, flew open.

Feyra ran her tongue round her desert-dry mouth, and struggled to sit up. She was still weak and sweating, but she knew that the contagion had passed. Her fingers, as she held them before her face, had returned to their normal hue. It must be night, as the cracks in the shipboard were dark and the lamp was back, hanging and creaking from the bracket, swinging with the ship in a queasy arc, throwing crazy shadows.

Her veils and hat had gone, lost as she had twisted and sweated on her makeshift bed. Her medicine belt was intact, but already loose at her wasted midriff. Feyra blinked twice and turned her aching head – her hair was a thick salty rope slithering between her shoulder blades as she twisted to see behind her. The impression of her body was pressed into the sacks beneath, dark with sweat where she had lain. There was an ugly black stain where the bubo in her armpit had burst and bled its dark matter out into the canvas; her gown, when she lifted her left arm, was likewise stained. She could not think what this might mean, for her attention was snatched, in that instant, by a voice.

She must still be trapped in her delirium.

The voice called again, hoarse as a crow's caw.

Her skin chilled at once, for at the third time of repeating she recognized the word it uttered; a word that meant she was discovered. Feyra waited, tensed, for the sacks and barrels to be thrust aside and for her sorry self to be discovered. But the raptor's croak continued, that one syllable repeated.

Feyra herself thrust at the sacks with arms as weak as twine, and with a supreme effort freed herself from her prison. Once she could see all before her she noted with puzzlement that the hatch to the deck above was closed, and she was alone in the hold. She stood, unsteady as a toddling babe, and walked forth, her progress hampered by the weakness in her legs and the roll of the ship. She walked slowly, as if through sand, one foot in front of the other, like the callipers, marking the space between her and the curtain.

Halfway across; beyond.

She reached out to the white fabric, and with a sense of dread, drew it back. As she did so, the ship slipped silently through the dark archipelago of a thousand islands known as the Peloponnese, where a sea captain had once carried off a Venetian princess.

The point of no return.

Feyra looked down at the casket and she knew she was right – the voice had been coming from the box. Suddenly weak, she could stand no longer. Her knees buckled and bent and her legs collapsed beneath her. She knelt before the sarcophagus as she had once knelt before a Sultan encased in a coffin of ice.

'Girl?' it said again.

'Yes, Box?'

Chapter 8

Feyra spoke again, her mouth as dry as tinder. 'Who are you?'

'I am Death.'

She choked, thinking then that the fever had killed her after all, that she was in some otherworld.

'What do you want of me?'

'Another soul.'

Dumb with horror, Feyra stared at the sarcophagus that spoke, trying to understand. Now she was close to the casket, she knew that she had seen the like before. It was wrought of pewter as she had thought and beautifully chased in jewel-coloured enamel. Geometric interlaced patterning in the Ottoman style twined with the gilded decorative calligraphy of *Diwani* script. She had seen a coffin just like this when the Sultan Selim had been laid in state in the Sophia, directly underneath the great dome where his mournful subjects lined past to look their last on him.

Here in this dank hold it was different. To contrast with the glory of the box there was a dreadful, underlying smell of human waste, and pomades of myrtle were tied at intervals from the silver rivets, a herb which she recognized for its power to contain evil miasmas. In the Sophia the dead

Sultan's face had been clearly visible through a panel of crystal – here the glass had been smashed away and replaced by a panel of opaque muslin, a weave broad enough to let air pass freely. The muslin drew in and out, periodically, vibrating slightly like the skin of a drum.

Something still breathed.

The thing within, despite his name, was alive.

A sigh emanated from the sarcophagus, and the muslin puffed and bellied like a sail. 'I did not mean to frighten you. I meant only that I wanted a friend, a companion. Four days now I have been enclosed. I am lonely.' The voice was male, and deep, it carried the rasp of someone who was wedded to his pipe, like her father. She began to be less afraid.

'I heard your speech and song. I thought you were one of the sirens they tell of who hug the shores of Greece, for we must be in those waters by now.' So Death was not ignorant of the sea. 'Now I know you are a mortal. I heard you suffer as I have suffered. I am sorry for you, that you are here, but glad for me.'

Feyra reached out her hand and placed it on the pewter in an involuntary gesture of pity. She expected the metal to be cool, but it was warm to the touch as if some fever raged within.

'What is your history?'

'I must ask you a question first. Are you loyal to our beloved Sultan Murad?'

Feyra had a thousand answers to this question. *He is a murderer. He is my brother. He wanted me for his wife.* Instead she fell back on formula. 'He is the delight of my eyes and the light of my heart,' she answered carefully.

'But are you *loyal*? For I cannot tell what I would tell, unless I know.'

Death was making a deal. Feyra had read the Persian tales, and understood the process – an exchange of clandestine stories as a testament of faith. A captive princess must bargain with her dark captor for her freedom. She had seen the illuminated marginalia of the texts in the Topkapi library; a dusky maiden, cross-legged in voluminous breeches, conversing with some monstrous chimera, her hands held high, her fingers spread like a fan.

Although she had never read of a lady gaming with Death before, Feyra knew what was required. She must tell him a secret before he would tell his. As if it were all a part of this unreality, she began, crossing her legs in the formal manner of the Ottoman storyteller.

'On the twenty-first day of the month *dhu'l-qa'dah* in the year of 982, it so fell out that I was appointed *Kira* to our beloved Sultan's mother, Nur Banu. When our beloved Sultan's father Selim Sultan died – may he walk in the light of Paradise – it so happened that our Sultan Murad was far from the palace in the Province of Manisa, where he was then the governor. My mistress Nur Banu, knowing that his jealous brothers would attempt to take the throne, took the notion to conceal her husband's death. She charged me with the task, and I caused the great kitchens to make a subtlety out of ice, a frozen coffin shaped just like the casket where you now lie, and in this way, in the heat of summer, we preserved his dead flesh. Over the next several days we took him out to prayer to be seen in his litter by the people, and even to the hippodrome to preside over the chariot races, propped in his golden throne. In this manner we preserved the fiction that he still lived. For twelve days Selim lived in his coffin of ice, for twelve more days than God had granted to his natural life, until Murad returned to

Constantinople. On Murad's accession to the Ottoman throne, Nur Banu acquired the title of Valide Sultan for her pains, and Selim was placed in a casket of silver and laid in the Sophia for all to see and mourn. So, it may be said, it was my privilege to aid in securing the throne of our beloved Sultan. This I have never told a living soul.'

Feyra waited for the ensuing silence to end. In the tradition of the sagas, the maiden would either be taken to the underworld, or another tale would be told in return.

'On the seventh day of this month of *sibtambir* in this year of 983,' she heard, with some relief, the voice from the sarcophagus begin, 'it pleased God that I fell deathly ill in the mountains on the way home from a long journey. There was no one to assist me but a shepherd. He put me on a hurdle and dragged me to a hilltop temple where the imams were skilled in physic. They looked at me but once before they gave me my own chamber and left me for dead. But when I woke from my fever I found myself attended by the Sultan's doctor, Haji Musa himself.' Feyra heard the name of her mentor with a jolt. She also registered the note of satisfaction in the voice; Death, it seemed, could still be proud. 'He came to me and asked me if I would embark upon a very important mission for the Sultan. He was afraid, I could see it in his eyes. I thought at first he was afraid of the Sultan, but it turns out he was afraid of me. Of what I had. It was the Plague.'

Feyra chilled. She knew, of course, of the dread pestilence of Constantinople in the year 747, when thousands of lives had been lost. The disease which had lain dormant for centuries, had, it seemed, returned. 'The Black Death?' she whispered.

'Plague, Black Death, it has many names. Although it had

not been in the city for many years, I knew the tales. I knew then that I was finished. The doctor knew it too. He made me promises; gold for my wife, preferment for my sons, good marriages for my daughter. He seemed to know all about me. He knew I had been at Lepanto.'

Feyra leaned forward a little. So Death knew the oceans, just like her father.

'He told me that if I agreed to the Sultan's plan I could defeat our old enemy single-handedly. He laid it before me thus: I could either die in that lonely hilltop place, and my family would live on in poverty never knowing my fate, or I could be a hero like the ones in the sagas, my name writ down in scrolls and sung in songs, while my family would live in riches. There was no real choice to make.'

Feyra heard a thump and rustle from within the coffin as Death shifted his weight.

'Could you give me some water? I am dry from my tale. There is a can by your side. Sometimes the sailors remember, sometimes they do not.'

Feyra looked down and saw a silver watering can with a thin pipe of a spout, curved like a billhook – like the ones the ladies of the Harem used to cleanse themselves. She applied it to the muslin panel and poured a thin stream through the cloth. She could only imagine the monstrous features beneath, but heard the smacking of lips as Death found succour.

'They took me in a litter down the hills, to an icehouse near the bay. It took a long time for they took a route well beyond the city walls. I did not see the doctor again but was attended by certain of the Sultan's men dressed in a black livery with black turbans and face masks. I never deter-mined whether they were soldiers or priests, for as much as they talked about their mission and their war, they talked also of Paradise and their sacrifice.'

They were Janissaries, black-clad, fanatical elite of the Sultan's soldiers. Taken from their Christian homes as boys and turned to the true faith, they were even more devoted to their adopted God than those who had been born into the bosom of the Prophet. But Feyra kept her peace and let Death speak.

'These soldiers of God placed me in this coffin. There was wadding of wool beneath my hips for my human functions, dried meat by my hands for my sustenance, and I would be watered from time to time. The box is large as you see, and I can move and turn, but I will not conceal from you my terror when they first nailed the lid over me. I thought I was never to leave my living tomb; but I was instructed that I am to emerge from it one last time. If I am still alive, I will rise from my casket at the end of our voyage, mingle among the people and give them my gift. In Venice.' He said the name of the city reluctantly, almost as if it pained him.

Feyra listened grimly. This was terrible confirmation of all Nur Banu had tried to tell her. The Sultan must be a monster indeed to contemplate such a dreadful scheme. She felt such nausea in her innards and bile rising to her throat that she might have assumed that her malady was returning, but she knew what ailed her was a moral disgust at what one human was planning to do to an entire city. She tried to keep the condemnation from her voice. 'And if you do not live so long?'

'The soldier told me that if I died my body would be cast into the waves,' came the answer. 'And furthermore, this man himself would lie in my casket, be wrapped in my shroud, would breathe my miasma, and carry the contagion himself.'

Realization dawned and Feyra's flesh crept. 'So this man is aboard the ship?'

'He is. And if he dies, another soldier of the Sultan will take his place. Every man on this ship has taken the pledge to carry this disease to Venice. We are all doomed, girl; you too.'

Feyra's fears gave way to her curiosity. 'But why this senseless series of sacrifices? Why should a man be taken?'

'The good doctor told me that, in the days of Justinian, the Plague was brought to Constantinople in a bale of silk from Pelusium. The Sultan could have done likewise but he wished for certainty; so the doctor counselled him that the best way to carry the pestilence is in the body of a victim. So when I told you that I was Death, I spoke true. My real name I cannot tell you, for I gave my promise in the name of the Sultan, the light of my eyes and the delight of my heart. If the plan were to go aright *or* awry, it is equally necessary that the source of the contagion is secret. The soldier told me that if the states of the infidel Christ knew what had passed, our nation would be condemned and we would bring down a crusade against Constantinople just as in days of old.'

Now Feyra understood why Haji Musa had been so fearful at their leave-taking in the Hall of the Ablution Fountain that he barely marked the passing of Nur Banu. Now the warnings made sense. The doctor, who had made an oath to save life, could not countenance the full infamy of a plan which would claim thousands. She voiced, at last, her horror, unable, now, to keep the condemnation from her voice. 'But, the *people* of Venice – the citizens?'

'What of them?' came the reply. 'The doctor was right about me. I was at Lepanto. The Venetian curs fired our ships. I watched them burn, girl. All those sailors. It was hell on earth. No. I welcome what I go to do. I embrace it. I am content.'

Over the next two days Feyra grew stronger, and began to believe that a miracle had occurred and that she had somehow recovered from this most dire of diseases. She did not tell Death of this, for she was chary of giving him hope of such a recovery. Their friendship grew over those days and at night, after the quartermaster had come and gone, she would draw back the white curtain and talk to Death.

By tacit consent they did not talk again about the mission and the contagion he carried. They talked of home, of places and things they would both know; the Bazaar, the fair at Pera, the regatta on the Bosphorus. He would talk, when he had the strength, of his own travels, and she was reminded, strongly, of her father. She asked him too, in a circumspect way, if he had heard of a fabled black horse, or a horse of another hue, but he had not. She even asked him if he had heard of a man called Saturday; she tried the words in Ottoman and Venetian; but at the sound of a Venetian name she could hear him attempt to expel what little spittle he had in a contemptuous spit; the muslin before his face darkened like a small bruise, and she let be.

The one topic she did not probe was that of his family.

She knew that, one way or another, he was going to die; and could not bear to hear that he had a daughter that sang to him while she spun the distaff in the kitchen, or a son who told him jests as they yoked their bull for ploughing, or a wife who curried his beard and kissed him as he left the house for prayers each morning. She just tried to ease his last days as best she could for she could not imagine the horror of his existence, to be confined in that space with his own wastes as disease ate him.

Now too, she knew why her father had asked her, a week ago at dinner, about the isolation of a patient aboard ship. It was she who had advised him about the curtain, she who had counselled him about the muslin panel, she who had prescribed a small, curtained enclosure hung about with myrtle.

It was she who had placed Death in this box.

'Girl?'

'Yes, Death?'

'Do you ever think about *Jannah*? What do you think it is like?'

Feyra thought for a moment. She had been asked the question before, in the Harem – the dying always turned their thoughts to what came next. *Jannah*, Paradise, was the destination he had been promised, and she was not surprised that he should wish to elevate his mind from his dreadful prison to the great beyond.

She did not know what to say. She could tell him that he would live in a meadow of flowers, drink sweet honey and dress in garments encrusted with jewels. But she believed in good and ill and a Prophet and a God who believed in them too so she could not, in all conscience, tell Death that he would be rewarded for smiting an entire city. She was saved from offering either a palatable lie or an unpalatable truth by a cry far overhead, above the deck, the sails and even the mast itself.

'Land ahoy!'

Chapter 9

'Death?'

'Yes, girl?'

'Have we stopped?'

'Yes. They have dropped anchor. We must be near.'

'Why have we stopped?'

'They are waiting for a storm. The soldier told me this too. Only then will we draw closer to the city and I will perform my final act.'

Feyra began to dread the arrival of the storm, because of the dreadful thing she must ask of herself. It would be terrible for any person to contemplate, but it went particularly against the grain for her, not just because the man in the box was now her friend, but because as a doctor she had sworn to heal; to cure not to kill. She longed to reveal herself and seek her father – but she could not, for his own sake, till the deed was done. One life, after all, was but a feather when weighed in the scales with the ten thousand that might be saved.

The moment came, early one morning, with a crack of thunder that shivered her ribs and rattled her teeth, followed hard upon by a flash of lightning so intense that it

found the cracks in the clinkers and lit the hold for one bril-
liant instant. Almost instantaneously Feyra felt a jerk and a
rattle of chain below as the rode was lifted and the anchor
was weighed. The great iron flukes scraped at the side of the
hold like a beast scratching to be let in, and the ship began
to move.

High above she heard the cries of the sailors, the creak of
ropes pulled taut, and the belly and snap of canvas as the
sails were raised. The ship began to pitch and heave, she felt
a strong pull forwards and *Il Cavaliere* was in full sail again,
full speed ahead.

Over these last days she had withdrawn a little from
Death. For one thing, she knew his condition was worsening
– his breathing was laboured, his speech confused. For
another, when the way ahead had become clear to her, she
could not bear to sit with him, knowing what she was to do.

As the ship gathered speed, she crossed the hold, lurching
and stumbling against the motion of the newly rough sea,
and drew back the white curtain for the last time. Beyond
the rushing of the winds and waters and the creaking pro-
tests of the timbers, there was an eerie silence from the
sarcophagus. Perhaps he was already dead. She hoped so.

She placed herself behind the heavy casket and began to
push as hard as she could. Her strength had almost fully
returned, and she had been eating and drinking carefully
from the supplies to restore it. But still it was more than she
could do even to move the thing an inch. In the end she let
the forces of nature assist her. The ship pitched and rolled to
such an extent that she was able to push the casket down a
steep slope as the ship rocked, and, when the slant of the
floor was against her, set her shoulder against the pewter to
stop the coffin sliding back.

At last she'd achieved her purpose and the casket was butted up flush against the gantry doors. Next, she took a heavy coil of rope and wrapped it around her wrist, to secure her to the shipboard. Then Feyra loosed the latches and threw the double doors open.

They were immediately thrust back at her, slamming against her forearms. She shoved them again, but was pushing against the four winds. With an enormous effort, taking one door at a time, she pushed them open in turn, judging it this time so the wind would snatch the doors and thrust them back against the ship itself, keeping them open with the blast. Her eyes were blinded by too much light, her lungs filled with too much air. After her dank, still dungeon, the freshness of the outside world made her gasp.

A roiling tempest sent heavy ropes flicking against the portholes like whips, and the sea-spray doused her with its freezing drench, fit to pull her into the depths. She looked down with sheer terror – she was among the dragon's coils now. The sea was pewter like the casket, and boiling so high that one moment she was in a leaden valley so low she could not see the sky, the next she was atop a silver mountain.

As she clung to the sodden ropes she was dimly aware of a tiny island lit by torches and enclosed around by walls, and heard a cry as the ship swept past. As she pushed the casket until first a quarter, and then a third of it protruded from the ship, above the clamouring, shrieking tempest she heard a more piercing cry.

It was Death.

He knew what she was about and began to hammer at the casket, crying out. She thought she heard an answering cry from somewhere above her, drowned out by Death's desperate pleas.

'No, girl, no! Leave me be! I must have my triumph. My family, what of my family? I beg you! If I do not fulfil my task they will not be rewarded!'

She tried to stop her ears and set her shoulders beyond the head end for one final push, but she heard every desperate word. 'I have a son, who wants to buy the farm next to mine! He is called Daoud and is just seventeen! I have a daughter, Deniz, who is twenty and wants to marry but has no dowry! My wife, my Zarafa . . . my love . . . dear God, don't let me fail them!'

Then she knew he was a man, just a man. They could call him the black horse, she could name him Death, but he was just a doomed mortal man with a family and a daughter as old as she. Feyra's tears were snatched and cast away by the winds before they fell, but she pushed grimly on. At last she stood back.

The casket teetered on the edge, balanced see-saw, and as she watched with horror, it reached its tipping point and began to fall into the roiling waves.

Then, all was confusion, as behind her, the deck hatch was thrown open and a succession of seamen tumbled down into the hold. In an instant her arms were bound behind her with the rope she held, while a figure flew past her and threw himself at the end of the sarcophagus that was still inside the hold. The coffin fell back down with a clang.

As the seamen heaved it inside Feyra let herself go limp. To fight further would only be to hurt herself. She did not, at first glance, know any of these men. They were not her father's regular crew and were dressed in the inky livery of the Janissaries, topped with black turbans.

As the sarcophagus was dragged to safety Feyra found

herself in its place, forced forward until she faced the silver wall of sea. Knowing she was now to suffer the fate she had planned for the casket, she waited for the shove that would send her into the deep, but heard a cry: 'No!'

She wrenched around to see the man who had shouted. It was the one who had flung himself at the coffin, and he now stood as soaking as she. His turban had been snatched by the waves and his dark hair blew about his face.

'You cannot kill her,' he told the men that held her, his dark eyes stern and commanding. 'She is the Captain's daughter.'

Now she recognized him. She knew him a little – his name was Takat Turan, and he'd sailed with her father often. Closer to her in age than Timurhan, she recalled that Lepanto had been his first battle, and that her father had saved his life. If it was this that had made him save her from the brink, she could use his obligation to her advantage.

She scarcely knew what she must look like – dashed by sea-spray, her shift and breeches bespattered with filth, and now soaked and clinging. She had watched the Concubines practising their alluring glances and the Odalisques simpering before the looking-glass. She had no such arts, but she used all the power she had ever hidden beneath her veils, and put every pleading effort into her gaze. 'Please,' she said, looking only at Takat Turan. 'Take me to my father.'

Takat looked above her head at the man who held her. 'Do it,' he said sharply.

The fellow shrugged. 'Very well. I'll take her to him. It comes to the same thing in the end.'

Behind her, Feyra heard the gantry doors being closed and secured. She willingly let herself be hauled up on deck and into the blinding light once again. She was frogmarched to the aft end of the maindeck, astern of the great citadel doors, given over to the captain's quarters.

As she was led to the night cabin on the starboard side, she wondered what her father would say when he saw her. As the door to the cabin was unlocked she was so eager to see him again that she did not even stop to wonder why he was under lock and key. But when the door was opened and she was propelled into the little room the reason became very clear.

Timurhan lay pale and sweating on his cot, and the fingers that clasped his heart as she entered were black.

Chapter 10

As the door closed behind her Feyra sank to her knees in front of the bed. She did not even hear the turn of the key in the lock.

The captain's cot, suspended by ropes from a swinging bar attached to the deckhead beams, nearly knocked her over as she knelt. The bed was a symbol of status, a larger version of the common seamen's hammock with wooden sides to maintain its shape and draped curtains to provide additional shade and privacy. But the rocking bed made her father seem as if he were a child in a cradle. Timurhan seemed diminished in her eyes as he lay twisted on the fine lawn coverlet; for a moment she was the mother and he the babe.

Feyra took the blackened hand and forced herself to regard her father with a professional eye. He was pale, and hot to the touch, his breathing laboured. She slipped a hand under his chemise and found the telltale swelling in each armpit. He knew her at her touch, for his eyes widened at once and he smiled weakly, trying to mouth her name with parched and cracked lips. Then the smile turned to distress as he realized what her presence might mean. The flicker of pain rent her heart and she embraced him hard and kissed his hectic cheek. 'Do not fret,' she said. 'I have had the sickness and it left me. You will heal too.'

Feyra forced herself to believe it. *This* was why she was not cast into the waves, *this* was why 'it comes to the same thing in the end': it did not matter to the Janissaries whether she perished at sea or in this septic cabin. Well, she would defeat the pestilence once more, this time on her father's behalf.

She stood, with difficulty, against the lurch of the ship and surveyed the cabin. There was a canvas drugget on the floor, painted to give the appearance of tiles, and carpets. There were paintings and pictures on the bulkheads and even a coalfired stove to provide heating in winter. But the aroma of woodruff and frankincense that sweetened the air was underlaid by a scent of putrefaction and decay. All this luxury served no purpose to her father now.

On the desk at the forward end of the cabin, Feyra found a crystal jug of water and a pewter one of wine. She swiftly poured a little wine into the water to cleanse it of any impurities, watching the grape must cloud like blood in the crystal. Then she took an ink sponge from the desk topper, tore off the stained blotter and dunked the sponge into the water. She carried it to her father and used the sponge to moisten his lips, squeezing it until a trickle fell into his half-open mouth, which made him cough a little – a good sign. Lastly she wiped the sponge around his face and his brow. Her ministrations seemed to give Timurhan ease, and it seemed to Feyra that his colour was better.

In contrast to her former prison, this room had lots of natural illumination – from portholes on the port side, through gratings in the quarterdeck above and from the portholes to starboard. The windows were so well glazed she could barely hear the screaming tempest outside, but the rain drummed at the portholes, each roundel of glass turned tabor. She glanced at her father – oblivious to the external storm and locked in his own feverish battle, he had fallen into a fitful sleep. There was little she could do but wait.

At the captain's desk a wooden globe spun on its axis as if all celestial forces had been puffed away and the four winds had dominion this day. An empty wine bottle rolled back and forth over the wood floor with the pitch of the waters. After a moment Feyra could not bear it and set the thing on its end on the desk.

She sat in the captain's chair and peered through the port-hole, wiping away the smoke of her breath. What she saw there made her wonder, for the second time today, whether she had died and passed into the beyond, for there, rising from the filigree of drifting mists before her, was a shining citadel set upon the water; with hoary spires reaching to the sky and ivory palaces crowding the waterfront. Even the driving rain could not diminish the strange beauty. The scale of the place was vast, and the harbour opened out into a wide square walled around by stone arches and pillars. A lofty tower stood tall over all, and a humped golden church, its painted colours varnished to jewels by the slick of rain, crouched in the corner of the square.

As she watched, the ship drew alongside two enormous marble pillars that rose high into the sky and Feyra felt the rattle and run of the rode chain as the anchor was dropped once more. She peered upwards, squinting through the deluge. One pillar was topped by some infidel saint, the other by a creature that she'd been taught to fear since childhood: a winged lion with a book.

She was in Venice.

A sound came from the cot behind her, and she turned to see her father shuffle to his elbows. A seaman to the bone, even *in extremis*, he had heard the anchor too, and knew the hour had come. 'Feyra,' he said, with a gasping effort, *'Death is coming . . .'*

She understood his ravings better than he knew. She nodded and turned back to the window, and watched the gangplank lowered. Her view was restricted, but she looked beyond it, through the twin pillars, to where the great square lay, mirrored with water. Despite the flood of the vast space plenty of citizens were still abroad, stamping through their own reflections matter-of-factly as if such floodings were commonplace.

She changed places to the next porthole, peering down deckside as she heard the scrape and boom of the sarcophagus being dragged to the head of the gangplank and set down. Feyra watched with dread as the rivets were loosened, and the myrtle leaves cast aside to be snatched by the jealous wind. The Janissaries stood back in a semicircle, their heads now bare of their turbans, their livery hidden under wine-coloured cloaks. They were transfixed but afraid, as the thing inside lifted itself with a painful effort, trembling like a new-birthed foal.

First he sat, than prised himself out of the coffin with shaking arms braced at each side. He was a dreadful thing to behold. His shrouds were shredded and flapped like bandages – a swaddled charnel-corpse come to life. Someone tossed him a cape which unfurled in the air and cast a dark shadow over him like a cloud. He fumbled it on, drawing the black hood over his swathed head. Across the back was emblazoned a winged lion stitched in gold. The beast seemed to move with the ragged gasps of his wearer, the bony notches of his wasted back seeming to animate the lion's wings as he struggled to breathe.

Now Death was clad, as was fitting, in black.

He stood for one instant at the top the gangplank, before stumbling down it, aided by the gradient and the winds at his back. On the dockside, Death fell to his knees, tried to pick himself up; couldn't.

Feyra watched, wishing she could turn from the pitiful sight but unable to tear her eyes away. She was torn by pity for the fellow and a fervent hope that he would drown now, face down in the waters, or be dragged back into the sea by the ebbing flood that silvered and soaked his heavy cloak.

With superhuman will, he raised himself up and staggered between those sentinel pillars. By some strange fall of the cloak's fabric it seemed that he was the only soul in that vast square without reflection or shadow. That and the voluminous black cloak, snatched and rippled by the winds, conferred on the dying man a malevolent, otherworldly appearance; he was the Reaper personified.

Feyra knew then that the galleas itself, and the cape with that dreadful chimera of the winged lion and the book, had been all part of the design. The citizens would see a Venetian ship, and an infirm man in an Admiral's cloak, and run to help him. Already, some people were wading across.

She hammered on the porthole, shouting, but the glass was sealed shut. Proof to storms and battle, the pane did not even crack. Her knuckles were raw and her voice hoarse but it did no good. She ran to the door and rattled the clasp, but knew already it would be no use. She looked up, desperately rattling the gratings in the quarterdeck, trying to force them open. Despairing now, Feyra picked up the wine bottle and smashed it against the porthole, but the bottle shattered in her hand, the green shards slicing her flesh.

As she sucked at the bitter blood on her fingers, Feyra

saw a woman with her son in her skirts. The mother set the child down, tipping his little tricorn hat over his nose against the rain. The boy clung to her skirts though, refusing to be left, so they went to the cloaked figure together.

Feyra no longer shouted, but spoke to the woman in a desperate undertone: *'Please, please please turn back. Take your child. Be on your way'*. But the woman, with her son trailing along behind, came right up to Death and offered a hand. As if time had slowed Feyra watched Death's black hand extend from his cloak, and close around the woman's white one.

It was done.

She saw the woman recoil from the face she saw beneath the hood, saw the white hand snatched away and wrapped around the little boy, pressing the little face into her robes with the hand that had touched Death's. A little knot of people came running, half wading, half running through the knee-high water to see what was amiss.

Feyra turned back to her father. She did not need to see the sequel to these events, nor tell him what had happened. He read all in her face, and fell back on his cot, defeated. The ship lurched again as the anchor was weighed and the galleass turned, the winds swelling the sails above, and the dock receding swiftly.

Framed by the porthole, Feyra watched the scene getting smaller and smaller. They diminished with the distance, that doomed little crowd of people clustering around Death, and she watched them till she could hardly see, until they were no bigger than the black spores of the Bartholomew tree.

Chapter 11

Feyra returned to her father's side – he was her only concern now.

She put away her other feelings. She'd been raised to hate the people of Venice, but she felt nothing but pity for that young mother and her child, and the others who had come to aid Death. And she had let *her* mother down; she had failed to warn the Doge of what was to come. But there would be time enough to repent at leisure. Her task now was to heal her father and get him home.

Having delivered its terrible cargo, the ship had now turned about and was sailing away from the city as fast as the canvases could carry it. Feyra knelt by her father's cot to comfort him with this news. For a moment she thought he had already gone from her, but as she took his hand he woke, and coughed a little again. She was heartened – coughing was the body's way of clearing foul ether from the lungs – and smiled at him. 'Be cheered, Father. We are going home. Soon we will see the Bosphorus again and Seraglio point, and the dome of the Sophia gold in the sun.'

Very slightly, he shook his head. '*Giudecca*,' he whispered, his voice a raven's rasp.

It was a word she did not know, but she knew that the

Plague could produce ravings. She patted his hand, but he grasped it and held it fast. 'Safe house,' he went on. 'Sultan promised.'

She nodded, smiling brightly, though in truth she could not believe that the Sultan would make any such provision. The men aboard *Il Cavaliere* were, surely, as expendable to him as Death himself had been, and every moment they spent in these waters put them in further danger.

Feyra took these unhappy reflections back to the port-hole. She wanted to see Venice recede, so they could be gone. The city held no beauty for her: her part in the terrible fate that awaited it made it a place of horror. She vowed, once she was home, never to leave Constantinople again. She would never come back here, never. Even the word 'Venice' was hateful to her; with its sharp syllables that sliced like a knife and hissed like a snake. She never wanted to look upon the winged lion again. He was a monster, and every league of sea that paid out between her and his dominion was a blessing.

But instead of cleaving the open seas, the ship was hugging a dun spit of land to the north of the city. There were few houses here that matched the opulent glory of what she had seen around that great square, and the brickwork was simpler, rougher; brown and speckled as a hen's egg. Here and there were ruins too, making gaps in the skyline like missing teeth, areas of grassy wasteland between. By one such wilderness the ship came aside.

Feyra had learnt to recognize the drop of the anchor and the lurch and halt of the ship, but still did not comprehend. Why would they stop now? Why not make haste home as swiftly as they could? What more business did they have here?

She sat by her father again and took his hand. The rain had abated and all was quiet.

Too quiet.

Quiet enough for her to hear the turn of the little brass key in the lock of the night cabin. She stood, afraid, as the door opened and a half dozen of the Janissaries filed in, dressed once more in their black face masks.

No one spoke, but one man took her arm and pulled her to the side. Four others took a rope at each corner of her father's bed and drew their scimitars with a metallic ringing. For a dreadful moment she thought they would execute him on the spot, but then each of the quartet laid hold of a rope and cut it cleanly, carrying the bed to the door like a litter.

Feyra counselled herself: they were loyal men who would follow the code of shipboard. Timurhan, even if incapacitated, was still their captain. Her captor pulled her along in the wake of the procession. 'Where are you taking my father?' she asked. But there was no reply from beneath the black mask.

Once on land, she could see their position – they were in the lee of the land mass, sheltered from the winds that whipped the seaboard, and with the ship now part hidden by a vast stone ruin. Here was a wall pierced by arched windows, and beyond, a wilderness of low walls with a well in the middle, populated only by the daws and kites that screeched from the eaves. Faded letters were picked out in gilt over the architrave, but only Feyra of the company could make them out.

Santa Croce.

A ragged stone cross, pitted and pocked by the elements, topped the jagged wall. At the sight of this symbol, the crew went into a huddle.

Feyra edged closer to the black-clad group on the deserted wooden pier.

'It was a place of their prophet, their Christ,' said one.

'We cannot cross the threshold, it is unclean,' agreed another.

'Our Sultan must have made a mistake; this is no safe house for us.'

'Our Sultan, the light of my eyes and the delight of my heart, does not make mistakes.' A clear and ringing voice.

'Look at it. No one lives here but the birds to shit on it. Their god left long ago.'

'We cannot stay here.'

'No, but this ruin will at least shelter us while we decide.'

Feyra followed them as they took her father within and they allowed her to make him comfortable. He was fortunate in his bed for the well-stuffed mattress was held firm by the sides of the box, and Feyra doubted he even knew he'd been moved. She ripped a strip from his sheet, and headed to the well in the centre of the old courtyard, tripping over the scattered stones broken up by the determined roots and grasses that had cracked them over the years.

Despite the torrential rainfall which had only just eased, the water level of the well was so far below that she could barely see a silver disc of cloudy sky lying at the bottom. There was an ancient rusted chain and pulley by the old stone bowl but no bucket, so she abandoned her idea of drawing water. She took the cloth back to the pier instead and dunked it in seawater – it would not quench her father's thirst but she could at least bathe his fevered flesh.

As she walked back through the ruined arch she was met by the Janissaries, standing in a semicircle. The cloth dripped in her hand, anointing her feet, and she stopped in her tracks, suddenly afraid.

She looked from one pair of dark eyes to another; none would directly meet her gaze. One spoke at last. 'Turn about,' he said. 'We are boarding the ship.'

'But –' she extended her hand to point inside the old church, still holding the dripping cloth. 'My father,' she said, as if they were all simple, as if they did not understand.

'He stays.'

It was she who had not understood. They were going to leave him. He was infected, and they would not have their captain back aboard. 'Then I must stay with him.'

'No. You are coming with us.'

'That's right,' said another. 'If death is to take us, I for one wish to enjoy the days that are left to me.' Now the first man looked at her, his eyes caressing her unveiled face, and the body to which her damp clothes still clung.

So she was to be a plaything for these men, all the way back to Constantinople. There was no one here to defend her honour. Her father was lying nearby on his litter, insensible even to the rain that had begun to fall on his face. She had longed to go home, but not like this. Then one man, who stood a little apart from the others, spoke.

'*I* will stay, as planned.'

He had silenced his fellows with his statement. At length one spoke, voice pitched high with incredulity. 'Why? There is no safe house. To stay here would be suicide.'

'Then I will follow the orders of my Sultan to the end as I have pledged, for he is the light of my eyes and the delight of my heart. And below our Sultan, I obey my captain. For he is our Sultan's deputy, and at Lepanto he saved me from much worse than this.'

He held up his left hand, where there were three fingers lacking, leaving him only his forefinger and thumb.

Now Feyra knew the masked man for Takat Turan, he who had saved her once today on the water's brink. Now, too, she remembered the story her father had told her.

When she asked him about this greatest sea battle of all he had told her not of the clash of the battleships or the bravery of the Admirals but a story of a boy, no older than her, brought aboard as a powder monkey to load the cannon. They had been boarded by the Venetians and Timurhan had found the lad literally pinned to the bulwark, for a Venetian dagger, thrown awry, had pinned his hand to the wood, and bit so deep he could not move. Timurhan had severed three of the lad's fingers with his own scimitar and pulled the bleeding boy to the forecastle and out of danger. He'd told Feyra the boy had not even cried, but, once the Venetian forces had been repelled, watched in stoic silence as the ship's doctor tarred and cauterized his fingers, only asking to save the Venetian blade as a keepsake.

Feyra could see that this courage had followed him to adulthood; and something else too, for Takat's eyes glittered with an indefinable fervour.

The fellow that opposed him gave it a name. 'You are mad!'

But Takat's tones were even. 'Nonetheless, if my captain needs me I will serve him until he dies.'

To find such loyalty in this dark time and this dark place touched Feyra deeply. Before she could shame herself by throwing herself at his feet, he went on.

'And furthermore you are forgetting the orders of our Sultan, the light of my eyes and the delight of my heart. For not one of you was destined to return. Remember: our work here is not yet done; we are part of a greater battle. This was but the opening salvo.'

Feyra read true loyalty in his eyes, and something more too, the fiery gaze of a fanatic. She wondered what more was to be done to this beleaguered city, but the other soldier began to argue.

'You have lost your wits! How long do you think it will take their officers and caliphs to find us? Have you never heard of the hellish methods of their torturers? The ways of Byzantium are nothing to it.'

Takat Turan shrugged lightly, as if such torments were nothing. 'Then let them come. For in the words of the Sultan, if they should pull my limbs from my body, and tear my eyes from my head and tongue from my throat, I will then be transported direct to Jannah, where I will walk and see and speak again, to praise the name of God.'

The other men shifted uncomfortably and began to talk among themselves. Then, at last, the one that had spoken first said, 'Please yourself,' and walked to Feyra. He found his way barred by the black-clad arm of Takat Turan.

'She stays too.' He spoke in slow and measured tones.

'What?' the other spluttered. 'Why should you have her all to yourself, you lecherous dog?'

'Your question shames you. I serve my God and my Sultan and my captain, and my purity would not importune a lady.'

His accuser stepped back a pace as if struck. Takat Turan took his moment and spoke to Feyra from the side of his mouth. 'Lady, go to your father and lie as close as you can by his side.'

She slipped beyond his protective arm, and lay down in the bed-cum-litter beside her insensible father. She was suddenly deathly tired and willing for someone else to direct her fate. She lay looking directly overhead, at the rain-fattened clouds scudding across the sky, listening to the angry voices ringing around the old stones.

'You may come to get her if you wish. See where she lies, by her father. You drew lots, I know, even to carry him from the ship. I *know* that my God will protect me for my purpose. Can you say the same? If so, come; pluck her out of his deathbed.'

Feyra waited, watching the clouds, for hands to grasp and arms to lift.

'And then, what?' came Takat's voice again. 'Which one of you will bring her aboard, and invite her to your cot? You might as well dally with the Plague maiden with her red apron and her broom.'

Not one man came forth to lay hands on her. Feyra dared to raise her head a little. The men shifted and some looked at the ground. Uncertainly, muttering and shamefaced, they retreated from the building, leaving the dying man and the two young people in the ruin.

From the archway Feyra watched as the anchor was weighed, the ropes hauled in and the ship shoved from the dock by impatient feet. Only then did she turn to Takat.

'Thank you.'

He bowed very slightly. 'All debts must be paid in time.' She thought then that he referred to what he owed her father and was glad. She smiled at him and it occurred to her that she had never before smiled at a man beside her father without the covering of a veil.

He did not return her smile, but instead looked out to

sea, through the broken archway of the great door, framing the shrinking ship. He had pulled down his mask so it rucked about his throat and she could study his face, his beard trimmed and oiled to a point, his lips unexpectedly full between the black hair. He seemed to be looking beyond the ship, beyond even the curve of the horizon and all the cares of the world. Instinctively she trusted him.

'What shall we do now?' she asked.

Takat Turan thought for a time. 'We must get your father to shelter.' He surveyed the ruin. 'Look. There is a place with a roof still – a gatehouse or some such. I will help you carry him.'

With much effort, her sinews straining, they half carried, half dragged Timurhan beneath the shelter of the old gate-house. Inside the shack there was a faldstool where the gatekeeper must have sat once, a bracket for a lamp which had long since been extinguished, and a nest of starlings under the eaves that screeched in protest at having to share their cot.

Feyra stroked her father's face but he did not respond. His breath was laboured and his fingers blacker than ever. She saw Takat look down at his captain and she could read his thoughts although he did not speak them aloud. He looked instead to the derelict roof and the sky beyond. 'I have a small parcel of food,' he said, 'but it is barely enough. Before night falls I must procure some more supplies.'

Feyra knew he would have to steal, but she did not care. She could no longer ignore the gnawing hunger in her stomach. As he turned to go she laid a hand on his arm to stop him.

'Wait,' she said. 'You cannot go abroad thus. You look

different to the citizens of this place. Unwind your turban too.'

He looked less threatening without it, younger, and the wind ruffled his dark hair about his face. 'Now go.'

The black-clad figure turned at the gate, on a divot in the stone where Saint Sebastian had once driven his sword into the ground. 'Hide yourself well,' he said. 'You'll see me again.'

She watched him until he had turned the corner. Over his shoulder she could see *Il Cavaliere*, far out to sea already, her prow set towards Constantinople.

For the next hours she crouched in the dank dark, her back against the cold stone.

She was colder than she had ever been; and however she sat the sharp flints stuck into her back. Twice in those hours she heard the citizens of the island pass, and peered through the stones to see two fat laundresses who held their baskets above their heads against the rain, and later a fisherman with a dog. She held her breath as the little cur actually trotted into the gatehouse and even sniffed at Timurhan's motionless foot, until she shooed him away and he bounded off at a whistle from his master. The scent of fish reached her through the derelict wall, transporting her back to the fish market in the Balik Pazari. She peered through the stones to see their silver scales glowing in the twilight as they lolled on the fisherman's shoulder. Her stomach growled afresh. She could have devoured both of them; eyes, guts, bones and all.

By nightfall she knew the truth. Takat Turan was not coming back.

She rose now, for it was too dark to be seen, and walked all the way through the old building to the other shore of the island. She looked up at the moon, and then down at the crystal ring on her finger. The tiny black horse was uppermost and she turned him till he faced away, below her fingers, so the red horse showed. She had failed to stop the black horse riding forth, and would never, now, find a man called Saturday, go to a house with golden callipers over the door, nor meet the Doge himself who was, incredibly, her great-uncle. It all seemed like an Ottoman legend, as ancient as it was improbable.

She watched the strange city across the water, windows illuminating one by one, pricked out like a constellation of stars as the citizens lit their candles and lamps. She knew that as the people lit their tapers and rush dips to light them to bed, somewhere in those houses a husband would notice the hectic colour of his wife's countenance, or a mother would note the unnatural heat of her son's cheek as she kissed him goodnight, and the dawn would bring the horror of the pestilence.

PART II

The Birdman

Chapter 12

Doctor Annibale Cason took extra care with his appearance that morning.

Newly qualified as the *medico* for the *quartiere* of the Miracoli in his home city of Venice, he had gained, with his new status, a manservant to dress him; but he could not stay still and let the man work. It was still strange to him to be dressed as if he were a babe, and he twitched and fidgeted, retied and rebuttoned, and at length dismissed his servant to be alone before his full-length Murano looking-glass. Today his garments were not merely a symbol of his status, but had to actually do the job for which they were designed. They were medical clothes and he wished to don them himself, for they could save his life.

Over his ordinary suit of clothes he pulled on long, supple leather breeches. As long as those worn by the fishermen in the lagoon, these were not to keep out seawater but other more noxious fluids. Worn beneath his cloak they would protect his legs and groin from infection.

Next Annibale swung a long, black overcoat about his shoulders with a sweeping flourish. He tied it tight about his neck, then flicked out the longer curls of hair that tumbled about his nape. He kept his curls long for a reason; his teachers at Padua advised that skin exposure was to be kept to a minimum in infected wards, for it was the air that carried disease. He turned up the high collar of the coat, so that his neck and throat were completely covered by the cloth and the join by his hair. The cape extended to his feet, and was coated head to toe in mutton suet and tallow. The suet drew the pestilence away and trapped it in the folds of the cloak, which was then smoked nightly in juniper smoke. The wax served as protection against droplet contamination, to prevent sputum or other bodily fluids from clinging to the cloak, for it was acknowledged that coughing carried the plague.

Then came the symbol of Annibale's profession, an ugly mask to cover his handsome features. A dreadful construction in the shape of a bird's beak, it was a mask that he had studied for seven years to be allowed to wear. Annibale knew the shape of the mask originated from the old-fashioned notion that disease was carried by birds and that by dressing in a bird-like mask the wearer could draw infection away from the patient and on to the clothes that the doctor wore. Annibale snorted behind the mask at this kind of ignorant assumption that now held no sway in the quadrangles of Padua, breathing in as he did so the heady scent of cinnamon and potash stuffed in the nose. The beak of the mask was filled with strongly aromatic herbs to overpower the miasma and dull the smell of unburied corpses, sputum, ruptured buboes and the other delights that he could expect today. The mask also included red glass eyepieces, which were thought to make the wearer impervious to evil.

Lastly Annibale donned the distinctive wide-brimmed black hat worn close to the head, and arranged it to cover the white domed forehead of the mask. He was not afraid of contagion for his own sake, but if he became ill, he would no longer be able to heal, and Annibale had no intention of stopping before he had even started.

Just before he left the glass he took up a wooden cane propped against the wall. The cane was used to both direct family members to attend or adjust the patient, and sometimes to examine the patient with directly. Besides, in wards of infection a *medico* could describe a circle about himself with a sweep of the cane that none would dare to enter. Annibale flourished it now, like a rapier, for the benefit of his reflection. But what he saw did not convince him. The ensemble looked too pristine and untried, fresh as it was from the tailors and maskerers, the bills of sale still attached to the folds.

For a moment he saw himself as others would see him, a harbinger of death. The plague doctor's clothing had a secondary use: to frighten and warn onlookers, and to communicate that something very, very wrong was nearby. The beaked mask in particular looked incredibly macabre.

Even on an ordinary day he was glad of the mask, for it covered his extraordinarily fine features. Annibale saw himself, as he saw everything, in scientific terms like a creature in a jar at the *Scuola Medica* in Padua. Of four cats pickled in a jar he could easily see which had the sharpest teeth and the leanest back and the longest leg. As a specimen he knew he was a fine example of *homo sapiens*, tall for a Venetian, with well-muscled, long, lean limbs, and a tumble of dark hair. His own face, though, was a mystery to him. He acknowledged he had regular features; but to him they seemed unremarkable, these dark eyes and the arched brows over them, and this straight nose with finely flared nostrils and the full lips beneath. However, they had a strange alchemy he did not understand, which acted on women in a way he did not welcome. Annibale liked order, and because he could not control the effect his features had he preferred to cover them up.

In truth, even when not wearing the beak, Annibale had cultivated a mask of his own; he adopted a brusque manner that gave him the impression of being proud and haughty, solely to keep women – and some men too – at a distance. When he spoke it was with ill-concealed irritation; he did not suffer fools and was known for being short-tempered.

The brutal truth was that Doctor Annibale Cason was a good doctor because he didn't really care who lived or died. After his mother had abandoned him as a babe, and the parade of numerous aunts that had raised him in succession had all died, he had no emotional attachments; and despite frequent proposals he had never married. He saw illness as a personal intellectual challenge, which almost had more to do with him than the afflicted, and was therefore extremely successful at treatment. He was known at university as a basilisk of a man, who could watch a babe die without pity.

In this his fellows did not give him enough credit. Annibale was not entirely heartless, but he kept a little circle of distance around him even without his cane. He had few friends and this suited him. Those he held close to his heart knew the real Annibale; they were few in number, and he had no need of more.

Padua was a wealthy city and, in his final year when the young doctors were released on the general populace, he had had to attend many rich women. There, in the city where he'd trained, the dreadful mask had served to keep him from the importunities of these bored matrons who were so taken with his comely face, that they would demand that he try their breath on his cheek or that he press his ear to their heaving bosoms to check their throbbing hearts. Today, back in his home city, the mask would serve its true medical purpose.

Annibale could not believe his luck. Born and raised in Venice, christened in the Church of Santa Maria degli Miracoli, the very church that now sounded the pestilence bell, he had been but one day back from Padua, had spent one night in his old bed in the family home, before the Lord had smitten the city. Now, at last, he would have the chance to put his seven years of learning at the University Medical School, where he had been one of the finest minds of his year, into practice. All the herbals he had read in the libraries, all those mornings spent in the botanical gardens, all those afternoons in the tiered wooden theatre watching his beloved mentor dissecting the cadavers of unlamented criminals, would now be put to use.

Ready now, he dismissed his reflection as he'd dismissed his man, barked instructions at his cook for that evening, and left the house, almost with a light step. He felt like a knight of old riding to battle and fate had provided him with the most deadly adversary of all to try his lance upon. He, *Doctor* Annibale Cason, was ready to take on the Plague.

He noted, on his way through the *calli*, that his foe had lost no time taking hold of the battlefield. The numerous red crosses daubed on doors, the lime boxes on each corner, the myrtle smoke snaking from every chimney, told him that the Black Death had set up camp, even in so short a time.

As he arrived at the Campo Santa Maria Nova, the place appointed for him to meet his superior, Annibale had no difficulty picking out Doctor Valnetti, who was dressed exactly the same as he. His mask was slightly different though, for as one of the six chief doctors of the *sestieri*, he had black eye-glasses painted around his red crystal eyes, a reference to his greater wisdom and learning. Although Annibale thought a great deal of the new-fangled invention of spectacles, he thought the twin black circles gave his superior a faintly comic air.

Doctor Valnetti was bustling around in an officious manner, bristling with the self-importance conferred upon him by a morning visit, along with the chief *medici* of the other five *sestieri*, to the Doge himself. He shook Annibale's glove briefly.

Annibale politely observed what his superior was doing – he seemed to be shuffling a pile of dried fish-skins, holding them for a brief second over the yellow fire pit in the centre of the *campo*, as one would smoke a haddock, and then placing them in a pile like autumn leaves.

Annibale looked closer and was reminded of one of his many aunts who used to make him *risotto con rana*. She would slice each of the frogs around the feet and up the back and peel the skin off like a chemise before throwing the membrane in the stockpot. He picked up one of the fish-skins from the pile on the pavings. It had limbs. Then he understood. Incredulous, he turned to his superior. 'Toads' skins? Really?'

Although he tried to sound respectful, Annibale reserved deference for where it was truly deserved, as in the case of his hero, tutor and mentor Hieronymus Mercurialis from the medical faculty at Padua. He could not keep the customary scorn from creeping into his voice.

'Well, not *all* toads – they are surprisingly hard to find,' answered the doctor breezily. 'But there are frogs in Venice aplenty, the canals are stuffed with 'em. So we make do. Such skins were proven to work the last time the Pestilence struck,' he concluded airily, neglecting to mention that this was a century past. 'They seemed to be efficacious in cleansing the air in the body's major vessels.'

Annibale narrowed his eyes behind the red eyepieces. 'You mean the *blood* in the body's major vessels.'

'Yes, yes,' agreed Valnetti. 'That is what I said.' He added, rather hurriedly, 'distribute these in your *quartiere*. Ease any symptoms as best you can. I'll see you here at sundown.' He handed the pile of the toad-skins to Annibale, who grasped at them with difficulty, for they blew about, dry and insubstantial as cinders. Valnetti clapped him on the back. 'I must say we were surprised to find a doctor to come to Venice, and I certainly didn't expect a Padua man. Most physicians are running as fast as they can in the opposite direction.'

Annibale shrugged and another frog's skin slipped from his grasp. 'I would rather die in Venice than live anywhere else.'

Valnetti snorted inside his mask. 'It might come to that.'

Annibale felt vaguely uneasy. It had been centuries now since any natural philosopher had believed that air, not blood, circulated in the veins. He, Annibale, had helped to prove the matter beyond doubt when, only last year, he had assisted in the transfusion of blood from a dog to a man, draining the cur's blood into the opened vessels of a convict. He could have told Valnetti so, leaving out, of course, the fact that the ensanguinated man and the exsanguinated dog had both died. But he didn't wish to waste his breath. Instead he raised the skins in his arms a couple of inches and asked, 'Is this it? Frogs' skins?'

'For now. I am, of course, developing some remedies of my own, but for today, do what you can. And – Cason?'

Annibale turned back, glad that Valnetti could not see his expression. 'Don't confuse them with your fancy Paduan theories. They are simple people, not intellectuals like us.' And the doctor disappeared like a magician into a pall of smoke.

The first thing Annibale did once he had turned the corner into the Calle San Canzian was to dump the odious frog-skins in the nearest lime box.

By the time he returned to the Campo Santa Maria Nova at the end of the day the Plague had beaten Annibale Cason in the lists.

Annibale had not anticipated just how unequal the struggle would be; he was battling not just the disease but everything else. He was battling with family feeling – mothers who would not leave their infected sons, wives who would not leave the sides of their husbands – so the disease was spreading apace. He was battling the medical establishment: the Council of Health were of Valnetti's mind and persisted in using the same remedies they had used in the last outbreak of 1464. But worst of all, he was battling the city herself.

Venice's palaces were teeming with servants who came and went as they pleased, taking the miasma in their breath and their clothes to the markets and the milliners and the tailors, while in the meaner houses families were crowded into one smoky room, breathing the same septic air.

Even the daubmen who marked the doors of the infected were taking the contagion from house to house, their persons and their paintbrushes unknowing vectors for the miasma. Cats and curs too who should – in truth – be culled, roamed freely; in the great houses spoiled lapdogs took the disease from one fond hand to the next, and in the poorer wards scavenging strays entered and left the houses of the diseased unnoticed by the distraught residents. There were not even any ratcatchers in evidence to curb the vermin.

Worse still, beggars stole corpses from the red-crossed houses and cradled them in the streets, pretending the cadavers were family members and begging for coin to ease their sorrow. The younger the corpse, noted Annibale, the greater the return.

Overlaying it all, Annibale even found the incessant bells unhelpful – at noon some edict had come down from the *Consiglio della Sanita* that the pestilence bell should ring the day long. The constant chimes from the Miracoli and San Canzian jangled on the nerves of the sick, struck fear into the healthy and were an irritant to the practitioners. Annibale was shorter than ever with his patients; it was his only answer to the pleading, weeping families faced with inconceivable loss. Unable to help them, his anger at himself translated itself into anger at them.

Annibale worked faster, refusing to acknowledge how much the day had affected him. In Padua, it was true that he had once seen a baby stillborn and had not been moved; but even Annibale's heart had received a jolt today, not to mention his pride. All his knowledge, from the first year basics of Galen and the four humours, to the final year sophistries of surgery, had afforded him no assistance at all.

It was twilight before he met Valnetti again, and as Annibale crossed the *campo* to greet him, his gait was

slow and tired, his feet heavy, as if they truly wore the saba-
tons and spurs of combat. His superior, however, a man of
twice as many years, exhibited a lightness of step and looked
surprisingly sprightly. 'A hard day I know,' said the doctor
before Annibale could speak. 'But it will go better tomorrow, for I have had my apothecaries hard at work.' He
tapped his beak with his gloved finger conspiratorially, then
swept his greatcoat back to reveal, with a flourish, what it
hid.

Behind him Valnetti pulled a little red wooden cart with
four wheels and a handle, with a grotesque caricature of a
doctor daubed clumsily on the side. The cart was fairly rattling with rank upon rank of tiny glass bottles. Annibale
picked one out with his gloved hand and held it to the light.
A green sludge clung to the sides of the crystal vial as he
shook it. 'What is it?'

'Four Thieves Vinegar,' answered the doctor proudly.
'Also known as Marseilles Vinegar. My own recipe. I have
altered the specifications a little according to my own
research. I am surprised that you do not know it. It has been
used time out of mind to treat the Black Death. What do
they teach at Padua these days? In my time at Salerno we
learned it at the very first lecture.' He sighed that he was
obliged to instruct Annibale and told the tale in a sing-song
voice. 'Four robbers in Marseilles were convicted of going
to the houses of Plague victims, strangling them in their
beds and then looting their dwellings. For this, they were
condemned to be burned at the stake, but the judges
were astonished by the indifference of the thieves to contagion. The miscreants admitted they were immune to the
Plague and revealed their secret antidote: a vinegar which
came to be named after them. The justices demanded to

know the composition, promising in return to spare them from the fire.'

'What happened to them?'

'They were hanged,' said the doctor briefly, 'but that is not really the point of the story.'

'No. No, I suppose not.' Annibale's scientific interest was piqued. 'And what *was* the composition?'

'Get out your tables,' said Valnetti importantly. 'You might want to set this down. In the normal way I would not share such knowledge with another practitioner, but if we are to achieve lower mortality rates in this *sestiere* than the other doctors can achieve, then we must work together, no?' He drew closer to Annibale and took a sheaf of papers from his sleeve, divided them roughly in half and gave a pile to Annibale. 'Bills of Mortality,' Valnetti said. 'Paperwork, I'm afraid. You have to fill in one for every soul we lose, even the poor.' He sniffed. 'To say nothing of our reward from the Doge, and strictly between ourselves, I have laid a wager with the other five doctors for a tun of Gascon wine that we shall lose fewer souls in San Marco than in the other sixths. Now hark.'

Annibale obligingly tucked away the bills and got out his notebook and pencil from his sleeve, although privately he thought that there was little his superior could teach him. It seemed, too, that Valnetti cared nothing for his patients – but was Annibale, who liked tilting with Death to see who was the better, any different? Discomfited, he began to write as Valnetti ticked off the components on his black-gloved fingers.

'Rosemary and sage, rue, mint, lavender, calamus, nutmeg. Garlic, cinnamon and cloves, of course; the Holy Trinity in the treatment of most maladies. White vinegar, camphor. And of course, the most efficacious (not to say expensive) of ingredients: greater and lesser wormwood.'

'*Artemisia absinthum* and *artemisia pontica*,' put in Annibale, stung at the earlier slight to his education.

'You steep the plants in the vinegar for ten days,' said Valnetti as if he hadn't been interrupted, 'then force it through a linen sleeve. Are you getting all this?'

'Yes, yes,' lied Annibale, who had stopped writing long since. The potion was a placebo; this random collection of herbs and unguents would neither kill nor cure. He looked at his superior dubiously. 'And I am to distribute these vials to each household?'

'*Gesu*, my dear fellow, no!' the good doctor exclaimed. 'They cost one ducat each, only to those that can afford it. Of course, if you can get two, so much the better. Go easy though; the apprentices have been working flat out, and cannot make more until tomorrow.' He lowered his voice and moved so close that their beaks clashed, like crows in conference. 'Here is a tip for you; if you find a mother with a sick babe – they will pay *anything*.'

Annibale stopped listening. He was looking at the painted doctor on the side of the little red cart – beaked and bespectacled, with gaudy red circles painted high on each cheek symbolizing health. He seemed a grotesque and a buffoon – like Pulcinella, the hook-nosed ancient of the *commedia dell'arte*. Worse, he was a vulture to pluck coin from the dead and dying, no better that the four thieves of Marseilles. He felt Valnetti slip the handle into his hand.

'You can pull the cart quite easily, look; *one ducat each*, remember, no less. My costs must be covered. Sell this cartload – it is the only one we have at present – and then be off to your bed. Cason? Cason? Where are you going?'

Sickened, Annibale had dropped the handle of the cart and walked away. This is not what he had trained for. He headed for the Fondamenta Nuove, the myrtle smoke swirling around him as if he were a Faustian spirit coughed from hell. There on the dock he could breathe again. He took off his mask and threw back his sweaty hair. He shook the smoke from his clothes, breathed the salt air, and began to question.

What if the citizens were not bottled together to die? What if they could breathe *this* air, not the choking smoke of burning myrtle? If he could just take them away, treat them as he wanted, not with witchcraft and superstition but with the sound medical precepts to which he'd dedicated his academic life.

He breathed out the horrors of the day in one long, defeated breath and looked right out to sea. On the distant horizon, through the sickly yellow mists from the plague fires which were rolling into the lagoon, there where the air was clear, he saw where the silver line of the sea clotted into a collection of islands. The glass island, the lace island. And beyond, the lazarets.

In the distant horizons of his mind, a vague notion clotted into an idea.

Chapter 13

When Feyra woke that first morning in Venice, she thought her father was already dead.

Heart thumping, she lay still for a moment by his side, suspended in the moment, afraid to look. But while the front of her body was warm, pressed next to his fevered form, her back was cold and stiff. The warmth gave her hope.

She rose from the litter and stretched. The starlings in the broken eaves were already awake and saluting the day. She went outside and saw a world transformed; a kindly sun shone, the rain and storm clouds were gone. The stones themselves revealed the crystals and fossils trapped in the wall and fairly sparkled, while the grass glowed and glittered with dew. Feyra's spirits lifted a fraction. Her father might yet live.

She went to the well in the middle of the ruin, and today had the time to work out the pulley system. Since the bucket was long gone she lowered a strip of her father's coverlet, baiting the chain like a fisherman. She lowered the hook to the distant depths and hauled it back up, dripping. She sucked the cloth dry, the water tasting surprisingly fresh and clean, thanks to yesterday's deluge. Feyra soaked the cloth again, returned to her father's side, and squeezed the water into his mouth, closing the rigid jaw with her fingertips so that he swallowed.

Then she sat in a sunny archway and removed her medicine belt, rubbing her waist where it had chafed and blistered her for days. She spread the knobbly leather belt on her knee and examined it. The vials in the holsters seemed intact – one of the little corks was gone, and she'd lost her supply of rue, not such a loss, for it was a common enough herb. The thought pulled her up sharp. It had been common enough in Constantinople. She was in a different terrain here.

The dried herbs in the little pockets had been soaked by seawater and rolled to a damp mulch, like the herbs the caliphs rolled and smoked in their *narghiles*. Feyra had several wondrous compounds here, from humblest lemon balm to powdered jewels. There was even, wrapped in a vine leaf, a greasy little knuckle of ambergris. Taking the vials and pockets and folds in all, she had about a hundred medicines collected painstakingly over months and years.

Feyra decided to make a last concerted effort to save her father. She rejected the notion of compound medicine – *murekebbat* – as she did not know enough about her adversary to tailor a cure. She decided instead to employ the practice of *mufradet*, the simple pharmacy of single plants. She would dose Timurhan with each medicine in turn, spaced by the sound of the bells which struck every hour, leaving aside the compounds that she knew to be strongly toxic. She began her regime with cinnabar – red mercury, which she knew in small amounts to be an excellent purifier of the blood. She took from a leather fold a fan of silver medicine spoons that she'd had made in a back street silversmith's in Sultanamet, of varying sizes connected by the handles to a hinged ring. She spread the spoons like a fan and selecting the tiniest, tapped out a minute heap of powder from the selected vial, and poured it though Timurhan's cracked lips.

With nothing to do now but wait, she knew she must take care of her own body. She broke off a small hunk of the bread Takat had left behind and forced herself to eat it slowly. Then, her growling hunger barely sated, she wandered the ruin, seeking the rue she had lost. She dropped to her knees and combed the damp grass with her fingers – the dew was refreshing and cleansed her grimed nails. She peered carefully at the grasses that grew around the old stones, the hardy flowers that squeezed between the masonry cracks and the herbs that fringed what seemed to be foundations for some ancient garden.

Feyra breathed in the myriad of scents as the sun rose and coaxed the leaves to unfurl and the petals to open. A skilled herbalist, she looked carefully at the shapes of those leaves and the colour and number of those petals. Some plants she could identify, some she couldn't. She did find more common rue for her belt, though, growing near the well.

She gave a little cry of triumph and knelt to examine the familiar feathery plant, with its glaucous blue-green leaves and yellow flowers. Her knees soaked and chilled in the waterlogged ground as she tilted the leaves to pick off the precious fruits, lobed capsules containing numerous seeds. Heartened, she searched further, and in one stony corner beneath a fallen corbel, found a real prize: a bush of wood betony, growing in its beloved shade. Here, as her searching fingers grasped and snatched at the tough roots, she found a more tangible treasure, a round, metal disc.

She rubbed the coin on her filthy breeches until she saw

a dull gleam of gilt. She carried it to her mouth and bit down.

Gold.

She examined the coin in the dappled light winking through the arched windows. On one side was a man with a beard and arms outstretched – she knew this man, he was the prophet called Jesus, and his sign was the cross. On the other side there was a man kneeling to another man. The kneeling man wore a strangely shaped hat, and the standing one had circle about his head. The circlet-wearer resembled the statue she had seen on one of the great twin pillars between which Death had walked. But the kneeling man's identity was a mystery.

For a moment Feyra held the cold metal as if it burned her; but then she tucked the alien coin firmly in the bandeau which bound her breasts. She had no idea of the value of the thing but it would surely buy a loaf for her father, perhaps some wine and flesh too. The thought made her mouth water.

The bell brought her to herself and she returned for her father. It was time for his next dose, and she blessed her luck. She would try a decoction of betony, which was proven to be most efficacious for sores, boils and pushes.

Perhaps it was the rising light, but her father looked a little better to her eyes after his treatment. She bowed her head and prayed over him, trying to remember the exact wording of the priests.

One of the main precepts of Ottoman medicine was the concept of *Mizan* – Balance. The balance was crucial to health, the duality and equity between body and spirit. One could not be well without the other, and the body had to be treated as a whole. With this in mind, when she rose from prayer, Feyra turned her attention back to her own well-being. Her own odours offended her and her hair was crackling with lice. She contemplated climbing into the well, but the salts of the sea would better cleanse her body and her clothes.

Taking her father's coverlet from his motionless body, she took it down to the deserted seashore. There she stripped beneath the blanket and lowered herself into the water, gasping at the cold of it despite the hot sun. Holding on to the little pier with one hand she scrubbed at her body with the other with a handful of salt and sand until the minerals stung her skin. Then, leaning forward, she dipped her whole head, scrubbing at her scalp with leaves of the tea tree from her belt to combat the lice, and wringing out the wet rope. Shivering, she combed the dark mass as best she could with her fingers, cracking any lice she found between her nails. Then she plaited it, like the Odalisques did, folding the strands in on themselves like a mackerel's bone.

That done, she dipped and scrubbed her clothes and veils and wrung them out, sprinting back to the protection of the buildings with her damp bundle. Once there, the coverlet wrapped around her like a dress, she hung the breeches, the bandeau and the shift around the wellhead, and draped the veils over the rusting wrought iron arch.

In the gatehouse she returned the coverlet to her father, thinking it might cool his fever, and sat shivering on the ground beside his bed, curled up as small as she could, clasping her legs to her, chattering chin on knees. For the next hour she shivered by her father, waiting as long as she dared before dressing again, almost weeping as she pulled on the still-damp clothes. Then, as her head emerged from her shift she was startled by the sound of bells: first one church on the island, then another, began to ring – to be answered by the churches across the water in the city, one, two and then all of them together. Had the alarm been raised? Were they about to be discovered?

Terrified by the bawling of the bells, Feyra lost all track of time and the rest of the day passed in a muddle and jumble of herbs and a muddle and jumble of prayers, until at last the light began to fail again. Feyra knew her father was growing steadily worse. Panicked, she contemplated what was, to her, a last resort.

Before the light faded and her courage too, she selected from her belt a scalpel sharp as a razor, fashioned by the same smith who had made her spoons. Then she slit her father's shirt up the middle with the knife, and removing the poultices from his swellings, pricked the left bubo. Seized with a sudden notion, she lanced the second swelling and collected the black blood cleanly in one of her vials. Then she laid some lemon balm from her belt over the cleaned wounds.

She leaned in close to her father's face in the dying light to look for signs of his reaction to the surgery. The bitter citrus of the lemon balm met her nostrils, and evidently his too, for, miraculously, he opened his eyes.

'She wore a mask,' he said, quite distinctly. He spoke as if he were picking up the thread of a previous conversation.

Feyra crouched by him in delight and took his forearm, kneading the frail flesh like dough. 'Who did, my dear, *dear* father?'

'She had a mask on a stick, it was a beautiful thing, wrought in silver and pearls. It was the head of a horse, I recall; she looked like a unicorn from the sagas. I had a little Venetian but mostly we spoke in mime like the shadow puppets – do you remember the shadow puppets?' His amber eyes were dulled now, but he knew her as he asked her the question.

Feyra nodded and squeezed his hand. Timurhan had taken her once to see a *Karagoz* shadow play in Beyoglu, spindly, curlicued silhouettes of a caliph and a concubine who moved and danced in perpetual profile as if they lived and breathed.

'I asked her if she liked riding and she held her heart and told me it was her passion. She showed me the ring she wore, a subtlety made of glass. Her fond uncle had given it to her – she pointed him out, he was the Doge. Then when we rode, there were lemon trees; they whispered their approval as we rushed by. The horses crushed the fruits under our hooves. I can still smell them, Feyra. I can smell them now.'

She smiled at him, knowing he could smell the lemon balm, hopeful now, knowing he would mend, that her surgery had worked.

Then he died.

Once again Feyra had to choose between well and sea, this time for a much darker purpose. She did not want to bury her father on ground consecrated to another god, and could not risk breaking ground in another place. She did not want, either, her father to rest in this sea. Although the ocean had been his home, she did not want him to be bloated by enemy waters and washed up on enemy shores. She chose the well because there he would be speedily interred under-ground as instructed by the Prophet, but insulated by stone from the unholy place around him. This ruin was abandoned – there seemed no danger that anyone would draw water from this forsaken shaft. And one day she might, God willing, be able to return and recover his bones, take him home and do him full honour.

It was impossible for her to drag the bed by its ropes so she rolled Timurhan from the cot in his coverlet, grateful that the counterpane encased him like a shroud and she did not have to look at his dear, dead face.

Still, it took her, in her weakened state, more than an hour to get him to the well. She took a last drink then hooked her father with his robes like a great fish, tipping him with an effort over the stone bowl, holding him in a last, terrible embrace, before letting him drop. Feyra shut her eyes, only hearing the chain paying out and the crash and splash as Timurhan hit the water. Then she looked down. The shrouded corpse looked for a moment almost as if it were standing, then the well waters, swollen by the rains, claimed the figure.

Feyra watched the water below bubble and flatten again. She fingered the ring on her finger and she thought for a moment of throwing it after him, so her father could have something of her mother. But her father was in Jannah and she was here, and it was all she had left that connected her to her family, to her mother, and, most extraordinarily of all, to the Doge.

It was all suddenly clear to her. This ring was her safe passage. She would go to the Doge. She had failed in her mission to keep the Plague from his door, but she could invoke the ring, awaken memories of his beloved lost niece Cecilia Baffo, and beg for safe passage back to Turkey.

She tied a *yemine* veil across her face again, suddenly ready to leave this place where she had shared her father's last hours, where she had passed her hands through the dewy grass, where she had found the betony and the coin. But just as she looked around for one last time, she heard a clunk and splash against the pier outside.

Feyra ran to the gate and peered through the little arch of the wheelhouse. A coracle had bumped up against the dock and a man in long robes stepped ashore, tying his painter to the sea-pole.

She hid in the gatehouse, breathless, and watched him through the great arched doorway. He was hobbling a little and on closer inspection, from his age and weight, she guessed he was gouty. As he drew within an armspan of her she could hear that he breathed with a slight wheeze – he'd either suffered from lung fever as a babe, or worked in a place where he breathed ill air. She did not think the latter was likely for she could see that his robes were made of vair and velvet. He wore, too, a black soft four-cornered hat. In Constantinople the wearing of a hat denoted status. And he wore it as if it were the same here. His face was kindly, his eyes benign, his beard grey. She was tempted to reveal herself and appeal to him in his own tongue, but something made her hold back, so she watched instead, while the man walked around the ruin. She held her breath, praying that he would stay away from the well. Her prayers were answered; he seemed to have no interest in it. He busied himself, instead, pacing one way and the other. He seemed to be counting under his breath, and every now and again he would stop, and take out a tablet and stylus, and mark his findings down. She heard an utterance clearly once, but it made no sense to her. He said, 'Sixteen by forty *passi*.'

For more than an hour he walked his strange measure, and once stooped to dig up a little soil, as if he too sought a cure. He placed the sample in his satchel, and before he left he lifted a small brick that he found on the sward to the light, tapped it once, and placed it in his bag too.

Feyra watched as the man returned to his boat. She considered, once again, asking him to row her to the city, but again something prevented her. As he rowed away, she breathed a sigh of relief and regret.

She had not been discovered, but now, for the first time since she'd left her home, she was truly alone.

Chapter 14

On his second day back in his home city of Venice Annibale Cason did not dress carefully in front of the mirror. He left the beak mask hanging over the looking-glass, and it watched him leave the chamber.

He did not march out of the house, nor did he go to meet Valnetti at daybreak in the Campo Santa Maria Nova, as he had been specifically instructed after his insubordination of yesterday evening. Instead he padded downstairs in his nightshirt, pulling from beneath it a little key that he'd worn round his neck for seven years.

The little gold key on the gold chain was warm from his sleeping skin. He'd worn it next to his chest since just before he went to Padua, a boy of fourteen, when the last of his many aunts died. Then and only then did the family notary give him the key to the Cason coffer, a bequest from the father he'd never known.

Annibale took his candle down to the wine cellar, his bare feet chilling on the stones. The wine barrels groaned and shifted as they fermented, and reacted to the changes in temperature that Annibale's presence brought to the room. When he was a boy and had come down here he had thought the cellar was haunted. He could hear then, as he could now, the canal lapping against the stones outside, for the cellar where the Cason family had kept their wine and salt for centuries was underwater.

The Cason family, of which Annibale was now the only scion.

He would be safe and secret here, and just as well; for it would not do for the servants to see the casket.

Annibale had been careful with the family fortune for all these years, not squandering the gold and roistering around town as his fellows did, but paying merely for his tuition, bed and board; and at the end of his seven years, his suit of doctor's clothes. So, when he rolled out the fourth barrel of Valpolicella from the left, the small coffer hidden behind it was almost full.

He set down the candle on the floor, dripping a pool of tallow to stand the taper in, the wax hissing like a cat at the damp stones. Then Annibale leaned forward to unlock the box without taking the key from around his neck; he had once sworn never to take it off. He inserted it into the lock and opened the lid of the oak strongbox. The brass bounding bands of the coffer fell back with a clang.

The box was stuffed with a shoal of the little gold coins known as sequins, dozens upon dozens of them. They sat in a little tray which formed a false bottom to the casket. Below the tray was greater treasure; a layer of golden ducats. He picked out one of the ducats and looked carefully at both faces, the Doge in his distinctive *corno* hat kneeling before Saint Mark on one side and the Christ on the other. He clasped the coin for a moment until it grew warm in his hand before dropping it back with its fellows and replacing the tray. There would be enough – more than enough for his purpose.

He took a mouseskin purse from the lid of the strongbox

and counted four gold ducats into it. He distributed a handful of sequins about his pockets then locked the coffer again.
Then he found an old brass goblet that had rolled beneath
the wine barrels and polished it on his cambric nightshirt
until it gave off a dull gilt gleam in the candlelight. Annibale
brought that along too. It was always advisable, in Venice,
to have a bribe in your pocket.

He went back upstairs and dressed in half the time he'd
taken yesterday. He left the house with the Cason casket,
once again with a spring in his step, but for a different
reason. Annibale may have lost the first sortie against
Death, but the battle wasn't over.

It wasn't hard to find a boat at the Fondamenta Nuove.
Trade and travel alike had ground to a standstill and the
boatmen and gondoliers that were well stood idle on the
dock. He picked a stout fellow who looked like a good
rower. The boatman raised an eyebrow at Annibale's
instruction, but a gold sequin shut him up.

As they headed for the islands he had seen the previous
evening Annibale stood firm in the stern. His years in Padua
had not robbed him of his sea legs; he had, still, that innate
ability born to all Venetians of being able to stand, static
and steady, in a boat. Masked once again, he stood like a
figurehead, looking forward, only forward, and the affable
boatman got no more conversation out of him than if he
was a mammet.

Annibale watched the island of Murano slide past, where
the glass furnaces now lay silent, then Burano where lace-
makers no longer sat in the doorways of the coloured
houses. On Torcello the bell of the cathedral tolled dole-
fully, numbering the dead; telling him that the Plague had
reached its shore. But when the boats reached the lazarets,

there was peace. Annibale directed the boatman to the island of Vigna Murada, the quarantine island.

As they drew near, Annibale could see a dun wasteland fringed by trees and some sort of walled structure. There was a long jetty terminated by a wooden boathouse. What they saw there made the boatman ship his oars and pull the collar of his coat over his mouth. On the boathouse, as tall as a man, was painted a ragged red cross.

'Wait here if you'd rather,' snapped Annibale, noting the boatman's reluctance to continue up the channel. The boatman tied up by three little steps, and Annibale, making sure that the mouseskin purse and the brass cup were still safely stowed in his sleeve, jumped out; concealing, still, the Cason treasure beneath his cloak. He flipped the boatman another sequin and ordered him, coldly, to wait.

At the head of a jetty was a gatehouse set into the great wall, with a door that looked very firmly closed. Just outside it sat two men, one old and one young, fishing in the lagoon. The greybeard was already watching the doctor's approach, alert; but the young fellow was staring into space with eyes of glass, a thin silver line of drool hanging from lip to lap like a fishing line. The boy's feet dangled well above the waterline; his arms were short and his torso abbreviated; only his head was the dimension of a man's, and seemed oversized on the squat body. His skull was oddly shaped, the bones malformed from birth, Annibale guessed. He had seen such dwarves before – most were drowned on delivery; others were taken for actors in the *commedia*, for some had all the normal faculties and could speak and sing. Annibale had seen such a wight at the court of Padua, where the Duke had kept it in his cabinet of curiosities, and had taught it to tell rude histories. But this one was clearly a simpleton. Annibale ignored the boy and greeted the elder instead.

'I am Doctor Annibale Cason from the *Consiglio della Sanita*,' he lied. 'Are you the gatekeeper of this place?'

The old fellow shrugged. 'I was, *Dottore,* till the plague maiden came. Then everyone took and gone. The *Consiglio di Marittima* decreed that no ships should come in and out of the city till we be clean again. Last one came past here Tuesday – in a terrible storm. A galleass called the *Cavaliere*. We shouted at it, waved torches, but it didn't stop.'

'Yes, yes,' said Annibale, attempting to stem the ceaseless flow. 'So everyone has gone? The marshals, the fortymen? The *bastazi* and their families?'

'Yes, *Dottore*. All gone and only one boat been by since excepting yourself, *signore*, which brought the letters from the *Consiglio*. They're smoking the mail now, of course – I got a letter this morning and I could barely read it it was so yellowed—'

'Of course,' interjected Annibale. 'So they've all gone then?'

'Everyone, *Dottore*. They all picked up their sticks, and went to Treporti. All except me and the boy.' The greybeard lifted his bestubbled chin. 'I am the gatekeeper, and, by God, I'll keep the gate. We live here, *Dottore*, my boy never known no different.'

Fled to the mainland. Annibale nodded to himself, the beak of his mask describing a sweeping arc before his face. It made sense. The rich always fled to their villas in the Veneto, the poor to Treporti. He glanced at the dwarf who was still fishing doggedly, without apparently marking the conversation at all. 'Can you let me see about the place?'

'Certainly, *Dottore*. I'll just let you through. Come *on*,' he shouted to the boy. Father and son left their rods and together the odd little trio went to the gatehouse, the grey-beard talking all the time, the boy trotting to keep up on his little legs. At the door the old man took out a ring of keys. The main gate led to a low arch, offering Annibale a tantalizing glance of what lay beyond. But there was business to attend to first. Annibale indicated a low door in the wall to their left.

'And this is your dwelling?'

'Such as it is, *Dottore*, such as it is.' The old fellow invited him in with a flourish as if he bid him enter the Palazzo Ducale itself, yet there was not much in the gatehouse beside a table, chairs and a smoking hearth. 'I got the job of gatekeeper of the Vigna Murada when I first married, San Matteo's day it was; a score of years ago. I came here with my wife but when we had the boy she took one look at him and was gone. Left as soon as she was churched, she did.'

Annibale glanced at the boy, but the grey eyes were as calm as the lagoon. 'What are your names?'

'I'm Bocca Trapani, and this here is Salve.' Bocca was not a Christian name, but Annibale suspected the gatekeeper was called so because he talked incessantly, almost enough to make up for his silent son. He could not have the fellow showing him around, he wanted to think. Salve was a name often given to the afflicted: literally, it meant 'to heal' or 'to save'; the gatekeeper must be devout. Annibale had an idea.

He took the chalice and purse from his voluminous sleeve. He laid the cup and the mouseskin gently on the wooden board, and gestured to the two men to sit. He noted that the boy immediately retreated to a shadow in the chimney corner, where he hid, peering out. 'Now listen to me well,' said Annibale. 'Here is my family treasure.' He indicated the purse with his gloved finger. 'May I trust you two honest gentlemen to watch it for me, while I look about on the Doge's business? And this –' he tapped the rim of the old brass cup which sang faintly back to him '– is a very old chalice. Some say –' he lowered his voice reverently '– that the Christ himself drank from it.'

The old man goggled at the worthless cup.

'I will be back in one quarter of the bells.' And Annibale left the little smoky house, walking through the arch into the Vigna Murada.

He had expected a purely functional place but here was a green lawn of lush grass, and a beautiful avenue of mature white mulberry trees, their gold-edged leaves waving against the cerulean sky. Here and there, set into the ground, were abbreviated pillars and great fallen stones which told the story of an older building that had stood here once. Just inside the retaining wall was a square of low stone almshouses, with a little church at one corner, and in the centre of all a great roofed building with arches open to the air, that the Venetians called a *Tezon*.

He had heard of this place and now imagined what would happen when a ship came in, reconstructing the scene, peopling the island in his mind. First the crew would disembark, and walk through a shallow pit of lime. Then they would carry the goods from the ship and pile them in the Tezon, marking the unique insignia or cognizance of the shipment on the wall above the pile of goods. Then the crew would be moved into the almshouses for forty days, the origin of the word *quarantine*. They would be expected to keep healthy and chaste and attend mass in the little church unless they were infidels. Each day of the forty, the goods would be carried outside the Tezon through the open arches, smoked with cleansing fires, aired, then piled back under the great roof overnight. Once the goods and the crew were pronounced healthy, they were allowed to leave and enter Venice proper, free to disembark and trade their goods.

Annibale knew that there had been an edict from the Council that all merchandise must be clearly marked with a cognizance because the black market on the quarantine islands was rife – the goods that went back into the cases after smoking and airing were sometimes not the same in quality or number as those that had been taken out. Annibale wondered how much money Bocca had made over the years, replacing luxury goods for homely ones. Well, soon enough he would have a measure of the gatekeeper's honesty.

Annibale walked through one of the great arches into the belly of the Tezon. Once his eyes had adjusted to the dark he saw a great yawning space, empty of persona and purpose, with nothing to tell of its past use but a few hollow barrels and a broken box or two. The walls, though, told their own story. Scrawled on every spare space was writing and drawing, some in Venetian, some in Ottoman, some in strange hieroglyphs unknown to him. The markings were in red, and if this had been a prison he would have thought them written in blood. He came closer to one scribble, rubbed it with his finger and sniffed his glove – the writings were in iron oxide, the same compound used to mark up the cargo. Some sailors, clearly bored by their forty days' enforced sojourn on the lazaret, had exercised their artistic talents – here was a gondola, there a perfect galleon, there a knight, there some kind of be-turbanned infidel king.

At one end of the great room Annibale looked back – each bay formed a natural niche and he could fit dozens of mattresses in here. All he'd need to do would be to close off the open arches, to keep the afflicted sheltered from the elements.

Ducking back outside, Annibale climbed the great boundary wall, the *murada* that gave the island its old name. Here and there, spaced along the wall there were *torresin*: observation towers where the marshals would stand to monitor the ships. He climbed one of them and looked over; there was a little wooded wilderness beyond the walls, and a *giro di ronda* pathway through the laurels and blackthorns. Then, beyond, a marshy expanse of salt flats that led to the lagoon, scattered with enclosed expanses of water which would be perfect for trout meres or laundry pools. Right on the horizon, as tiny as this island had been to his eye yesterday evening, was Venice, shrunk down at this distance to a spiky pewter crown cast into in the middle of the lagoon.

Annibale climbed down the stone steps, walked around the back of the Tezon and found a well – a good-sized wellhead with a decorative rain drain. Wells of this design had seven layers of rock and sand filters between the drain and the bowl, so the water to be drawn was clean and fresh. The stone bowl featured the ubiquitous winged lion carved in relief, but the book he held was closed.

Annibale leaned in to look, momentarily distracted. Usually in such depictions the book in the lion's paw lay open, with the greeting of Saint Mark, '*Pax tibi, Marce,*

Evangelista meus', clearly etched in stone. He wondered what the closed book meant; perhaps that something was sealed, or hidden.

Reminded, he dropped to his knees and dug up a clean square of turf in the soft ground, placing the Cason casket deep in the earth by the well, covering it completely so it was unseen. But he felt eyes upon him and thought for a breathless moment that the lion was watching him back.

As he got to his feet, a large grey cat hurtled out of the wilderness of long grass as if shot from a mangonel, slowed to a saunter, and sidled brazenly right up to Annibale, nudging his hand for a stroke. The creature was destined to be disappointed.

Annibale continued along the row of almshouses. He looked into one empty dwelling – two rooms, one above the other, with a fireplace, good light and ventilation. There were probably above a hundred family houses here. All of the houses were in good condition except one in the corner, which looked run down and ruined. Annibale guessed it had once been blasted by cannon – not all ships called in to the island by the officers acceded readily to the Republic's strict quarantine laws.

Where two rows of almshouses adjoined there was a small square church topped with a cross. Annibale walked over to it and went inside, followed by the cat. He didn't have much time for religion. He had been raised to be devout, but at Padua had been taken to hear a few radical underground lectures by those who set science against God. He could sometimes, secretly, see their point.

He turned about in the centre of the little nave. There was one good window of Murano glass, with shaped and coloured panes in a pleasing design of four ships flying the scarlet and gold pennants of Venice, riding curly periwinkle waves. But apart from a few rude wooden benches, and a rough wooden cross on the plain altar there was nothing here – not a chalice nor a book. It seemed God was long gone from this place; birds had made their nests in the crossribs.

Someone, though, had been sweeping the floor – he could see the twig tracks of a broom in the dust, and a white stain where someone had tried to scrub some of the birds' leavings from the pew. Annibale kept this snippet of information, bottling it like a specimen in the cabinet of his mind.

Outside he looked up at the architrave; gold letters read *San Bartolomeo*. Saint Bartholomew. A good name for a church; a better one for a hospital, he thought.

He went back to the gatehouse. The old fellow was watching the humble chalice on the board in front of him as if it were about to perform a miracle. The simpleton, still occupying a shadow in the chimney corner, watched his father.

Annibale picked up the mouseskin purse. It was lighter than before. 'My thanks,' he said. 'And for your pains I make you a gift of the chalice. May it bless you and give succour to your son, for did not Christ himself bless the afflicted? My ducats, of course, I will take back.' He bored the father through with his red gimlet eyes.

Bocca looked at him, his eyes as round as the ducats. Annibale saw a flicker of guilt there and knew, suddenly, who had been sweeping the church. He fingered the coins through the mouseskin; there were three, not four.

'Wait,' said Bocca, twisting with shame. He opened his dirty palm. 'Here is a coin I . . . found . . . on the floor. It must have jolted from the purse when you set it down.'

Annibale swooped upon it, snatching it up in his gloved hand. He saw the man visibly recoil from his beak. 'Why, thank you, Bocca. Honest men are rare. In return for your rectitude I will offer you a rare opportunity. I have been granted this island by the *Consiglio della Sanita* for a Plague hospital. Your help would be most welcome, so you may stay and work for me.'

Bocca knelt and kissed Annibale's glove. 'Oh yes, *Dottore*, let us stay. We will give you all the help you need.'

Annibale was pleased with his own cunning. He needed Bocca, who had known the island for twenty years, and the man and his idiot would now be loyal, and not question his credentials.

'Good then. I will return tomorrow, and in the meantime, do not let any other person through these gates. From today, this island will be known as the *Lazzaretto Novo*.'

Annibale walked through the gates with a flourish of his black coat, pleased with the morning's work.

Back on the jetty the grey cat followed him still, trotting after him delicately over the wooden slats to the boat. When Annibale stopped the cat wound about his legs looking up hopefully. Annibale picked it up by the scruff of its neck. One of the rules of his island – for in his mind, it was already his – was that there would be no cats or curs to spread the pestilence. The cat dangled calmly in his grip and he lifted it so he could see its face before he cast it into the sea to drown.

It was a mistake. The red eye-glasses met the jade

black-slabbed eyes and Annibale read utter trust there. Cursing, he threw the cat into the boat instead, much to the boatman's surprise, and took it all the way back to the Fondamenta Nuove before setting it free in the *calli* of Venice.

He was royally scratched for his pains.

Chapter 15

Feyra set forth from the island later than she'd planned, delayed by the visit of the strange old man.

The light was already fading a little, silvering the lagoon and greying out the city across the water.

As soon as she'd left the ruin and begun to walk along the seaboard she felt vulnerable despite the fact that she once again wore her veil and her medicine belt. She took the foreign coin from her bodice and turned it over and over in her hand. She took a deep breath. True, she was utterly alone, but she still had her wits and her knowledge and one gold coin. It was enough. It had to be.

She walked down a stone walkway on the city side of the island towards a huddled settlement of houses. As she approached, she saw a black crescent-shaped boat crossing the silver channel between the island and the city. The boatman was headed to a small pier with a parti-coloured pole. Her heart beating faster, she arrived just after he did. He'd decanted some passengers, and she noted with interest that two of the women travellers had scarves drawn over their faces against the sea fog. Perhaps her own veil would not be such a cause for comment, and her father's coverlet, which she'd wrapped about her as a makeshift cloak, covered the rest of her alien garb.

The boatman was standing on the jetty now, calling out a word she did not know, in long, mournful, drawn out syllables; '*Traghetto! Traghetto!*' Feyra gathered her courage and went over to him. He held out his hand, and she put her coin into it. He gazed at it astonished, and then back at her. Then he gabbled out something else she did not understand.

Panicked, Feyra just pointed at the coin and him. He narrowed his eyes, shrugged, and held out his hand again. She said, carefully, 'It is all I have.'

He looked at her again, more kindly. ''Tis more than enough. Your hand.'

She held out her hand and he helped her into the boat. He was only the second man in her life to hold her hand.

It was the end of the day and Feyra was alone in the boat. She supposed that just as many workers at dusk crossed from Constantinople to their homes in Pera, so did the people did here, from Venice to her satellite islands. There were no seats in the boat as there were in the punts on the Bosphorus, so when the boatman pushed off from the shore she nearly fell and was obliged to take his hand again. She was freezing despite the coverlet, nauseated by the motion of the water, and exhausted by having to keep her balance. The boatman steered the boat expertly with one long oar, whistling as he went, and it was with relief that she watched the city she had dreaded coming closer. For the moment she wanted nothing more that to be off this boat.

They were to land, it seemed, far from the place where Death had disembarked. Although she could still see the tower that was the North in her compass, it was distant and hidden in part by tall buildings. From her time in Constantinople she knew that the greatest men lived in the greatest buildings. To find the Doge she needed to find the great court where *Il Cavaliere* had dropped anchor two days ago.

When the boat reached the dock, the boatman leapt to shore to hand her out of the vessel. She nodded her thanks, and he looked at her kindly again. When she took her hand away from his her coin was back in her palm. She turned to protest, but he'd already pushed off again, whistling once more.

Calling down blessings on him, she tucked the coin away and plunged into the darkening streets feeling much more optimistic. Her feet were on solid ground and there was still kindness in the world, even among strangers.

But her optimism faded with the light. This was a hellish place. She would walk for what seemed like hours, only to fetch up in the same spot. Dreadful ghoulish noises bounced from the stone walls, lamplight was refracted by the water and sent back a warped glow to cast dreadful shadows. Mists swirled about her, making it even harder for her to find her bearings. Augmenting the natural sea-mists were man-made fires that belched acrid yellow smoke on every corner that made her cough. Already feeling breathless and trapped by the choking smoke, Feyra felt enclosed by the tall skinny houses and tiny alleyways, unlike Constantinople where the dwellings were low. And here the infidel was ever present: shrines of the baby prophet and his mother were lit by candles at every corner and ragged red crosses were painted randomly on the doorways. And yet, godless trollops lolled in those same doorways; twice she saw women with their breasts bared, leering at the passers-by. Shocked, she averted her eyes only to be met by some more dreadful sight as pairs of figures embraced in the shadow of an archway. Feyra, raised in the Harem, was no prude; she knew what she was watching. At least the Sultan took his pleasures behind closed doors – in Constantinople one would be stoned for public fornication.

Worse than the human inhabitants were the grotesque half-creatures she saw; birds, beasts and demons seemed to loom from the sickly mists. It took Feyra some time to realize that she was not delirious: the citizens were wearing painted masks. From childhood she had heard the legends that the Venetians were half human, half beast. She knew that this could not be true, but in the swirling fog of this hellish city she almost believed it. The creatures seemed to stare at her down their warped noses, from their blank and hollow eyes. And overlord of all was the winged lion – he was everywhere, watching from every plaque or pennant, ubiquitous and threatening.

Feyra did not know whether she shivered with fear or with cold, for her clothes were still not fully dry from their earlier dousing, and the briny splashes that she'd endured in the strange black boat had soaked her further. As she stumbled from alley to alley, she would, more often than not, fetch up at a dead end, facing another glassy canal, lapping at her feet, mocking her. She'd crossed a thousand tiny bridges until she crossed the mother of them all – a great wooden structure crowded with the malign citizens. It did, however, seem to bring her, at last, closer to her goal. In the twilight she could see the great needle tower once again, and determinedly set her course.

Feyra decided to stay, as far as she could, next to the great channel she'd just crossed, a broad silver canal that snaked through the centre of the city. Once she'd crossed the bridge she appreciated the futility of the last hour she'd wasted. She could have wandered until dawn in the place she'd disembarked and never found the tower, for it was on an entirely different island, separated by the great watercourse. But with the waterway as her guide, in short measure she fetched up in a vast square. She could see the great tower once again, and the crouching gold church she remembered.

As Feyra crossed the crowded great square, unnoticed, there was another tribulation – the horrid grey birds clustering about her feet, hampering her steps. When startled they took to the wing and flew in her face ruffling her veil with their filthy feathers. She had to steel herself not to run.

At length she reached the tower, thinking perhaps that the Doge might dwell here, for the Topkapi palace boasted the tallest tower in her home city, and the Sultan dwelt just beneath it. But the walls of the tower rose blank and windowless into the mists, topped by booming, unseen bells. The golden church seemed grand enough with all the gilding and the paintings, but it was clearly a temple. That left the great white palace, topped with delicate snowy pediments of stone.

She ventured into the stone courts where a crowd gathered about a giant staircase topped by twin white statues, and she joined the throng. Presently the great doors at the top opened and a stream of servants came out carrying flaming torches and platters piled high with bread. The crowd snatched at the loaves and she could smell the delicious yeasty aroma – her stomach twisted, her mouth filled with saliva. The Doge must be a merciful man to give alms to his people, she thought. A morsel fell to the floor and she snatched at it, stuffing the sweet warmth into her mouth. The bread was so good it brought tears to her eyes. With renewed strength she saw her chance, and ran up the steps to the very top, where she was met with the crossed pikes of two ducal guards. She said, as clearly as she could. 'I wish to see the Doge.'

One of the guards looked her up and down. 'Certainly, *signorina*. I will just fetch him. And would you like a goblet of wine while you wait?'

Feyra was about to decline graciously, when the two men began to guffaw with laughter. Through their still closed pikes she saw a stone lion's head set into the wall, with a black slit of a letterbox for a mouth. It seemed to be laughing at her too. Desperately, she redoubled her efforts. 'Please, I must see him, *now*.'

They only laughed harder. Then, into the sudden interested silence that had fallen across the crowd below, she cried, in desperation, 'I have a message from Valide Sultan of Constantinople!'

They guards stopped chuckling as if struck, and she realized her mistake.

She should have used her mother's Venetian name.

The word Sultan was enough.

Suddenly afraid, she began to back down the stairs, slowly, carefully, as if to flee would be to break the spell. 'Are you . . .?' one of the guards began, realization dawning.

'She *is*!' exclaimed the other, across him.

'Are you a *Turk*?'

Feyra shook her head, retreating further, the crowd below suddenly still, watching the drama play out on the stone stair. She tripped and tumbled backwards, losing one of her yellow slippers, falling down four more stairs. Her side stabbed and she gasped with the sudden pain and the sight of the shoe left in the middle of the steps, brightly lit in the torchlight, the yellow shoe of the muslim, with its unmistakably upturned toe.

'See, the yellow shoe!' shouted a voice from the crowd.

'She is a *Muselmana!*'

Feyra picked herself up and ran.

The crowd tore off her coverlet, snatched at her veils and ripped her breeches, trying to catch her for the guards. She pulled away desperately, trying to close her ears to the epithets and insults about her people; such vitriol and hatred against the Turks as she had never heard before. Her veils were soaked with spit, her side bleeding where one of the glass vials from her medicine belt had cracked in the fall. But like an animal pursued, she threw off the grabbing hands and pulled free.

She raced across the square, chancing a look upward as she ran. There she saw a sight to terrify her – emerging from the gallery of the temple were four vast bronze horses, their mouths agape and foaming, their forelegs flailing.

The four horses were already here.

Almost more afraid of them than the mob, she redoubled her speed. The dark alleys and ways she'd feared were now her friends, as she darted away, pursued by the crowds. The two guards behind were hampered by their heavy half-armour, which clattered helpfully to give them away. Not knowing where she went Feyra ran through the night, over a dozen, a hundred bridges. Once or twice she heard the clash of the armour far away or close, fooled by the echoing waters and the treacherous whispering stones. Once, at a deserted canal, pursuer and pursued found themselves on parallel bridges, and for a heart-stopping moment Feyra and the guards were eye to eye. Now she was at a disadvantage, for they knew the route to her, and she did not know how to evade them.

Holding her bleeding side she chose her direction; and chose wrong. She found herself, once again, at a dead end; a waterway too deep to ford and too wide to leap. She turned, in despair and ducked into a dark little square and here the malign city bested her at last. The square had three blind sides and only one exit, the one from which she had come. Behind her in the alley, the armour clattered closer.

She could run no more. Exhausted, she collapsed and waited for the guards to catch up with her. She shut her eyes, panting, a warm moist patch of her veil pulling in and puffing out of her open mouth with her ragged breath. She prayed, briefly, thinking she had come to the end.

When she opened her eyes she saw an answering gleam of gilt across the square. An inverted V shone out above a doorway, a shape that was both familiar and dear to her. Feyra rose and walked across the square, peering through the swirling mists. She stopped at the threshold of a pair of double oak doors. She had not been mistaken. Above the door, etched in stone and gilded in, were a pair of callipers.

A house with gold callipers over the door.

Suddenly she heard the cries of her pursuers and the clatter of their weapons. She hammered desperately on the door to match their rhythm, for the alchemy of the streets meant she did not know whether they were a few alleys away or hard by. The door opened, and a man stood there. His greying hair was ruffled skywards in wayward spikes, his thin mouth had fallen open, and a pair of newfangled spectacles dangled from his ink-stained hand.

'A man *called Saturday*,' she gasped. 'I seek a man called Saturday.'

'I am he,' said the man, 'but you may not beg here.'

He began to close the door but she wedged her one remaining yellow slipper painfully in the gap. '*Please,*' she said. She wrenched the horse ring from her finger, searching for the words in Venetian; 'For this ring. In the name of Cecilia Baffo, your friend.'

The terrible pressure on her foot eased. The curious man looked at the ring, then at her, then past her into the street, right and left, with quick, bird-like movements. Then he grabbed her forearm and pulled her through the doorway.

Feyra could see nothing in the dim candlelight, but she heard the clunk as the oak doors close behind her.

She was safe.

Chapter 16

'Cecilia Baffo,' said the man called Saturday. 'Forgive me. I have not heard that name in years.'

Feyra stopped eating and looked at him. He had a far-away look in his eyes, magnified hugely by the spectacles. He turned to look at her, and the candlelight turned the glass circles to flat gold coins, and she could no longer see his eyes. His thin lips, though, curled into a smile. 'It's good?'

She nodded, her mouth so full she was unable to speak. He had brought her a plate 'stolen from the kitchen'. There was a small loaf, a lump of cheese and some shreds of dried fish, and she stuffed it all down as fast as she could. Feyra knew that she should eat slowly and chew well after her long fast, but she did not care. She had been raised in a palace and yet this was the best meal she had ever tasted.

They were in a small plain bedchamber, with a truckle bed, a chair and a cross hanging on the wall. On the cross the little prophet she'd seen on the coin hung, twisted and dying, with a crown of thorns about his head. She'd deliberately sat on the bed with her back to him to eat her meal, but she was so exhausted, so hungry, so cold, she would have closeted with the Devil himself.

Now warm with food and relief, she studied this curious man. He wore a waistcoat and shirtsleeves, knee breeches, stockings and soft leather slippers. The reason that his hair stood out from his head in such a peculiar fashion was because he rubbed and ruffled it constantly. His cheeks were sunken and sprinkled with ashy stubble. His long, sensitive hands were stained with ink, but also flaking with scaly, dry skin and red raw where he scratched them nervously. He took off and put on his spectacles constantly, sat and rose again, as if he could not be still. When he spoke it was in a rush of words that twittered forth from him with nervous energy and the manner of his speech and his twitchy demeanour added to the bird-like impression.

'I knew Cecilia Baffo,' he said. 'Once, long ago when she was a young woman, I was her drawing master. I was in the employ of Duke Nicolò Venier, on the island of Giudecca.' He stopped his pacing. 'You know it?'

Giudecca. 'I do,' said Feyra quietly.

'Duke Nicolò wanted to raise his only child in possession of all the arts becoming to young ladies, so that she would one day marry so well as to fulfil all his hopes. I was a young draughtsman with a precocious talent. We were the same age. I was captivated by her; I never thought she would look at one such as I, but for a time her attention *was* caught by me.'

Feyra looked at him anew. She imagined him when the skyward grey hair had been black and the features taut and shaven of the stubble. She could believe that he had been handsome once.

'She was just coming into her inheritance.' He cocked his head at her. 'Not her wealth, but her beauty. I had never seen a creature so beautiful; so gold of hair and blue of eye, with a waist as tiny as a greyhound's.' While he spoke he fidgeted and twitched before the little window, looking out to another place and time as a thousand stars pricked through the sickly fog. 'I was born on a Saturday, and in Venice if you are born on that day you are considered to be blessed by God, and named after the day. My father was born and named likewise, so I was doubly blessed with the name Zabato Zabatini. All my life, I had been waiting for this wondrous luck to manifest itself – we were not especially rich, nor noted. But I remember thinking, in those moments with Cecilia, that my namesake luck had come to roost at last.' He turned back to Feyra. 'I was powerless in the face of her beauty; and one day, in the schoolroom, we were caught in an embrace.'

Feyra's eyes widened. For the first time she thought about her mother as a young woman, the Cecilia Baffo that she had never known: headstrong, beautiful and playing with her power, a woman who could seduce a young drawing master for sport, then run away with a sea captain after knowing him for an hour. For the first time, too, she questioned her mother's lightness of conduct. Had she given herself to this man, before her father, before Sultan Selim? She did not know how to ask Zabato the question; she did not wish to.

But he answered it. 'It was just a kiss. But Nicolò Venier was furious – terrified that I would take her maidenhead and would destroy his marriage prize and all his hopes of alliance. He dismissed me and moved Cecilia at once to their summer palace at Paros, where he began marriage negotiations at once. It was there, I suppose, that she was taken by the Turks.'

Feyra knew the sequel to this story very well; and knew too that the fire that had been lit in her mother by this strange, skinny man had not been easily put out.

'And now she is dead.'

'Two weeks ago. In Constantinople.'

Zabato sat again. 'So it was all true,' he breathed. 'I heard that she had been taken by corsairs.'

She nodded. 'My father. He was a sea captain. He brought her to Turkey.'

His eyebrows, black as his hair had once been, shot up. 'And gave her to the Sultan?'

'Yes.'

Zabato looked directly at her. 'Was she happy?'

Feyra considered. 'Yes.' And she believed it. With the Sultan Cecilia had found both conjugal contentment and an outlet for her fierce intelligence in Byzantine politicking. She had probably been happier as Nur Banu than she would have been as Cecilia, the wife of a penniless draughtsman, or even Cecilia, the wife of a Turkish sea captain.

The thought of her father reminded her of what else she had to tell. 'I am her daughter.'

Zabato was still for the first time that evening. He looked at her face, peering at her features through the thin *yemine* veil. 'Yes,' he said, slower than his accustomed speech. 'Yes, you are.'

She told him then, haltingly, the rest of her history; of her mother's end, and her father's, of the disappearance of the ship and Takat Turan too. She showed him the crystal ring and she saw that he recognized it.

Zabato shook his head, as if blinking the tears away, and rose again, pacing at once. 'I wrote to her at Paros. I even wrote to her at the Sultan's court, sending my letters with our merchants, even with our ambassador. I wrote last to tell her of my situation here in this house, I told her I was ever her devoted servant, but I never knew if she received my notes.'

Feyra was in no doubt. 'She must have.'

He nodded quickly, once, twice, three times. 'Yes. Yes. Yes. And now that you are here, you will have all the help that Zabato Zabatini can afford you. What must I call you?' He held out his hand.

She looked at it, not sure what to do. She touched it briefly with her fingers, then pointed to her chest. 'My name is Feyra Adalet bint Timurhan Murad.'

Zabato let the hand drop and shook his head. 'That will not do. If you are to hide here it is important that your origins are not known. The Turks have never been loved here, and the hatred burns hotter than ever since Lepanto.'

And will be worse still, thought Feyra if what my father has done ever becomes known.

'We should give you a Venetian name,' Zabato said.

'Cecilia?'

Zabato inclined his head. 'Of course. And for your family name you may take mine, Zabatini, for I will tell the household that you are my niece.'

'I can stay here?'

He shrugged his bony shoulders. 'Where else?'

'I want to see the Doge. He must help me to go home.'

'To *Constantinopoli*? No and no and no!'

Feyra went cold. 'Why?'

'There are no ships coming to Venice, nor leaving, while the Plague is our guest, by order of the *Consiglio Marittima*. You must wait her out.'

Feyra swallowed. How long was she to be a prisoner in this place? 'But the Doge? I can see the Doge?'

Zabato spoke gently. 'I am not acquainted with the Doge, although Sebastiano Venier is brother to my old master. I worked for *Nicolò* Venier, but he turned me from his door thirty years past. My luck departed with my love, and I moved from post to post since.' He saw Feyra's face fall and leaned forward, inky hands together, elbows on his knees. 'Tonight we lost our maid. It is for this reason that I answered the door.'

'Plague?' Feyra caught her breath. If the pestilence was already inside the house then this kindly man and all his household were probably already doomed.

'No. She fled to her family on the mainland.' He stood again, and indicated a bundle of cream-coloured clothes slung over the back of the chair. 'Here are her clothes. Rest now, dress in these at daybreak.' He tossed them on the bed.

She fingered the strange fabric and looked up. 'Can I wear a veil?'

Zabato Zabatini shook his head. 'No. A veil will give you away at once.' He saw the expression in her eyes and tried, once again, to brighten them. 'You shall have our maid's wages as well as her clothes. One sequin a week, and bed and board. In time, we will contrive a way to get you to the Doge or get you home.'

She wanted to thank him, but had nothing to give; so she gave him the only thing she had. 'Your hands,' she said. 'Rub them with this.' She passed him a little jar of salve from her medicine belt. He peered at it doubtfully through his eye-glasses. 'Camphor and gum dragon. Every night. And in the morning, drink the juice of a lemon.'

He looked at his hands and back at her, then smiled his thin smile. 'Rest now. I will call you at daybreak and direct you to your duties.'

Just as he was leaving she found the words for the question she wanted to ask him. 'Why are you doing this?'

He turned back in the doorway and the smile died. 'Cecilia was just toying with me, trying her teeth. For me it was more. You see, I *loved* her.'

In the morning Feyra was awake and dressed before the knock on her door.

Zabato Zabatini stood on the threshold. 'Sleep well?'

'Yes.'

The mattress had been lice-free, and soft; and, spared the rocking of a ship or the anxiety of her father's health, she had indeed slept for several dreamless hours. He stood back as far as the dim little hallway would allow. 'Let me look at you.' She felt his eyes upon her; kindly, not predatory.

She felt uncomfortable in the maid's clothes. The fabrics themselves were soft and forgiving, although stiff under the armpits with the sweat of the previous owner, but the style of gown was unseemly. There was no looking-glass in her room, but Feyra could still clearly see the many faults of the dress. The throat was far too exposed, with the neckline cut almost down to her nipples. There was no opportunity for her to wind her bandeau about her breasts either, for the bodice was underpinned by a tight-laced corset which made her bosom seem enormous. The sleeves were tight on the upper arms and a cuff of simple lace at the elbow barely fell to her forearm, leaving a great expanse of her wrist exposed. The voluminous skirts, shored up by half a dozen petti-coats, nearly filled the little room with their girth, and yet in length barely fell to her calves, showing a great deal too much stockinged leg. Feyra was evidently taller than the absent maid too, which meant the bodice was lower, the sleeves shorter and the skirts higher. Her bulky medicine belt which she had strapped on under the skirts, made the kirtle flare even more at the hips and her waist seem even smaller. There was a soft lace cap to be worn on the head, and by the time Feyra had bound and plaited her hair under it and viciously tucked all the tawny curls away, it only served to leave her entire neck and shoulders exposed. Her own clothes were no good for anything but the fire. Instead of the yellow slippers she put on the leather boots that sat under the chair. They were a little small and down at heel, but the leather was surprisingly soft. Her soiled, single yellow slipper she slipped under the bed, the only remaining memory of her original garb.

She straightened up and presented herself to the man called Saturday. She felt cold, uncomfortable and exposed, but Zabato seemed pleased with her appearance.

'A proper Venetian maid,' he said, and beckoned to her. 'Come, I will tell you your duties. Do not speak to anyone, for your accent gives you away. I have told the household you have an affliction of the tongue. Especially do not speak to my master – he has no particular quarrel with the Turks but he has a very heavy task upon him at present, and it troubles him day and night. In time, however, we may, with your permission, take him into your confidence; as he *does* know the Doge. Personally.'

Feyra was puzzled. 'Master? Are you not the master here?'

He laughed, an odd, snorting sound, with a bitter edge. 'No. I told you that my luck departed with your mother. Times have been hard, and I have ever been someone else's servant. Come.'

Feyra followed him out of the room and down the

narrow stair. Soon she would have to be silent, so she asked her last question. 'And your master's name?'

The stair was narrow and winding, so Zabato answered over his shoulder. 'His name is Andrea Palladio.'

Somewhere in the deep belly of the Doge's palace, the two guards who had let Feyra escape stood in a windowless room. Seated before them, at a dark wood desk, was a blond-haired man who asked a lot of questions; but really his tone was so pleasant they began to believe that they might escape the whipping they had expected. On the other side of the desk sat a smaller man with a quill in his hand and the four-cornered hat of a scribe upon his head. The scribe scratched at his paper as the elder of the two guards described the fugitive.

'She was dark.'

'Skin or hair?'

'Both, *signore*.'

'Darker than a Venetian?'

'Darker than some, I'm sure, *signore*,' said the younger. 'But really, she could almost have been a southerner, but for her clothes.'

'Any distinguishing characteristics?'

The guards looked at one another.

'Anything *different* about her. Besides her garb, I mean. We have your description of the yellow slippers.'

'Well, *signore*, she was . . . that is to say . . . when the people ripped away the veils . . .'

'She was fair,' blurted the second.

There was a brief, intense silence. 'You're telling me she was *beautiful*.'

'Yes, *signore.*'

'You're telling me, that we are seeking a *beautiful Turkish woman?*'

The first guard, the elder and cleverer of the two, began to be afraid. There was something in the inquisitor's tone that made him think again of the sting of the whip. 'Well, perhaps,' he said, 'now you mention it, her skin *was* dusky; swarthy almost.' He looked at his partner.

'That's right,' agreed the second. 'And her nose was somewhat large . . .'

'With a hook in it!' finished the first triumphantly. 'It tended downward as much as her *infidel* shoes curled up.'

The blond man nodded with approval, as the scribe scribbled ever faster at his drawing. When he was done the inquisitor turned the drawing around to face the guards.

'Would you say,' he asked, his voice honey once more, 'that this resembles her?'

The guards peered at the drawing. There was a hideous hooknosed crone, black-skinned and swathed in veils and billowing breeches. Her nose turned down to meet her upturned shoes. Both men nodded enthusiastically.

The inquisitor picked up the drawing in his ringed hand and gave it to the older guard. 'Take this personally to the pamphleters in the Campo San Vio,' he commanded. 'Have one posted on every corner of every *sestiere* by sundown.'

Chapter 17

In the first light of dawn a man in a bird mask walked the silent streets of the Miracoli, his black greatcoat sweeping the pavings.

He stopped at a door with a red cross on it and tapped it with his cane. A family, cloaked and hooded, carrying few possessions, filed out silently and followed him.

He went to the next painted door and did the same. Soon there was a little band following him, winding through the streets, swelling in number.

At the Church of the Miracoli, the procession stopped as Annibale raised his cane. He entered the church where he had been christened, but he did not genuflect, nor gaze at the considerable marble marvels of the interior. Instead he climbed the small stair to the stone arch that arced over the street like a dun rainbow to a little convent tied to the church. From the latticed windows he could see the families huddled below, waiting for him. He felt a sudden jolt of panic. But he had put this thing in motion, now he must see it through.

He walked across the arch to the little door beyond and rapped on it, as respectfully as he could, with the knob of his ebony cane. An elderly nun in a black habit and white wimple opened it. *La Badessa*, the Abbess of the Order of the

Miracoli, with whom he'd had a long conference yesterday. 'Are you ready, *Dama* Badessa?'

She nodded, serious. 'Yes. We are ready.'

'And you are sure?'

She gave the ghost of a smile. 'We are a pastoral order, *Dottore*. If the families go, we go too.'

Annibale turned, and the Badessa and the sisters followed him downstairs. He waited while the Badessa genuflected before the marble altar. She shut and locked the aumbry set into the altar wall which contained the Host. After bowing once to the tabernacle she burned two wads of holy oil before the golden cross and laid the cross down on the marble. On her way back to her nuns in the aisle the Badessa did not do reverence to the supine cross. The priest had died the night before, and for the moment, this was no longer a church, but a beautiful, marble mausoleum. God was gone, and now the sisters of the Miracoli must be gone too.

Outside, Annibale led the way, like the pied piper who had stolen the nurselings. But his growing band had attracted attention – *Dottore* Valnetti, pulling his cart of false, bottled hope, dropped the red handle and ran after Annibale. Annibale set his teeth behind his mask. He'd known that this moment would come.

'Annibale? Where are you taking these people?'

'To my new hospital.'

'What the . . . Which is where?' Valnetti spluttered.

Annibale was silent.

'These are *my* patients.' Valnetti's voice grew louder.

'Mine too.'

'You can't *do* this, Cason.'

'And yet, I am.'

'But why?'

'We differ in our methods. I have tried yours, and now I am going to try mine.'

Valnetti started to wheedle. 'We can reach a compromise.'

'I do not think so.' Stony, Annibale swept past Valnetti, but Valnetti shot out a restraining arm.

'My family is from Genoa, you know.'

'So?'

'There's a legend there.' Valnetti stumbled to keep up with Annibale, speaking fast and loudly. 'A shepherd called Nicholas, who was little more than a child, had a vision from God and led thousands of children across the Alps to crusade against the Muslim infidel.' He ran to overtake his junior. 'They fetched up in Genoa, all these lost children, in their multitudes. Nicholas believed that the sea would divide, and the baby crusaders all sat on the shore waiting for it to happen.' He stopped Annibale with an out-thrust arm, gathering a bunch of the younger man's black coat at his chest. His out-thrust beak clashed with Annibale's. 'Nicholas was not a visionary, Cason, he was just a stupid child.'

Annibale batted him away and walked on, silently. Valnetti was stranded in the steady stream, some of the followers barging him a little as they passed. He tried to appeal to one, then another, but gained no answer and had no choice but to trot after Annibale until the company reached the Fondamenta Nuove.

As Annibale directed the families into the waiting boats Valnetti could do nothing but watch. When the younger doctor jumped into the largest boat, he delivered his parting shot.

'I'll have you struck off the *Consiglio Medico*,' he warned.

Annibale shrugged. 'It's a duty of care.'

Valnetti snorted down the long nose of his mask. 'Since when?'

Annibale did not even have to think about it. He put out his foot and pushed the boat from the dock.

'Since now,' he said.

At the head of the little flotilla, once again a figurehead, Annibale had the worst cases with him in his boat as the forerunners. When they reached the Lazzaretto Novo he saw that Bocca had carried out the instructions he had given him during the previous week. The red cross had been scrubbed from the boathouse; there would be no doleful markings here. A brazier had been erected on the jetty. When it was lit, the boats were to stop here; when it was dark, they should not come near. Bocca had dug a shallow pit at the gate's threshold, and filled it with potash at Annibale's instruction, so that each visitor's feet would be purified before entry and on leaving.

Annibale told the other boats to wait and he took his little band of desperately ill patients through the gates, some on litters carried by the less afflicted, some still able to walk, some stumbling with crutches or leaning on their fellows. Annibale led them into the Tezon, settled them in their beds and gave each one water. Then the great doors were closed.

Returning to the boats he fetched the families one by one and settled them in the almshouses, with strict instructions not to enter the Tezon, no matter how much they might long to visit their loved ones. Two houses were left unoccupied: the little ruin next to the church and the corner house by the *torresin*, which he'd taken for his own. He left the children playing under the tree walk of white mulberries, and took himself off to the Tezon.

But first he looked into the little church. There was a figure there, kneeling. Annibale retreated, not wishing to disturb her prayers, but the Badessa turned and stood. 'Come in,' she said.

He walked forward a little tentatively, and slid the broad-brimmed hat from his head. The beak he left alone. 'Forgive my mask,' he said to to her. 'It is for your safety more than mine.' But he bowed awkwardly to mitigate any disrespect; not towards the altar but to her. 'I do not wish to disturb you.'

She spread her gnarled hands. 'I am not saying anything which cannot be continued later.' She pointed a knobbled finger to the rafters. 'Our conversation will take a lifetime; it will not be concluded today.' She smoothed her habit over her ample hips. 'What are you doing here, *Dottore*?'

He fiddled with a splinter that protruded from the pew and smiled ruefully, inside his mask. 'Honestly? I don't know.'

She smiled too. 'I think I do. You are about to embark upon a great undertaking.' She sat down on one of the benches and invited him to do likewise. 'When you came to me yesterday, and tended to poor Father Orlando, you reminded me that our order of the Sisters of the Miracoli was instituted for the *incurabili* – the incurables, whom God had smitten with leprosy and other untreatable conditions first brought back from the Crusades. Those first patients knew there was no cure for their afflictions. The first sisters knew it too. But what they believed in was the Miracle.' She looked at him. 'When you came to me with this idea of yours, it humbled me. It was for this that I and the sisters came with you. We were in the business, then, of delivering miracles. And, it seems, we still are.'

Annibale, listening, said nothing.

The Badessa clasped the simple wooden cross that hung about her purity. 'Son. I heard Valnetti's story, and men say it is true. Nicholas and the Children's Crusade sat on the shore and *waited* for a miracle. But there is another story told too, a greater story, part of the greatest ever told. A man once led his people to the promised land, and there was an ocean in his path. He did not sit and wait for the waters to cleave; he crashed his staff upon the ground and *demanded* that the seas part.' The Badessa rose, and the coloured glass of the single picture window turned her simple habit to motley. She turned and looked down at him. 'And they did, *Dottore*. They did.'

Over the days, the little island buzzed with activity like a hive of bees. The sisters of the Miracoli did wondrous work filling in the arches of the Tezon with wattle and daub. The boy Salve, despite his afflictions, seemed to understand simple instructions and had been a great help; more, if truth were told, than Bocca. There was a wattler among the families of the Miracoli, and he had directed operations, while the sisters of the Miracoli, well known for their robust and practical rule, were not too otherworldly to soil their hands.

Annibale sent some of the sisters to purchase good linen from the market across the water on the mainland in Treporti where the sickness had not yet reached. Bocca and Salve were directed to draw clean water from the well each morning, and to fish the lagoon every day, as well as stocking the pools with trout and cultivating clusters of oysters on great knobbly ropes. One of the nuns, a beefy woman named Sister Ana who was skilled in rearing fowl, bought a brace of broody hens and a cock and rowed them back in a little coracle, wearing the live birds slung over her shoulder like a squawking stole. Annibale believed that if food could be freshly grown or fished it could not be infected with bad air.

One of the families included a schoolmaster who began a schoolhouse in the little church for the boys, while the nuns, in rotation, kept their rule with masses sung at the canonical hours, and a daily service for the families at which Bocca was never absent, and Annibale rarely present. Bocca had donated to the Badessa, with great pride, the chalice that Annibale had given him, as a vessel for the Host. Thus a humble bronze cup from a disused wine cellar became San Bartolomeo's finest relic.

Annibale oversaw every detail of his little utopia. The nuns began to dig a herb garden in the good drained soil beyond the well, and Annibale made drawings for them of the Botanical Gardens of Padua, so his medicines could be grown and his unguents prepared on site.

The wives sewed mattresses for their loved ones, stuffed with rue and heather for their medicinal properties at Annibale's direction, with which he lined the hospital floor in neat ranks. The afflicted were to be kept in the Tezon, their families in the almshouses, and never the twain should meet. No one could pass from the Tezon to the almshouses save Annibale, in his protective clothes. All was financed by the Cason treasure, which was gradually emptying from its hiding place by the well, as the stone lion stood sentinel.

Every day, Annibale would pause in his work, climb the

torresin in the south-eastern corner of the wall, and look across the water to Venice. When the wind was in the right direction he could hear the city's plague bells ringing incessantly, tolling the passing souls. The six doctors of the *sestieri* were losing their battle. Through his glasses Venice looked like it was on fire.

Annibale was aware of the precariousness of his position. He was aware that he had commandeered an island that was the property of the Republic, and he could only hope that when his methods were proven, the Council would let him be. Valnetti did not like to be crossed, and he suspected that the doctor had already been to the *Consiglio della Sanita* to report Annibale's conduct. And, every day, looking out to the roseate sea through his red smoked lenses, he expected someone to come and stop him.

Chapter 18

Cecilia Zabatini settled quickly into her new life as a maid in the house of the gold callipers.

In a very short time she got to know the long tall house with its myriad of connecting stairwells and passageways. She became used to the darkness of the back rooms and the blinding brightness of the front salons, where the arches and rounds of the glazed windows let in sunbursts of light, refracting into dazzling rainbows. At the side of the house was a quiet square with a well in the centre, where the main entrance for visitors was marked by the callipers over the door. At the front, facing the shining canal and its bustling traffic, there was a watergate; at the rear, a tiny, dingy courtyard overlooked by three other great houses. The courtyard was the trash pit for all the slops of all the houses – human and kitchen waste ended up there, to be swept into dung carts once a week by the midden-men. It had a foul smell and the new maid, considering the place insanitary, avoided it as best she could.

The household accepted the tall, quiet girl; she was intelligent and helpful, she did not need to be told what to do but anticipated the need for a task to be done before she was asked. They were kind to Feyra partly for her own sake, partly because she had an affliction of her speech, and partly because she was under the protection of her uncle Zabato, a man they liked and respected, who was, moreover, their master's dearest friend. The two footmen were kind to the new maid for an additional reason – any fool could see that she was beautiful, however much she tried to hide it.

The cook, who went by the name Corona Cucina for she was, as she boasted, Queen of the Kitchen, missed very little that went on in her kingdom. She quickly noticed the footmen's glances and decided to act. She chucked Feyra kindly under the chin on the first morning she came down and tutted. '*Gesumaria*, dearie, you look like you're fit to work the *ponte delle tette*, flashing your bubbies for the gentlemen! Let me give you some lace fillings for that neckline, and a longer petticoat too.'

The cook hauled Feyra off to a chamber in the cellars, not unlike Feyra's own, and looked around in her cupboards. She found the girl a longer underskirt which fell, thankfully, near to her ankles. 'And here –' Corona Cucina tied a scarf of lace about Feyra's shoulders. Holding the knot with one meaty hand she rootled in a little drawer with another. 'I'm sure I have an old pin somewhere – ah, here – it will serve to fasten it.'

The kindly cook pinned the brooch through the knot to hold the collar fast to the dress. Feyra looked down at her bosom. The brooch was a little tin cross, with a tiny figure hanging from it.

Wearing the sign of the shepherd prophet was not the only adjustment Feyra had to make. Without her veil the smells of the house assailed her; the fish bones boiling down to stock on the kitchen stove, the beeswax polish of the pantry and the rancid mutton tallow of candles in the *studiolo*. The choking, tarry scent of the coals she had to carry made her cough; even the musty leather and paper of the books in the little library, set on a high mezzanine all around the study walls, made her sneeze.

Once she had a shock; when sent to fetch salt from the little cellar under the house, she brushed against something bristly in the dark. When she raised her candle she saw a whole pig, hanging upside down by its trotters, flesh pale and tongue lolling as the blood dripped. Feyra dropped her candle with a clatter and ran, retching, to the little court-yard in the middle of the house. Corona Cucina bustled out to her and rubbed her back as she vomited, asking what was amiss. Forgetting herself, Feyra choked: '*Porco*.'

'He's nothing to fright you, dearie. Can't hurt you in that state, can he?' The cook stroked Feyra's clammy cheek. 'Fancy you running from a porker as if you were a *Muselmana*!'

Feyra froze. There was that word again.

Muselmana.

The word that Nur Banu had left out of her lexicon, the word she had heard on the steps of the Doge's palace, when she had left her slipper on the stair. She blinked, and looked at the cook's concerned face. Corona Cucina was kind; now was her chance to learn. '*Muselmana*?' she asked, making her intonation as Venetian as she could.

'Ay – they hold pig's flesh in horror. And that was how we Venetians could bring the body of the blessed Apostle Mark –' Corona Cucina drew a cross on her ample bosom with her forefinger '– from the land of the heathens to rest here in Christian Venice in the Basilica. They placed the Saint's corpse in a large basket covered with herbs and swine's flesh, and the bearers were directed to cry "*Pork!*" to all who should approach to search. In this manner they bamboozled the *Muselmani* and brought our Saint home.'

Feyra's puzzlement must have been written on her face, for Corona Cucina raised her voice as though she was simple. '*Muselmani*! Those as goes to church on yellow shoes, and wears their heads bound in turbans! *Dio*, your uncle said as you were dumb, not simple.' She pinched Feyra's chin. 'Well, they don't know what they're missing, for when that porker has hung for a week I'll make pancetta and shred pie that'll make your mouth water. You'll like the pigling right enough then.'

From then on Feyra avoided the little courtyard whenever Corona Cucina was cooking pork. Even to breathe the aroma was a faithless act; almost worse than wearing the cross.

The prevalent smell in the whole house, though, was ink and paper. Her unseen master had reams of it all about the place, tumbling from his desks, spread upon the map chest and even the dining board. She peered at them once or twice. She did not understand the annotations, but the drawings held no mysteries for her. She had seen the like many times in the company of Mimar Sinan.

They were plans.

This Palladio, like Sinan, was an architect.

Feyra was beginning to tune her ear to the Venetian accent. Her fellow servants spoke a little differently to the pure and noble language that her mother had taught her. There were so many Zs in the dialect that they sounded all together like a hive of bees and waved their hands around so much that they sometimes hit each other in the narrow passages of the house, or knocked the candles from their sconces. But during the two meals the servants ate together in the kitchen in the morning and evening, Feyra watched, and listened, and began to adjust.

She rarely left the little square, but when she went to the market she found that Venice by day was a different city to the one she had encountered at night. There was, it seemed, no plague yet in this ward; Zabato said it was raging worst in the district called Cannaregio so if she bought her goods at the Rialto and came straight back there would be no danger.

So Feyra got to know her sixth, or *sestiere*, of Castello, well. She noted the constant presence of the shepherd prophet on every corner, above every church door. In her faith it was not permitted to express God in art; it was considered not only impious but impossible. But here the Christians lived with their deity as though he was their neighbour and it was impossible to avoid him. He seemed only to have two manifestations: a babe in his mother's arms or a near-corpse hanging on his cross like offal. The beginning and the end of his life; there was nothing in between. Even in the market, where butchered beasts were sold hanging from wooden gibbets, the shepherd prophet hung above them, higher than all.

Mostly Corona Cucina went to market, as she did not trust another soul with her precious ingredients, but now and again her legs and feet pained her so much that she had to sit in a chair and raise her legs. Feyra caught a look at them once – the feet were as big as eel-boats, misshapen about the toes with huge swellings on each side. Furthermore, the vessels on Corona's lower calves stood forth like black and blue cords. Feyra had seen such veins and pushes in the Harem, and wondered if she would ever have the courage to offer her remedies in return for the cook's kindness.

She greatly missed the practice of medicine, not just for the status, but for the way in which her opinion had been sought, her skills utilized. Here she was the humblest of the servants and her duties were to clean, fetch and carry and set the fires in the master's rooms.

After one day of work she ceased to wear the crystal ring of the four horses on her hand. Her work was hard and physical and she knew that at some point the ring would be cracked or damaged. She pulled a piece of ribbon from the hem of one of her many petticoats and hung the ring around her neck, tucked firmly in her bodice. Feyra thought of the Ottoman tradition of wearing amulets to preserve health – a verse from the Qur'an writ small and twisted into a little scroll, the name of God on a scrap of paper worn in a bag, or a pendant like the five-fingered hand of Fatima. Amulets were secret and personal; they were worn under the clothes and particular to their wearer. Well, the ring would be her amulet, the only thing about her person now that had come with her all the way from Constantinople. It struck her, too, how much she was learning about her mother since her death – it said something of her mother's cosseted life that she could have worn a ring of glass for the whole of it.

In Venice, even among servants, Feyra saw that women got the worst deal. They did not seem to have been schooled, any of them; and when the men came to play cards in the kitchen in the evening, the women had to retire to their rooms. In Venice, she was sure, no woman would have been encouraged, or even permitted to qualify as a doctor.

Some things were the same here as at home. Corona Cucina was very like the kitchen wives that she'd known in Topkapi: kind, loud, brash and bawdy. She talked incessantly and at times Feyra had to stop her ears to the stream of stories about what the cook got up to in her young days, or how various members of the household conducted their courtings and couplings.

And yet, Feyra could not help but warm to the enemy. She thought of the young mother who had given her hand to Death, the boatman who had not taken her coin, and Zabato Zabatini who had taken her into this place. At these times she remembered, with a shock, that she herself was half Venetian. She had a foot in two nations however wide the seas between.

Feyra might have prided herself on fitting into Palladio's household, but it was not only the two footmen who had noted her presence. News of a beautiful new maidservant in the *sestiere* travelled fast, especially in a city cut off from the outside world. Once again she had to become used to the gaze of men. Her few trips to the market had excited some keen interest among the stallholders and she would have been horrified to discover that she was the toast of more than one drinking session at the market locanda. Accustomed now to her Venetian dress, the veils and the swathed clothes of her homeland seemed part of another life, but one day as she hurried through the market, Feyra was brought to a standstill by a sun-yellowed pamphlet tacked to the wall.

She drew closer, heart thudding, holding it flat to study it, the paper bubbling under her suddenly damp fingertips. The figure depicted was grotesque – a female and a Turk, wearing a veil, voluminous breeches and upturned yellow slippers. Protruding from the headdress were wiry black curls like corkscrews, and a hooked nose curved over the *yashmak*. Feyra could not read Venetian as well as she spoke it, but she recognized the word *Muselmana*. This, she was sure, was meant to be her. She tore the paper quickly from the wall and crumpled it into her basket. Looking from left to right to check that no one had seen what she had done, Feyra failed to notice the tall, cloaked figure watching her from the edge of the square.

Chapter 19

Annibale had just seven nights of peace on his island.

It was Bocca who alerted him, and came running from the gatehouse. Fiercely partisan since the gift of the chalice, he apprised Annibale of every passing bark or coracle, whether they were of note or not.

Today Annibale saw at once, from the old man's shambling speed, and the expression on his face as he called, 'Ship ahoy, *Dottore*, ship ahoy!' that this was a craft of quite a different colour, even before Bocca elaborated.

'Longboat, *Dottore*, forty-oar, hoving from San Marco.'

Annibale hurried through the gate, although he was not so flustered that he forgot to dip his feet in the potash. He could see a speck on the horizon, and marvelled at the keenness of the gatekeeper's eyes, although his own were hampered by his smoked lenses. The barge came closer till he could see the diamond dips of the oars, down and pull, down and pull, all forty in perfect synchronicity. The boat appeared to be made of some light timber for it seemed gilded by some trick of the sunlight. As the craft grew nearer Annibale realized that he had made no mistake – the barge was, in fact, made of gold; and as soon as he saw the face of a lion on the prow, with his mane spread like sunrays, he knew it was over.

This was the *Bucintoro*, the barge of the Doge.

A man stood in the prow, his magenta cloak bellying and cracking in the wind like a sail, the sea breeze ruffling his short blond hair. He was not especially tall, nor muscular, but he carried an air of great authority.

'Are you Annibale Cason, *Dottore della Peste?*'

'I am.'

'I am the Camerlengo to Sebastiano Venier, His Serene Highness the Doge of Venice.'

Annibale was glad of the mask. He looked at the Camerlengo. The chamberlain was suited in black beneath the cloak, in a suit of clothes that seemed to be made of hide, some sort of supple black leather. He was a younger man than Annibale expected, with the blond hair and blue eyes of a northerner. He was neat, cleanshaven, with his hair cropped short as a Teuton; and his voice was cultured and low. There was nothing threatening about him, and yet everything; and suddenly Annibale was afraid.

'Is there somewhere we can speak privately?' the Camerlengo asked.

'Yes.' Annibale looked at the semicircle of guards. 'All of you?'

The Camerlengo smiled pleasantly. 'Just me.'

Annibale began to relax a fraction, and took courage. 'If you wouldn't mind, Camerlengo, could you walk through this pit?'

The Camerlengo lifted his wine-coloured cloak and walked obligingly through the potash. Annibale followed him through the gate.

Once inside the walls, Annibale led the way across the lawns, giving the Tezon a wide berth. He tried to imagine what the Camerlengo would be thinking and tried to see the place through his eyes. It was a sparkling autumn day – the sun was shining and there was a fresh coolness in the shadows and a breath of winter in the air. The mulberries were turning to rose and amber. He could see the children running around by the schoolhouse, and hear the chime of the little bell of San Bartolomeo calling Tierce for the nuns. The rich dark loam of the neatly dug herb garden with its botanical sectors in circles and squares made a pleasing contrast with the verdant turf, and the area of wilderness that he'd had scythed and marked off for a graveyard was yet to receive its first body. Things had been going so well. Annibale pointed with his cane. 'My house –' he stopped himself, for the title sounded overly proprietorial '– the place where I stay is this way.'

The Camerlengo stopped and drew in a deep breath of the cool autumn air. 'It is a fair day, is it not? Shall we take our ease here? I spend overmuch of my time in the great chambers of government.' There was no hint of a boast in the statement: the Camerlengo's power was complete. 'So I take the air whenever I can. And certainly it seems sweeter here than in our stricken city. Better to be out than in on such a day, don't you think?'

He sat down on the ancient fallen pillar by the mulberry walk, and Annibale sat warily beside him. He did not think the question required an answer, but the Camerlengo thought differently. 'Don't you think, Cason?' he repeated.

There was an edge of threat in the idle question. Annibale turned to him and the sun caught the ice in the blue eyes. The Camerlengo expected his question, this conversational nothing, to be answered with a considered reply; and, by implication, all future questions too. Annibale wondered if the chamberlain ever left those great painted salons of the

Doge's palace to descend down to the dungeons and apply his inquisitorial skills with rather more pressure, assisted perhaps by the fire and the irons. His eyes wandered to the guards beyond the gate. They stood on the jetty in a neat semicircle, hands clasped before them. They did not loll or jest as men-at-arms at ease were wont to do. These, he knew were the *Leoni*, the elite guard for the Doge and his household. So Annibale waited for the next question, knowing he was powerless.

'Are you aware of the *Consiglio della Sanita*?'

Annibale knew the Council of Health very well, and had been, more than once, to the immense white building next to the *Zecca* Mint in San Marco, which served as the Council's headquarters.

'I was lately there,' said the Camerlengo, 'sent by my master the Doge, in search of *un vero Dottore*. Do you know what he meant by that?'

Annibale knew exactly what *he* meant by a 'real doctor' but whether his opinion was shared by the Doge, he knew not. Some of his customary arrogance surfaced. 'Yes. Me.'

The Camerlengo gave the ghost of a smile. 'It is interesting that you say that. For I have to tell you that when I was at the Consiglio there was a doctor there, named Valnetti, complaining about you very vociferously. Do you know this man?'

'I do.' Annibale began to understand the Camerlengo. He was a man of fierce intelligence, but gave nothing of this away. Instead, he asked questions, allowing his subjects to reveal themselves. He elected for complete honesty. 'He is a fool.'

The Camerlengo sniffed. 'That was my impression also.

And I must say, one shared by the Doge. So –' he brushed the skirts of his robe with his long fingers. He had very neat, square nails. 'This island of yours. How does it work? The afflicted are in that great building there?'

'Yes,' said Annibale, encouraged by his interest. 'And their families in the almshouses.'

The pale eyebrows raised. 'You brought the families too? For sentimental reasons?'

'No.' Annibale was quick to reject the suggestion. 'Because they might also have been exposed to the miasma, and may develop the disease secondarily. When you cut out a canker, you must take it all, the tumour *and* the healthy flesh that surrounds it.'

The Camerlengo made a little moue with his mouth at the metaphor. 'I see. And have they developed the disease?'

'Not so far, no.'

The Camerlengo seemed impressed. 'And how are you treating the infected? Do I take it you do not approve of Valnetti's remedies?'

'Four Thieves Vinegar? No. I find it somewhat . . . old-fashioned. I treat my patients with the latest surgical interventions – I was lately schooled at Padua.' The Camerlengo gave a nod. 'For instance, I respect the proven Galenic theories that we all know to be truths: the four humours and the necessity of balancing these. I leech the patients to draw off the evil humours, and I have also begun to lance the pushes that appear in the groin and under the arm. This seems to have some efficacy.'

For once it seemed that he had given the Camerlengo too much information.

'There have been deaths?'

'Not so far.'

'And the families – are you taking measures to protect them from infection?'

'Of course. We have contained the infection and we take certain measures to ensure the miasma cannot leave the isolation area. For instance – there is a smoke chamber that I pass though each time I enter or leave. And there is a further pit of lime and potash at the doorway.'

'Would you say, then, that it would be possible to put these measures in place in the house of an individual?'

'Of course.' Annibale began to guess where these questions tended, and felt brave enough to ask one of his own. 'Is it your wish, that is, do you wish me to be the Doge's doctor?'

'No, not that. He has no fears for his own health. But there is a man that is very important to him, a man that he wishes, at all costs, to be kept alive.'

What man's life could possibly be worth more to Venice than that of the Doge? Annibale asked himself.

'Are you wondering who it is?' The Camerlengo seemed unable to break the habit of his constant questioning.

'Yes.'

'His name is Andrea Palladio.'

Somewhere through the mists of memory, the name chimed. Annibale was astonished. 'The architect? Why?'

'My Lord Doge has commissioned him to build a church on the site of an ancient monastery on the island of Giudecca, a ruin where once Plague miracles were performed by means of a blessed well there. Signor Palladio is undertaking to build a church that is great enough to appease the Lord, and have him turn his vengeful eye away from Venice.'

Annibale barely suppressed a snort.

'You find this singular? Yet the Doge believes – saving your presence – that the Almighty has a better chance of saving the city than the medical professionals – the ones he has met at any rate.' The Camerlengo did not reveal whether or not he agreed with the Doge; he was here to serve his master's will, and serve it he would. 'He does, however, need a medical man he can trust, to protect the architect from the pestilence until his work is done.'

'He is a well man? The architect?'

'Tolerably, I believe. He is elderly, but is that not an affliction that all of us must one day face?'

Annibale looked at the Tezon, and thought of the stricken within. It was a preposterous notion, that he should make a daily visit to a man who was hale, when his patients already manifested the black fingers and boils of the pestilence. He stood, suddenly impatient.

'Regretfully – and I am sensible of the great honour you do me – I must decline. I cannot waste my time on a man who is well.'

The Camerlengo craned up at him, squinting his blue eyes against the sun. He did not argue, but merely asked one more question.

'What am I going to say now?'

Annibale looked towards the gateway at the phalanx of guards. The *Leoni* had not moved at all during the course of the entire interview. He looked back at the Camerlengo, sitting placidly on the mossy pillar, still as his stone seat. Annibale sat down again, defeated. 'You are going to say that my rights to the island have been revoked, that I must clear the place of myself, my patients and their families, and that I must be taken by your guards.'

'And if you agree to doctor the architect?'

'That I may keep the island as a hospital, and go in peace for as long as I am tending Signor Palladio.'

'Precisely. I congratulate you on taking the point so quickly.' The Camerlengo felt in his leather glove and drew out a metal plaque. 'This,' he said, 'is the seal of my Lord Doge. You may produce this at any time in your dealings in the city, and it will be as if your word is his.'

Annibale looked at the seal in his palm; an exquisitely cast brass roundel bearing the Doge's image and the winged lion, finished with a tab of wine-coloured ribbon. He weighed the seal in his hand. The Camerlengo had known that Annibale would agree to his offer. Now the chamberlain stood.

'That's settled then. You'll come with me?' It was not really a question.

'I will have to instruct my deputies,' said Annibale carefully. He did not name the sisters of the Miracoli; he was not entirely sure of the legality of their defection from the city.

'Do it then.'

Annibale found the Badessa and told her he would be back by the end of the day and then followed the Camerlengo to the great barge. As the guards dipped their oars he watched his island recede with a qualm that clenched his stomach. He could not identify the feeling, for he had never had it before; but as the barge speeded away he thought it might be something akin to homesickness.

Chapter 20

It was a whole week before Feyra even saw her master.

She saw evidence of him – the drawings grew and spread and changed in both composition and position. His platters and cups were emptied and left to clear. But her first encounter with him was not a chance glimpse in a corridor, or a retreating back in a doorway, but altogether more dramatic.

Light was a crucial commodity in the house of the gold callipers. Feyra was charged with filling the sconces with fresh candles, setting the bobeches below to catch the wax lest it drip on the precious drawings, restocking the tallow cabinets, and trimming the numerous lamps. The master wished to draw at all hours, and even in the dark of night the rooms must be as bright as day. Her last task before retiring was always to carry a great white bubble of blown glass full to the brim with water, known as the fishbowl, to the architect's *studiolo*. She understood its function, and admired the science of it; if a candle was placed behind the glass bowl the water acted as a lens; the flame was magnified, the light augmented as it passed through the water, and the drawing table completely illuminated.

Late to bed one night, she was carrying the great bowl from the kitchens to her master's room, when in the inky hallway she was halted by a thin rectangular frame of gold, as tall as a man, suspended in the blackness.

She walked towards it, still carrying the brimming bowl and saw the outline flicker. She knew then that what she was seeing was not a cosy hearth blaze but a conflagration.

She forced the door open and was almost beaten back by the heat. The great table, for the first time ever, was empty of drawings; they were all crowding the fireplace, curling and burning in the inferno, fiery ashes rushing up the chimney. Without thinking, Feyra poured the contents of the bowl over the long plan table, then pulled the whole fabric from the board and threw it over the fire, dousing the blaze at once, stamping on any stray embers with her leather boots.

Coughing from the black smoke, Feyra turned in the sudden dark to grope her way to the casement and threw it open. Then sticking her head out of the window, she gulped down a mouthful of clean air under the spangled stars.

When she drew in her head a voice spoke from a chair in the corner and she nearly jumped from her skin. As her eyes adjusted to the moonlight she could see the white-edged outline of a figure. 'What are you doing?' it said.

'What am I doing? What are *you* doing?'

In shock Feyra forgot to speak Venetian, and railed against the seated figure in Turkish. 'You must be crazy! How can you build a fire that way? The chimney was not even drawing the flame! How can you sit there and watch it burn like that? The entire house could have burned down! Don't you know that if the tapestry above the mantel had caught, the whole house would have burned to the ground?

And it's such a tall, silly spindle of a house that the servants in the attics would have been trapped! Do you not care?' She stopped for breath and there was a silence from the chair. She could not make the figure out at all apart from the glow of a winter-white beard.

'Who *are* you?'

Realizing her mistake, Feyra matched his silence with her own. Heart pounding, she reverted to Venetian. 'I am Cecilia Zabatini, the new maid.'

'Really?' The voice from the dark sounded amused. 'I am pleased to make your acquaintance. I like you better than the old one already. Light the lamps, then,' Andrea Palladio told her. 'If we are to exchange pleasantries, it is better that we may see each other.'

Feyra snorted, still angry. 'How can I light them? I can't see them.'

Palladio's voice had a wheeze of a squeezebox, and a gravel in it. It rumbled out of the dark. 'There is one in a sconce between the pilaster of the principal door and the orlo. There are two on the architrave of the mantel. Another in the void between the secondary and tertiary window, and three above the frieze and under the cornice. Light one and you will see the rest.'

Here were words that Nur Banu had never taught her. 'I don't understand what you say.'

'Find me a taper. I'll do it.' Feyra found a leaf of paper that had been spared the flames and screwed it into a stick. Her master rose from the chair and shuffled past her. He took a light from the smouldering fire, and went about the room touching the paper to each candle. As the room warmed into light she recognized him at once – he was the very old man who had come to the ruin on Giudecca, just after her father had died; pacing and peering and prodding and writing in his tables.

She watched him return to his chair with his shuffling, gouty gait. He sat heavily as if the weight of the world were upon him. She went to the fire and prodded the ashy part-charred parchments. They were covered with drawings and diagrams and every one was destroyed. She peered closer and picked up a glowing shred of paper. The drawings had been torn across and across before they'd been burned, as if he'd wanted to obliterate his work entirely. She looked up, a fragment still dangling from her hand. 'Why did you burn all this?'

He sighed, so heavily that his breath stirred the ashes. 'I cannot do it.'

'What cannot you do?'

'Build a church.'

She froze with the shred of paper in her hand. Something Zabato Zabatini said to her wakened in her mind. As casually as she could she asked: 'For the Doge?'

'Not for him. If it were only Sebastiano Venier I had to please, I could do it well. No, for a more exacting master. For God.'

Feyra dropped the fragment and straightened up, brushing her cindered fingers on her skirt. She was not entirely sure whether she should leave him to himself, but she'd revealed herself and shouted at him and now there was no way back. Besides he seemed inclined to talk and he was her only route to the Doge. She took a deep breath. 'What have you done so far?' she asked.

'I have measured the site —' he waved his hand towards the fireplace '— scribbled enough lines to reach Jerusalem if you laid them end to end. And had my poor draughtsman draw enough to come home again. Every one of them but a worthless scratch.'

Feyra thought about the draughtsman named Saturday and those inkstained fingers which he'd scratched raw. 'And what will he think about what you've done?' she asked sternly.

'He knows me well enough by now. You are acquainted with Zabato Zabatini?'

'I am his niece,' Feyra said carefully.

He looked straight at her and she saw tiny candles burning merrily in both his eyes. 'You most certainly are not. For one thing his sister is unmarried. For another, you just gabbled like an infidel. Are you a Moor? Or a Roosian?'

He did not seem angry, more amused. Feyra steeled herself to tell the truth. 'I am from Constantinopoli.' She prepared herself, wearily, to recount her story.

But it seemed that Palladio, caught up in his own conundrum, was not interested in her history. Instead he said, musingly, 'Ah. *Constantinopoli*. There are many wondrous temples there, I'm told.'

He could have said nothing more certain to secure her regard than this. She came eagerly right up to his chair. 'Oh, there are! There are many mosques. Besides the wonders of the Hagia Sophia, there is the Süleymaniye which stands on a hilltop over the Golden Horn; it is the largest mosque of Istanbul with four minarets. Then there's the Fatih mosque which includes medreses, hospices, baths, a hospital and a library.' She was suddenly back there, wandering the pavings warm from the sun. The Fatih, more than any other building, exemplified to Feyra the concept of *Mizan*, for it dealt with the soul as well as the mind and body.

'Then there's the Beyazit Mosque at the centre of a huge complex. It has a great dome supported by four pillars.' She described the dome with her hands, reaching high in the candlelight. 'Such workmanship!' She could not stop, consumed suddenly by an overwhelming nostalgia. 'Then there's Eyüp, the oldest of all. It lies outside the city walls near the Golden Horn, at the supposed place where the standard bearer of the Prophet Mohammed is buried. It is so magnificent that the faithful have flocked there for centuries.' The great Sinan would not sit about wallowing in self-pity, burning his drawings, Feyra thought. 'In Constantinople the architects are obsessed by their vision,' she declared. 'I have known one who does not eat from dawn to sundown. Once the light has gone and he cannot build more, *then* he breaks his fast.'

'Would that I had his passion – for mine has quite gone, it seems,' Palladio mused, with the self-absorption of unhappiness. He rose and began to fiddle with a casement catch. 'For all of those temples you named I can match them with churches of my own. See –' suddenly spurred, he began pulling out the drawers beneath the long map table, and pulling reams of plans from their depths. 'Here,' he read the notations, 'Portal for the Church of Santa Maria dei Servi. And here: Façade for the Basilica of San Pietro di Castello. And here: the Refettorio of the Monastery of San Giorgio Maggiore. The Convento della Carità. The façade for the Church of San Francesco della Vigna. I could go on. And now, *now*, I get my very first commission from the Republic of Venice, and I cannot draw a meaningful line.' He drove one fist into his palm with frustration.

Feyra looked at the scattered plans. 'Why must this one be any different?'

Palladio threw up his arms and put his hands behind his white head. 'Because it is an offering. I am caught in a contract, the seals have been set and the papers signed, and there is to be no breach of it.' He sat again, heavily, letting his hands drop. 'The Doge thinks that if I build a miracle of architecture worthy of His glory, God will spare our city. He thinks that the Venetian people have sinned and God has smitten them for it.'

Feyra, much interested by this new perspective on the disaster, did not reveal that the disease had come to Venice through the dreadful design of one mortal man sitting in the Topkapi palace. She thought of her former profession. 'What of the doctors? There must be some here.'

'The Doge sends one such to me tomorrow, to keep me well. He thinks a doctor may save *me*, but only God may save *us*.' Palladio clasped his rough hands, as if in prayer. 'Oh, it matters not, I have my contract, and I must complete it. Only I cannot.' He looked at her. 'What do you do when you cannot get something right?'

Feyra thought of the many times in the Harem when her remedies had not worked. 'I go back to the beginning,' she said simply. 'I think you have to find your beginning.'

'*Find my beginning*,' he mused, and sat still for so long that Feyra wondered if she should go. She began to look about her. Her eyes lighted on a single drawing, pinned on the wall, untouched by fire. She rose and went over to it.

It was a drawing of a man, with wild hair and fiery eyes. She felt herself blushing. He was unclothed, a man in his prime, with eyes of fire and hair like sunrays. He had twice as many limbs as other men – all outstretched like a spider, one set delimited by a circle, the other by a square.

A man within a circle within a square.

'Why did you keep this?'

The architect broke out of his reverie and looked up slowly. 'Because it is not mine. It is by a fellow called Leonardo, from Vinci, near Florence. This is the drawing that started it all for me. This –' he rose, his voice full of realization '– *this* is my beginning.'

Suddenly animated, Palladio snatched a candle from the nearest sconce and limped up the tiny winding stair to the mezzanine. The circle of saffron light spread across the spines of the books, illuminating the letters just as the ink of his own drawings had gilded in the flames. He pulled one ancient tome out of the stack and blew the dust from its pages. 'There's my old friend,' he said, and brought the book down to her, flinging it on the table with a thud and an accompanying cloud of dust. She spelled out the long word across the front. She thought at first it said 'Venice', but concentrated hard on the other characters and spelled 'VITRUVIUS'.

'You read Latin?'

Feyra had pored over some monastic herbals in the Topkapi library but could only make out but a few words. 'No.'

'He was the original master builder, when the Romans ruled all.' He smiled a little. 'When your country and mine were one empire.'

Feyra watched as he turned the pages – noticing his hands as he turned the leaves gently. They were as ink-stained as Zabato's, heavy and square, with short stubby nails and hardened horny fingertips. They were the hands of a labourer not a nobleman; and yet she found his speech easier to understand than any one else in the house. She suspected that he had not been born as a nobleman. She looked at the book over his shoulders. 'Where does it begin?'

He rapped his forefinger on the first diagram. 'With this, a circle within a square.'

She frowned. 'Is it the answer?'

Her master sighed. 'Vitruvius is my beginning and my end, my alpha and omega; his geometrical rules govern everything I do; not only that but the universe beyond.' He swept his arm to the open casement, a gesture that embraced the cosmos, directing Feyra to the night outside, velvet and baubled with stars. 'I have built my life upon Vitruvius's shoulders. He is my inspiration.'

Feyra looked at the stars, the same stars that shone on Constantinople. She thought of the minarets and domes of Mimar Sinan. She remembered then Nur Banu working at the plans for her mosque with the earnest, turbanned man, making suggestions for a staircase here, a false arch, or an ornamental screen. Feyra looked at the book of Vitruvius again. The circle within a square. Now the shape was different, assuming three dimensions, transforming before her eyes. It was not meaningless. It was a dome.

'Perhaps – your god does not want the same thing as before. Perhaps he wants something different.' She spoke carefully. 'The fellow I told you of. His name is Mimar Sinan.'

'An infidel!'

She corrected him sternly. 'An architect.'

Palladio inclined his head. 'It is late. Come to me in the morning. I have that tiresome doctor attending me at noon but come to me before that. I would hear more of this Sinan.'

As she bowed and backed from the room she could see Palladio, in the candlelight, turning the pages with his stone-hardened fingers, rapt. He had taken a clean sheet of paper and a stick of charcoal, and was drawing, again and again, a circle within a square.

Chapter 21

When Feyra went to Palladio's *studiolo* the next morning, the room looked entirely different.

The walls were scrubbed, and the only evidence of the fire was a sooty stain on the tapestry that hung above the mantel. The plans were packed away again and the only drawn material in evidence was the book of Vitruvius, open at the circle and the square, and the picture of the man with many limbs pinned on the wall, staring down from his geometrical prison. The great chair had been shifted to the middle of the room. Palladio invited her to sit in it while he stood. Feyra duly settled herself, and their visit to Constantinople began.

The architect bid her sit still with her hands in her lap and close her eyes. Then he asked her to imagine herself back in Constantinople, and to walk from her house. He limped around her as she spoke, firing questions at her like an archer at a mark. Feyra, intrigued, acquiesced.

In her mind's eye she crossed the threshold of the little house in Sultanamet that she'd shared with her father and set off down the worn, warm cobbles. 'Take me somewhere,' she heard Palladio's distant, gravelly voice say; and she went left to the Bazaar Quarter and through the spice market. She was so immersed in her daydream that she

could smell the acrid leaves and feel the fallen herbs underfoot though her thin yellow slippers. She walked until she
reached the Imaret gate. 'Where are you?' asked the voice.

'I am at the Süleymaniye Mosque, the greatest edifice
Sinan ever built, for the tomb of Süleymaniye.' Now she
passed under the vast shadow of the Muvakkithane
Gateway, dwarfed by the massive ornamental marble postern. 'And now I'm in the *avlu*, a great monumental
courtyard on its west side. There's a long row of continuous
arches . . .'

'A colonnaded peristyle. Go on.'

With the architect occasionally interrupting with questions, Feyra walked round the whole complex in her mind,
describing its columns, courtyards, minarets in minute
detail.

'And what of the church itself?' he asked.

'The main dome is as high as heaven, and gilded within,
as if someone has captured a lightning flash. The interior is
almost a square.'

'A circle in a square,' breathed the voice, softer than
before. 'Go on.'

'The two shapes together form a single vast space. The
dome is flanked by semi-domes, and to the north and south
arches there are windows with triangles over them,
cemented with a rainbow of tiny tiles.'

'And how are the domes supported?'

Feyra turned around beneath the dome. 'There are supports built into the wall, but they are hidden by the arches
of the galleries.'

'He's masked the buttresses, to give a more harmonious
interior. Clever,' said the voice, warm with admiration.

'There is a single *serife* . . . gallery . . . inside the structure, and a two-storey gallery outside. The inside is clad with subtle *Iznik* tiles and the woodwork inset with simple designs in ivory and mother-of-pearl. But the jewel in the casket – the tomb of Süleymaniye – is clad in white marble.'

Feyra was in the grip of her dream, revolving around under the jewel-studded roof. She felt as if she were in heaven. A sharp rapping sound brought her crashing down to earth.

'*Damn,*' cursed Palladio. 'It is the doctor.' Flustered, Feyra rose. 'Come –' her master opened a small door by the staircase. 'Wait in the *cabinetto.*'

The little room held all Palladio's supplies, his pens and inks, ramparts of charcoal and pillars of paper. Feyra held the door closed with her little finger curled in the keyhole, but her curiosity got the better of her and she let it open a crack and peered through.

The sight before her made her heart thump so hard she almost fell into the room. Her master was seated in the chair she had just left and over him arched a dreadful monster; clad in black, with a curving beak poised to strike.

Chapter 22

'I do not think you are even ill.'

Annibale looked the old man over. The architect was clearly wealthy by the quality of his velvets and the size of his rooms, and the chair he sat in was good oak. Although his beard was white, his eyes were bright as pebbles.

'I'm not,' admitted the old man. 'Yet. But I cannot afford to become so, and the Doge claims that you are the best plague doctor in Venice.'

Annibale was without vanity; he'd been told by his mother that he was a beautiful baby, then by his aunts that he was a beautiful child, then by numerous women that he was a beautiful man. In Padua, the plaudits changed from the physical to the intellectual as his tutors told him repeatedly that he had the best medical mind in his year. Then the Camerlengo of the Republic himself had sought him out. So now he merely shrugged. He was irritated to be taken from his work; irritated to have been outplayed by the Camerlengo. He did not trouble to hide it. 'And you,' he said sarcastically, 'are the most important man in Venice, because you are building a church.'

The old man sat a little straighter. 'Not just any church. A church to beg the Lord to save us from the Plague.'

Annibale thought about the streets he had just passed

through. Valnetti and his colleagues were clearly failing to hold back the tide. In some *quartieri* there were crosses on every house now, lime boxes on every corner, myrtle smoke snaking from every chimney. 'Beg hard,' he snapped. He adjusted his mask, already preparing to go.

The old man gestured to the beak with his roughened hand. 'Does that thing work?'

'So far. And whether it does or it doesn't, the people expect it, which is more.' Annibale straightened up and told a lie to expedite his exit. 'The truth is, *Maestro*, that if you have dodged the pestilence for these many days, you will, in all probability, not catch it now.' He relented. 'But this you may do. Get yourself a square of good linen – I mean with many close-woven threads, like good Egyptian cotton – smoke it on the fire each day and tie it over your nose and mouth if you should walk the streets.' He glanced back at the old man. 'In fact, if you are a mason, it would serve you well to do this anyway, for that cough will kill you before the Plague does. That, or keep away from stone.'

The fellow smiled into his white beard. 'I can't keep away from stone. It is my life.'

'Then what was once your life will be your death,' snapped Annibale.

Now, the old man chuckled. 'So long as I can finish my church first, He may come and get me.'

Annibale snorted, and the old man looked at him keenly. 'You don't have faith? You don't attend church?'

Annibale shot him a look. 'I'm too busy in this world to concern myself with the next. In your profession too you would better serve God by serving mankind. Before you build your church you should build some better hous-ing. The Plague has taken such a hold principally because of cramped rooms, no sanitation and no ventilation. Health begins with the home.'

The old man's eyes brightened and he looked at the doctor properly for the first time. 'You are *absolutely* right,' he said emphatically, as if he had found a kindred spirit. 'Go on.'

Annibale opened his mouth to vent his fury at the Republic and its shoddy housing provision for the poor, but he closed it again. He needed to get back to his island; his island and his patients. 'If you'll forgive me, I must return to those who have *actual* need. I'll see you in seven days,' he said shortly, and swept from the room with a flourish of his coat.

Unfortunately the drama of his exit was ruined by the fact that he chose the wrong door. He found himself in a small antechamber in which a maid was fiddling about with some chores. She jumped a little, her cheeks burning, and shot him through with an amber glance before lowering her strange topaz eyes respectfully.

He automatically appraised her appearance as he did with everyone he met. Her skin was unblemished and her cheeks fairly glowing with health. She was a fine specimen; at least Palladio's servants did not seem to be pestilent, and that was half the battle. 'Your pardon,' he barked at her, his manner rendered even ruder than usual by the farcical situation, before backing out and leaving, this time by the right way.

Chapter 23

Feyra spent each morning in the *studiolo* with Palladio.

Her tasks were reassigned and Zabato Zabatini was directed to come to his master in the afternoons only. No one in the household made comment: the master was working again.

Feyra told him of the new mosque Sinan was building for her mother, a place that would be Nur Banu's tomb. During these conversations, Zabato Zabatini would often loiter about the room and Feyra would feel his eyes upon her from behind the eye-glasses, as if her voice or her features brought Cecilia back to him.

She soon forgot Zabato, though, for now Palladio's questions became more direct. As she'd seen the mosque being built, he asked her how the dome was constructed, how it was supported, even how the masons cut the stone. He became obsessed with the concept. How did one turn a circle within a square to a sphere within a cube? For to build a true dome, aesthetically pleasing and following all the geometrical precepts of Vitruvius, the dome must have an equal space beneath it, a void that the worshippers would fill with their faith.

Sometimes he drew, sweeping lines and marginalia crammed with detail. Sometimes she did, and found that the pen answered in her hand for she been trained to draw anatomy. Again and again Feyra's eye would be drawn to the Vitruvian man pinned upon the wall. His geometry informed every one of the drawings around him and his expression exemplified the meeting of Feyra's discipline and Palladio's architecture – anatomy and building.

Sometimes Palladio would ask about Sinan himself, and she tried to recall as much as she could about the turbanned, quiet little man. And there were similarities between Mimar Sinan and Andrea Palladio: bearded, kindly, utterly obsessed with their creation, the two could have been brothers-over-the-sea. Yet as often as Palladio would ask about the new build, he would ask about the old.

Again and again Palladio asked Feyra to tell him of the Mosque of Eyüp, where the standard bearer of her Prophet lay enshrined. He seemed captivated by immortality through building, the notion of pilgrims streaming to worship centuries after the architect was dead and gone. He did not seem to make a distinction between his god and hers, and Feyra began to wonder if he had a point. If Sinan and Palladio were two sides of the same coin, like the coin that she wore in her bodice, perhaps the god of the West and the god of the East were likewise. Perhaps Palladio's Almighty and her Allah were looking-glass gods.

She chided herself for the impure thought, and would climb the stairs each night and pray loud enough to drown out the constant bells. She'd learned the canonical hours from Corona Cucina and those alien times now measured her days – Matins, Prime, Tierce, Sext and Nones. The cook was forever telling her rosary beads and Corona Cucina's unswerving faith reminded Feyra of the Salaah, her own rule of prayer. She swore to keep it in her heart and head even if she could not wash and kneel at the five required times, the Eastern reflections of the canonical hours; but the demands of her tasks and the hours of the household's meals did not accommodate her, and she soon forgot.

When she did remember, she prayed fervently and hopelessly, clutching her yellow slipper. She would have prayed even harder had she known that one evening, in a dark corner of the Doge's palace, an unseen hand had slipped a piece of paper into a letterbox. The box itself was a mere slit in the wall, but it was set into a great stone relief of a lion's face and positioned where the creature's mouth would have been. Behind the stone mask was a strong box in the office of the Camerlengo, a coffer opened only by the chamberlain's hand. On this occasion, the denunciation that the lion consumed contained just a few lines written in an awkward hand: directions to the house of the gold callipers, and the name of Feyra Adalet bint Timurhan Murad.

Chapter 24

As time passed Feyra reflected more and more on the concept of *Mizan* – the balance.

She'd always believed that the sickness of the mind was as detrimental to the human spirit as sickness of the body, and Palladio was a case in point. Feyra had cured Palladio's malaise, and unlocked his passions. She still spent her mornings with him, talking of the great edifices of the East, but his afternoons and evenings were spent drawing new plans for his domed church with Zabato Zabatini.

Tradesmen came from the scriveners with reams of new-smelling paper and pots of ink, sticks of dusky charcoal and blotting sawdust smelling of wick wood. And the draughtsman drew until he dropped, well into the night, with Palladio peering over him or pacing behind him, talking and waving his hands to describe the arches and pillars in the air. And, on the paper, a miracle began to rise, an earthly twin of Palladio's ethereal vision, set down in black and white, each dimension perfectly to scale, each measurement exquisitely described, exact plans to be given to the masons and committed to stone.

For the first time Feyra appreciated Zabato's skill. While Palladio's drawings were a caprice, a fantasy, Zabato tethered them to the earth, drew them with no passion but exactitude, made the fantastic possible.

Feyra no longer worried for Palladio's mind, but she was now worried for his earthly shell. She would listen to the music of his chest as he leaned over the plans and knew that if the Plague entered this house now, he would be taken. She thought about the visit of the Birdman physician. She could hardly believe that the doctors in Venice went about so garbed, like they were wild shamans of the savages, and she was astonished to discover from his conversation with Palladio that he was known as the best plague doctor in Venice. She had only agreed with some of what he'd said – what he said about housing certainly chimed with her conception of *Mizan*, and a face mask may well protect her master from the miasma of the streets – but she found his dismissal of Palladio's peril a little too glib. Preventative medicine for the well was as important as curative medicine for the sick, especially for one whose malady of the lungs might make him more susceptible to airborne diseases. Very well, if the Birdman doctor would not care for her master, she would.

One morning Feyra took courage and went to Zabato Zabatini and told him what she wanted done. She found him in the *cabinetto* cutting the alabaster sheets of fresh paper to size. He listened to the long, long list in silence, then took off his eye-glasses and rubbed his shock of hair. 'Feyra,' he said. 'What you ask is impossible.' He set his glasses back on his nose. 'Our master is in full flow with his church, and will not tolerate any upheaval in this house.'

Feyra set her chin. 'How are your hands?'

Zabato Zabatini spread his fingers before him and looked at them as if he saw them for the first time. The scaling and soreness had completely gone – the flesh was supple and clean.

Feyra raised her brows.

He sighed. 'Very well.'

Feyra did not go to Palladio that morning. Instead she set Corona Cucina to make a great crock of potash and goose-fat, which she used to fill in the cracks about each window, and she tied each casement closed with twine. Winter was coming, and there was no argument from the household. Once Palladio began to visit the site on Giudecca Feyra directed Zabato to take him there in a gondola with a *felze*, a black tented cover, so that he would not be exposed to the air. In the great chamber she had her master's bedding washed and smoked and the curtains rubbed with camphor. Feyra made a firepowder of equal parts of wood aloes, storax and calamite. She mixed the components in a mortar with rosewater of Damascus, and fashioned the paste into small, oblong briquettes to set on the household fires.

She shut off the tradesmen's door which was reached by a tramp through the foul courtyard, and insisted instead that every visitor to the house, great or lowly, should enter by the principal door in the square, under the sign of the gold callipers. The great door led into a small atrium that housed coats, hats and canes, before another pair of doors which were kept open. Feyra had the little coat room cleared, the stone flags swept and covered with rushes steeped in rue and potash, then sprinkled them with cassia, vinegar and rosewater. In the wall sconces she set candles she had made herself, from wood ash, mutton tallow and water, each one impregnated with woody shreds of frankincense from her belt. Each visitor had to pass through the smoky hallway, and clean their feet on the rushes and herbs.

Feyra directed sternly that when the door to the street was open, the doors to the household were closed; when the household doors were open the door to the street was shut.

Palladio, if he noticed these measures, did not comment. He was not troubled by anything so long as it did not interfere with his work.

And nothing did, until the night it seemed the Plague had indeed come for him.

Chapter 25

It was the dead of night, and Feyra was birthed from some nameless nightmare at the sound of a sharp knock on her door.

Bleary-eyed, she opened it to find Zabato Zabatini, dressed in a nightshirt, blinking in the light of his candle. *'Come and see,'* he said.

She flinched at the phrase, unable at this hour to place it, but she came without question and followed him down through the crazy shadows of the candle-lit staircase.

Zabato whispered to her fiercely as they descended. 'My master is in a fever, and there is a swelling protruding from his flesh as big as a medlar.'

Feyra stumbled a little, numb with foreboding. She steeled herself. 'His fingertips – are they black?'

The wild head of grey hair before and below her shook from side to side. 'I do not know.'

Two floors down from her own attic room was her master's chamber, a place where she laid and cleared the fire each day, with a great bed and four posts. She drew aside the heavy camphor-impregnated curtains of the bed. There he was in his nightcap and gown, twisted and fevered on his bed, his beard and hair damp with perspiration. But she was encouraged. His complexion had flushed and reddened, not become dark or sallow as a Plague-drained visage; his fingers, when she took them up, were pink and when she pressed their stone-hardened tips the blood rushed back into the white bruise with his heartbeat. Instructing Zabato to hold the candle still she examined his armpits. Although damp with sweat, they were unblemished.

Without a thought for propriety she was about to raise his gown to check the groin, when she saw the swelling that Zabato had mentioned. It protruded from the side of his Palladio's left knee, yellow and firm as a quince. She was instantly relieved. This was not Plague. But the relief was short-lived, for her master was old, and in the grip of a grave fever.

Corona Cucina, who had entered with some grappa for the master, set down her tray with a clatter by the bedside, and took to crossing herself so fast that her hand was a blur at her bosom. 'Is it Plague? Is it the end?' she wailed.

'No,' said Feyra shortly, and handed her back the grappa. 'Take this – it is no good to him. Boil it till it bubbles then bring it back.' She thought she knew the cause of the swelling. Palladio had gout. She had recognized his malady the very first time she had seen him limping around the ruin on Giudecca the day her father had died. This swelling of the knee, from the fluid that had accrued at the joint, was infected and must be lanced. She sighed as she took off her medicine belt and laid out what she needed. If she had had the care of this man she could have managed the gout and Palladio need never have reached this pass.

She heated her silver scalpel in the blue heart of the candle, then laid it by to cool. Then she brought out a little of her precious wood betony, and some of the lemon balm for healing. She tore a strip of the master's linen and powdered it with lime. All was ready.

With a dreadful sense of repetition she lanced the gouty swelling and watched the greenish pus drain off. She waited and dabbed it once with Corona Cucina's steaming grappa. Then she took her needle and thread and drew it through the liquor to wet it. 'Mercy!' said the cook, watching closely. 'You are never going to sew our master like a cushion?'

'Hold his leg,' said Feyra in answer, 'and pour the rest of the grappa down his throat if he wakes.'

In Ottoman society alcohol was forbidden, but it was permitted in hospitals to be used as medicine. In the Topkapi palace the imperial pages of the third court used to pretend to be ill in order to be admitted to the hospital and drink the wine. Feyra smiled grimly at the memory and heated the needle in the flame, this time without cooling it – the heat would better cauterize the flesh – then she began to sew the wound, neatly, stitch by stitch. As Haji Musa had taught her, she looped the wine-soaked thread beneath each stitch to anchor it. Once the thread was tied and cut, she opened a leather capsa from her medicine belt and poured a little ground glass over the wound, laid betony over the whole and tied the leg with the limed linen. Palladio did not seem sensible of any of it.

'I will stay here the night,' Feyra said to Zabato, and he nodded, escorting Corona Cucina, protesting loudly, from the room.

In the grey hours Feyra's head bumped the footboard as she dropped at last into sleep and she woke with the Matins bells to find her patient sleeping too, cool to the touch, breathing evenly, his cheeks rosy, not hectic.

Relieved, she crept downstairs again, to be shooed back

to her attic by Corona Cucina, who, alone of the household, knew how she'd passed the night.

Feyra was woken by raised voices.

The sun was high in the sky so it must be the hour of noon. She huddled into the well of the stair and recognized the clipped, arrogant tones of the Birdman.

She crept down two floors and listened at the door of her master's solar. She had learned that as a servant she was invisible to company, so she laid her hand on the door's handle and entered the room.

Sure enough, the physician was there in attendance. At her entrance the Birdman did not look round, but curved over her master on the bed like a scavenger that expects carrion and is frustrated to discover that his prey is still alive. Feyra stood close by, making small and unnecessary adjustments to Palladio's bedclothes, listening.

'Who has done this? Are you retaining another doctor? Is it Valnetti?'

Annibale was incensed, and his anger had made him irrational. It could not be Valnetti. He had only seen sutures like this once before, with a loop to each stitch, when a doctor from Persia had visited Padua. He got as close to the wound as his mask would allow. Even through the beak the bitter smell of grappa reached his nose; the physician had treated the thread, prepared a betony poultice, then sewn Palladio up as neatly as a Burano lacemaker. The wound seemed to have been cauterized too. Not Valnetti, then, for he had no more skill than a butcher. 'If you are retaining another physician I cannot keep you safe.'

And if Palladio had admitted another doctor, what of

Annibale's deal with the Camerlengo? If he did not have the care of the architect, would he have to give back his island? He had noticed as he entered, the smoke of frankincense in the small hall, the cleansing herbs underfoot, and that the windows were sealed with fat and ashes; exactly the measures that he should have put in place here himself. Guilt fuelled his anger even more.

Palladio spoke in conciliatory tones. 'I am not retaining another doctor,' he said, but his eyes went past the physician to the servant girl standing by the bedpost.

Annibale spun round to face her and saw a telltale blush stain her cheeks. He covered the ground between them and pushed his beak into her face. 'Who taught you to stitch flesh like this?' He tipped the bird head to one side as he examined her features. 'Where are you from?'

The maid began to back away.

'Wait, wait!'

But the girl did not. She turned and fled.

Chapter 26

Palladio was at the house less and less.
He had engaged his masons, and a gang of builders, and his church was growing apace.

His and Feyra's roles had now reversed. He would describe his church to her, how the foundations were laid, the pillars founded and the buttresses piled. He invited her to the site to see the walls growing from the ground, but she could not face visiting what would always be to her her father's grave. She was further horrified to hear from Palladio that the builders' gang were having trouble with hordes of visiting pilgrims who came in their droves with buckets and jurdens and other vessels to collect the water from the well, believing it to have miraculous healing powers. The legend had grown out of the story of Saint Sebastian the Doge had recounted and Palladio had been forced to hire guards for the site, to put an end to the nonsense.

Feyra caught his tone and looked at him sharply. 'What will you do with the well?' she asked.

'Wall it in,' answered Palladio briefly.

Feyra thought of her father's bones, interred for ever at the heart of a Christian church. Her own heart a stone, she said instead, 'Do you not believe in miracles?'

Palladio thought for a moment. 'No.'

She thought of her mother, of her father. 'Neither do I.'

The news of the fate of the well greatly depressed Feyra's spirits. The danger and desperation of her escape from Giudecca had forced her to put aside her grief for her father, and it came upon her now, rushing in like *acqua alta* with a force to knock her off her feet. She felt the loss of him as an actual physical pain, located just below her heart. Her growing misery was compounded by apprehension. For as the week passed and the Birdman's next visit neared, she began to fear the doctor's retribution. With Palladio and Zabato away at the site, she felt even more fearful. And it was clear that the Birdman had the ear of the Doge.

Palladio stayed at the house every Friday for his appointment with his physician with an ill grace, for he was impatient to be at the site. When the next Friday dawned Feyra crept downstairs, dead-eyed as the mackerel Corona Cucina was preparing in the kitchen for breakfast. She breathed in a wobbly breath. Usually Friday – fish for every meal – provided a respite from the aromas of heathen flesh that the Venetians feasted upon. But today the sea-scent nauseated her. She skulked in the hallway at noon, hoping that someone else would open the door to the doctor and when she heard a rap at the door, and a commotion in the hallway as the Birdman came to roost at the house, she hid. Nearly doubled up with nerves, she tried to regulate her breathing, but her heart leapt to her mouth as she peered from the shadows of the hallway at the little party at the doorway.

For it was not the Birdman.

It was a stranger, with clipped tow-coloured hair, and he was not alone, but accompanied by a semicircle of guards in the half-armour she recognized from the Doge's palace. The stranger had his back to her, and more terrifying than his escort was the insignia on his back, the winged lion, jaws agape, watching her. When the man turned, he smiled, but the smile did not reach the ice blue of his eyes, and he was scarcely less frightening than the lion. 'Good *Dama*,' he was saying to Corona Cucina who had answered the door, 'would you be so kind as to gather all the persons in the household in your master's room?'

It was not a question but an order.

Feyra was vastly relieved that she was not alone. Corona and she had to crowd into the *studiolo* behind all the other household staff, from the kitchen maids to the midden-men to the footboys.

In his customary oak chair sat her master, stroking his beard, Zabato standing fidgeting behind him. Palladio seemed outwardly calm, but Feyra knew that he was simmering with impatience. It was a measure of the man that had gathered them here that Palladio had received him at such a time, when his work was in full flow. Feyra was beginning to realize that everyone in this city bowed before the Lion.

Hiding behind Corona's bulk, Feyra was no longer afraid that this strange meeting had anything to do with her. The stranger waited for the door to close, before he spoke. 'I believe that most of you know that I am the Camerlengo, the chamberlain of the Doge?' No one answered the question, nor was expected to. 'I have received information,' he said in a low, musical voice, 'that there is a fugitive among you.'

Feyra's heart plummeted. 'A Turk and an infidel was seen fleeing in this direction some time ago. A search proved fruitless, but in these last days we received a denunciation, posted through the Lion's mouth, in an unknown hand, telling us the identity of the Turk that hides here.'

Feyra's heart knocked against her ribs, and was met by an answering knock against the door outside. She darted her gaze around the room. All the household were here. The stranger must have posted another of his men outside the door. She was trapped.

'I will not try your patience by questioning all of you here,' stated the Camerlengo mildly. 'All the menfolk may move to the fireplace.'

The crowd around Feyra thinned out as the men of the household moved to the left of the room. 'And now every maid who has entered the household in the last month may stay where they are. The rest are to move to the fireplace.'

Feyra was rooted to the spot, unable to move as the others melted away from her. All the eyes of the household were upon her, but she only felt the single piercing blue gaze of the stranger. She could sense him appraising her amber eyes, her skin, the tawny curls escaping from her cap.

'There's no need to be afraid,' he said gently, in a manner that implied the very opposite. 'Just tell me your name, and where you come from.'

Feyra was dumbstruck. After her time in the house she could speak the Venetian dialect passably well, but in no way would her accent fool a native, and she was still careful to speak to no one save her master and Zabato, and a few words to Corona Cucina. She looked desperately at the two elderly men who had sheltered her – one who knew her history, one who did not, both of whom knew her provenance. Palladio was utterly still but his eyes held a warning; Zabato twitched, wringing his hands.

The Camerlengo moved closer. She could smell the sweet woodruff scent that he wore. 'Come,' he said. 'Won't you speak?'

Zabato stumbled forward, tripping and then righting himself. 'She is my niece!' he piped in a high, panicked voice. 'She joined the household lately for our maid left us, when the pestilence came.'

The Camerlengo did not turn his light eyes from Feyra's face for an instant. It was as if he had not marked Zabato at all, and yet he had clearly heard every word. 'Is this true?'

Feyra had just opened her mouth to give herself away when she felt a painful shove at her back as the door opened and the Birdman came in.

He strode into the room with a force that almost equalled the Camerlengo. 'What is the meaning of this?' he demanded, his tone amplified by the dreadful beak mask.

'Just an interrogation, Cason. Calm yourself.'

'Calm myself!' The Birdman fumbled in his black cloak and brought forth a round plaque, which winked in the sunlight as he held it high. It seemed to be wrought of some kind of yellow metal. 'What is this?'

The Camerlengo smiled. 'Come, Cason, you know very well. It's the seal of the Doge. I gave it to you myself.'

The beak nodded in a tall sweep. 'And *why* did you give me this?'

The Camerlengo was silent.

The Birdman answered his own question. 'So I could

protect this man here from pestilence.' He pointed at Palladio with a black-gloved finger. 'You came to my island, did you not, and told me that the Doge himself wished for me to visit this architect every day, and keep the pestilence from his door?'

The Camerlengo inclined his head.

'Then how may I do my work when you have trailed half of the city into his *studiolo*, carrying the Lord knows what upon their breaths and clothes? The Lord Doge gave me leave to treat the architect. I choose to isolate him. I must ask you to all leave.' The red glass eyes stared round. '*Now.*'

'But . . .'

The Birdman held the seal high. The Camerlengo opened his mouth to respond, but in the end gave a jerk of his blond head that sent his *Leoni* guard scuttling from the room. The household followed, staring at Feyra as they passed, their eyes full of questions.

The Camerlengo paused for a second, as if he would say more; then he strode from the room. He did not look at the Birdman again but his gaze found Feyra in his shadow and he favoured her with a final, blue stare.

'He knew.'

'Of *course* he knew.' The Birdman answered the architect scornfully. 'He knows everything.'

Zabato paced, shaking, his hands fluttering like clipped wings.

'Can you stop him doing that?' the Birdman asked Palladio, as if Zabato could not hear.

'Leave him be,' said Palladio. 'The Doge may be pious

and gentle, but his guard dog is not. Little wonder he is feared. And he'll be back.'

Feyra, shaking, leaned weakly against the wall, trying to make sense of what had happened. She would have bet the Sultan's dagger to a hen's egg that it was the doctor who had denounced her, but he had saved her instead.

'Now we must hide Feyra,' said Zabato Zabatini.

Palladio was still seated, dazed. 'Who is Feyra?'

Zabato pointed to the shadows. 'She is. The maid you know as Cecilia Zabatini.'

Palladio looked at her, with a chastened expression. She saw then in that one glance that he cared for her, that he was aware how much he owed her, and that he was ashamed he had never troubled to find out anything about her. 'Of course we will hide her,' he said.

'But where?' Zabato's teeth were chattering with fear. 'This house has many nooks, but the Camerlengo would find her in a heartbeat. And there are some in the household who would not shelter her, knowing she is a Turk. Even Corona Cucina; as you know, her husband was killed at Lepanto.'

Feyra swallowed. Even Corona Cucina, her friend and advocate?

'I could get her to Vicenza, perhaps.' This from Palladio.

'No,' countered Zabato. 'She now has a connection to you. If she is found in your house her presence would endanger your family there.'

The Birdman let a small silence fall. He had taken no part in the discussion; it was nothing to do with him. 'Well – I must away to my island.'

Both of the older men turned their heads as one to look at the masked man.

The Birdman retreated a pace, gloved hands outspread. 'I cannot take her. I have a hospital to run.'

'A hospital on a Plague island, where no one dares to come.'

'What would I do with a maid?'

'She is skilled in physic. You owned it yourself.'

The Birdman was insistent. 'I absolutely refuse. I must be gone. I will see you in a week.'

Palladio rose. 'In a *week*,' he said slowly, measuring the syllables. He came right up to the Birdman, until his nose almost touched the beak. 'In the Camerlengo's presence,' Palladio observed evenly, 'you said you had been here every *day*. But you have not. You have visited *weekly*.'

There was an uncomfortable pause.

'How would he like to know this?' wondered Palladio aloud. 'How would he punish you?'

The doctor had gone incredibly still.

'And yet,' went on Palladio, 'if you take *Feyra* –' he used her name with care '– then you may come here at each new moon, just once in every *four* weeks and the Doge will not be the wiser from me.'

The Birdman moved suddenly, snatching up his cane. 'Very well,' he barked. 'But she must come *now*.'

'The house will be watched,' warned Palladio.

'The watergate,' suggested Zabato. 'I will find a gondola with a *felze* such as my master normally uses.' He turned to Feyra. 'Fetch what you will from your rooms.'

Feyra ran to the attic, her mind spinning like a windlass. But there was nothing for it – she must go. She had little to pack: she had only the clothes she stood up in, the ring around her neck, the coin in her bosom and the yellow slipper beneath the bed, with the sequins she had so far earned jingling in the toe. In a trice she was downstairs again.

Following Zabato Zabatini, silent but for the hissing torch, Palladio, the Birdman and Feyra made their way down a dark and winding stair that led to a place that Feyra had never been, as she had never left the house by boat.

She stood on a damp dais. Beyond the stone stage was a wet dock; a green limpid square of canal water, where in former centuries the family's gondolas and barges would have been moored.

Zabato opened the doors to the dock with a pulley and handle, and they watched as an ink-black gondola with a tented black cover came towards them, negotiating the everyday traffic of gondolas and *traghetti* criss-crossing the sparkling canal. A burly man at the tiller raised a hand and drew in to collect his passengers. The doctor stepped into the craft first, looking left and right for spies on the water with a lateral sweep of his beak.

Zabato smiled at Feyra wanly, twitching as ever, and she could see he would be sorry to see her go. Palladio drew her aside and tenderly took her hand.

'I hope I will see you again, and that you will see my church one day, for it sprang from your brain as much as mine.' As he handed her into the gondola his eyes looked dull as stone.

Then the curtains swung closed and she was alone in the blackness, the Birdman's beak curving towards her, glowing out of the dark, the colour of bone.

PART III

The Lion

Chapter 27

A nnibale did not speak for the whole of the gondola ride to the Fondamenta Nuove.

He did not say a word as he handed Feyra into a bigger rowboat at the seaboard, and only spoke to the boatman to give him directions to the island. He was silent with the fury of being outsmarted twice in one week. It was a sensation he was not used to, and did not enjoy.

He wondered what on earth he was going to do with this girl; but by the time he'd reached the Lazzaretto he had calmed down a little. She did not chatter – she conducted herself with decorum, sitting there in the bow of the boat like a *Maria di Legno*, one of the wooden Virgin Marys common to every church in Venice.

Annibale had not been used to womenfolk since the last of his aunts had died. His mother had been an occasional, unreliable presence in his life, but he never spoke of her. The one function of a mother was, surely, to be a mother, and in abandoning him she had failed even in that. After her defection her history had become so shameful he could not bring himself to utter her name. The Badessa and the sisters on the island were his only female company, but they were practical and devout, most of them elderly and none of them handsome.

Feyra's appearance, on the contrary, was distinctly disturbing.

He handed her out at the jetty, then stalked ahead, not waiting for the girl until they reached the great gate and the trench of potash. 'Walk through this, *carefully*,' he directed curtly, knowing he did not have to explain himself.

Bocca stood sentinel at the gatehouse as the doctor entered. Annibale did not even slow his pace. 'Do not say a *word*,' he said through his teeth, knowing how broad the gatekeeper's humour could be. 'She is my maid, nothing more.'

He walked purposefully to the very middle of the green lawn, then stopped and turned so rapidly that his beak nearly knocked out Feyra's teeth.

'What is your name?'

'Feyra Adalet Bint Timurhan Murad.'

'Where did you learn your doctoring?'

'From Haji Musa, chief physician at the Topkapi palace in Constantinople.'

'You were his assistant?'

'I was a doctor,' she corrected gravely.

He was silent, amazed, for besides the goodwives and cellar wenches that would rid a woman of a unwanted babe, or provide a vial of poison for an unwanted husband, women and medicine did not marry in these lands. 'How did you come to Palladio's house?'

The girl appeared to consider her reply. 'On shipboard,' she said carefully. 'My father was a sea captain and he . . . took sick with the Plague.' She spoke good Venetian, but with a thick and not unattractive accent. 'Then I nursed him when we reached Venice, but he died. I sought employ at the architect's house, and he took me in.'

He expressed no sympathy, but went right to the meat of the medical matter. 'And you were not infected?'

'I nearly died from the Plague aboard ship, but my boils burst and I lived.'

'So you had the pestilence and survived.'

'Yes.'

'Yet your father did not.'

She was silent for so long that he felt obliged to speak. 'I will show you the island,' he said stiffly. 'It is a work in progress, but it runs quite effectively.' He was not quite sure why he felt obliged to excuse his work to her, and pointed curtly to the great, roofed building in the middle of the island.

'There's my hospital, known as the Tezon.' He could not suppress a tiny timbre of pride in his voice, and went on to show her the rest of his kingdom. He did not know why he was guiding her himself, using his precious time when he could have turned her over to the Badessa at once, which had always been his intention. For some reason, too, he hurried past the cemetery. Pride again, he supposed, for there had been more deaths lately, enough to give him midnight misgivings about his methods. 'These are the almshouses, where dwell the families of the afflicted.' He looked at her sideways but she did not comment, she just studied the houses with a considering eye and smiled at some of the children playing on their step. Her smile suddenly made him forgot what he'd been going to say.

She walked on ahead of him. 'And this?'

Annibale shrugged and hurried on through the botanical garden, pleased with the geometric rows and the nuns busy at their horticulture, and stopped at the well. He explained the rain cistern and the seven filtrations of mineral salts and sand that made Venetian water the purest urban water in the world. But he could see the girl was looking at the stone lion with his closed book, with keen interest. 'And these sisters, in the black habits, are the sisters of the Miracoli.'

'They give succour to the patients?'

'No. Only I enter the Tezon. They give aid to the families, and help me run the island. They run the gardens and stock the trout ponds and the eel leets, do laundry. They row to the mainland for supplies, tend the chickens and goats, and maintain the garden. I will leave you in the care of the Badessa. You may board with the sisters and you will help them in their daily tasks.' He looked at her through his mask, at the exposed flesh of her throat. It mattered nothing to him that she was a Turk, but he knew that the women-folk of her culture went about veiled, and wondered what it cost her to be so exposed. It would be a relief to have that face hidden – to him as well as her. 'You may cover your face if you like,' he said curtly.

Feyra looked into the blank red glass eyes, trying to fathom what lay beneath.

In Turkey great store was set by the notion of *feraset*, physiognomy. The human body was the clothing for the soul, and therefore it followed that by studying physical traits it was possible to deduce character and temperament. But the Birdman who had made this place was covered head to foot, even more swathed than she herself was used to being, and his face was a dreadful beak. She could only judge him on his speech and actions and the Birdman had offered her sanctuary – not just geographical, but a deeper retreat too. Here, it seemed, she would be allowed to cover her face. It was the first kindness he had shown.

Feyra looked at the nearest nun, busy, bending over the herbs, digging. A simple string of wooden beads fell before her face as she dug, and on the end of the string hung a little tin cross, winking in the sun. It was just like the one Corona Cucina had given her, the one she still wore at her bodice, with the miniature shepherd prophet dangling from the cross. She unpinned the little brooch from her lace shawl, and dropped it down the well. Then she wound the lace around her head and turned to him.

'I will not help them,' she said. She pointed to the Tezon. 'I will help you.'

It only took the Birdman the space of one hour to know what a gift he had in Feyra. By the time four bells had rung he called her to him. 'Very well,' he said. 'Henceforth you will be my nurse.'

Feyra said nothing. It was a demotion from her role at the Harem, but a promotion from being a maid.

'What did the architect pay you?'

'One sequin a week.'

'Then I will pay you the same.'

If Feyra thought she'd been promoted, she was wrong.

Her tasks were far more onerous than those she'd carried out in Palladio's house. She spent her first day changing the soiled mattresses of the afflicted, giving them all food and water, changing the dressings and poultices of the numerous suture wounds that she found on each patient. She was impressed with some aspects of the organization of the Tezon, but found it far from a model hospital. True, the Birdman had isolated the patients admirably, the smoke cabinet at the great doors fumigated the doctor as he entered and left, and he kept the afflicted tolerably comfortable on their pallets. His medicine cabinets were well stocked, his botanical gardens fruitful. Supplies of food and water were left outside by the gatekeeper. But the patients were laid together as close as herrings in a crate, and no one, it seemed, had the care of their minds.

From the conversations she had with them, it was clear that some were even unaware that their families were hard by. As she found her feet Feyra resolved to implement changes as she went along. And this was as good a place as any to earn more sequins to fill her yellow slipper. Once the pestilence was passed and the shipping began again, she would have enough to take her home to Turkey.

On that first day, sitting with her patients in the Tezon, she looked at the Ottoman script scrawled on the walls in the iron oxide. They were manifests only, just the words for silk or spices, copper or cotton, but they were like the greatest sagas of the poets to her. Similarly the cognizances of the ships, scrawled here and there, insignia she'd seen on her father's ships and his order papers since she was a girl, were as beautiful to her as the *tugra*, the golden calligraphed signatures of the Sultans.

There was even, fittingly, on the eastern wall of the Tezon, a wonderfully rendered drawing of a ship of the Ottoman type, just like the one her father used to take to sea. She remembered standing on Seraglio Point, when she was no more than eight, watching it hove in across the sound. She felt her homesickness like a blow to the stomach, and it was a great comfort to think of the yellow slipper of sequins; it would take her home again.

By the end of the day Feyra knew the island well. Even the little cemetery in the wilderness beyond the well was not forbidden to her. In quiet moments she would dig graves alongside the sisters companiably enough, in silent respect for those that had gone, both faiths mouthing their parallel prayers. She drew water for the patients from the well where she had dropped her crucifix, impressed by the clarity of the water. She looked at the stone lion and he looked back at her but, strangely, she was not afraid of him here on this island. His mouth was as closed as his book. It was open jaws she feared; open jaws that might receive poisonous letters.

She could not think who could possibly have denounced her. It was not the Birdman. And no other member of Palladio's household had known her identity save Palladio and Zabato. Had Corona Cucina somehow discovered her from her medicines and her accent? It seemed too fantastic to be true. And just how long would it take for news of her presence on the island to filter back to the mainland? If the Camerlengo and his guard were determined to find her, how long would it be before they thought to look here?

Feyra went about her work the rest of the day drawing as little attention to herself as she could manage. The one place she did not set foot in was the church. Saint Bartholomew was the Christian saint that gave his name to the Damascene tree, the tree whose spores poisoned her mother, and for this, as much as the other reason, she would not go in.

But as much as Feyra would not enter the church, someone else was just as anxious to keep her out.

'She cannot room with us.'

The Badessa was waiting for Annibale at the end of

Feyra's first day. He stuck out his beak belligerently, and shook the smoke of the atrium cabinet free from the folds of his coat.

'Why?' he demanded, already knowing the answer.

'She is an infidel.'

Annibale sighed. He had thought it such a neat solution. The nuns all roomed in the customs house behind the church which had a great upper room. 'But she will not be living in the church itself. That was never suggested.'

'It does not matter. The customs house is one of the church buildings. She cannot live among us.' She touched his arm. 'I will be her friend. I try to be a Samaritan, as our Lord taught. I have, if you have noticed, given her some cloths for her head, and sandals for her feet. But she may not bed in our dormitory, nor enter our church. If you asked her, she would probably say the same.'

As the sun lowered Annibale showed Feyra the little cottage, next to the church but outside the retaining wall. It was the house that had suffered the cannon fire, the house that was so tumbledown that he had not deemed it fit for a family nor for himself. He was especially curt about it, telling her before he left that there was an idiot boy, a mute who would make the place good. Crossing the green he shouted for Salve, bellowing at him to get materials and tools and mend the roof. He saw Feyra watching their exchange from the doorway of her little ruin. She gave him a look, and said nothing.

Feyra's house reminded her sharply of the little gatehouse where she had lost her father. Upstairs there was a jagged blue rag of sky showing through the roof, and she knew she should set her bed in the lower room before night fell. She dragged the mattress downstairs; but the sight of the pallet beside the stone door jamb recalled her father's deathbed to her even more. There was even a nest of starlings in the ruined eaves, and she lifted the nest carefully and took it to the blackthorn woods. She saw the Birdman watching her cross the green with the nest in her hands, but she studiously ignored him.

When she got back, her bed had been rearranged in the lower room, closer to the hearth, the coverlets neatly folded. A little fire had been set in the fireplace, the sticks placed neatly in a conical stack, and already smoking like a volcano. A broad piece of canvas had been placed across the unglazed window against draughts, and a little man, mis-shapen and warped in body, stood in the shadow of the chimney stack.

Feyra tried not to stare. His head seemed disproportionately large in relation to his body, like a giant babe. His limbs were malformed, but he was clearly agile, for he had achieved more in the brief moment that she had been in the woods than she had done in the whole of the preceding hour. She saw an expression of fear and diffidence in his eyes, and took his little twisted hand in hers and looked directly into his face. 'Thank you,' she said.

From then on, Feyra had a friend on the island. In quiet moments in the Tezon she would return to her little house and sit companiably with Salve while he did repairs. She spoke to him kindly over the following weeks, without a reply, and was astonished when one day he began to talk back.

'Does the doctor know you can speak?'

'No.'

She could tell that speech was not a custom with him –
that he had some malady of the lantern jaw and tongue.
'And your father?' She had met the gatekeeper by the well;
he had been friendly enough, but she had barely said one
word to his thousand.

'Never . . . gives . . . chance.'

Salve had few words indeed but was not as simple as the
Birdman had decided. Feyra took trouble with him and he
began to talk more. She noticed, though, in company even
with his father he was as silent as ever, and from the doctor
he simply hid.

It seemed that the Birdman had no time for the community on the island; his attitude to Salve exemplified his
attitude to the little neighbourhood that occupied the
almshouses. He had gone just so far as to recommend that
everyone that could tolerate it take up the pipe, and so
men and women went about in a personal cloud of smoke.
But beyond this the doctor had no truck with the families
at all, and the citizens of his island only gained his notice if
they fell sick.

As time passed Feyra ceased to be afraid of the Birdman,
so she felt brave enough to challenge him about it.

'Why did you bring the families here?'

Feyra was at his shoulder, by the great medicine cabinet
at the back wall of the Tezon. She asked the question with
no preamble.

Annibale thought of the Camerlengo, who had asked the
same question. 'Because they may have been infected by
the miasma of their relations. You see, if you cut out a
canker . . .'

She was not interested in his metaphor. 'Do they get word of them?'

'What?'

'Do the *families* –' she spoke as he did to the dwarf '– get word of their *loved ones*?'

'No, of course not.'

She looked at him.

Annibale had thought that having her face covered would be a relief to him; but he still had to endure what he called to himself 'the look'. Her amber eyes would gaze at him, not with censure, nor with pity, but with something of the flavour of both and 'the look' always left him with an overlying notion that he had in some way disappointed her. He felt moved to defend himself. 'You think I have time to—'

'I do. And the sisters of the Miracoli do.'

Within a week she had made arrangements.

She had shown great interest in a letter Bocca had brought him from the *Consiglio della Sanita*. The content, that all new medicines developed to fight the Plague must be registered, and their constituents listed with the *Consiglio*, was of no importance to her. She did however peer at the paper itself over his shoulder, making him uncomfortable with her closeness.

'Why is it discoloured?' She pointed. 'And why is there this white slab, here?'

He looked where she pointed. The letter was in a close hand, written by an official secretary, and the paper brown as a speckled hen, except in one long rectangle, in a diagonal across the script, where the paper retained its original alabaster, and the ink showed black as pitch. 'It has been smoked,' he replied. 'This is commonplace at times of

Plague, so that the pestilence is not passed from one *sestiere* to the other with the mail. See, here are two seals –' he turned the letter over '– one from the sender, the red one, and the orange one from the Council of Health.' He showed her the two circles of wax.

She was interested. 'And the white place?'

'Where tongs have been used to hold the letter above a smoking cabinet.'

Within a week she had instituted a similar system whereby she would smoke letters between the families, and hand them to the patients herself. Annibale watched as she stood over the afflicted while they read the notes, or read them aloud to the sicklier ones in her accented Veneto. To his amazement they smiled, even the dying, and he could see, by the way her amber eyes narrowed above her veil, that she smiled too.

Annibale discovered she knew all of the patients by name. 'Number one needs a poultice,' he had told her in passing.

She had stood in his path and given him 'the look'. 'Which one is number one?'

'The fellow at the very end.'

'That is Stefano. He is Tommaso's brother.'

'Tommaso?

She gave him the look. 'Number fifteen.' He was genuinely surprised.

'It might be a kindness to lie them together.'

She made other changes too – more often than not without asking. He knew she thought he was too keen on surgery and cut the patients for no reason. She would never pick up the knife, unless she had to. He told her to leech the patients daily, for he bred leeches in one of the leets by the salt flats and had an endless supply. But she looked at the slivers of liver grey undulating in their jar with distaste and he never once saw her bleed anyone.

Instead she began to isolate the patients, not just from their families but from each other. She hung curtains between them for greater privacy, great squares of linen steeped in camphor. She washed the patients daily and encouraged the families themselves to do likewise. When Annibale questioned her, she quoted at him the saying of Mohammed. 'Clean yourself,' she intoned sternly, 'and God will purify you all.' The extraordinary girl even had the nuns lining up by a deep little pool beyond the black-thorn to take their plunge. Annibale, shocked to catch a glimpse of holy alabaster thigh as he stood on the *torresin* one day, was perplexed by the relationship between the Badessa and Feyra. The two women thought each other infidels, but the Badessa not only lent her support to the postal service Feyra had instigated, but laid down the daily ablutions as the rule of law. Annibale tolerated Feyra's caprice until she turned her topaz eyes on him and uttered the outrageous words, 'You could do with a wash yourself.'

Feyra also set great store by what she called *diata* – diet. She encouraged the nuns to grow as much produce as they could and marked off a little field beyond the gardens expressly for growing vegetables. She ploughed it with a handshare, with only the little dwarf to help her, and tilled it herself. She cleaned out the ovens below the customs house where the nuns had made their dormitory, and had them baking bread day and night, stoking the ovens with mulberry wood and nutshells. 'In Constantinople,' she told Annibale seriously, 'if you drop a piece of bread in the street, somebody picks it up. Bread is sacred, it supports life and health.' The Badessa, who had to be persuaded to let Feyra into the customs house beyond the lychgate and light the ovens, was heard to comment gratefully that for the first time in weeks, the sisters were warm at night.

The Badessa was complicit in another of the changes that Feyra had brought to his island. Feyra told Annibale that in the hospitals of Constantinople, it was commonplace to have music played day and night. Some of the hospitals, she told him, even had their own band. With her usual dispatch, within a day of imparting this information, she had the sisters of the Miracoli intoning psalms, motets and hymns upon the green, whenever they were not about their observances.

And the music was not always sacred. Feyra would find out the patients' favourite songs. She would winkle out their favourite folk ditties, or rhymes from the nursery if they were not long out of the schoolroom, or sailors' macaroons if they were old seagoers, and have the families sing outside the walls, at a safe distance. She even sang to the patients herself as she took their pulses, a strange, melodious drone, the rhythm of which became progressively slower and slower. She maintained, when asked, that such chants regulated the heartbeat of the afflicted.

Annibale thought it all nonsense, but even he had to admit that to hear the island ringing with song amidst all the death was lightening to the heart, and he would not wish her oddly beautiful voice silent in the Tezon. And he would have put a stop to the changes at once if he had found them medically detrimental. But if he would not admit it to Feyra, he had to be honest with himself: since she had come to the island, the Bills of Mortality, that he had to write in his own hand in the evenings by his lonely fireside, had markedly diminished in number.

Among all the death there was life. Soon after Feyra's arrival on the island Valentina, a newly married girl, had begun to puke and swoon. The Birdman did not concern himself with women's troubles but Feyra, who had seen the signs many times before, knew that she was with child. The raven-haired Venetian girl was young to be a mother, with the waist of a weasel and narrow hips no wider, and Feyra saw trouble ahead for her when her time came, but that was in the future. Hope must always be good.

Sometimes Feyra wondered what the Birdman looked like for she never once saw him without his mask. Sometimes she saw the mask itself, lying outside the private dorters she had constructed in the Tezon, and then she knew he must be performing one of his many surgeries; close work which would be hampered by the beak.

It was on one of those occasions that she made one of the changes she did not consult the doctor about. She put her hand deep in the beak and pulled out the dusty, ancient, and – in her opinion – ineffectual herbs. She took off her medicine belt and reached in capsa and pocket and flap for the herbs she sought. Stealthily she placed them within the beak, with a good bunch of lemon balm near the nose, just as had been there before. It would neither make nor mar him, but would hopefully mask the scent of the other plants she had placed there. Then she put the mask back exactly as it had lain and fled.

Feyra presumed that he left the mask off inside his own house, which lay directly opposite hers across the square lawn beyond the Tezon. Sometimes she could see his light on at night: a golden square suspended in the black velvet. She imagined the Birdman poring over medical texts and envied him; her hands itched to turn the pages of a book. She wondered if he slept in the beak, and the thought made her giggle. She wondered how old he was. Sometimes he spoke like a seasoned greybeard, but other things he said made her think he was quite young and not long out of medical school. He never conversed, only spoke to give curt orders and was not interested in her beyond her medical knowledge. In this way he reminded her very much of Palladio.

She wondered about the architect, and Zabato, and was anxious for news of them when the Birdman returned from the city at the end of each month. He had kept his contract with Palladio and visited the architect at each new moon, and told Feyra how he seemed when she asked, but said no more.

She wondered if they ever thought of her. Palladio had wanted her for her knowledge of Constantinople, and for Zabato she reminded him of the woman he had once loved. And now the Birdman wanted her for the physic she could give. So many Feyras, so many compartments of her being. She wondered if she would ever be in the company of someone who would want to know the whole Feyra.

Chapter 28

Feyra tried to counsel herself against feeling safe.

She'd felt safe at home in Constantinople, and had been sent away from everything she'd known. Then she'd felt safe in Palladio's house before being forced to flee. This island was the last place she'd expected to feel at home, but somehow, she did. She had her house, she had her tasks, and she had her Birdman.

The nuns had gone from tolerance to civility to friendliness. The Badessa had unbent so far as to talk about her girlhood in Otranto. The name of this Italian coastal town was well known to Feyra; all Turks knew it for it was a place where the Ottomans had once besieged and then massacred the entire population. Neither woman alluded to the massacre during their conversation, and it had happened years before the Badessa was even born; but Feyra, walking back to the Tezon after their brief conference, was left with the distinct impression that it was the Badessa was trying to apologize for something.

Salve the dwarf had also become a firm friend. The quiet, sensitive boy would come to her in the evenings sometimes and showed a wisdom that his limited speech belied. Little by little, she tried to teach him to express what he wanted to say. Some of the things he said jolted her; she'd been used to speaking to him as a child, but a child he was not. She liked him – better than his father Bocca, who looked at her sometimes in a way she did not like. She knew the gatekeeper for a devout, and wondered if, while the nuns had the tolerance to ignore her faith, he had not.

Sometimes Feyra thought of the crew of *Il Cavaliere*, and of Takat Turan who had been her champion. He would be dead of the Plague by now, she thought, and mourned his bravery. But now they all, even her father, seemed to come from another life; insubstantial as ghosts or the silhouettes of the *Karagoz* shadow theatre that she used to attend in Beyoglu. She still saved her sequins in her yellow slipper every week, but thought less and less about Constantinople. And as the growing belly of Valentina Trianni, the young pregnant wife, marked the passing months, the people on the Lazzaretto Novo became her life.

Especially one.

The Birdman was her constant belligerent and her foil. He was the barb in her side and the fly in her liniment. But her discussions with him, and the battle between them for the rule of the Tezon among all the dead and dying, made her, conversely, feel more alive than she'd ever been. They laid siege to the hospital; she was Saladin, he was the Lionheart, and the Tezon was their Holy City. Neither East nor West could prevail, and the supremacy exchanged hands almost daily in a constant stalemate.

For months Feyra had argued with the Birdman about his methods. She knew that in Padua there was a fashion for surgery, and the skills of herbalism had receded, but she did not know how his incessant leeching and draining could help the patients. And he could not see how carrying letters between the almshouses and the Tezon, or singing a childhood ditty, could lift the spirits of the sick. Feyra did not tell him how she knew for certain that the draining of the plague boils was ineffectual; she had tried it as a last resort to save her father, and it had failed. She knew that the Birdman based his entire medical philosophy on the principles of Galen, the Greek pagan; but she found it a house of cards. She had tried to point out to the doctor that the mortality rates of those he cut were significantly higher than those he let be, but he would not listen.

He argued that it was a matter of balance; that the bleedings and leechings and drainings would reassert the natural balance of the humours. In this she found some common ground and attempted to explain the concept of *Mizan*, the balance of body, mind and soul, but here they found themselves in opposition again. He favoured intervention every time.

They were forced to agree on one point: that none of the remedies championed by the *Consiglio della Sanita* for the Plague had any efficacy whatsoever. The Birdman told her the story of a physician called Valnetti and his decoction of Four Thieves Vinegar and she scoffed along with him; but as she laughed a thought occurred – if a person *believed* that they had been given a cure, would the strength of this belief have a physical effect? Could the mind really affect the body through faith alone? So, as she scoffed, she admitted, privily, that what this charlatan, this Valnetti, was practising was the logical conclusion of *Mizan*: the medical manifestation of mind over matter.

Because of their differences, and because of the fact that the Birdman thought that midwifery was not part of his remit, when it came time for Valentina Trianni to be delivered, Feyra fought alone to birth the baby in the little house by the well, with just the girl's mother to aid her.

The little wife twisted on her bed, her swollen belly undulating alarmingly, while her husband hunched over the fire downstairs, trying to ignore the appalling screams. She had laboured since noon the previous day, and now it was near midnight. Valentina was drifting in and out of consciousness, her blue-black hair spread out on the pillow like the rays of a dark sun.

Feyra struggled in the candlelight as her own magnified shade mocked her upon the rough plaster wall; a shadow-play of an incompetent physician. The problem, she knew, was the girl's frame; her pelvis was narrow but the babe was large. Here on the Lazzaretto the islanders ate well – for Feyra knew good diet to be the best physician of all – and breathed the fresh salt air. If Valentina had given birth in a slum the child might have slid forth like an oiled kid; but here the babe had outgrown its dam. So when the church chimed the midnight hour with the dull clink of a goatbell, Feyra wiped her hands and told Valentina's mother that she was going for the doctor.

She saw the relief on the old woman's face, but was not insulted but glad; she knew then that she'd been right when she'd argued with the Birdman – believing that a cure was at hand was almost as efficacious as the cure itself; the physician himself as placebo. Still it cost her something to come to the Birdman that night and acknowledge that after six-and-thirty hours of labour she was at risk of losing both mother and child, and that, in this case, surgery was the only recourse.

With renewed energy she ran through the chill night – the doctor's window leading her like the North Star. She rapped on the wooden door, once, twice, but there was no reply. Taking a breath of cold night she lifted the latch and walked in.

A young man sat there, hunched over the fire. His tumble of dark curls fell forward, partly hiding his face, the firelight finding the copper filaments in his hair. He was staring into the flames so intently he hadn't heard her knock. But when she entered he jumped up so suddenly that his chair fell over.

'Where is the doctor?' Feyra demanded.

The young man put a hand to his cheek involuntarily, as if he had been caught naked. Comprehension dawned. '*I* am the doctor,' he said.

Feyra took a step back. His voice was the same, but softer, less abrasive; as if peeled to softness without the hard shell of the mask. '*You* are the doctor? But you look –' she did not know how to finish the sentence. Young? Handsome? Surprised? Guilty? And, she thought, *cornered*.

His hand twitched towards the beak mask where it hung on his fire hook and she wondered if he hid behind his mask as she hid behind hers.

'What do you want? What's amiss?' he asked, and she knew him then for her Birdman: rude, abrasive, abrupt.

'It is Valentina Trianni,' she said. 'She is come to the time with her child, but the babe will not be born.'

Without another word he reached for his cloak; and the mask.

Feyra watched him as he examined Valentina, curving over the girl with his beak as if she were his prey. But Feyra did not see the mask any more, only his unforgettable face, burned into her consciousness like a candle flame. She knew what he would say.

'The babe must be cut free.'

She had been right. But she also acknowledged that that was why she had fetched him. 'Bindusara,' she said at once, like a reflex.

'Emperor of the Indies, cut from his mother's womb,' finished the Birdman, and their eyes met across the heaving belly. 'And Saint Raymond Nonnatus – the procedure gave him his name. And in both cases . . .' he said, and stopped abruptly. Again, she knew what he would not say.

In both cases, the mother did not survive.

But there was no choice. The Trianni babe was breech, and would not turn. Valentina might well die; but if they did not act she would die anyway, and the babe too. Annibale barked at the mother to leave the room, but she would not leave her daughter until Feyra assured her that she would look after Valentina, and that just by being in the room during the procedure she was endangering her daughter. Once the old lady had gone the Birdman removed his mask.

For once Feyra was happy just to assist. She gave Valentina as much juice of the poppy as she dared, but the poor girl was in such agony she could not be still to take the draught, and the black decoction ran down her cheeks. Feyra cleaned the distended belly with rosewater steeped with mint and borage, but stood back as the Birdman made the wide incision just above the pubis, dark blood springing up in an admirably straight line. The babe spewed forth almost at once, and as Feyra lifted it two little eyes opened and a mouth formed to cry as the Birdman sliced through the cord. Feyra cleaned the babe with linen, and placed her finger between the tiny lips to clear the mouth. The babe suckled instantly. Valentina had lost consciousness at the cut. Feyra laid the bundle by the dark head, and continued her work. She cleaned the wound and took up the wine-soaked thread for the sutures. She bent her head over her task and sewed as neatly as she could by the light of the candle. Remembering Palladio, she set the glass bowl that held the rosewater before the candle flame, and the light spread through the makeshift lens. As she sewed, she looped the thread under each stitch to anchor it as Haji Musa had taught her. She could feel the Birdman watching her. She then laid a poultice of cinnabar and rosemary above the wound to draw infection and laid the coverlet tenderly over the girl. Then there was nothing to do but wait.

The babe, as if exhausted by his violent entry into the world, slept by his mother's head. Feyra expected the Birdman to go, but he stayed and watched with her, his shadow joining hers on the wall. She knew he did not seek her company, but was waiting, dispassionately, for the medical outcome. They did not have to wait long. On the stroke of Matins, Valentina opened her eyes, and, as if prompted by some indefinable bond, her baby woke too.

The Birdman and Feyra walked back across the green in companionable silence in the pitchy dark. Across the lagoon the dawn was a white line on the horizon, the spring grass dewy underfoot. As they passed the Tezon she turned to him in the dark. The wards of their hospital were the lists where she and Annibale jousted every day, and she could not resist a sortie. Valentina's father lay within, recovering from his own battle with the Plague, so she said mischievously, 'And perhaps you will now agree with me that old Gianluca Trianni should be told about the birth of his burly grandson? That the news will do him more good than any potions we may give him?'

The Birdman regarded her down his beak. 'And perhaps *you* will agree with me that the morning will be soon enough? For even you must own that Doctor Goodtidings is an inferior physician to Doctor Sleep?'

Feyra smiled and inclined her head. She saw his window ahead, golden with firelight, as she'd seen it a hundred times. Her own house was dark. She did not want to go home, not yet. At his door they stopped by tacit consent.

'Would you like to come in?'

This time he took off the mask as if it were a relief to him. She revised her earlier opinion – he did not love to hide, he found it onerous. She looked at him anew. This was him, her Birdman. No; Annibale – for tonight she had learned his name; and only then because Luca Trianni had wanted to thank the *Dottore* by naming his new son after him. She found it difficult to adjust. *Annibale*. She would be surprised if he was older than she. When they stood together they were exactly the same height, and she looked at him eye to eye. He looked tired, but elated.

'Sit,' he said. 'I suppose you don't drink?'

She shook her head.

He poured the wine. He gestured to the chair on the other side of the fire and she fell into it, exhausted.

He raised his glass – to himself as much as the babe. 'To Annibale,' he said.

When Feyra had burst on upon him he had been staring morosely into the coals, feeling for the first time in his life that he had bitten off more than he could comfortably chew. He had been so sure that his hospital would be a success, but the Plague was gaining pace. There had been more deaths lately than the little cemetery could hold, and he felt that he was losing his grip. In the long-fought battle with death he felt that death was gaining on him. Then he had been handed this surgical triumph by this extraordinary girl.

Of course, the danger was not over for Valentina Trianni. The surgery was a major procedure, and the risk of secondary infection was great; but he, Annibale Cason, had performed a *non natus* procedure, and, for now at least, both mother and child had lived. He acknowledged that he was not concerned overmuch for the young mother. He was more interested in Feyra. He studied her across the firelight. Tonight she had given him back his belief in medicine, his belief in himself. He wanted to give her something in return.

He noted her skin, the colour of cinnamon, the amber of her eyes, the tiny reflected fire burning in each. She looked at him directly, and he felt, again, the power of her gaze. Tonight, it seemed, she admired him, and that warmed him even more than the fire.

'So you are Annibale.'

'Yes, Annibale. Annibale Cason, *Dottore della Peste*.'

She inclined her head a little. 'What does your name mean?'

'I have no notion,' he snapped, annoyed with himself for using his full title.

'Mine means "justice drops from my mouth",' she said.

She was well named, thought Annibale, for her mouth was particularly beautiful – it was full and rose-coloured and the top lip was slightly bigger than the bottom.

She looked into the fire again. 'In my country the meaning of your name is everything. We never name a child without very careful consideration. It is very important in my faith. I am surprised you Venetians do not know the significance of yours.'

Annibale stretched his legs out before him until his boots were nearly in the fire. 'There is little to know. We are mostly named for saints and days.'

Saints and days. Then she remembered, as she looked at the lightening sky. 'It is Valentina's birthday. The feast, she told me, of Saint Valentine. And,' she said, 'there is Zabato Zabatini, named for a lucky day.' She wondered about her old friend and his master, and the church that grew around her father's grave. 'And your Saint Nonnatus, we now know why he was called so.' She looked at him. 'So you see, some of your names have meaning, even if yours does not.'

He was silent for a time. 'I did not speak truly,' he said, with difficulty. 'I know why I am called Annibale.'

She waited.

'Annibale was a general from Carthage, and in the second Punic campaign he rode war elephants across the Alps into Italy against the might of Rome. When he set off, he had no idea what he was riding into, or if he would ever reach his destination.'

She too was silent. She remembered the reciprocal tradition of storytelling, and how she had exchanged stories with Death. 'In the Ottoman Empire,' she began, 'the camel traders have stopping places along their trade routes called caravanserai. Sometimes they are hundreds of miles apart, over desert or mountain range, but they travel safe in the knowledge that there will be a place where they can shelter and find succour at the end of their journey. Even if they have never been that way before, they are sure that there will be such a place; that sooner or later, they will find a caravanserai.'

Annibale sat forward, interested. '*How* do they know?'

'They do not know. They have faith.'

He sat back again. 'I think Annibale did too. That is why my mother named me so.' She could see that it cost him to talk of her. 'She liked the story. She said no one could know what lay beyond today, but you had to hope, and be brave, and trust that all would be well.'

The Camerlengo eyed the man before him. He was wearing the slashed doublet and red hat of a gondolier, and they were never the most honest of men. But the fellow's eyes were wide, his speech clear. The Camerlengo knew a liar when he heard one, and did not think he heard one now.

'You are sure?'

'Sure as I'm standing here, your honour. Cosimo, his name is, and he works the Tre Archi bridge. Thursday last it was – he said he picked up a woman from the address you were asking about. He remembered the fare because the fellow that called for him particularly asked for a *felze*.' The man eyed the Camerlengo and felt moved to explain. 'A covered gondola.'

The Camerlengo was accustomed to being taken for a foreigner. 'Was there anyone travelling with her?'

The gondolier shrugged. 'He didn't say.'

The Camerlengo raised his pale brows. 'Yet he told you this much?'

'He was boasting about it in the locanda. Said he was going to be rich.'

The Camerlengo steepled his hands. Gondoliers were

notoriously greedy and venal; moreover, they had no sense of collective loyalty. He knew once a bounty had been offered it would not be long before one of their number came knocking on his door. Yet something did not quite add up.

'Why, do you suppose, has he not come to claim the bounty himself?'

'That I don't know, your honour.' The gondolier shuffled his feet. 'Can I have my ducats now?'

The Camerlengo eyed him, then rose. 'Why don't you take me to him first?'

The Camerlengo could have taken a consort of *Leoni*, but he did not. He chose instead the two guards who had first let the girl go. He chose them deliberately, for he knew and they knew that they owed him their lives. He did not wait for his cap or cloak, but walked straight down the stone stairs as he was, in his black leather garb, with the guards at his heels and the gondolier trotting before.

The gondolier nosed his boat through secret and unknown canals, stagnant waterways so narrow that the sun would only strike them at midday. The way he took was a considerable shortcut but the Camerlengo, seated in the prow, was silent with impatience.

At Tre Archi he strode after the boatman without saying a word, the plague smoke swirling about his heels. Under a small *sotoportego* in a poor part of the *quartiere*, he watched the gondolier count the doors to his colleague's house. twelve, thirteen, fourteen, fifteen . . .'

The man's voice died. Number fifteen was barred with a rough plank of wood, and on the door was painted a red and ragged cross.

The Camerlengo said nothing for a moment. Then, in a

voice of absolute calm, he commanded the guards: 'Enquire of the neighbours. You –' he turned to the first guard '– take sixteen. And you –' he turned to the second '– take fourteen.'

In a moment they were back.

'He died,' said one.

'Last night,' said the other.

The gondolier began to back away from the fury that leapt in the chamberlain's eyes, but the Camerlengo thrust out his glove and caught the man by the scruff of the neck. With one fluid motion he lifted the bar, kicked the door open and thrust the man inside the pestilent house, bolting the door behind him.

Chapter 29

From that day onwards Annibale and Feyra were friends. In the evenings after their last rounds of the patients the two of them would cleanse themselves, leave the Tezon and go back to Annibale's house.

Feyra noticed more about him, the way his voice rose when he was excited, and his nostrils flared a little when he spoke. She noticed too that he wore something about his neck upon a chain, just as she wore the ribbon that held her mother's ring about her own neck and wondered if he wore a remembrance of his mother too. In the morning Feyra was often dead-eyed in the Tezon, yawning behind her veil, for each night she went back to her own house later and later, crossing the green sometimes as the water-white line of dawn showed on the horizon, unseen except for one pair of eyes – the old eyes of the Badessa, opening the church for Matins.

It did not occur to Annibale that their meetings compromised Feyra. To him their evenings were a professional arrangement; so when the Badessa warned him about the propriety of spending time alone together he was short with her. 'We *work* in the evenings. We speak of medical matters. We prepare our potions and ointments. When else are we to do such things, in the hours of the day? There is no difference than if she were a man.' But he believed it no more than the Badessa did. The truth was his evenings with Feyra were the best part of his day.

Feyra would cook a simple supper. The ingredients were only what could be bought in Treporti or grown on the island, but the way she put them together and the flavours she brought out were new to Annibale. Afterwards he would take a glass of wine and they would sit by the fire. By tacit consent neither of them would wear their masks; Feyra left off her veil, as she had done in her father's house, and Annibale hung his beak by the door. Then they would broach medical topics or talk of herbs. Feyra would teach Annibale how to make the syrupy *serbets* and juleps, or the doughy paste known as a *ma'cun*. Sometimes they would prepare a posset of unguent on the big butcher's block Annibale had bought for the purpose.

They would pore over medical texts together, Annibale helping Feyra as she stumbled over the Latin. She was interested to note that one book of incredibly detailed anatomical drawings that Annibale showed her, was by the same Leonardo da Vinci who had drawn the Vitruvian Man. In return she would tell him about the work of the great Ottoman physician Serafeddin Sabuncuoğlu, and the *aqrabadhin* medical formularies in the libraries of Topkapi. When she mentioned the most treasured manuscript of the Sultan's palace – *Al-manhaj al-sawi*, Jalal al-Din al-Suyuti's masterful discussion of medicine as expressed in the sayings of the Prophet – she was delighted to hear that the volume was not unknown to him. Padua, it seemed, had a world view of medicine.

Feyra told Annibale of the six non-naturals that made up the balance of *Mizan* in human life: 'Light and air,' she said, counting these building blocks of health upon her fingers, 'food and drink, work and rest, sleep and waking, excretions and secretions, including –' she coughed a little '– baths and sexual intercourse, and lastly dispositions and the states of the soul.'

In reply, Annibale told Feyra of the balance of the four humours; a subject on which they found some agreement – the black bile, red blood, white bile and pale phlegm representing the sanguine, choleric, melancholic and phlegmatic temperaments. For a moment she thought she saw a connection of enormous significance between the humours and the four horses her mother had described. They were black, red, white and pale, too. She asked Annibale if he had ever heard of four horses of these colours, ever read of them in one of his many books. He shrugged. 'In church as a child, perhaps. But I have had little to do with scripture since. I remember they were said to carry Death.' The conversation left her feeling uneasy. She touched the ring at her bosom, almost as a charm to ward off evil.

As they grew closer, they would broach other subjects. Soon they were exchanging histories. Feyra did not break her mother's confidence, but she told Annibale about her parents and slowly Annibale began to talk about the mother who had abandoned him. She was a woman who, it seemed, had hurt him so much that, although his outward shell was healthy and handsome, his soul was more damaged than any occupant of the Tezon. Feyra soon perceived the reason for his discomfiture.

'She was a courtesan?'

'No,' he said savagely, 'not at first. My father was a gentleman of Venice, and when he died she left me – just a boy – in the arms of my aunts. And I scarcely saw her between the ages of five and twenty. She would appear for only a day or two in all those years. Clean, sober, her carriage correct and her manners impeccable, she would suffocate me with love. And then in another day, when she'd found some new patron or drunk all the wine in the house, she would be gone. More often than not we would only know she had gone because one of my aunts would miss some coin or a jewelled pin or pearl comb. She'd sigh and say, "Well, Columbina has gone again," and I would search the house for her, and sure enough, she would have gone without a word.' Annibale was silent too for a moment, the firelight playing on his stern face.

'When I was a boy,' he went on, 'I would cry for days. I would never understand how someone who showered me with kisses and comfits could just go away again. I used to smell her perfume; it would stay in the house for days after she had gone.' He laughed bitterly. 'It lingered longer than she did.'

'So you did miss her?' Feyra prompted gently.

'When I was a boy, yes. When I grew to a man I ceased to care.'

Feyra said nothing, but wondered if this was true. 'When did you last see her?'

'In my first year at Padua. She came to my rooms and told me how proud she was – pressed me to her bosom, charmed my fellows. She apologized for her long absences, promised that we would start anew, that all would be different, that she would be the very model of a mother.'

'And what happened?'

'She was gone the next day. And my silver scalpels too.'

Feyra's mother had been elevated to queen and empress, whereas Annibale's mother had found herself back in the gutter, but she knew that the distance from the concubine who was her mother to the courtesan who was his was not so great a step. 'My mother was no better.' Feyra admitted the truth to him and herself at the same time.

He let out a hissing sigh, to rival the crackling fire. 'Born of sin, children of whores,' he said viciously.

Feyra was shocked at the harshness of his words, but she felt she owed it to her mother, to her father, to defend their relationship a little.

'Perhaps it is not so great a sin,' she said, 'if there is love in the case.' She spoke carefully, looking down at her hands in her lap; so she did not see the fire leap a little in his eyes.

What she had said led Annibale to hope.

They had arguments, of course, and often found themselves violently opposed to each other in matters of medical practice. These they both enjoyed as much, if not more, than the matters when they were in accord. But such arguments never strayed into the personal, and were quickly forgotten.

One of their most furious disagreements was over the Ottoman practice of variolation. Feyra argued that engrafting small amounts of infected blood or other contaminated matter into a healthy patient ensured, in nearly all cases, partial or complete immunity to the full-blown disease, especially in cases such as the pox. She described seeing Haji Musa open four veins in the forehead and chest of a young boy, and insert into the wounds small amounts of mucus taken from a smallpox patient. The boy grew healthily into adulthood, despite every other member of his family contracting the disease.

Annibale argued that the practice was forbidden by the Catholic Church for good reason: that it killed as many as it preserved. He forced Feyra to admit that in some cases the inoculated patients died of the very malady the physicians had been trying to prevent. They returned to the subject many times, and never found the least agreement. Their arguments always finished in the same way. 'Mohammed said that God did not create a sickness in this world unless he produced the cure as well,' stated Feyra. 'Might not the cure be found *within* the disease?'

Annibale would shake his head. 'In reply to Mohammed, let me invoke Maimonides; he is credited with observing that the perfect doctor is one who judges it wiser to let well enough alone, than to prescribe a cure that is worse than the malady.'

Their other major disagreement was over whether or not patients should pay for medicine. Annibale abhorred the practice, citing Valnetti and his fellow profiteers, who benefited from people's misery. He would quote the physician's code which stated that doctors should work for their stipend, cover their expenses but not profit excessively from their medicines.

Feyra was more pragmatic. 'But what if by selling medicines a doctor can provide better care for his patients?'

'I fund this hospital,' retorted Annibale sharply. 'My funds are adequate; and I have no need of more.'

Here he did not entirely speak the truth.

The Cason hoard, which he had long since dug from the wellside and placed beneath the floorboards under his own bed, was dwindling alarmingly as the hospital reached its first anniversary. After this last conversation with Feyra Annibale climbed the stairs and took up the board.

He set the casket on his knee and fitted the little key from the chain about his neck into the lock. He ran his hands through the remaining gold, feeling the cold metal discs slithering against his fingers. There was now only a thin layer of ducats to gild the bottom of the box. He estimated that the coins would get him to Michaelmas, no more. He shut the lid with a thud and buried it once again beneath the floorboards, his worries along with it.

Feyra was changing.

Annibale was the first man she had ever met whom she did not want to keep at bay. When she was with him her coverings, those layers and layers that she lived beneath like the raw white heart of an artichoke, seemed laborious to her. At night she dreamed scalding, private dreams of taking off her clothes for him. Sometimes he would be there as she undressed, and he would take hold of her scarves and veils and wind her round and round like a Dervish, unwrapping the reams of diaphanous fabric until she was dizzy and exposed, standing completely naked before him.

Always she woke with burning cheeks, and knelt at once to pray, but no amount of prayer could rid her of the will. For the first time she understood the impulse that had driven her mother to ride away into the night with her father. But she was not a Venetian princess, she could not beckon an infidel sea captain across a ballroom with a lift of her white glove. She had to wait for him to beckon her.

And one night, he did.

They were sitting, as they always did, at either side of the fire. Feyra was peering at a woodcut by Andreas Vesalius, trying to make sense of the Latin labels, when Annibale spoke. His tone was casual.

'The Trianni girl, mother of little Annibale. Did you say she was with child again?'

Feyra lowered the woodcut. 'Yes. Another babe to be born in the spring.'

'They should have a house of their own. There are too many of them now in that cot.' She was silent. 'Insanitary, your friend Palladio would call it.'

She waited.

He leaned across the fire, towards her. He was very close. 'Your house,' he said. 'Perhaps you would not be so sorry to leave it?'

'It is . . . very cold,' she murmured.

'The roof is unstable,' he added, his voice a warm whisper.

'It leaks day and night,' she whispered back, feeling disloyal to the faithful Salve who had made the roof entirely waterproof.

'And the church bells?'

'They wake me every hour of the night.' She began to smile.

'You should come and live here.'

She was silent, afraid to breathe. She wanted to be sure. 'As your mistress?' she whispered.

He was untroubled by her directness. 'Yes. Will you come?'

'Yes.'

Chapter 30

As Andrea Palladio walked up the fifteen steps to his church on Giudecca, his pleasure at the sight of the growing building was a little lessened by his own breathlessness.

He'd had a headcold and had been feeling wheezy all week, his chest tight and pressed. He'd left his house knowing that if he waited in for Cason's Friday visit, the doctor would declare him unfit. Palladio just wanted to be at work. He had begun to acknowledge that this church would be his last building, and he wanted it to be his legacy.

His immortality and his mortality met each other, abruptly, on the steps. The wheezing in his lungs reminded him that he was sixty-nine. He could no longer blame the decades of stone dust he had breathed in, and not wholly breathed out again. He was getting old.

Zabato stuck his shock-head out of the doorway. 'Master, may we continue? The light is dying.'

On the last step Palladio was brought up short by a sharp and sudden pain. Petrified, he staggered, his flesh suddenly freezing. It felt like a celestial hand was squeezing his heart, which leapt like a snared coney. *The light is dying*, he thought in a sudden panic, *and so am I*. Surely the Lord would not take His builder before he had completed His contract?

In a moment the pain was gone and Palladio could walk again, taking deep gulping breaths of relief. Zabato, ahead of him, had noticed nothing. As Palladio walked under the great lintel his heart slowed again but he still felt weak and sweaty. He had found of late that he was talking to God more, since he was building Him a house. It was not a spiritual dialogue, just a conversation, such as he would have with any great lord for whom he was building a dwelling. He'd had a hundred exchanges such as these with his friends the brothers Barbaro when he'd built their great villa at Maser, and he did not see that the Almighty should be any different. So he consulted his heavenly patron on the style of the pillars or the pavings of the pavimentum and did not expect an answer. But now he asked for something in return, his first prayer of supplication.

Give me time, Lord, he prayed. *Only give me time.*

It was late afternoon by the time Annibale traced Palladio. He'd gone first to the house in the Campo Fava and rapped with his cane at the door with the golden callipers. The fat cook opened the door, and told him that her master had gone to the site of the church on Giudecca. 'He's there every day,' she said, 'him and Zabato come home like a pair of ghosts, so white they are with the stone dust.'

Annibale nodded, noted that Feyra's septic measures of cleansing herbs and frankincense candles had been well maintained in the atrium, exhorted the cook to continue in this way, and left. It would be no trouble at all to go the Giudecca on the way home. He walked to Zattere in search of a *traghetto*, a spring in his step, and thought of Feyra.

As he stood steady in the boat looking ahead to Giudecca

he pictured her now as she looked when she crossed the green to the Tezon. She always looked straight ahead like a ship's prow, the *Maria di Legno* again, never turning in her purpose. He thought of her skin, the colour of cinnamon, the amber of her eyes. He could not believe that by tonight she would be living in his house.

Ever since she'd told him the meaning of her name he'd become obsessed with her mouth, that strange, upside-down mouth, with the top lip a little fuller than the bottom. He wondered how it would feel if he was lying on top of her, his body cushioned by her body, his mouth cushioned by her mouth.

He was jolted from these thoughts by the bump of the *traghetto* against the jetty. Annibale tossed a sequin to the boatman, jumped ashore as lightly as a gleeman, and noticed the church for the first time.

As someone who had grown up with the topography of Giudecca, and had become used to the jagged ruins of the convent of San Sebastiano, the progress of Palladio's church was striking. What an exquisite site for a church! Already it was the tallest building on the island, but as yet a rect-angular stone prism without spire or campanile. Because of this, to Annibale's eyes, the church resembled a temple of the East; an impression supported by the wide plinth at the entrance. The façade could be a temple of Jerusalem, a Parthenon of Athens or – he shivered with joy – a shrine of Constantinople. Annibale counted fifteen steps to the doors, and ran up every one.

Inside was a mess of earth and stone. There was a chok-ing white smoke of dust and a deafening cacophony of stonecutters hammering and chipping and men shouting as blocks were raised by complicated winches and pulleys.

A cruciform pathway was marked off by pegs and parti-coloured ropes, and at the centre of this, where the Christ would have hung, stood Palladio and his shadow, that scruffy draughtsman fellow. Annibale beamed upon them both, forgetting his mask. When they saw him, Palladio smote his forehead.

'Forgive me, *Dottore*. I had forgotten it was Friday. You find us debating what to do with this well.'

Annibale poked his beak down the crumbling shaft. It looked ancient. 'What is your dilemma? Fill it in, surely.'

'That was my feeling also,' said the architect, but he still rubbed his beard indecisively. 'And yet it is still a focus of the faithful – my masons turn pilgrims away daily, who come in search of a Plague remedy. I thought I might still incorporate it in the design and yet Zabato tells me that the well would be directly below the centre of the dome. Of course, nothing must detract from its glory, so I fear it must go.' Palladio looked down, looking where Annibale looked, laughed a little. 'You are my physician. Should I drink some of the water? Benefit from the panacea before the well is buried for ever?'

Annibale laughed. 'Please yourself, my dear fellow, for it will neither kill nor cure you. When do you begin the dome?'

'Today.'

Annibale looked up to the sky. It was the blue of a duck's egg, dotted with tiny clouds with a darker indigo beneath their feathery bellies. It seemed impossible to span that sky, to enclose a sphere of it, but today Annibale believed anything could be done. Palladio could do it.

He studied the old man – perhaps it was the outdoors, but the architect had never looked better to him – his colour was even, his wind sound, his eyes bright. He opened his mouth to ask after Palladio's health but ended up asking something entirely different.

'What does your name mean?'

'Forgive me?' The old man seemed perplexed.

'Your name. Palladio. What does it mean?'

'It was given me by my first master, Gian Giorgio Trissino,' said Palladio. 'It refers to the wisdom of Pallas Athena.'

Annibale smiled. Everything amused him now. 'I thought it would be something like that. So what is your real name?'

'Andrea di Pietro della Gondola. But Palladio is easier for people to remember. And I want to be remembered; for this church in particular.' He seemed to shiver.

'You will be,' Annibale assured him. 'You will finish it with ease. You have been wise enough to keep yourself in good health.' Annibale was well disposed to Palladio, well disposed to the world. He even responded politely when the draughtsman with the wild hair asked after Feyra. It was a joy to hear her name, a joy to talk of her. 'She is well,' he said, 'and sends you both greetings.'

Now he had spoken of her, he wanted to go on talking; to say her name over and over, to recount every little utterance she had ever spoken to him. He had to leave before he gave himself away. He made his excuses and ran for the *traghetto* as if the Devil were after him.

As he was rowed across the lagoon, Annibale watched with pleasure as the shadows elongated in the late afternoon, each increment of length bringing him closer to the night and to Feyra. He barely even waited for the boatman to tie his boat at the little jetty before he jumped out, overpaying him handsomely, and marched past the gatehouse greeting not just Bocca but the dwarf, too. He gave a little shiver as he passed the hospital building; he knew she would be within, about some task. So close.

For once he did not enter the Tezon but went straight home. He did not want to see her with the patients before tonight, to be by her side but not touch her. He had set a little bed in the corner by the fire, so the dying embers would warm her in the night. He had laid out his best coverlet to cosset her body, and his best palliasse stuffed with straw to cushion her flesh. He ran his hand over the smooth sheet where tonight they would both lie.

Unwanted, the voice of the Badessa of the Miracoli came to his mind. When he'd told her airily that the cot by the church would be free for the growing Trianni family, she was stern with him.

'What do you want with that girl?' she asked him. 'She is orphaned, unmarried, far from home. You are unmarried. All of this is to say nothing of the difference in your faiths. She is bound for eternal damnation, but *you* may still be saved. There is no question, therefore, of your offering proper suit to her; and if you share your hearth with her you are placing your immortal soul in peril. Let her be.'

'There is no question of such a relationship,' he lied. 'She will room downstairs by the fire. Would you deny me a maidservant?'

'And yet she is *not* your maidservant,' the Badessa reminded him firmly.

Annibale lost his head and began to shout. 'No. She is not.' His voice rang around his own head within the beak. Too loud. 'She is my fellow. She is a *doctor*.' It was the first time he had said it and he surprised himself.

Now, in his house, he twitched and fiddled, pottered and

paced the rest of the day away. He thought of Feyra with the patients, veiled and industrious, and wanted her here, now. He knew exactly how he would take her in his arms, how he would kiss her strange and wonderful mouth. Annibale, who never prayed, prayed for the light to fade.

When night had fallen at last and her knock came, he nearly shot out of his chair. He opened the door so swiftly the fire belched smoke. As it cleared, it revealed a dreadful apparition.

It was as if Feyra had aged a century's half; her dark curls dyed too-black by some artifice, crow's feet spreading about the eyes that were dulled from the amber of flame to sludge green, her cheeks brightened by two spots of too-red rouge high on the sunken cheekbones. She was wearing a gown of raggedy red velvet and so cut down to the nipples that it would never have been deemed decent. He stared in horror. He could not move.

'Annibale,' she said. 'Will you not let me in?'

It was Columbina Cason, his mother.

Chapter 31

Feyra's hand shook as she raised it to knock at Annibale's door that night. This was the beginning of their new lives.

The door opened and a woman stood there, in a travelling cloak with a mask in her hand as if she had only just herself arrived. Feyra stood, stunned to silence, and the woman raised her chin with the poise of a lady. 'Yes?' she said haughtily.

'I am here to see the doctor.' Feyra could see Annibale hovering in the background, and she looked to him with entreaty.

The woman registered her accent, and narrowed her green and cat-like eyes. 'And *you* are?'

Annibale came forward hurriedly. 'Feyra is my nurse at the hospital.'

'Well –' the woman shifted her weight from hip to hip in a way that was both provocative and proprietorial. 'My son does not need a nurse. His *Mamma* is home.' And she shut the door in Feyra's face.

'I have changed.'

His mother had sat, unbidden, in the fireside chair that he

thought of as Feyra's. He said nothing, but she must have sensed his disbelief.

'I *have*, Annibale. That old life, I've said goodbye to it now. I want to be here with you. I want to be a mother at last. I know I've wronged you – abandoned you more than once—'

'How did you find me?' he cut in sharply.

She lowered her cat's eyes. 'I had gone to Treporti with a merchant . . . companion. There I heard that a doctor called Cason had a hospital on this island. My companion took sick and I didn't know what to do. But I knew that if I came to my son he would save me. Oh, my sweeting! *You* did all this; you brought all these good people here, you rescued them.' She sank to her knees before him, kissing his hands. 'I knew you could rescue me too!'

He found he could not take his hands away but waited, sick at heart, until she sat again, sniffing prettily at the pomade that hung from her wrist, and arranging her skirts. Her eyes were completely dry.

'I think you and I should start again, dearest. I have not had an easy life, you know. Your father—'

Annibale went suddenly cold. 'You *were* married to my father, were you not?' He thought of everything he'd ever known, his name, his nobility, the Cason treasure hidden in the floorboards beneath his bed.

'Of course! But the thing you must know is that I was a courtesan, not just afterwards, but before.'

He blinked, his eyes dry from the fire, trying to understand. 'You mean, when my father met you . . .'

'Yes. I used to ply my trade near the Campo d'Oro. You were conceived in a gondola at Carnevale. When I knew I was gravelled with you, Carlo said he'd marry me. I was beautiful then, Annibale, you cannot imagine.'

He could not. Only one woman was beautiful to him, and besides beauty for him was not the mask but the person within. He looked at his mother's mask, where it hung next to his beak on the fire hook, in an unholy union of courtesan and bird. A flawless, painted face; gazing at him from his mother's past.

He learned that when she'd left him and his father she had gone to live with her new lover in one of the great Villas in the Veneto. When she'd found her patron bedding both the kitchen maids at once she'd moved on, leaving for Rome with an artist who had been painting the frescoes of the villa. There she'd become the mistress of a priest, before running away to Messina with one of his acolytes.

After a while Annibale stopped listening and constructed, instead, an alternate truth. In her youth she was stunningly beautiful, beautiful enough to snare a minor Venetian nobleman despite her low birth. He suspected her last lover, the merchant, was no more than a cloth hawker, with a pitch in Treporti market. Her clientele had declined with her beauty, and all that remained was a flawed character unable to attract a companion for the autumn of her life. Eventually, sick of the sorry tale, he slept where he sat, his slumbering brain crowded with unhappy dreams. In the morning his bottles of fine wine were empty and rolled beneath his stumbling feet, the fire was dead and his mother was snoring on the fireside cot he had readied so tenderly for Feyra.

He left her there.

∞

Annibale's evenings were much changed. Instead of his medical discussions with Feyra, discussions that made him feel as if he could vanquish death and cure the world, he had to listen to his mother's tales of disgrace and decline, to her mourning for her youth. Annibale was suddenly, horribly lonely and yet was constantly in his mother's company. He was isolated and yet he had never been so touched physically since his mother had left him as a child. Her intimacies were stuck in that time, preserved in amber – she touched him as if he were still an eight-year-old boy. She ruffled his hair and pinched his cheeks, nibbled his neck and rubbed his middle back as she might have done if she had been there when he'd been ill as a child. He found himself unable to repel these embraces but her importunities sickened him for they were a dreadful mockery of the intimacy he'd hoped to have with another. He had given his mother his own bed in the chamber upstairs, so he had the added torment of sleeping each night in the bed that he'd made for Feyra.

Annibale advised Columbina to go about masked and the mask she had with her, a full-faced model that tied about the head, was the one that he thought he remembered from childhood. It was of a beautiful, made-up courtesan's face, white as lead paste with a pearlized sheen, complete with painted cherry lips and patches upon the cheeks. It gave her an eerie, blank look of a beauty she no longer possessed. Her clothes fitted badly, and their bright colours would have better complemented a more youthful complexion. Even her name now seemed too young for her. *Columbina Cason* was a name for a cocotte, or a precocious, capricious beauty. She had long outgrown it.

Elsewhere, too, Columbina Cason wore a mask. She

called on every family bringing charity in the name of her son; pots of stew or fresh lemons, or comfits for the children. She sewed mattresses with the nuns. She even hoisted her gowns and dug in the garden. She attended daily mass, charming the sisters with her pitiful life and her penitence, and went to confess her sins to the Badessa almost daily, finding in her constant shrivings yet another opportunity to talk about herself.

Columbina had noticed the strange, shrouded girl who worked so closely with her son, so silent and industrious and competent. Jealous, she attempted to flatter the girl, but the foreign chit was the one person on the island that seemed immune to her charms, save, perhaps, the simple dwarf. Columbina had caught the freak watching her once or twice and had stooped to slap his ugly face for him. The silent girl had come to the midget's side immediately and given him a salve to soothe the graze Columbina's ring had caused. The older woman had the uncomfortable feeling that the girl's amber eyes could see right through her.

From then on, instead of ignoring the *Muselmana*, she'd begun to cross herself whenever she saw her and spit in her path, as was just and right behaviour from a good Christian woman, although she was careful not to do this in the presence of her son. Some of the younger nuns began to follow her lead and the increasing isolation of the infidel girl satisfied Columbina that she was doing God's work.

The Badessa of the sisterhood of the Miracoli was a good judge of character and she had not been convinced by Columbina Cason.

The Abbess knew real faith when she was in the presence

of it – Bocca the gatekeeper, for example, was truly devout – but she had learned much in those endless shrivings and the doctor's mother, to her ears, had no more devotion than her son. And seeing the graceful and dignified way Feyra bore Columbina Cason's insults made her ever more well disposed towards the infidel girl.

So when Feyra had appeared a week or so after Columbina Cason's arrival, hovering at the church door, she had greeted her warmly. The girl looked terrible. 'Is something amiss?'

'Nothing,' Feyra said, lightly, her looks giving the lie to her words. 'Only that you must tell the Triannis that they may not move to the tied house just now. I will need it a while longer.' She turned to go, but not before the Badessa had seen something glint in her eyes.

The Badessa called her back. The girl would not cross the threshold, nor would the Badessa allow her to, so the older woman came outside. 'Are you well?'

The girl had composed herself by now. 'Quite.'

The Badessa was not usually one to interfere, but she meant what she had said to the doctor. 'If I may . . . I divine that something has prevented you from sharing a roof with our doctor, and I am bound to say that this may be a blessing.'

The heretic turned her great eyes upon her. 'Would it have been so bad when there is love in the case?'

The Badessa looked at her with pity, but spoke firmly. 'What you are speaking of is *sin*, sin against the Christian law.' She relented, as they walked together to the lychgate. 'You are of different faiths; but there may be a way to bring you closer together. If you read and study the Christian Bible, the Book of Books, you could, in time, become part of the family of God. Then, and only then, would it be possible for the doctor to formalize his arrangement with you.'

The girl's strange yellow eyes opened wider. She looked as if the thought were terrible to her, and yet, in a heartbeat, a change came across her gaze like the breeze rilling the lagoon. 'Yes,' she said. The words came in a rush. 'Yes. If you permit it, I would like to borrow a . . . Bible.'

Feyra had no intention of entering the family of the Christian god and his shepherd prophet. She knew her mother had made just such a change the other way about, but the idea was loathsome to her.

And yet, when the Badessa had mentioned the Bible something her mother had said chimed in her memory – the Bible was the Book of Books, and in there she would find what she needed to know about the Four Horsemen. Now her evenings were her own, she had been thinking more and more about the mystery, trying to remember her mother's long forgotten words. Now she needed occupation; she decided to solve the riddle of the four horses.

Before her own fire, a poor cousin to Annibale's cosy hearth, she looked at the book where it lay in her lap. It was bound in crimson velvet with silver clasps, and the edges of the pages were exquisitely burnished to a smooth gilded sheen.

Feyra laid open the book as if it burned her hands. The vellum was as smooth and milky as could be rendered by the parchmenter's art and the quires beautifully stitched at the spine. It was obviously a book of great value, and it was no little thing for the Badessa to place it in her hands.

The calligraphy was close and black, the text illuminated in jewel colours, the naïve pictures depicting angels and demons, promising glory and damnation. This book had legitimized violence against her people and atrocities against her faith and yet she leafed through the pages determinedly. She struggled with the Latin, but it brought her closer to Annibale, however fleetingly, for she was reading in the language that he had taught her. Odd, she thought, that the language of Western medicine was also the language of the Christian faith, when sometimes, according to Annibale, the two were set in opposition to each other. He had told her once of the objections of the Curia of Padua to the various treatments for the inoculation of the pox developed at the medical school there, on the grounds that they were ungodly.

Feyra leafed through the pages, peering at the letters until the black print swam before her eyes, and the gilded figures in the marginalia began to dance before her gaze as if they were animated. Finally she found what she was looking for; in a book called Revelations. There they rode, as if leaping from the pages – a black horse, red horse, white horse and pale horse, all mounted by grinning skeletons.

The Four Horses of the Apocalypse.

She found the Latin hard, and had got no further than the first phrase, when she was chilled by the memory of her mother's final ravings.

'"*Come and see*"!' she read aloud, and was frightened by her own voice. '*I looked, and there before me was a black horse! Its rider was holding a pair of scales in his hand. Then I heard what sounded like a voice among the four living creatures, saying, "A quart of wheat for a day's wages, and three quarts of* barley for a day's wages, and do not damage the oil and the wine!"'

This made no more sense to Feyra than when her mother had choked out the words on her deathbed, but as she read on she swallowed painfully as she understood for the first time the gift that her father had conveyed to Venice. For the black horse brought pestilence. She read, with growing consternation, as the Great Tribulation her mother had warned of played out. Behind the black horse rode the red, harbinger of fire and bloodshed.

'When the Lamb opened the second seal,' read Feyra, 'I heard the second living creature say, "Come and see!" Then another horse came out, a fiery red one.'

Then came the white horse, bearing a conqueror with a bow and a crown, bent on War. And finally, the pale horse, the green of bile, bringing Death, despair and the End of Days.

She closed the book, as if by pressing the covers together she could keep the horrors contained within. She closed her aching eyes too and struggled to remember what Nur Banu had said. She had said that *four* of the horses would come, not one. Four horses, like the quartet of bronze beasts with the flailing hooves she had seen on the Doge's Basilica.

In the Bible the pale horse followed the black but on her ring, when she examined the crystal band warm from her bodice, the little red horse was following hard upon the black, with the white next and the greeny-pale horse last.

Feyra cursed herself for not remembering the signs her mother had taught her, for not repeating the message to the Doge as she had vowed. Once her friend Death had entered the city she'd assumed failure. The black horse had bolted from its stable and there had seemed no sense in closing the door. But now she began to wonder, with a hollow dread, whether there was more to come.

With Annibale beside her she might have shrugged the prediction off, but now she wondered what more ills could blow across the sea from Constantinople to this beleaguered city. Shipping was still forbidden, the crew of *Il Cavaliere* had sailed away, and she was the only person from that ship left alive in Venice. The mission had to be at an end. And yet she wished she had not seen that terrible vision written down in black and white. It had left her with a terrible feeling that perhaps it wasn't over.

Feyra did not go to bed that night. She sat, watching the book on the mantel as if the horsemen could escape from the pages and spring to life. When she heard the bells of Matins she went to the church, and left the book on the threshold.

The Badessa, leaving the little church of San Bartolomeo before dawn to lead her sisters back to their dormitory, nearly trod on the Bible. She picked it up, her old bones creaking, and exhaled a long sigh of failure. Then she went to bed for the few precious hours before Prime, shaking her head over one lost sheep.

Chapter 32

Over the next few days Feyra tried to forget the Horsemen. She decided instead to make amends for the only one of their blights that she understood. She would collate all the information she had gathered from her own and Annibale's knowledge and experience and discover a cure for the Plague.

In Constantinople the most learned doctors had often made a potion known as a Theriac, a cure-all antidote that was one of the most complex forms of medicine in the canon of the apothecary. Theriacs had as many forms as they did purposes. They were often only available to the very wealthy due to the cost of the numerous constituents, and only the most competent physician would attempt a decoction.

But Feyra was not afraid. She needed employment. She took out her medicine belt and examined the herbs and unguents and powders – some from Constantinople, some restocked and replenished from Venetian soil, and some new treasures gleaned from the darkest reaches of the blackthorn woods outside the walls here on the island, or from the strange plants that thrived on the salt soil of the flats.

She had two aims: to heal those already afflicted and to

prevent the well contracting the disease in the first place. Her potion must simultaneously lower fever and reduce boils, cleanse the blood, and overall it must give hope to the mind too: there must be that within each little bottle which made the taker believe, without question, that the liquid in this little prism of glass would give him back his life. She decided to name the medicine *Teriaca*, a Venetian version of the original word borrowed from the Greeks. She was well pleased with it, but all she had was a name.

She began work.

Her home became an alchemist's den, crowded with bottles and limbecks and cauldrons and crucibles. Although she tried to concentrate, she would look up at every sound, every creak of the door, hoping that it would be *him*, lifting the latch to tell her that his terrible mother had gone.

But days turned into weeks, and the weeks into a month; and she still did not see Annibale outside of the Tezon. As far as she knew, he visited Palladio each Friday and on those days she barely left the hospital, for it was then that the malign presence of the doctor's mother made her life outside intolerable. She used the time wisely. Over those precious Fridays she conducted trials on the patients, asking permission of those that could speak, and administering to those that could not, suspecting that any chance of a cure would be welcome to those within the icy reach of death. She also offered the liquid to some of the families in the almshouses, who had had a member recently infected by Plague. Her findings interested her greatly.

Knowing what she now had, she was ready to make the medicine in bulk. She collected a stack of vials from the Tezon, stuffing them with sea salt to rime overnight. The next day, a Friday, she took a satchel of the purified bottles to the well to fill them with the water she would need for her solution. When she hauled up the bucket, sparkling and dripping with the crystal water, she calibrated the bottles carefully, stoppered them and laid them in smoked linen, ready to take home for the addition of the secret ingredient. She heaved the clinking bundle on to her back. The stone lion with the closed book watched her.

'Not a word,' she said.

It was almost dark by the time Annibale returned to the island. He had deliberately delayed his return from Venice on this particular Friday. On his way back to the island, he calculated that he had not seen Feyra's face for a month now and it was agony to him to be near her and yet not to be able to be close to her. She had been quiet and reserved around the hospital, working harder than ever. She was civil to him, but he could see she was hurt and he found this so unbearable that he became even more abrupt. He was also forced to face the truth.

Whether his mother went or stayed, he knew he could never again ask of Feyra what he'd asked that last happy night by the fireside. He could not dishonour her by taking her as his mistress any more than he could offer her marriage. The Badessa had been right: the gulf between them was too wide. He would have her for a year, two years, perhaps, until the pestilence had gone and then what? He could not have her passed from man to man until she fell down the abyss that had swallowed Columbina Cason.

He had become accustomed to his mother's presence in the evening, to the constant invasion of his person, to her incessant chatter, her selfish, self-obsessed stories of woe.

He would sit silently staring into the fire, trying to conjure the face he missed so much: her upside-down mouth, and the topaz of her eyes. He had resigned himself to an eternity of such evenings and was surprised to get back to his house to find his mother gone. His first thought was that she would have relieved him of some of his medical valuables, but there was nothing missing except her cape and gloves and the eerie, white-faced mask no longer hanging from the fire hook.

He hurried out in the night and went back to the gatehouse, where Bocca and his son were breaking bread over their meagre fire. 'Has a boatman come?' he demanded.

The tone of the doctor's voice was enough to bring Bocca to his feet. 'Yes, *Signor Dottore*. I lit the brazier at Sext, and fetched your lady mother from your house when the bark came. I assumed you knew of her departure.'

For a fraction of a heartbeat Annibale felt like an eight-year-old again, abandoned and bereft, but he nodded, glad of the mask. 'Of course I knew of it,' he snapped. 'I just wished to know that she was safely dispatched.' He left abruptly, discomfited by the scowling face of the dwarf staring at him from his customary shadow.

As he crossed the green he felt an enormous relief. He could never be intimate with Feyra in the way he had planned; but was it too much to hope that they might, in time, be once more friends? He convinced himself that if he could only sit with her again, look upon that face, and talk of the things that mattered to them both, he would be happy. Halfway across the green he stopped. He would go to her house now, knock on the door and beg her to come with him to his fireside.

Then he saw the well, its pale stone glowing from the

dark. The lion, with the closed book held close in his paws, gazed back at him with blank stony eyes. With a sudden jolt of panic, he turned and ran not to Feyra's house, but to his own.

He burst through the door and raced up the stairs, tearing off his mask as he went. He scrabbled under the bed and lifted the loose floorboard that hid the Cason treasure. The board came up easily, as if it had not long been laid in place. The cavity below was empty, the casket gone.

Annibale's head drooped in despair until his forehead touched the floorboards, the useless golden key hanging redundantly from his neck.

Chapter 33

Annibale was at his wits' end.

Paradoxically, with his mother gone, the gulf between Feyra and he had widened.

There was nothing left of his fortune. The coin in his pockets would last no more than a few days. Now, because of his mother's theft, San Bartolomeo's hospital, and his utopian island, could not survive beyond the end of a week.

The families would have to go home, the dead and dying would remain here, and the sisters would return to the Miracoli. He did not know what would happen to Feyra – he supposed that he must get her to the mainland and find a ship to Turkey, perhaps from Ancona or Ravenna. He cursed himself for believing in his mother, for believing that she could change.

Left with no choice, he asked Feyra if she would visit his house that evening, praying that his own resolve would not weaken at the sight of her lovely face.

She came as she was asked, but did not sit in her long-accustomed chair, for she knew who had been filling it in her absence. Instead she stood, noting sadly that for the first time since they were alone in this house he had not removed his mask. And nor did she.

'First of all,' said the Birdman in subdued tones, 'let me

set your mind at rest. I must tell you that I will not be renewing the offer that I made to you lately.'

Feyra swallowed. She had known this, but to hear it was as if he had made an incision in her heart. She felt her eyes pricking with tears and was silent, lest her voice give her away.

'Secondly, I am sorry to have to tell you that the Cason treasure is all gone.'

He did not tell tales, but he had forgotten how well she knew him.

'And your mother?'

The bird mask looked down at the floor. 'Gone too.'

She said nothing.

'Consequently, the island must be closed and returned to the Republic. The hospital will be shut within seven days. I will pay you to the end of the week, and do my best to find you a passage back East.'

There it was. The moment she had worked for, all those little golden sequins that she had collected in her yellow slipper, whispering as they tinkled together with the promise of home. In the last lonely month she had begun to think of the life she could have if she returned to Turkey. Not to Constantinople, of course, but to some outpost far from the Sultan's eye like Antioch or Tarsus; she could perhaps set up a physician's practice of her own. She wanted to sail away and never look West again. But instead she said, 'It does not have to be that way. I have made a concoction – an antidote – which I have named Teriaca. Let me sell it, to fund the hospital.'

The Birdman drove his fist into his palm, but spoke calmly. 'I have told you, many times, that I will not advocate preying on the minds and purses of the sick with useless charlatan remedies.'

'And each time we have discussed the subject I have told you that, if by controlled sale of a remedy a doctor can better the facilities for his patients, or fund further researches, then it may be permissible. I am not speaking of exploitation – I am speaking of legitimate sale, for my potion is far from useless.'

'How can you possibly know?'

She took a deep breath. 'Over the last month of Fridays I have been conducting trials. My linctus has proved most efficacious.'

'You've been interfering with the prescriptions of my patients?' he spoke harshly, the beak amplifying his rage.

She lifted her chin, glad of her own anger. 'Yes. To *great* effect.' She held up her hands. Here they were, arguing again, just as they used to. 'If you let me, you will be able to carry on here as ever. For ever. Do you really want to give all that up for the sake of this game of bones you're playing with me?'

The Birdman was breathing hard. His eyes seemed to be raking her up and down behind their prisms of smoked glass. She followed his gaze. In the year she'd been here, she'd completely reverted to her Ottoman style of dress, gradually covering herself, month by month, with loose breeches and a long shift, a loose *ferace* gown of cinnabar red thrown over all, a most practical colour for her work in the Tezon.

'Well,' he said after a time, sounding at last like the Annibale she knew, 'you can't go like *that*.'

Annibale jumped ashore at Treporti, already weighing his last few coins in his pockets. As he swept through the crowded market people made way for the doctor. He glanced at the townspeople professionally – there did not seem to be any pestilence among them yet, and the doors of the little white sunbaked houses were unadorned by crosses. This was not a commission he wanted to entrust to anyone else, but for a while he hovered between the pitches, not entirely sure what he was looking for.

Mamma Trianni had told him to get samite or silk, of whatever colour pleased him, and she would do the rest. He did not know the differences between these materials, but had not admitted as much. He made his way to a brightly coloured stall where reams of fabric ruffled and streamed in the wind like pennants. Without knowing it, he picked a bale of cloth exactly the green of his eyes, the hue of bottle glass, which had a watery sheen to it as he turned it to the sunlight.

The clothier appeared at his elbow. 'A fine choice, *Dottore*, the emerald. Indigofera from the Indies for the blue, fine English weld for the yellow, mixed together and fixed with good Venetian piss to make green.'

Annibale took a step back, still clutching the bale. 'Would this stuff do for a gown?' he barked.

'Yes, *Dottore*.'

'How much would I . . . would my seamstress need?'

'That depends.' The fellow scratched his chin, and readjusted the tape measure draped around his neck. 'Is she a large dame?'

'What? No, no, she's as slim as a greyhound. About this around . . .' Annibale put his hands together as though they clasped Feyra's waist.

'And will you be wanting stuff for a bodice? Petticoats? Stomacher? How about some crystal beads for the embroidery?'

The clothier could be speaking another tongue. Annibale, flustered, said *yes* to everything, and came away with a very large parcel and very little money.

On the way back to the boat he had a sudden thought: Feyra should have a mask, not for anonymity but for sanitation. He swerved to the maskerer's stall and quickly chose a horse's head in pearlized white. He was halfway back to the island before he recalled why the horse's head had leapt out at him – he vaguely remembered a question she'd asked him once.

Leaving his parcel at the seamstress's house, he kept the uncomfortable exchange as short as possible. 'Do your best, for she must look like a noblewoman.'

Mamma Trianni laughed a wheezy laugh through her few teeth. He noted that when he had recommended that the families took up the pipe to keep the miasma at bay, this old dame had obeyed with alacrity. 'Don't fret, *Dottore,*' she said. 'I know exactly what I'm about. She shall look like a Dogaressa before I'm done.'

Extricating himself as quickly as he could, he hurried to Feyra's house, where he found her packing her bottles for the next day.

He'd spent the last of his remaining ducats at Murano on a boatful of virgin bottles – purified in the fires and never used before, they would preserve the integrity of the ingredients of her mysterious linctus, whatever they might be. He'd noticed with interest that the burly, firetanned glassblowers had put in place their own safeguards to protect them from the Plague that had not yet reached their isle – the bottles were pushed out to him in a little coracle and he was directed to throw his coin in the salt sea, to be purified by the brine before being fished out by one of their number.

Now Feyra placed the bottles neatly into a leather case, the sides cured stiff and rigid, so the bottles would stand. He noted the concoction within – her secret antidote, for she had not shared its constituents even with him – was exactly the same colour as her dress.

She straightened up when Annibale entered.

'I have been thinking,' he said without preamble. 'You need a story, something like Valnetti's Four Thieves – a holy tree or a magic well, or some such. Some legend to make the people believe in your cure. People don't understand medicine, but they do understand folklore.'

'Very well,' she said, in agreement at once. 'How about the well of the lion with the closed book – it's true I drew the water for the potion there.' She actually smiled. 'And I will tell you no more.'

His heart leapt at her smile but he merely shrugged. 'Our concern at this point is not what is true, for the whole business is a tissue of lies and I do not like it.'

She came so close to him then that he could almost feel her warmth. 'I would not sell this concoction if I did not truly believe it in my heart to be effective.'

'Very well. The Lion's Well is good enough – the emblem of the lion should appeal to Venetian ears. Besides, holy wells are good fodder for the gullible – there's one on Giudecca, precisely where Palladio builds his church. Pilgrims swear the water protects them from the Plague.'

Feyra made no reply to this, but before long they were seated, and unmasked, and talking as they used to, speaking over each other and gesticulating and arguing their points as they concocted the legend of the potion she called Teriaca.

'I was walking by the well one day, and I saw the lion and the book—'

'No, the lion *spoke* to you.'

'Yes, that is better. The lion spoke to me and said: "I am the symbol of Venice. Within my well is a water that will cure my people; water blessed by . . . "' She tailed off.

'Saint Mark,' finished Annibale.

Feyra remembered the story of the unfortunate Saint wrapped in pork like a Christian feastday dish. 'Saint Mark when he came from the East—'

'The Holy Land. It is *always* the Holy Land,' interjected Annibale.

'Saint Mark when he came from the Holy Land. He wrote his blessing in my book with his bolt from heaven—'

'Celestial lightning?' Annibale suggested. 'With his celestial lightning, and then bid me close my book for ever—'

'To keep the secret!' Feyra finished in triumph.

Annibale made her tell the story over and over again, to perfect her Venetian accent. She was clearly immune to the Plague as she had walked among the sick all these months not protected by a mask as he had been, but she would be in great danger if she was discovered to be a Turk. Feyra, remembering too well her flight from the Doge's palace, listened carefully to his instruction and bent her tongue around her tale with a Venetian twang.

Mamma Trianni walked to the blanket box beneath the little window and opened the lid with great ceremony. Silk folds of an incredible green tumbled out like a waterfall. The colour was exactly the green of the lagoon on an overcast day, an iridescent, verdant hue of shifting waters. The old woman pulled the dress free with the help of her daughter Valentina, and held it up so that Feyra could admire the exquisite workmanship of the bodice and sleeves. She took it from Mamma Trianni reverently – it was incredibly heavy – and saw that the real artistry was in the green stomacher, sewn with more tiny crowded crystals in amazing curlicues which mimicked the waves of the Adriatic.

Feyra undressed quickly, and the green silk dress slipped over her easily, cool and heavy against her warm skin.

Mother and daughter stopped chattering as Feyra walked to the window. 'Is it all right?' she asked tentatively. There was no looking-glass so she could not see what they could see. But just at that moment Annibale walked in, and her doubts vanished.

Annibale stood, mouth agape. His Feyra was transformed as completely as caterpillar to butterfly or cygnet to swan. She had crossed an ocean from Byzantium to Venice and been reborn as a Venus of the West. The green gown fell to the floor, accentuating her height, and her golden shoulders rose from the crystal bodice. Her waist, nipped in by clever invisible tailoring, seemed tiny. The dress was all one colour and the single, strong hue made the warm tones of her skin glow, and gave heat to her amber eyes. Mamma Trianni clucked around her, making tiny, unnecessary adjustments to the perfection.

'It is my turn now,' said Valentina, standing. 'She'll not be long, *Dottore*.'

Annibale leaned at the doorframe, rapt.

'Now: hair. First, let us get it all down.' The veil was snatched away and Annibale saw Feyra's hair for the first time, falling, whispering, loose on to her shoulders. He'd tried to guess at its colour from the small curls escaping from her veils, but those tiny clues were so confusing – sometimes the filaments were the colour of copper, sometimes dark as squid's ink, sometimes burnished like cherrywood. Now he could see the full spectrum of the amazing golds and browns in her hair.

'*Esumaria*, so much of it! And all those colours!' exclaimed Mamma Trianni, echoing his thoughts. Annibale watched as Valentina bundled the shining mass loosely into a net to sit at the nape of Feyra's neck, bounded in a coif of seed pearls, with a few curls escaping around the ears.

For the first time he could see that the plain ribbon Feyra wore around her neck held a ring. For a moment he worried that it was some token of a former love, but however she had come by it, its simplicity with the green dress and the bundled hair was stunning.

Once Valentina had finished, Annibale handed Feyra the magnificent mask, pearlized white and shaped like a horse's head. He had chosen it hoping to please her, but could not interpret the gasp she gave when she laid eyes upon it.

Annibale thought how much she was once again changed when she held the mask in place: the visor erased all expression, but through it Feyra's eyes glittered, still alluring. Her beauty frightened him; she was a creature now that would enslave any man, no longer the girl that had been his Feyra by his fireside. However, he said nothing of this, merely asking, 'Ready?'

Annibale gave Feyra his arm across the green and she took it as seemed fitting. He carried her case of bottles for her too, as far as the jetty, the bottles clinking in counterpoint to her nervous, pattering thoughts. The skirts dragged at her hips and she wondered how the Venetians managed all their Carnevale debauchery when so hampered. She looked at her escort and saw him eyeing her as if she were a stranger.

'I do not like this. I do not like you going,' he said.

'Then you go.'

'You know I cannot. I neither approve of the potion, nor will I take the credit for it. Moreover, as a doctor of the Republic I must register the ingredients of any cure with the *Consiglio della Sanita*, and to them would go the bulk of any profits.'

She opened the gate and emerged from the shadow of the postern. 'I will not place myself in any danger,' she re-assured him. 'I am a harmless goodwife selling a homemade remedy. And you must own that I look Venetian enough, even for you.' She thought of what the Badessa had said, of how she could change, accept God, become assimilated herself into the Christian West. Would she look like this if she was Annibale's wife in truth? She bit her lip a little, making the rose of her mouth even deeper.

He stopped walking, turned. 'I *never* wished for you to look so,' he protested vehemently, as if it were suddenly more important that she should know that about him than any of his instructions about safety in the city.

On the jetty she handed him her yellow slipper full of sequins. She gave it to him swiftly before she could change her mind, for the gift of her hard-earned wages represented her passage to Turkey. Now she would never go home.

'For the hospital,' she said, 'until I come back with more.' Then she got swiftly into the waiting bark, hampered by her unaccustomed skirts, her green kirtle spreading to fill the boat like a single lily's pad on the water.

Feyra watched Annibale standing there, getting smaller and smaller as the bark rowed away, expressionless in his beak mask, but wringing the yellow slipper in his telltale hands. She had been right to give it to him. She had thought that she could not leave her patients, but the truth was that, even though all hope was gone, it was him she could not leave.

Chapter 34

Annibale had sent Feyra forth in a strong-bottomed dory which could accommodate both her heavy case and the green dress, so as the boatman neared Venice he had to navigate carefully between the canal traffic.

A heavy mist of sea fog and Plague fires combined hung low over the water so the city's spires poked above the gloom like swamp rushes, and Feyra had to peer through her mask to divine their direction. She saw that the dory was pulling into the city almost exactly where *Il Cavaliere* had dispatched its dreadful cargo all those months ago. There was the white filigree palace and the great twin pillars Death had walked between.

Now she was seeing his works.

The numerous barges were not crowded with pleasure trippers but filled with shrouded bodies, already powdered with snowy lime to begin their decay on their journey to their graves. Here and there a peevish wind lifted their shrouds to reveal a blackened hand, a rictus jawbone. Now the drift of yellow fog had risen to hang in a sickly pall over the city, pollarding the tops of spires and belltowers. The Plague had taken hold in Feyra's six months' absence, and the need for what she had to sell was great. She sat a little straighter, and held the horse mask to her face. Today she had a part to play.

She leaned forward, 'Which is the *veduta della Sanita et Granari Pubblici*?'

The boatman pointed. ''Tis that big white building, *Dama*, with all the hawkers before it.'

Feyra peered though her mask holes at the long low building – she could barely see its pillars and porticoes for the massing crowds before it. There were pitches and stalls crowded on to every inch of the foreshore. 'Who *are* they all?' Feyra breathed.

The boatman laughed bitterly. 'Sellers of dreams, *Dama*. Promises to keep the Plague Maiden from bedding with you. They'd tell you a rush dip was a moonbeam and charge you for it.'

Feyra kept her chin high as the boatman handed her out of the dory. There was nothing for it but to put her case down beside the rest, and set out her stall.

By noon she'd sold one bottle – to a gentleman who'd clearly thought she was selling something else besides – and given another away. Her story of the Lion and the Well went unheard and unheeded, drowned beneath the barkers and sellers shouting their own desperate slogans and pitches. One seller sold faggots of firewood; juniper, ash, vine and rosemary, guaranteed, he shouted, to raise a smoke hateful to the Plague. Another favoured a powder to be thrown into the flames made of mastic, laurel and cypress. A lady nearby in a dress almost as fine as Feyra's sold smelling apples moulded from gum Arabic, fragranced with roses and camphor and artfully coloured with red and white sendal. There were cures for every budget – from a concoction of spikenard and rhubarb for the poor to a powder of real emeralds or an amethyst etched with a healthful symbol for the rich. Some remedies were downright bizarre;

one enterprising fellow, who seemed to be selling severed pigeon wings, was singing the virtues of his cure in a sweet baritone.

Feyra felt degraded by this company. She saw the same woman visit almost every stall with a silver goblet, desperately trying to exchange the cup for a potion to protect her only daughter from the disease. Having determined the child had not yet been stricken, Feyra gave the second bottle of Teriaca to her, along with some directions for best use. She did not take the cup.

By the afternoon Feyra was desperate. She could not bear to return to the Lazzaretto with a full case, and tell Annibale that he must give up his hospital. She had been so sure that she could save the island for him.

She looked about her. Annibale had been so anxious that she would fit in in Venice that in her mask, cloak and gown she looked no different to all the other high-born dames she saw skirting the stalls. Her gown was a little finer, perhaps, her carriage taller, but she was Venetian to the last detail. She remembered what Annibale had said: if all potions looked the same then in order to sell yours you needed something that no one else had. The man who sang and twirled his pigeon wings had long since packed up and gone home, every plume sold. Quality and efficacy meant nothing in the first instance. Quality and efficacy would keep a customer coming *back*. But for a *first* sell, you had to stand out.

Feyra had a sudden, desperate flash of inspiration. She would tell the people something much more terrible than a seller's lie. She would tell them the truth. She found a discarded fish crate and set it on its end. She took a single bottle of Teriaca out of her case, threw off her cloak and mask and stood on the box.

'List to me well, people of Venice,' she called above the hubbub, 'to the story of the Sultan's Secret.' She caught the attention of the little knot of people nearest to her; they turned to listen, and began to shush those about them. Feyra continued in her best Venetian accent, but using all the conventions and mannerisms of the Ottoman storytellers to draw in her audience. *Begin with a secret*, she remembered. *Tease them, tell them something they don't know*. 'That's right, I am in possession of a secret that comes all the way from Byzantium, that no other living soul knows. I know how the Plague came to Venice, and I alone know the cure!'

Her heart beat faster, her voice carried out over the heads of the now silent crowd. Steeling herself, she went on. 'The Turks gave you the Plague! That's right, the Ottoman Sultan sent the Plague to our good city!'

'How do you know this, *Dama*?' shouted one of the crowd.

'My husband, God rest his soul,' she choked out the treacherous blessing, 'worked at the Quarantine island of Vigna Murada.' She had remembered the old name of Annibale's Lazzaretto. 'The fortymen apprehended a ship lately come from Constantinopoli, and took the crew ashore. It was their mistake. Within seven days all the fortymen were infected with the Black Death, and the heartless infidels gathered supplies and waited for them to die.'

Now the crowd had multiplied, and was listening, rapt. Feyra lowered her voice a little, drawing them in. 'My husband was the last to die, left alone to resist the enemy. The ship prepared to sail once more, but even in his sickness, my good husband prevented one man from reaching his ship, by stabbing him to the heart. His cowardly compatriots left

the Turk, a faithless infidel called –' she thought quickly '–
Takat Turan.'

There was silence from the crowd – she could have whispered now and they would have heeded her. But she spoke
clearly, warming to her theme. 'The two men were alone
on the island, one Christian and one heathen; one stabbed
to the heart, one sick unto death of the Plague. My husband,
my dear . . . Annibale –' she let her voice crack into a sob
'– asked Turan how it was that none of his compatriots had
succumbed to the terrible disease they were carrying.
Turan showed him the answer – it was *this*.' She held the
bottle of Teriaca high. The liquid inside, as green as her
dress, was illuminated by a fortuitous sunbeam that penetrated the fog, shining out like a hopeful star in the pestilent
gloom. 'In those last hours my husband persuaded the
Muselmano it was not too late to make amends. They
crawled together to the little church of San Bartolomeo, set
there upon the island, and there my husband asked Takat
Turan to accept the true God. My husband, too noble to
come home and give me the pestilence, wrote down every
word of this history, and the constituents of the potion too,
and left it among his effects rolled and scrolled and bound
within this our wedding band –' – she pulled the crystalline
ring from her bodice '– so that I would find it. Being somewhat skilled in physic – I mean in the domestic sphere,' she
hastily amended, 'for do not we women cook in the *cucina*
for our menfolk every day?' – there was a sickening titter in
the crowd – 'I made the decoction in its exact parts as
stated.'

The crowd rumbled with interest. 'How do we know it
works?' called one woman.

'I am living proof of it,' sang out Feyra, clear as a bell.

'For six moons now I have walked among the Plague wards, untouched till a good Badessa told me God wanted me to share my gift with you good people for the meagre price,' she said, sick at heart, 'of one sequin a vial. So little a price to pay for a life.' She opened her hand and saw that her palm was bleeding where her nails had bitten into it. She stood waiting, the picture of youth and health, her arms outspread in entreaty, one hand wounded like the crucified shepherd prophet, the other holding the magical vial.

It was enough.

She was knocked from her box in the rush.

Amid the shouts and the jostling panic to exchange money, she heard the real reason she'd been successful. Over and again she heard the Turks derided, named as devils, demons and curs. Over and over again she heard terrible lies, passed from one mouth to the next, of their religious practices; she heard insults against their women, curses rained down upon all of her people. Only the thought of Annibale and all the good she would do with the money could make up for the fact that the reason for her success was hate.

Annibale quickly overcame his scruples in the face of Feyra's success. For a week she returned to her pitch and told the same story, embellishing it, honing it, choking on every word. The crowd grew and changed every day, and she served teachers, clerics, and once a Republican guard in the same livery in which his fellows had once chased her from the Doge's door. She even saw, once, a doctor in the crowd towing a cart of his own cures, his beak recalling Annibale to her, except that his mask had black spectacles drawn around the eyes. He appeared to listen intently, and cocked his head like a sparrow when she uttered the name 'Annibale'. Feyra faltered in her tale and felt a sudden sense of danger pool in her stomach. She had made so much money this week that she was attracting attention. Perhaps it were best that she did not return for a few days.

After her bottles were sold she had to call upon one of the Consiglio's constables to help her, so great was the baying of the disappointed crowd. He advised her that it would be too dangerous for her to walk down the waterfront, so she ducked into the little streets where the sun could not penetrate. After some minutes of wandering she found herself in a familiar ward. Why not? she thought, and turned her steps to the little square where there was a house with gold callipers over the door.

She knocked with some trepidation: after all, she had fled the house as a Turkish spy, and although she did not doubt Palladio's welcome she knew that others might not be so pleased to see her again.

It was Corona Cucina who opened the door, and Feyra stood nervously, conscious that some of the tale she'd woven all week was a reality for this dame, who had indeed lost her husband to the Turks. But the cook sketched a curtsey, and said humbly, 'How may I aid you, *Dama*?'

'Why, Corona Cucina,' exclaimed Feyra with a nervous laugh, 'don't you know me?'

The cook's eyes widened to saucers, she clasped Feyra to her in a bear's hug, then held her at arm's length. 'Turkish, my arse! I always knew you for a Venetian! Come and see the master. He'll be right glad to see you.'

At sunset Doctor Valnetti parked his cart before the great doors of the *Ufficio della Sanita et Granari Pubblici*, the headquarters of the *Consiglio della Sanita*.

He demanded two things of the constable on guard: firstly, that he should be allowed to see the Tribunal without delay, and secondly that the fellow should look after his cart. It was still full to the brim with little bottles for he had sold exactly one vial of his Four Thieves Vinegar today. He might as well, he thought, as he mounted the wide white marble steps to the great chamber, let the varlets steal the vials, for after today, it seemed, the bottles had no value, thanks to the woman in the green dress.

The *Sala della Consiglio della Sanita* was a magnificent room that ran the whole length of the top floor of the *Ufficio*. Bottled crystal windows let the lowering sun into the gloom, and lit the vast dark frescoes depicting the seven stages of alchemy. Here and there gilded elemental symbols or figures of magi sprang forth in burnished relief, the leaden paint turned to gold.

At the far side of the room, behind a long oak desk scattered with fat ledgers, sat three ancient fellows, gowned in scarlet. Seeming as old as Time, their slack jaws melted in multiple waxen folds into their tallow chins.

This was the Tribunal of the *Consiglio della Sanita*.

The oldest of them paused in this counting of the day's tithes, his hand quavering in the air. 'Is it Valnetti?'

'Yes, Tribune.'

'What is it, *Dottore*? We are finishing the day's business here.'

Valnetti strode forward over the vast wooden floor and recounted the mysterious widow's story. The three ancients listened in silence. When he was done, Valnetti felt compelled to refine his point.

'In short, business is suffering because of this widow in the green dress selling her "Turkish cure"; this *Teriaca.*'

One of the tribunes stroked his sagging chins. 'Does it work?' he asked aloud in his quavering voice.

'So she says. Does it matter?'

'But Valnetti, you know the rules,' put in the first, querulously. 'If she were a doctor, then she would have to register each ingredient over a hundredth part of the decoction, and pay the tax. But from what you say, she is a private citizen.'

Valnetti held his tongue. He was an indifferent doctor but he had made a great deal of money over his years as a physician by being a creature of instinct. He had pricked up his ears when the widow had uttered the name he most hated: *Annibale.* That and her tale of the island where Cason had built his hospital was too much of a coincidence; Valnetti was as sure as he could be that his young nemesis would prove to be at the bottom of this. But he kept his peace for now, until he could be sure.

'If she were practising medicine with a licence, now,' the second went on, 'then of course, that would be different.'

'Of course,' echoed the third ancient. 'Then you would be able to collect your tithe from her. It would be no small income if she sold the scores of bottles that you say.'

Valnetti gritted his teeth. 'But if her medicine leads the market then *you too* will be losing money hand over fist!'

There was an agonizing pause before the first tribune spoke again. 'He's right you know.'

The second drew a great wheezing breath and let it out again with a sigh. 'Very well, Valnetti. Then find out where she comes from; if she is connected to a hospice or medical practitioner then perhaps we can demand that she registers this . . . what did you call it?'

'Teriaca.'

'Teriaca. An odd name.'

'How shall I discover her whereabouts?'

'My dear fellow, this is Venice,' said the third tribune. 'Have her followed.'

When Feyra emerged from Palladio's house after an hour, so buoyed up was she by the success of the day and by the old man's company, she did not notice the watcher in the shadows.

She thought over her conversation with the architect and smiled into the dark, shaking her head a little. He was unchanged, so obsessed with the church that grew brick by brick on Giudecca, telling her in great detail about each joist and buttress, that he had forgotten to ask her why she was here, and dressed like a Venetian to boot.

He did ask after the doctor, though, and confided in her that he felt a fluttering sensation in his heart. She'd given him some white willow bark to chew from her medicine belt, and also gave him a small green vial of Teriaca. Feyra had eyed him sternly till he'd taken the draught down. She had left him cheerful enough, exhorting her to visit his site one day. She'd smiled, but knew she never would. She would not set foot in a Christian church. After all the lies she had told this week in the foreign god's name, she feared terrible vengeance if she should cross the threshold of his house.

But as she hurried down the *calli* in the direction of the Fondamenta Nuove, the smile vanished from her face. She could hear footsteps in the darkness mimicking hers. She held the horse mask to her face and pulled up the hood of her voluminous riding cape. Perhaps she was imagining things, but there the footsteps were again, slowing and speeding to match hers, stopping when she stopped.

She changed direction when she could and doubled back, but still they came. She cursed the impulse that had led her to Palladio's house. In her unease she took the wrong turning and fetched up in a tiny alley, enclosed by dark and looming palaces. She ran down it, but it was a dead end. High up on the wall was a shrine of the mother and child, lit by a guttering candle stub flickering like a warning beacon.

She looked up at the tableau, rooted to the spot. She had seen other such scenes since she'd been in the city, on practically every corner. But the eyes of this mother did not look kindly upon the son who reached up to her shining face: this was an icon of an older Christianity. Here mother and son, their faces exactly alike except in size, their heads backed by circles of gold, looked straight out, accusing her of borrowing a god that was not her own.

Retribution was coming.

Her pursuer was behind her, close.

Terrified, she turned at last and saw a black figure standing at the end of the alley, tall as a hanging tree and faceless under a black cowl.

He walked towards her, slowly now, confident that she was trapped. His cloak lifted in the breeze and fear clutched at her throat. Was this Death, then, still stalking the alleys, come to collect her new-forged debt to the Christians' god?

He came close. 'Feyra Adalet bint Timurhan Murad,' he said, in her own language. 'I have been seeking you for a long time.'

He threw back his hood.

It was Takat Turan.

Chapter 35

'I was the one who denounced you.'

The words dangled around them both like corpses on a gibbet.

Feyra's eyes widened. She looked into Takat Turan's face. He was thinner than she remembered, but still neatly groomed, his beard trimmed and his hair oiled. It was the eyes she remembered most clearly, dark as chips of jet and glittering with a nameless fire. She remembered how he had saved her from the crew of *Il Cavaliere*. '*Why?*'

'For seven days I was sick unto death. I could not return to you or your father in the infidels' ruin. When I was well enough to go back to the temple where I'd left you, there was nothing but a gang of masons building there and you were gone. I feared you dead, yet a boatman remembered you but not your father.' Takat Turan bent his head, and his respectful pause was strangely at odds with what he'd revealed. 'From then on I watched and waited and found you eventually in the house of the architect.'

Feyra felt suddenly angry. She turned on him. 'Why did you do it? Why would you place me in danger? You who defended me, you who served my father until his last hours?'

Takat Turan spread his hands as if he were surprised. 'I

thought to get you nearer to the Doge. Is that not what you wanted? If you were arrested you would be taken to the belly of his palace, where the dungeons are.'

'To be tried and tortured?' She was aghast.

'If that is what our master requires, we must bear it as we may.'

Feyra began, suddenly, to feel afraid. His utterings sounded reasonable, but their meaning was insanity. Now she could put a name to the fire in his glittering eyes. He was a true fanatic.

'How would that help me to meet the Doge?'

'Meet him?' Takat Turan laughed. The incongruous sound echoed down the alley and back. 'You mean *kill* him! Is that not why we are here?'

Feyra took a step back, her shoulder blades pressed against the cold stones of the palazzo behind her. She willed herself to be silent.

'But then you slipped away, and I did not see you again. I gathered together everything necessary and as the day drew near, was about to act alone.'

He opened his cloak and took out a small, muddy ball. She noticed again his missing fingers.

'Persian naphtha,' he said, 'beloved of the Crusaders, the most incendiary substance known to man. You see, all is ready bar the details.' He took hold of her shoulders in an iron grip. 'And then God decreed that I should see you again, in heretic weeds, telling heathen lies to gather money for our enterprise. I commend you. I knew you would not run, I knew you would finish your father's mission, once he had told you the whole of the design of the Sultan – the delight of my eyes and the light of my heart.'

'My *father*?' Was it possible that Timurhan had been

complicit in this second crime, to burn the Duke of Venice in his own palace and fire his city? Or had her father known only of the Plague? Feyra forced herself to remain calm. She could not afford to reveal how little she knew. 'And now?'

'The second stage of the Great Tribulation,' he whispered, the sibilants in his voice hissing in competition with the votive candle. *'It is time to purify with fire.'*

Feyra looked into his eyes, burning with tiny reflected flames, and began to shake. 'When?' she choked out.

'Tomorrow night. There is a feast among the infidels – the great square will be crowded with the filthy citizens. They have been visited by the pestilence but some survived. The unquenchable fire shall harvest them. The Doge will burn, his palace will burn, and all the city too. And now *you* have been sent to aid me.'

Feyra's head beat with her pulses, but she kept her voice steady. 'How will we gain entry?'

'That is the easiest of the matter. We get ourselves taken by the guards.' He took hold of her arm in a vice-like grasp.

She pulled back. 'And what will become of us? The Sultan's faithful?'

'We shall burn too. But we shall be saved, and transported to Jannah, according to the will of God. Come –' he clapped his hands. 'There is much to do and only a day to do it. I will take you to my dwelling place; it is safe, and no one will find us there, for it is close by a church.' He smiled at the irony, as if they spoke of inclement weather.

He is mad, Feyra thought.

'Your infidel coin will buy the kindling that we need for the oil and the fuses; yes . . .' He turned to look at her once again, and she saw that he was bent on one purpose alone, the service of his earthly and his heavenly master. 'And your disguise and mastery of their filthy tongue will aid me – for I have not their language, nor your innocent looks.'

He marched her to the mouth of the alley, and on to a larger thoroughfare, over a bridge and by the side of a canal flat and still as a smoked mirror. She was close to Palladio's ward but she knew that to run to the architect would avail her nothing – Takat already knew the house and would find her there at once. She must get back to the Lazzaretto and to Annibale and pray that Takat did not know of the island's existence. She knew these streets and must pray that he did not. She tried to walk steadily, but as they passed a tiny *sotoportego* Feyra twisted away from his grip and ran.

She was reminded of the first time she had fled through this city, but this time she ran from an even greater danger than the guards. The great skirt of the green dress hampered her legs, her ribs pained her, but finally she reached the waterfront. She ran across the last bridge in the direction of a knot of friendly boatmen.

Takat Turan loomed out of the dark and barred her way. She screamed before she could stop herself, and the boatmen turned to watch the struggle. As Takat put his hand over her mouth she bit it as hard as she could and shouted, in her best Venetian, 'Help me! He is a Turk! *Muselmano! Muselmano!*'

The boatmen, seeing a Venetian woman attacked in the dark, hurled themselves across the bridge, and fell upon Takat Turan. Thrown clear, Feyra clung to the balustrade of the bridge and watched as Takat was pinned to the other side. His head was punched repeatedly until it lolled back on his shoulders, his lips and eyes swelling and oozing gore. Stray curs came and twined around his feet to lick the pooling blood. Feyra's hands flew to her mouth.

'Say something,' bawled one of the burly men, his great oar arms crushing Takat's neck, his spittle falling on Takat's swollen face. 'Say something so I can be sure, before I turn you in.'

Takat spoke then, venomously. 'I curse you and your Devil's city. All of you will burn.'

Only Feyra understood the words, but the boatmen understood the accent well enough. 'Take him to the constables,' said one. Takat Turan went suddenly limp. As he was dragged away, he looked back at Feyra, a little smile playing about his lips. She could feel his eyes on her long after he had passed round the corner, the flame still burning there.

Feyra waited until he was out of sight before she gave a loitering boatman her directions to the island, low-voiced, confident that no one but he could hear the name of her destination. Once she was seated in the coracle she began to shake. She had put Takat Turan exactly where he wanted to be: in the gaols, right in the belly of the Doge's palace. But she also knew he would not act until tomorrow; he would not deviate from his plan. He needed the citizens to be gathered for their festival, so he could inflict as much damage as possible.

At the Lazzaretto Novo Feyra barely paused to pay the boatman. She ran through the gatehouse with scarcely a greeting to Salve, running only for the square of light that was Annibale's window. She knew he would be waiting up for her, as he did every day, to count their sequins, guilty as usurers, before the fire.

Feyra burst through the door and found him just as she had the first time she laid eyes on him, sitting hunched, staring into the fire, his curls tumbled forward. Her heart failed for a second but there was no time for nostalgia.

'I need you to help me,' she gasped. 'Your Doge is in danger.'

He stood at once. 'What do you mean? What has happened?'

'The Red Horse is coming.'

Feyra's boatman rowed back to Venice with the speed and satisfaction of someone who had been paid twice for his labour. He went straight back to the Fondamenta Nuove and from there walked the short distance to *Dottore* Valnetti's house, there to give up the whereabouts of the woman in the green dress.

PART IV

The Red Horse

Chapter 36

Doctor Annibale Cason walked through San Marco at sundown.

His beak mask went almost unnoticed among the revellers preparing for tonight's celebration for the feast of Saint Mark. By his side was his assistant, a young man of exactly the doctor's height, carrying his master's bag. He was dressed simply in a dark frock coat and breeches and a cambric shirt with no cravat, and he wore no hat on his curls, but women still turned to look at him, for in these times he was a sight for sore eyes.

Today, Saint Mark's day, was also known as the *Festa del Bocolo*, the feast of the rose buds, for on this day men gave long-stemmed red roses to the maids who caught their fancy. It seemed that the tradition had not halted for the Plague, but the Venetian maids and wives too, even the ones who had already been given a tribute, looked at Annibale with the coquettish glances of the young or the hungry eyes of the more experienced. It reminded him of why he'd donned the beak in the first place. As he passed, the roses they had been given were dropped and trodden, unnoticed, underfoot.

They'd been up late into the night, and Feyra had told him everything, from the day her mother and father met at

Paros, to her mother's deathbed confession, to the day that she'd buried her father. She told him of the ring of the four horses and her mission to see the Doge. She told him of Takat Turan, who had vanished from Giudecca and re-appeared like a spectre earlier that night. He'd been stunned by the story, humbled by the burden she had carried alone. She had told him of her father's part in the tale shame-facedly, and he had wanted, very much, to take her in his arms and tell her that her father's crime, and the blight upon the city, was not her fault. She had done nothing but try to atone since she had come to Venice, and now, when she ap-pealed to him to prevent further bloodshed, he could do nothing but aid her.

Feyra trod carefully, disorientated by the doctor's beak and her view of the world through the eyepieces. She was seeing the city as Annibale saw it, and it was unsettling. The distance that the beak placed between a doctor and the out-side world seemed a very great gulf indeed; little wonder that compassion rarely passed beyond the mask.

They neared the campanile. At the foot of the great red bell tower was a gilded cage as big as a barge. Within the cage, pacing back and forth, was a huge lion, the emblem of Venice made real. Feyra stopped and looked closer at the monster. The fur was patchy brindle, not burnished gold, and the shaggy mane looked fleabitten and bald in patches. Only the dull eyes had lustre, lent by the dying sun which turned them as amber as her own, but nothing could disguise the animal's misery.

'It is the Lion of Saint Mark; the *real* one,' said Annibale. 'The *Consiglio* keeps a live beast caged here in perpetuity.

When this one dies they will get another. He is supposed,' he said with heavy irony, 'to be the luck of the city.'

Feyra had not expected to feel sorry for her nemesis, but she had not known a lion could look like this. He already looked defeated. She left him pacing, and they crossed the broad thoroughfare to the Doge's palace.

Together Annibale and Feyra reached the broad white stairs, with the great alabaster giants standing sentinel and gazing down at them from blank marble eyes. As they ascended, Feyra's knees shook a little as she remembered the first time she had climbed these stairs, and recognized the same two guards who had chased her that night.

At the head of the stairs Annibale touched his forelock and addressed the two impassive guards who crossed their pikes in his face. '*Dottore* Annibale Cason,' he said humbly, 'to see the Doge'.

The guards looked not at him, but at Feyra in the beak mask. 'Your token, *Signor Dottore*?' asked one.

Feyra held out the Doge's seal, shining on the palm of her black glove. The guard reached out and turned it over. She examined the metal roundel with him; the Doge and Saint Mark on one side and the shepherd prophet alone on the other. Just like the design of the ducat she wore in her banded bosom beneath her doctor's cloak.

She waited. She couldn't believe that she was finally going to see the Doge. Sebastiano Venier, Admiral of Lepanto and Duke of Venice: her great-uncle.

To Feyra's surprise the token was enough, the halberds parted and they were ushered through. One of the guards beckoned a servant liveried in wine and gold to lead them. She felt a nudge at her back and walked forward, remembering that Annibale, as her servant, would follow at her heels. As she walked she rehearsed the story of her mother's death, the sarcophagus on the ship, her father and Takat Turan, and the coming of the fire.

The servant took them through a palatial stone passageway, which opened out into an enormous chamber. Feyra had seen many wonders in the Topkapi palace but never been in a room as vast as this: the single chamber was as massive as the belly of the Hagia Sophia. Every inch of the walls was covered with paintings of pastoral scenes and the ceiling had been transformed likewise to a cerulean heaven powdered with stars and studded with chubby angels. High in the clouds, roosting like starlings, nested a line of dozens of Doges with their dates of birth and death written on scrolls about their throats. Feyra shivered. If she could not get her message across to the Doge he might be depicted there with his date of death written down as today.

Footsteps sounded from an unseen inner chamber, the door opened and her heart leapt. Then hope flickered and died, as the Camerlengo entered the room.

'*Dottore* Cason?' he said. Feyra remembered his well-modulated tones from his inquisition of her in Palladio's house: the man who spoke in questions. Her blood froze in her veins. She nodded, the beak slicing down in front of her face like an executioner's axe.

'Is it the architect? Is something amiss?'

She was silent, and Annibale could not speak either, for then the Camerlengo would know him for the true doctor. She shook her head, the beak sweeping from side to side this time, her heart beating so hard she could hear it within the mask. There was an awful moment of silence, as the Camerlengo shifted his feet impatiently. 'As you know, I act as a conduit, shall we say, between the larger world and His Excellency himself. My Lord Doge follows me hard upon, but first may I know of your purpose here?'

Feyra felt Annibale pull at her arm. She was torn between removing the beak and pushing past the Camerlengo, and running towards the footsteps she now heard approaching. But just then a commotion erupted from the left.

A small doorway, which led on to a tiny stone arch of a bridge, was suddenly filled with the bulk of a guard. He was pulling a prisoner who was shackled to him, followed by another guard behind. The Camerlengo turned his blond head in irritation. 'Will you forgive me?' he asked Feyra. 'A prisoner for questioning. Take him to The Room and await me there,' he ordered the guard, nothing in his voice suggesting what would lie ahead for the prisoner. 'Is it not clear to you that my Lord Doge will have confer- ence here? Do you think we have need of such a distraction?'

Feyra turned too. Annibale was tugging her arm again, desperate to take advantage of the diversion to make their escape.

The Doge's footsteps came closer.

The prisoner came into view, his eyes aflame, and she knew.

As she watched, horrified, the fire in his eyes seemed to ignite at his heart and his jerkin exploded. The fire spread down his arms and the guard to whom he was shackled screamed as the naphtha consumed his body. The hapless man ran to the voluminous draperies at the window, drag- ging his burning captive behind him, tearing the velvet down and wrapping them both in it as the flames engulfed them. But the draperies caught too and the flame leapt from them up to the painted ceiling, where the pigments ignited and burned merrily, crackling as they rained droplets of fire on those below.

As Annibale dragged her away, Feyra saw the Camerlengo run to the inner chamber and saw, beyond the door, a shadowy figure in a tall white hat before the billowing smoke hid them from view.

As they ran from the chamber, Feyra and Annibale forgot their pretence and shouted to all in their path to clear the palace. Annibale shoved her towards the great white stairway and they clattered down the stairs, matching each other step for step. Just as she reached the bottom, Feyra remembered the last time she'd been on this stair and the kitcheners bringing bread for the poor.

She grabbed Annibale's arm. 'The servants!' she cried above the screams and the smoke. They doubled back into the palace's cellars and kitchens, giving the alarm and clearing the legions of servants out into the square. Pigs and chickens reprieved from the chopping block scuttled out into the air between their legs. Outside they were met by a cacophony of screams and cries, the ringing of bells, the babble of prayers, all overlaid by the nightmarish roaring of Saint Mark's Lion.

Feyra and Annibale turned back to look at the inferno; the traceries of the palace windows were now silhouettes of black lace against the topaz flames. The white and rose bricks were blackening rapidly. She had never known before how noisy fire could be: that flames could roar louder than a lion, that timber screamed as it warped and fell, that glass shrieked as it melted. Feyra watched, almost hypnotized by this strangely beautiful, yet terrible sight, unable to look away although the floating cinders stung her eyes. There was nothing she could do to help the Doge although she had seen the Camerlengo run to save him; it was the city herself that was now at risk. She could turn and run through the square with Annibale and escape, but she knew she would not and neither would he. They were healers and savers of lives and the inferno screamed at them to stay. In unspoken agreement Annibale and Feyra jostled to the lagoon's edge to help to fight the fire, joining the rapidly forming bucket chain.

Matters were already being well organized by a tall man with white hair and a beard; his long robes tattered and blackened, shredded at the hem like a pedlar's. He might have been a priest or a hermit but he was organizing the people as if he were the general of an army, and like the best of generals, he was not just giving orders but was first into the fray and nearest the fire. Following his pointing arm Feyra fell into line between Annibale and him, and helped pass the buckets of salt water.

During those hours as her arm muscles cracked and her hands blistered, she began to admire the human spirit, exemplified in the lines of Venetians who had flooded from all parts of the city to help. As the effort to fight the fire swelled, the containers that passed through Feyra's exhausted hands were changing; not just buckets now but ewers, chamber-pots and even a child's bath. The fire, the vast drama that played out before her as the great white palace burned, was shrunk down to these humble household containers that she held in her hands; she *knew* these people, through these cracked jugs and christening cups with their children's names writ on the side.

As the interminable night wore on Feyra almost fell asleep where she stood, her face burning in the white heat of the roaring flame. The beak mask was long gone, burned or trampled or used for bailing, she would never know. Her feet chilled to blocks of ice by the freezing water that slopped on to them from the buckets. But it seemed that the fire was gaining headway and eventually the white-haired general turned to the line. 'The fire will spread to the Basilica,' he bellowed. 'We must take down the counting house. Menfolk, to me! Bring hammers and rams.'

The night changed from then. The men began to attack the antique walls of the old *Zecca*, the mint and counting house, in an ecstasy of destruction. The ancient stones were pulled down under their hands till a gap appeared against the yellow sky, a gap the fire could not leap.

Feyra looked desperately for Annibale, and caught sight of him once or twice in the thick of the men, shrouded by smoke, his face as black as a moor's. She shed her cloak, organized the women on the bucket chain, redoubling their efforts for the lack of the men. Between the dousing she would also tend injuries where she could: minor burns, smoke on the lungs, and even a woman bleeding from the head where a molten lead tile had fallen from the skies and struck her.

Once back in the line, Feyra was struck by the irony of it all; she was striving with these people to save their great golden church, a church with the four bronze horses bursting forth from the gallery, turned to gold in the fire. Watching them rearing above the flames she knew that this was their work, that of the four the red horse had dominion this night. Why should she save these four-legged demons? And Saint Mark, whose feast his citizens celebrated this day, who lay within there wrapped in his blanket of pig's flesh? Let him cook there, like a Saint's day feast himself. But she did not stop the relentless pass and toss of the buckets, never slowing in her rhythm.

By dawn they were gaining. Having devoured a great dark bite of the palace, the ravenous fire seemed satisfied and dwindled to a few pockets of flame, the temple and her sentinel horses smoking but safe. As the sky silvered to day, the sun rose on a different world. All was black – the palace, the citizens, and even the sky rained sooty cinders. The only colour was the red rose petals of Saint Mark, strewn about, blowing in eddies with the ash.

Feyra dropped her bucket at her feet and staggered to the corner of the church. The menfolk were dispersing and she looked desperately for Annibale. She saw him, leaning on the corner of the Basilica. He was doubled up, coughing, his face as puce as the stone. She dragged him clear, sat him down on a fallen pillar and looked at him closely, as he caught his breath. In all his doctoring he had kept his face covered; now he was exposed not just to the miasmas of the city but the thick smoke too. The fire was doused, the Doge, she hoped, was safe and Takat was dead. It was time for them to go. She held out her hand. 'Let's go home,' she said.

Annibale had barely risen, still speechless and wheezing, when a fellow, trailing smoke like a comet, ran round the corner from the Riva degli Schiavoni, and stopped, panting, at the feet of the tall hermit. The old man addressed him.

'Tommaso,' he said, laying his long hand on the man's heaving shoulder. 'Calm yourself. The fire is beaten and we have won the day.'

'Not so,' said the man in the blackened livery. 'The fire has taken the *Piombi*, and the prisoners have all cooked in their cells like fowls in the *forno* and the blaze now spreads along the nether bank to the Merceria.'

'The Rialto!' The hermit strode away, and those who were still able followed him.

Feyra turned to Annibale. 'Palladio!' she said.

They hurried after the crowd of citizens and past the Basilica. Feyra glanced up one more time at the bronze horses. They were glowing as if heated in the forge, the four of them striking forth with their fiery hooves, their red mouths open, as if the Basilica were a vast gilded chariot that they pulled with their supreme strength. Their temple was untouched by fire. The horses had protected their own.

She turned away from them, intent on protecting the architect, whose house in the Campo Fava lay in the path of the fire. They raced the spreading blaze through the market, which had been more than usually crowded with sellers because of the Saint's day. Turning for an instant Feyra saw the pitches and stalls were burning merrily behind them; the glassblowers' wares cracking and bursting in the heat, spewing molten jewels of multicoloured glass on the pavings.

Before they reached the old bridge she and Annibale broke away from the crowd and hurried to the little square with the house with the golden callipers over the door. Behind them the pall of smoke followed like a stalking shadow. Feyra hammered on the door, and when the cook appeared, she spoke for Annibale as she could see he was still in want of breath.

'Corona Cucina,' she said. 'Rouse the household and get everyone to safety. There has been a great fire and it burns this way.' She held up a hand to dam the cook's torrent of questions. 'Is your master here?'

'He is, and Zabato too.'

Feyra pushed past her and walked straight into the well-remembered study. She found Palladio in his familiar posture, bent over his drawings in conference with Zabato, the two grey heads together as she had so often seen them. She was filled with a sudden determination that they should be safe, these two men. They looked up at the interruption.

'Feyra?' Palladio's dark brows drew together as his eyes went past her to the doorway. 'And who is this?'

Feyra realized that Annibale's face was unknown to him.

Annibale strode forward. 'I am your doctor, and I'm about to fulfil the task I was charged with. There has been a fire in the Doge's palace and it is spreading through the Merceria to the Rialto.'

Palladio moved surprisingly quickly. He took up a soft leather pack which gave the telltale clink of his tools. 'Zabato. Get the household across the Accademia.'

His draughtsman stood too. 'Where are you going?'

Palladio strode to the door. 'If the fire spreads across the Rialto, the other half of the city will burn.' He turned at the door. 'We have to destroy the bridge.'

Feyra and Annibale could barely keep up with Palladio as he swept before them through the *calli*.

Soon the great bridge loomed out of the dark, a great black arch against the saffron sky of slatted wood rising out of stone piles. Feyra could make out the tall shape of the hermit, lofty against the night, organizing the buckets ready for the conflagration and even recruiting children to stamp on stray sparks that drifted close, threatening the great wooden structure.

Palladio went right up to the hermit, and began to talk, waving his arms and gesticulating toward the bridge. Feyra heard little of their conversation against the crackle of timbers, but then he turned back to them. '*Dottore*, come with me. Feyra, over the bridge with the rest.'

Feyra did not budge, her flesh chilling with foreboding. 'What are you going to do?'

Palladio laid down his pack with a clink, took out a chisel and handed it to Annibale. In his own hand he held a heavy-headed hammer. 'The important thing is to take out the piles. Then the whole bridge will tumble.'

The two men slipped into the water and attacked the bridge from below, even as women and children crossed over it to the safety of the other bank. Palladio concentrated his efforts on the two great joists supporting the piles at either side of the bridge. The two men hammered away but the fire was gaining. The hermit had directed the men to destroy the little row of wooden cots by the bank, but the fire soon beat them back. Then several of the menfolk, including the hermit himself, waded into the water to help. Feyra bit her fingers till they bled, and listened with dread as the structure began to groan, then creak, for now she worried that the bridge could collapse on top of them. In front of her she could see the reflection of the flames turning the water to fire, but she still did not turn. The sun had fully risen before the beams came free, and as the arch began to lurch she could wait no more and waded in to pull both men clear with a strength she did not know she had. As the great structure began to collapse, she heard gasps and screams from the gathering crowd on the opposite bank for the loss of the symbolic wooden bridge was a calamity.

Feyra wondered what it meant to Palladio to destroy something when he lived to build. But when the old man straightened up his eyes were shining with a fire that was not entirely reflection and there was a certain relish in his expression. 'What is destroyed can always be built anew,' he said, and smiled.

Annibale waded up to them. 'Come. We must get to safety.'

Once Palladio was dispatched to his bed, his house untouched, Feyra and Annibale staggered back through the square in the direction of the Riva degli Schiavoni and home. Their eyes red-rimmed, hair clogged with ash, faces and limbs blackened with soot, they stumbled through the cinders and roses.

In front of the ruined Doge's palace, an artist had set up his canvas, readied his palette and was beginning to thumb his paints. As the two doctors passed him he began to draw with his charcoals in furious strokes, attempting to capture the aesthetics of devastation.

In the cage at the foot of the Campanile, the Lion of Saint Mark was a charred and smoking skeleton. Trapped, as he had been in life, within his blackened bars.

Chapter 37

Feyra looked down at Bocca the gatekeeper, twisting and sweating on his bed in the gatehouse.

'What happened to him, Salve?' Feyra asked.

The little dwarf stayed in his customary shadow. He would not speak while the doctor was in the room.

It had been an uncomfortable morning for Annibale. Exhausted from lack of sleep, his lungs paining him from the smoke, and charcoal in his saliva every time he spat, it would have been bad enough; but he felt naked without his mask, especially here on the island. The inevitable explanations, the fascinated glances of his islanders, especially the women, made him ruder than ever; and Feyra feared the lash of his tongue would fall upon Salve.

She turned to Annibale. 'Get some rest,' she urged. His eyes were almost closing and he swayed where he stood. 'You are no use to anyone like that.'

He turned without a word and went out. Once he had gone Salve came from his corner.

'What happened?' Feyra asked him again, gently.

'Doctor not here.' Salve struggled to form the words. He pointed to his ailing father. 'He drew water. Took to Tezon.'

One of Bocca's daily duties was to draw a barrel of water

from the well of the lion and book, and take it to the Tezon and leave it on the stoop.

Feyra chilled suddenly. 'And then what?'

'Took it within.'

Feyra's heart sank. Instead of leaving the water at the door as was his daily commission, Bocca had taken it beyond the smoke chamber and the doors, to dip the cups for the patients. An act of vanity or an act of kindness – it mattered not, for it had been enough to infect him. Feyra turned over the gatekeeper's fingers. They were black. She went to wake Annibale.

Feyra felt terrible that in her zeal to protect the islanders with her Teriaca she had, somehow, neglected to dose father and son in the relatively distant gatehouse. When Bocca had been stretchered to the Tezon and made as comfortable as he could be, she went straight back to the gatehouse. Salve was watching the fire from his shadow, as if he did not know what to do. Her heart went out to him, seeing him as he was: a child without a mother, his father perhaps to be taken from him too. She sat on the settle on the other side of the fire, the seat that was Bocca's.

'Well?' said the shadow.

'Well enough,' said Feyra carefully for she did not want to lie. Bocca's fever raged, and he might not last the night. She felt a responsibility for the boy, left without a working wage. She reached into her bodice.

The coin was still warm from where it had nestled by her heart so long. Word had spread before they had left the charred city that the Doge was alive, and would address the people at sunset once he had taken his rest. She had helped to foil the second part of the Sultans's plan and turned back the red horse. Now she would do all she could to save Bocca and his sorry son. She held the ducat to the light and looked at the likeness of the Doge. Odd, she thought, that her great-uncle had been next to her heart all the time, and she had never got to meet him.

She gave the coin to Salve. 'This is for you, for you will not have your father to provide until he is well. Do not worry.'

He took the ducat across the fire into his misshapen hand. It barely fit in his palm. His eyes grew as round as the coin.

'Why . . . give . . . this?'

'I want to look after you. Come to me tonight, I will make a special decoction for you, to keep you safe.'

In the gatehouse, now alone, Salve turned over the ducat in his hand. He held it to his lips, her words ringing in his malformed skull.

When Feyra opened the door of her house that night, she was expecting Annibale. She had quite forgotten that she had invited Salve and had to look down to see her visitor.

She invited him inside warmly. He had not been to her house since the days when he had mended it for her, when she'd first come to the island. He looked about him with an appraising eye to see how his work had held and she felt, suddenly, that she had been a poor friend to him since then. She invited him to sit. He did not.

'You said . . . look after me.'

'Yes,' she said. 'Take this.' She took up the bottle from the decoction table that she had made up that afternoon, with especial guilty care. She held out the vial, confidently in her hand. 'It will save you from your father's contagion.'

He took the little bottle and their fingers touched for an instant. The vial was huge in his hands, and he turned it nervously, as if screwing his courage. '*You* look after *me*,' he said, as if repeating his catechism.

She nodded slowly. 'I look after you.'

'What if . . . *I* look after *you*?'

She looked at him, and he looked back, his hooded, uneven eyes unwavering. For the first time she noticed that his eyes were a muddy blue, like lagoon water after a storm. Slowly, slowly, it dawned on her that she was receiving a proposal.

She took a breath, heart thudding, giving herself time. 'I thank you, Salve, but . . . that is to say . . . I mean, are you even . . .?'

'Seventeen.' The warped palate of his mouth had trouble forming the word. Feyra tried to mask her surprise. She could not have pinpointed his age at all. His deformity made his appearance juvenile but at other times their conversation and his skill at joinery suggested he was a much older man.

She felt a surge of sympathy for him so strong that tears started to her eyes. She had been wrong that morning. He was not a child. He was a man, a man trapped in this attenuated form. She thought of the thousand little cruelties he had probably endured daily at her hands, times when she'd been offhand, times when she'd been so caught up in her misery about Annibale that she had slighted or ignored him. She'd sometimes noted Salve's preference for her, but thought he'd been showing her gratitude for her defence of him from the cruel blows of Columbina Cason.

But now she knew he'd felt something deeper. She had thought once that Salve's hatred of Annibale proceeded from what he'd suffered at the hands of the doctor's mother, but now knew that she had been wrong about this too. She did not want to laugh at him, or to dismiss his suit; perhaps if she confided in him his feelings might be salved.

'I am sorry, Salve, I cannot. I love another.'

He knew it already. 'You love doctor.'

She admitted the truth for the first time. 'Yes.'

And then she saw her terrible mistake. What she had done was not to salve his pride but to break his heart. Instead of just refusing him, she had held to his face a dreadful looking-glass that showed him what he could have been if the shepherd prophet had favoured him. It was worse, so much worse now, since the fire when the beak mask had been burned. Now he could see Annibale's face, see what he could have been, what he could not ever be.

Salve turned, but too late for her to miss the hurt in his eyes, and left her house, still clutching the little bottle of Teriaca.

As Salve passed the well of the lion and the book he dropped the Teriaca down the shaft. Then he strode to the Tezon as fast as his short legs would carry him.

If he thought about the words Feyra had spoken to him, they would curl about his heart like a serpent and squeeze it till it burst; and then he would bleed to death. He must concentrate on his purpose. He wanted the one man who had ever been a constant to him, because despite his father's blaming and belittling of him, Bocca had cared for his freakish son, he had put meat in the misshapen mouth and clothes on the warped back. He had not left as Salve's mother had left.

Salve had to stand on tiptoe to reach the door of the hospital. There were only three patients left in the long room, lit by a brazier burning cinnabar and myrrh. The second curtain he drew revealed Bocca.

Salve stood over the body, and it was only then that he let the tears fall. Bocca could not hear him now so he might as well speak. He uttered the first word he had ever said to his father. '*Papa*,' he said, listening to the word unfurling in the darkness.

Then he lay down beside the still-warm corpse, holding his father close, waiting for death.

Chapter 38

Feyra wept bitterly over Salve as she had never wept for a patient before.

She had neglected and belittled Salve more than anyone else in his life, by befriending him and then taking her friendship away when she'd replaced it with another. It would have been much better to have let him alone, to have never forged a friendship she had not the care to keep. She said his name over and over. She cried until her veil was soaked, and then prepared him herself for his laying out beside his father. She kissed his misshapen cheek, and the rigor of death relaxed and unfurled his hand. In it was her ducat. She kissed the coin too, and slipped it back into her bodice, where it had lain so long.

Having slain the gatekeeper and his son, the Plague seemed to abruptly quit the island.

News from Venice had it that four of the six *sestieri* were now clear of Plague. Feyra suspected that the purifying fire that Takat had spoken of had turned against his purpose, purifying the miasma left by the dead.

As the Tezon emptied as the last cases died or healed, Feyra began to wonder what the future held for her and Annibale. He did not once renew his proposals to her, but she thought she could be happy if she was just here as his colleague and friend. But a hospital could not run without patients. Nowadays she was more often prescribing bark for toothache, or borage for moon-cramps, than her Teriaca.

One spring day when she climbed the Murada, she saw a tall ship pass, cleaving the sunlit waters. She identified it as a Cypriot vessel. A cloud came over her sun, and fear settled in her stomach like a stone. Trade was recommencing between Venice and the wide world. She craned into the far distance and imagined Palladio's church, on its distant island, growing into the sky. She knew that, one day soon, the church would be completed, the Doge would have no further need of Annibale, and the Republic would want their island back.

The following day the Badessa came to them in the herb garden, where Feyra and Annibale were reseeding the botanical beds; a task that they had created for the Tezon was all but empty. Feyra straightened up, hand on her lower back, as the Badessa, followed by her nuns, circled the beds.

Annibale stuck his spade savagely into the ground and did not look at the Badessa. 'You're going back,' he said.

'Yes,' she replied gently. 'Sister Immaculata went back to the Miracoli yesterday. The *sestiere* is clear of contagion. They are appointing a new priest to replace Father Orlando. A good man, I believe.'

Annibale sniffed. 'I'll arrange a dory for you. Bocca . . .' he let his voice trail off.

The Badessa nodded. 'We said masses for his soul, and that of his son. And Sister Ana has already lit the brazier for a boat.'

Annibale nodded in turn, curtly. 'We'll see you off.'

Feyra hesitated, unsure of whether to follow, but found herself invited by the Badessa's beckoning hand.

She walked with the older woman, arm in arm across the sunny green to the gatehouse, and at the gate the Badessa stood back to watch the sisters file though. She reached into her sleeve and handed Feyra a heavy book wrapped in canvas. 'In case you need it,' she said, and walked through the gate before Feyra could refuse. Feyra did not unwrap the book; there was no need. She knew what it was.

At the jetty the nuns got into the strong-bottomed dory one by one, the Badessa too. She turned in the boat.

'Before I go, *Dottore* Cason, there is one more thing. Sister Immaculata visited some of the houses of our island families. Some are empty still, and sound, but some are rotting, and some being taken over by vagrant villeins. If your little community does not go home soon, the Republic will billet families on the dwellings. Many people have lost their houses in the fire.'

Annibale's expression, even without his mask, was unreadable. 'And you have told the families so?

The Abbess's brows nearly vanished into her wimple. 'Of course. They cannot live here always. Even if you can part the waters, you cannot hold back the sea for ever,' she said gently. 'One day it will rush back in.'

Feyra understood. Their strange, infected paradise was coming to an end.

Chapter 39

Dottore Valnetti's anger kept him going, for he had little else to give him succour.

His *sestiere* of the Miracoli was a ghost town. Half the houses were empty, the others stuffed with the dying. He had not been able to shift any more of his Four Thieves Vinegar, and began to drink it in the evening for its alcoholic content alone, for he could no longer afford wine. The tun of Gascon wine which he might have won for having the least Plague deaths in his *sestiere* seemed as remote as a rainbow, for he seemed to scribble Bills of Mortality every day – it was now his sole function as the physician of this ward.

Perhaps because of the other ingredients in his linctus he'd begun to have strange, hallucinatory dreams, all filled with a mysterious dark lady in a green dress, swirling about like a sprite or a jinn. He would wake with a gnawing hunger but no money for bread and no servants to get him any. He'd spent his last coins on the greedy boatman whom he'd paid to take the lady in the green dress to the Quarantine island now known as the Lazzaretto Novo.

Annibale Cason's island.

He had known that Cason was behind it. He was as convinced as he could be that the sorceress was Cason's creature, and that she was somehow funding his lunatic enterprise with her 'Teriaca'. Having Cason and his green witch dragged before the *Consiglio* was now Valnetti's one mission in life. Hatred was his driving force, but he could not eat his hatred.

So when he was offered a strange commission for gold, he took it willingly.

'The *Salamander*? Who is the Salamander?'

Valnetti had had to open his door himself, for his man-servant was long gone, taking the doctor's silver tableware in lieu of wages. He looked down at the small and grubby boy.

'The Salamander,' the boy said, tasting the word, 'is a legend in Cannaregio. He survived the fire, so they call him the Salamander for this and for other of his lizardy properties, *signor.*'

'Like?'

'Well, there's his scaly skin, and he lives in a bath of oil of olives like a lizard in an olive grove, his tongue is forked like a lizard and he—'

'Yes, yes,' interrupted Valnetti testily. 'And have you seen him?'

'No. But my friend Luca has. He saw him through the window. Terrible he was, all burned skin and dreadful eyes, black as sin. Luca said he hissed at him like a demon. For he cannot speak our language.'

'He cannot speak Venetian?'

'Only a few words, *signor.*'

'Then how am I meant to treat him? You're wasting my time,' Valnetti said loudly.

'No *signor*, I'm not,' protested the boy. 'He pays to buy

him bread and fishes. Only us young 'uns, though; he won't have a grown-up near him. The oil for his bath took days to collect: bottles and bottles he needed, sent an army of us out to all the markets. And he has local children running in and out to teach him Venetian, the ones that can bear to look at 'im, that is. He's looking for somebody, and he wants to know enough words to find them. Some of the lads come out fair jingling with coin.'

Valnetti had been about to shut the door. 'Coin?' he said, loudly enough to drown the sound of his own rumbling stomach.

'Foreign coin it is, but bites like gold. See?'

The doctor took the coin from the boy's dirty palm and held it up in the spring sunlight. Currency was one of the doctor's favourite things and he fancied himself quite the expert. The coin was a *sultani*, an Ottoman coin, with a turban-headed caliph stamped on one side in gold relief. Round the turban were little toothmarks where someone had bitten the Sultan.

The boy held out his grubby hand, and Valnetti surrendered the coin reluctantly. 'And he gave you this, did he, this . . . Salamander?'

'Yes, *signor*,' came the reply. 'One for going, and one for coming back again, with a doctor.'

'And where does he reside?'

'One of those empty houses, *signor*, the ones the families left when they went to that island. Next to the church of the Miracles.'

Valnetti considered. Infidel coin it might be, but gold was gold. He fetched his cane and hat. 'Show me,' he said.

Even without his guide Valnetti would have found the house without difficulty. A small army of Venetian children circled it like seagulls, afraid and curious all at once. It sat in the shadow of the Church of Santa Maria degli Miracoli, a church he passed every day. But today something was different.

Valnetti lifted his beaked mask as if he smelt the sound. Singing.

The sweet singing of the sisters of the Miracoli was issuing from the lofty windows of the adjoining convent for the first time in a year. The sisters were back.

Valnetti remembered well that Cason had spirited the sisters away to people his island and run his hospital. Did this mean, then, that Cason's hospital was now closed? The song sounded in his head like a victory hymn.

One of the taller urchins seemed to be guarding the door of the house, his back as straight as a fire iron. At the sight of Valnetti and his little guide he opened the door with an ominous creak to reveal a rectangle of pure blackness. For a moment there was stillness and silence, then a gold coin spun out of the darkness past Valnetti's beak. The boy that had summoned him caught it, and ran. Valnetti, encouraged by the gold, walked into the black.

For some moments he could see nothing at all. He walked further into the pitch, foetid odours rising to his nose and nameless vermin crunching beneath his feet. Somewhere in the room something was breathing in a rapid, laboured way.

Then Valnetti saw a flat reflection as if from a pool, and saw a rippling surface broken by something that resolved, as his eyes adjusted, into a figure. The doctor fumbled in his coat for his tinderbox and struck a light, his heart beating painfully. What he saw almost made him drop the taper.

There was a man in a hip bath, a man who at first glance seemed to have been skinned. His hair and brows were gone, his nose melted away to two black holes. His peeled flesh was the scarlet of the demons that frolicked on the frescoes of next-door's church, and yet here and there was scaled in white where his hopeless flesh had attempted to heal itself. His chest and groin were the most burned, his torso ridged with dunes of arid flesh. The place where his man's parts had been was, mercifully, immersed in the oil, for Valnetti, who had seen many sights in his years of physic, could bear no more horror. The burned limbs stuck out of the bath like monstrous claws, the fingers and toes nibbled and merged by fire into unnatural numbers never meant by God. But the black eyes still burned from the bald red head, eyes so dark they seemed to have an infinite blackness that sucked Valnetti into a soul so murky he could not look upon what dwelt there.

The Salamander's tongue flicked out continually to moisten the aperture where the lips had once been, a tongue not thick and pink but black and pointed like a poker's end, giving him an even more reptilian appearance. Here and there black hairs protruded from the desert flesh as if a fowl had been carelessly plucked.

This man had been badly burned, so badly it was a miracle he lived.

The flame seemed to agitate the creature in some way, so Valnetti, with relief, put the light out. Instantly he felt reprieve, but he could still see the dreadful creature before his eyes, stamped before him on the darkness.

'Help,' it said, in an awful growl, the word corrupted by

the warped tongue, the lack of lips and something else, buried deep below in the man he must once have been: an accent.

'Well . . . that is to say,' Valnetti stammered, 'you are taking the correct measures'. As always when afraid, he took refuge in flattery. 'Oil of olives is most efficacious for burns.' To his own ears his voice sounded as thin and high as a bat's squeak. He began to back away. He would forgo his fee willingly if he could just get away from this hellish place.

'Must find green lady.' The creature from the dark spoke haltingly, but clearly enough.

Valnetti stopped.

'Bring . . . death.'

A light leapt in Valnetti's little eyes. Was it possible the Salamander and he were of the same purpose? '*She* is the one you seek?'

'Journey.'

Valnetti needed to be clear. 'You are looking for the green lady, you bring death and you need to be well enough to make the journey to her.'

The thing in the hip bath nodded.

'You tell, I kill you.'

Valnetti snorted, for the Salamander could barely rise from his oily sump, but the creature hissed at him from the pitch, and there was something in the dreadful sound that made the laugh die on his tongue.

'I can help you,' he said hurriedly. 'I know where she is. I will bring a vial of the juice of the poppy, which will manage your pain upon your journey. I can arrange for a litter to take you a little way to the canal hereby, and have a boat wating to take you thence. But it will cost you –' he wondered how far he could push it '– thirty *sultani*.'

The thing gave another nod.

Valnetti eagerly bent as close as he dared to tell the Salamander where the green lady dwelt. How much more satisfying to let this creature solve his problems. How much more convenient to let the Salamander take care of the green witch and bring her her death. How much less bother than to wade through the painstaking processes of indicting Cason through the *Consiglio della Sanita*. Despite the Salamander's physical infirmities Valnetti had absolutely no doubt that the creature would complete his task before he allowed himself to die. It was the only thing keeping this cinder of a body alive.

As Valnetti left the dank house to make the necessary arrangements, he had a spring in his step. The Salamander had offered him an opportunity to vanquish Cason and his sorceress without getting his hands dirty, and with refreshingly little *bureaucracy*.

Bureaucracy was, really, one of the most tiresome things about Venice.

Chapter 40

The sisters' departure was the first of many leavetakings from the Lazzaretto Novo.

One by one the families returned to their homes to pick up the thread of their lives in Venice and the *quartiere* of the Miracoli. Only the Trianni family was still in the almshouses, and that for a very peculiar reason.

The Badessa had sent word that there was a little local difficulty. The Trianni house, the one right next to the church of the Miracoli, was currently occupied. Feyra questioned Sister Benedetta, the nun who had brought the message, as the burly sister tied up her boat to the jetty. 'I suppose it is to be expected?' she asked. 'Many have been made homeless by the fire, and you cannot blame a family for seeking shelter.'

'Except it is not a family,' rejoined the sister matter-of-factly. 'It is a demon; reportedly a fire demon that has assumed the form of a lizard.'

Feyra stepped back, looking at the nun for signs of a jest, but Sister Benedetta's expression was completely serious. She shrugged her broad shoulders. Demons were her business.

'We will watch and wait and pray, and send word when

the lizard demon is exorcized from the house. But the Triannis should wait, for a week at least.'

Feyra received the news of her friends' stay of departure with relief, but it was tempered by a small and secret disappointment. She did sometimes wonder what would happen when she and Annibale were alone on the island.

That night she dreamed of him, of the heat of him, the weight of him, suffocating, sensuous. She woke gasping, as if someone had laid a hand across her mouth and stopped her breath. The shame poured from her with the sweat. Feyra rose from her bed and crept downstairs to where the fire still burned. She saw the Bible the Badessa had given her, propped on the mantel. She did not want the book in her house, but could not bring herself to burn a gift given in kindness.

In Constantinople the name of God was sacred. If inscribed on paper the paper itself, even the merest scrap, became a thing of great value. Because people wore such scraps about their person, they were often found dropped upon the ground and the citizens of Constantinople would pick up the sacred shreds and tuck them into the walls. Some walls on the busier thoroughfares were saturated with the name of God. Feyra did not want to burn the Bible; although the god named there was not her own, she feared the sacrilege.

Too hot suddenly, Feyra stepped out into the night, just as she was, in her long shift. The ground was cold beneath her feet and she felt a welcome shiver cross her burning skin. A fat spring moon shone to equal the sun, the firmament was baubled with stars and she could see every silver blade of grass as if it were day.

She walked the square of green to the Tezon, her skirt trailing in the dew, soaking and dragging as she went. Inside the empty hospital, the moon lit the atrium of the cavernous space and the ghosts of those she had treated there fled to the shadows. Around the door she could see, as she had seen every day, the scrawled *graffiti* on the walls. The markings seemed to glow faintly in the moonlight; and she saw again the Ottoman ship and the calligraphy that had once been such a comfort to her.

The *graffiti* on the walls spoke of a past tolerance towards the many peoples who had come to trade here, of a relationship of mutual benefit, of the give and take of commerce. This Venice had been a crucible of nationalities and races and religions with as many colours as a prism and she could only hope that, as the Plague faded, this Venice would return. She couldn't help thinking that along with the four horses, the Sultan had sent a fifth: with the cessation of trade he had cut off the city's very lifeblood.

Feyra reached up and touched the word that was clearest to her: *Constantinople*. Once it had meant home. Now this island was her home.

On the way back, Feyra looked up at Annibale's house. The lights were out. In the Trianni house too; all was dark. She decided to walk on and went to the gatehouse. There, the door was standing open; she saw Salve's chair in the chimney corner next to the empty hearth.

She walked right through the gates and out on to the jetty where she had, only this afternoon, waved off Sister Benedetta. She looked out to the lagoon, to the silver pathway of water paved in moonlight, leading to the horizon where the sea met the night. As she watched, the pathway was broken into numberless radiating ripples of light.

A boat.

Feyra watched, suddenly absolutely still, her pulses thudding in her throat as she realized the boat was rowing away from the island, not towards it. She peered into the moonlight. There was a boatman in the craft, but no passenger. What was the meaning of it?

Feyra took a step forward, and saw in front of her a pair of footprints shining on the jetty. They were prints that no human could have made. One was cloven like a two-toed foot or hoof, and the other had three.

Like a lizard.

She crouched down and put her hand to the print. It was still wet and gave off a familiar smell. She dipped a finger in the print, raised it to the moonlight and rubbed it together with the thumb. Then she held finger and thumb to her nose and sniffed once. It was oil of olives.

Swivelling right round, still in her crouching position, she looked back to the gateway. The strange footprints continued to the gatehouse and beyond. She stood too suddenly, and swayed for a minute. Someone *had* disembarked here. She was standing in their footsteps.

Feyra followed the footprints through the gatehouse and lost the trail on the grass. She shook her head. Sister Benedetta's talk of lizard demons had infected her mind: what she needed to do was to sleep.

The first thing she saw as she opened the door of her house was the pages of the Bible scattered all over the room. Then she saw a pile of clothes on the floorboards, a voluminous cloak and a shirt and breeches.

Then she saw the demon himself, stretched out and skinless before the fire, as if the flames had birthed him.

Feyra collapsed, falling into a chair. When she opened her eyes she wished them closed again.

She could see now, that the thing on the floor was a man, but he had been skinned of all flesh. He spoke, a strange strangled sound, for his lips were gone.

'Forgive me. I cannot bear clothes upon my skin, nor shoes on my feet.'

Feyra recalled the forbidden etchings of Andreas Vesalius, declared diabolical by the Christian Church, that she and Annibale used to pore over in the evenings. She recalled the corpses stripped of their skin to show the workings of muscle and sinew, but animate, standing and walking with waking eyes in their heads. This monster had stepped from a book of science, but in his warped hand he held a book of faith, the remnants of the Bible the Badessa had given her.

Feyra knew herself then to be in a nightmare for she understood the demon's tongue. She looked away from him at the pages of Latin scripture scattered around the room.

'Did you do this?' she whispered.

The thing seemed agitated, and rocked its scarlet head. 'I cannot find it. I tried, but I cannot.'

'What can't you find?'

'The white horse. Janissaries are raised Christian. My father was a tower commander in Iskenderun, and a follower of the shepherd prophet. So I knew this infidel book well before I was brought to Constantinople and the light of the true God.'

The familiar name penetrated the fog of Feyra's nightmare. 'Who *are* you?'

He turned his terrible, lashless, browless eyes upon her, burning from their skinned sockets with a fire she had seen before. 'Don't you know me?' he asked.

She nodded, slowly. 'I know you,' she said. 'You are Takat Turan.' In the Doge's palace, she had seen, with her own eyes, the fire spreading across his chest. How could he possibly have survived? 'But – the fire . . . I thought you had died in the fire.'

'I did.'

She knelt then, appalled by his suffering. 'What will give you ease?' She remembered the prints on the jetty suddenly. 'Oil of olives?'

The thing nodded. 'And a physician gave me juice of the poppy.'

Feyra reached for the medicine cabinet, holding her breath, for his exposed flesh stank of putrefaction. She poured the black linctus directly into his mouth, and though it ran down his scorched cheeks, he swallowed some of it. It seemed to give him a little renewed strength.

'I wish to ask a boon of you.'

'Of me?'

'I'm dying.'

This was not the time for lies. 'I know.' Suddenly everything fell into place like a tile of mosaic. 'The fourth horse,' she said, 'is Death.'

'Yes. And now I will greet him face to face.'

She pressed him further. 'But it is not just *your* death, is it? There is more to come before that. The first horse, the black horse, was Pestilence. My father brought that here on his ship. The second horse, the red one, was

Fire. Death is the fourth, the pale horse. What is the third?'

He was silent, his eyes closed.

She repeated, urgently, 'What is the white horse?'

'There is no time. The die is cast. But I must ask my final request of you. I need you to send my bones back to Constantinople. I must be buried among the faithful, and collect my reward in Paradise. Will you promise?'

Feyra stood, her pity gone. 'Tell me of the white horse.' Her voice was cold as stone. 'Tell me first or I will bury you beneath the stones of the church. Here, hard by, there is a temple of Saint Bartholomew.' She leaned close over his dreadful face. 'I will lift the pavings of the very altar and inter you there, I *swear* it. Tell me. The white horse. What else is coming to Venice?'

'And if I tell?' he croaked, fading.

She forced herself to speak gently. 'You will be placed in a casket and sent to –' she thought again. Not the Sultan, for he would not do honour to this man who had given his life for him '– to Haji Musa, the physician of Topkapi. He will give you to the priests and have them pray for you and do honour to your grave. Now *tell* me.'

'There is a room in the Topkapi palace,' mouthed the dreadful lips. 'The Sultan's own chamber. I saw it once when I received my orders. There is a marble floor, set with the designs of the seven seas and all the lands.'

Feyra grew impatient. Takat's mind had begun to wander, as she had often seen at the end.

'He has fleets of ships, my master, cast in many metals,' went on the terrible whisper. 'The ships are as high as his knee. He can move them, just like Allah can move mortals with his hand.'

Feyra set her teeth; he did not have much time left. The crossing of the lagoon must have cost him, and she could hardly bear to think of the pain of every splash of the salt spray on the flayed flesh. She took him by his greasy shoulders, and gave him a little shake, her fingers penetrating the soft tissues.

'Never mind the metal ships. *Tell* me, quick and plain.'

He swivelled his eyes to her. 'The white horse is War.'

Her flesh froze. 'Say on.'

'The Sultan's design was to weaken the city with Plague and Fire. The first horses were just the forerunners. Now, with the spring tides, he is sending an armada to take Venice. It will be the biggest sea battle ever seen. Lepanto will be nothing to it.'

Feyra could see how much it hurt him to talk, the remains of his lips drawn back against the blackened and broken teeth in a permanent snarl, but she had to persist. 'When?'

'The attack will begin on the twenty-ninth day of *mayis*. The day has significance for the Sultan because of the events of 1453.'

Feyra frowned. '1453?'

'You may know the date better in our own reckoning. 857.'

Feyra breathed out slowly. All Ottoman children learned this date in the schoolroom, as the greatest triumph of the Empire over the Western world. 'The Fall of Constantinople,' she breathed.

By now, the thing could only nod.

By the Christian calendar this fateful date was two weeks away. She must act, once again, if she was to save the city from the final Tribulation.

But there was to be no saving Takat Turan. She gave him more poppy, but he was sinking fast and no longer had the strength to keep the decoction between his lipless mouth. She anointed his scaly body once more, but as the fire died in the hearth, so did he, as if the Salamander could not live without his sustaining flame.

Feyra took a shovel and went to the well where the ground was soft, and dug the grave herself. She rolled Takat in his own cloak and dragged him on the cloth to the well, rolling him into the hole. While she was covering the body with the earth, the peaty smell of the loam masking the stench of the cooked flesh, her mother's ring fell from her bodice and swung free on its ribbon.

In the grey of dawn she turned it until the third horse was uppermost, looking at the little prancing white shape set in the crystal.

She felt eyes upon her. The stone lion on the well was watching her from above his book. Feyra dropped the ring and spoke to him. 'Did you know this was going to happen?' she asked. 'Did you foresee this?'

The lion was silent.

'Well, you had better keep this secret too.'

And, suddenly angry, she shoved the spade into the earth until it bit deep and stood, wavering and upright, where she'd left it.

Back at the house she did not look at the oily floorboards as she picked up the scattered pages of the Bible, leafing through until she found the Book of Revelation that she had marked before. '*I heard the second living creature say, "Come and see!" Then another horse came out, a snow white one. Its rider was given power to take peace from the earth and to make men slay each other. To him was given a large sword.*'

She went to throw the pages on top of the smouldering ashes in the hearth, but stopped herself and tucked them instead in a crack over the mantel. Then she walked to the blanket chest below the window. She'd put away the green dress, with a sprinkling of camphor in the folds against the moth's tooth. She had thought she would never again wear it, but she'd been wrong about that, just as she'd been wrong, so many times, when she thought the charge of the Sultan's horses was over.

Feyra dressed carefully in the predawn, smoothing the green dress over her hips one more time and winding her hair around her fingers and pinning it up in the Venetian style. For when the sun was fully up she must go to Venice to visit Palladio.

It was time, at last, to see the Doge.

PART V

The White Horse

Chapter 41

Feyra was back from the city in good time to say farewell to the Trianni family.

Mamma, who had sewn Feyra's green gown, and Papa, who had been snatched from the jaws of the Plague in the Tezon, were helped into their boat first, kissing the hands that had helped them in gratitude. Valentina got in next, now with two babes, little Annibale and a girl she'd named Cecilia at Feyra's suggestion. She kissed Feyra on her cheek just above her veil. 'I won't forget,' she said, as her husband wrung Annibale's hand in thanks.

Now is the time, Feyra thought, as they watched the Triannis' boat sail away. Tomorrow, Sunday, Palladio's plan was to bring her to the consecration of his church. The Doge himself would be in attendance. There was no knowing if the Doge would hear her; would believe her story or would clap her in chains. She and Annibale only had the certainty of tonight.

She unhooked her veil and turned to him.

They were face to face. Here was Feyra, there was Annibale.

He looked at her, half questioning, half smiling, as if he knew exactly what she wanted, as if he'd been expecting it. She was so close to him she could almost feel her flesh against his. Wondering at her courage, she took him in her arms, and he did not protest. She lifted her lips to his mouth. She was about to close in for the kiss when she felt the heat from his face, a sickly heat that she had felt on her cheek a dozen, a hundred times, when she leaned into her dying patients to determine if they still breathed.

The heat she felt from Annibale was not passion, but pestilence.

Chapter 42

Andrea Palladio stood at the back of the congregation and listened to the consecration of La Chiesa del Santissimo del Redentore: his church.

The service was already in progress, but Palladio had not truly heard a word of it.

There was a constellation of richly dressed clergy and nobility crowded at the front in their stifling velvets. There below the altar was the Doge in his golden chair, wearing his *corno* hat and looking every one of his eighty-one years. Below him, on a gilded stool, his cropped head as golden as an archangel's, sat the Camerlengo. Standing in his scarlet robes before them both was Bishop Giovanni Trevisano, Patriarch of Venice, his voice so sonorous and monotonous that Palladio wondered that he did not send the congregation to sleep. He had built the Patriarch a house once in Vicenza, and the man was an utter bore.

It was a warm spring day and the church was packed. The smell of human sweat was overlaid by the choking sweetness of incense belching in white clouds from the silver censers. Palladio was rammed shoulder to shoulder with his neighbour on his left and his right, and his irritation was only slightly offset by the little shiver of pleasure that neither the stout dame on his right nor the fellow on his left

– who must, by his reek, be a fisherman – knew that *he* was the architect of this wondrous place.

Palladio lifted his eyes up to the heavens, away from the crowded pews.

Not interested in the service, he just looked at his church. It was magnificent, and his pride was so great that he felt it literally swell his chest.

The projection of the spaces and masses within the church corresponded beautifully to the exterior façade. The tripartite scheme was reflected in the sequence of the nave, sanctuary and choir. And their separation was reflected not just in changes in floor height but variations in ceiling type, with the paired half-columns giving unity to the magnificent space, soaring from floor to ceiling. There were no frescoes, few paintings and little statuary. Unlike every other Venetian church, the beauty lay not in the decoration but in the building itself. It was not just beautiful, it was *clever*, so clever in its geometry. Palladio hoped that even if the common herd did not see it then God would understand – for were not the heavens and all things in nature constructed along geometrical lines? The golden section itself was exemplified by the curl of a fern, the spiral of a snail, the shell of the humble nautilus. He shifted his feet and looked down.

There he was. The nautilus.

Palladio had had the church paved in red and white *terrazzo* marble and in one of the tiles that the masons had brought him the architect had found a perfect nautilus. The head mason had asked him if they should discard the tile, as it was imperfect, but Palladio insisted that the fossil should stay. It was there now, beneath his feet, and he had set the nautilus tile in pride of place, not hidden, but in the aisle where it could be seen.

When he had first been given this commission he had thought himself trapped in Venice like the nautilus in stone. He had wanted to run from the Plague, to turn his back on the only commission the Republic had ever given him, his greatest work and the start, he hoped, of many. It seemed perfect to him that the nautilus sat at the very heart of the church; it was a jest that he was sure the Almighty would understand.

Above all, Palladio felt enormous relief. The church was not his any more; it belonged to the people and now it was up to the citizens of Venice to make it their own, Sunday by Sunday, week by week, year by year. He might never step into it again, for he never revisited his buildings. They were like a book, once written, closed by the author and never picked up again. His legacy was now out of his hands.

But he was satisfied that this church was good enough for God, for as the church neared its completion the Plague had lessened its hold on the city. He had heard it said on the streets that the Plague had been defeated by the fire that had purified the miasma of the city and that the new miracle linctus of Teriaca had prevented any new cases. But Palladio knew the truth: it was the dome. Feyra's dome, Sinan's dome, *his* dome. He had captured a cerulean orb of heaven and bound it in a sphere to rival the infidel builders of the East. He had completed his contract with the Lord: a church in exchange for Venice.

He knew too, that after this commission, he alone would be entrusted with the rebuilding of the city, so that Venice could emerge from the flames like a Salamander, peeled of her old skin, cleansed and new. There would be so much to build, he thought with excitement. Palladio put his hand to his forehead as if he could shield his thoughts from God, as he recalled the indecent relish with which he had pulled down the old Rialto Bridge. His dearest dream now was to build the bridge anew. He could see it in his mind, a white stone rainbow arcing over the Grand Canal, another keystone in his legacy. And who was more likely to get the contract than Palladio, friend to the Doge?

The thought of his benefactor jolted him out of his reverie with a start.

Where was Feyra?

She had come to him two days ago, resplendent and Venetian to the seams in her green dress, to insist that she meet Venice's duke on a matter of death and life. She would not tell him the meat of the subject, saying it was a great matter for the Doge's ears alone, but he felt he owed so much to her that he had told her to meet him on the steps of the church this very morning. At the close of the service he was to be presented with the order of *La Proto della Serenissima*, Chief Architect of the Republic. He foresaw no difficulties in presenting Feyra to the Doge for in that green gown she could stand up with any monarch alive, but he was worried that she had not turned up as she had promised.

There would be ample time to get to the hospital island and back in time for his investiture. Palladio began to shove his way through the crowds down to the waterfront to hail a boat. The church door was jammed open by the press of people who crowded the steps outside so that he could barely pass. They crammed the foreshore and lined the banks all the way to the Venier Palace and back.

These were not just simple peasants. More than once he saw the wig of a lawyer, the beak of a doctor, the ruff of a teacher. Mothers brought their children. Grown men brought their aged parents. These were Venetians from all walks of life. The only thing they had in common was the look in their eyes: humble, observant, calm, a strange peace coupled with a peculiar determination.

Crafts of every sort crowded the canal, sailing to the church from every direction. One enterprising fellow had even built a raft, which he paddled from Zattere where the less adventurous citizens stood on the bank to get as near as they could to the church and the blessed ceremony. Palladio was astonished, flattered, until he realized that they were not there for him, or even for his church. As he sailed away from his own church's consecration, he realized what it was he was witnessing.

It was faith.

Chapter 43

Feyra had got her wish.

She had indeed shared Annibale's bed on the first night that they were alone. But God had played a terrible trick on her, a just punishment. For she was merely trying to keep the man she loved alive.

She would never know whether the smoke of the fire had corrupted his lungs and let the pestilence in, or whether, having lost his mask, he had breathed in the infected miasma of the Tezon. The truth was that it was *she* who had brought him into harm's way. Once he began to care for her, his own life and health became important to him for the first time, and when *she* asked him to put it at risk, and go into the city unmasked, he had done it without question.

All her intimate ministrations hurt her. The first time she touched Annibale was to smooth the curls back from his hectic forehead in a terrible parody of a lover's caress. She first held his hand to check his fluttering pulse. She unbuttoned his chemise, as she had so long dreamed, only to expose the dreadful swellings in his armpits. She moistened his lips, not with her kisses, but with a sponge soaked in vinegar and water. She would go for long walks in the blackthorn wilderness, not to sigh and moan as lovers do, but to seek, desperately, any new root she had missed, any new flower whose juice might make a remedy.

As with her father before, she tried everything: all the herbs in her medicine belt and all the concoctions in her cabinet. She even leeched him, as she had never done with any of her patients, watching in disgust as the grey undulating creatures fed upon Annibale's dear flesh. But if he believed in these measures, then she owed it to him to try. She lanced the buboes too, but the surgery was no more effective here than it had been on her father. From Annibale's grey pallor she seemed to have merely weakened him further. His eyes were closed, his pulse weak and fluttering in his throat as if he had swallowed a moth.

Then she tried everything of which he would not have approved. She sang the Venetian folk songs she had learned in the Tezon, in the hope that his feckless mother might have sung him at least one such at her knee. She even read a passage from the fractured Bible, pulling the crumpled pages she had stowed in her wall, tangling her tongue around the Latin in the hope that his god was listening.

The only thing she did not try was her Teriaca, knowing that it was far too late for her remedy. She remembered how he had scorned her methods, how he had oft debunked the theories on which her physic was built. What she would give to hear one word from him now, even uttered in anger! He seemed pale, so pale; his face now alabaster, flecked with beads of moisture like a statue in the rain.

She unhooked her face veil to feel his last shallow breaths on her cheek. She would have torn it off for ever, there and then, if it were only for herself; but she would not endanger him further with the miasma of her breath, so she replaced it again. Then, exhausted, she curled up beside him, praying to the God she had neglected, that if he did not wake, neither would she. But her prayers were not answered. At dawn she woke curled into Annibale's back, just as she had with her father.

And it was there that Palladio found her. She was lying with the doctor. They nestled together like the chisels in his pack. They could have been any couple, handsome, well-matched, lying in their marital bed.

But he'd known something was wrong as soon as he'd landed on the abandoned island, walked across the deserted green, peered into the great empty barn-like building at the centre, and peeked into almshouse after vacant almshouse. And now in the last house, he had climbed the stairs and found them.

He knelt carefully on his good knee and lightly touched Feyra's cheek. She turned to him, almost as if she'd expected him. 'I could not save him,' she whispered, as if she did not want to wake the still form. Her eyes were brimming, her veil soaked with tears. 'I tried *everything*.'

Palladio thought of his church, his dome and the people crowding the banks. 'Not *everything*,' he said. 'There is yet one more thing to try.'

He held out his hand to her and she rose reluctantly from the bed, looking back at the body she'd left, as if it were the other half of her, loath to leave him. *'Come and see.'*

He saw her react to the words as if she'd heard them before. Hope flared in her eyes.

She fingered her veil. 'Should I don the green dress?'

He looked at her – her headdress, her breeches, her face veil. She looked unmistakably Ottoman.

'No,' he said. 'You'll do very well as you are.'

Chapter 44

Feyra stood and looked up at the great church, tears starting to her eyes. Palladio had not taken her back home, he had brought her home to her.

The incredible dome, the sentinel minarets, the façade of a temple; she was back in Constantinople and yet in Venice. A church that looked like this, she could enter with impunity. As if in a dream, she began to climb the fifteen steps, past the guards posted at the doors, guards who wore the emblazon of the lion, guards exactly like the ones who had thrown her from the doors of the Doge's palace, then admitted her in her doctor's weeds. Like that latter time, they uncrossed their halberds before her face, this time at the behest of the architect who accompanied her. Unlike that time, both men recognized her at once.

Feyra crossed the threshold of a Christian church for the first time.

The interior was dim after the sunlight, candlelit and smoky with incense. New candles, waxy and white, stood in serried ranks waiting to be lit, while banks of older candles still burned in thanks for the delivery of a city. The candle-light gave the church a warm glow and Feyra was grateful for its welcome, for it was a daunting place for her.

She walked on, to the centre of the cruciform. Below her

feet was a black marble star, denoting the centre of the dome, and she imagined the well beneath where her father lay. She sent a blessing down to Timurhan in her own tongue and his.

Then she looked up.

She turned around and around below the dome. It was a vast and perfect hemisphere, undecorated but painted with a nacreous sheen, like the inside of a shell. She recalled all the mosques she visited in the East, the Harem, Palladio's house, the Tezon, Annibale's house, everywhere she had ever stood until now.

She knelt, and put her hands together as she had seen the sisters do as they prayed for their miracles. She looked up at the altar; at the cross she'd once worn, the cross she'd once cast down a well.

'Please,' she said, in her own language.

Then she said it in Venetian, in case this god did not understand her. 'Save him. Bring him back to me.' If all gods were one god, would not he answer?

But the cross was silent, and she felt a fool. She got up from her aching knees. She should not have come to this place. There was no god, in this church or any other. The temples of Sinan and Palladio were empty.

As she got to her feet, she realized she was not alone. A man was kneeling in a niche, his eyes closed. She recognized him from his *corno* hat, the hat that she had seen depicted in the pamphlets that burned on the streets of Constantinople, the hat that featured on the ducat she wore in her bodice.

She was so muddled by grief that she almost let the Doge be, but a few more moments would not make a difference to Annibale now, and he had always lived for the saving of lives. If she could halt the white horse, it would be a fitting legacy for her love. She went and stood over the Doge until he felt her presence and turned.

'Who are you? How dare you interrupt my private devotions?'

As he stood, furious, she recognized the tall, old hermit who had taken charge of the citizens on the night of the fire. She had been cheek by jowl with him for that whole night.

She had waited for this moment for so long. She looked at the old man, into his bearded face and was reminded of her father. Both men of the sea, they had the horizon in their eyes.

Feyra opened her mouth, but before she could speak, the church doors burst open and a black-clad figure with cropped golden hair strode down the aisle, followed by the sentinel guards. 'Stand aside!' he commanded. And Feyra's arms were seized by the guards. She twisted desperately to the Doge, who took a step back.

'What's amiss?' he asked his chamberlain.

'This,' said the Camerlengo, breathing heavily, 'is the infidel woman we have sought all this time. She arrived at the same time as the pestilence. She well may be an assassin, sent by the Sultan.'

'This . . . child?' The Doge walked over to Feyra, as the guards began to march her roughly down the aisle in the wake of the Camerlengo, who kicked open the great doors to the light.

With a last desperate effort, she twisted from their grip and turned in the aisle to face the Doge. Reaching into her bodice, she held up the crystal ring her mother had given her. With her other hand she tore the veil from her face.

The Doge's voice rang out around the stones. 'Stop!'

The Camerlengo turned too in the doorway, unsure. He voiced the first question he had ever asked of his master. 'But . . . why?'

'Because,' said the Doge, 'she is a Venier.' He did not even glance at the Camerlengo and the two guards. 'Leave us,' he said.

The great doors boomed closed. The Doge lifted a hand to Feyra's cheek, and let it drop.

'Cecilia?' he said.

'I am her daughter.'

'But you are . . .'

'I am a Turk, yes.' Feyra took refuge in urgency. 'There is little time and you must know this. At this very moment Sultan Murad III of Constantinople is mustering a great fleet against you – he comes to take the city. It was one of his Janissaries who fired your palace; one of his sea captains who brought the Plague to you.' She took an unsteady breath. 'I am that sea captain's daughter, and came on that very same ship. And my mother, Nur Banu, Valide Sultan, was once Cecilia Baffo of Paros.' She paused for breath again. 'She told me of her son the Sultan's design on her deathbed, and charged me to warn you of the four horses that come to Venice bringing dire times. I failed to warn you of two of these tribulations, but if I may save you from war and then death, I will.' She held the ring out to him again, untying it for the first time. 'My mother couched the warning in these terms because of the ring she gave me as a surety. Do you see the design of the four horses? I think,' she said, carefully, as she saw his expression, 'that you know this ring?'

The Doge took the thing from her, and touched the little horses with his fingertip. 'Yes,' he said wonderingly. 'I gave it to her myself, one summer, long ago, in Paros.' He paused and looked at her. 'You have risked many dangers to bring me this warning,' he said gently, 'Now, how can I serve you?'

'I just want to be allowed to go home.'

'To Constantinople?'

'No,' she said violently. 'No, that's not my home!' She began to back away, down the aisle.

'The ring?' The Doge held it out to her.

She waved it away. 'It is yours.'

'No,' he said, following her. 'It is yours.' And he placed it on her finger, right there in the aisle, as if they wed. 'For you are a Venier.'

She looked at the ring on her fourth finger, just as her mother had worn it.

'Where is your home?' asked the Doge gently.

'On the Lazzaretto Novo.'

'On the hospital island?'

'Yes.' She pushed open the great door to the outside world.

The Doge shouted after her. 'With the doctor?'

Feyra stopped. *Of course.* The Doge had appointed Annibale in the first place. 'No,' she whispered. 'I live alone.'

Chapter 45

Feyra did not know how long she sat and held Annibale's blackened hand.

On her return from the Redentore the sun had been high in the sky. Now it was low enough to gild his dead face like a reliquary.

She had lived, in those hours, their life together as it might have been – living and healing together, perhaps travelling to the teaching hospitals of London, Bologna, Damascus; perhaps opening a hospital together. She did not, in that imagined span of years, speculate upon how their features might have combined in their daughters and sons. She did not want children, never had, she just wanted Annibale. To be with him, wed to him in whatever way their faiths allowed.

She took the Venier ring from her finger, suddenly obsessed by the notion that they should be betrothed before Annibale was interred. It was a lady's ring so she had to place it on his smallest finger and the crystal shone against the blackened skin. Black bile, red blood, white bile and pale phlegm. All had drained from him now; all humours equalized, all temperaments quieted, all balance gone. The spinning top had fallen.

Even this did not bring tears to her dry eyes. Grimly she

saw that the pale horse was uppermost on his finger, and then she understood. Now she knew that the final horse, the pale horse of Death, had not foretold Takat's death or even the death of Venice, but the death of Annibale.

The lowering sun shone directly in her face and the light brought tears to her dry eyes. She roused herself – the light was fading – she must wash the body and lay him out. Tonight she would watch him in vigil, and tomorrow she would bury him.

She collected a batch of new white tallow candles from her cabinet and laid them by the bed. Then she went downstairs and out to the cemetery, the gnarled roots tripping her and the winding thorns tearing at her robes. She trod carefully around the graves, imagining the skeletons beneath.

The ones she hadn't saved.

At the newest pile of earth swaddling Takat Turan's grave, she stopped and planted her foot squarely in the fresh soil. She remembered her promise to him to send his bones home. She had no intention of keeping it. She regarded the mound of earth. 'Rot there,' she spat, and walked on.

She collected the lime barrow from where it rested against the *murada*, and wheeled it to Annibale's doorway. In the morning she would fold his body into it.

Then she went to the well to draw water to cleanse Annibale's body. The stone face of the lion watched her with his knowing glance. She was tired of him. 'Is this what you meant all along?' she asked the lion. 'Was this your great secret? Well, well done, your prophecy has come to pass.'

She sent down the bucket with a rattle. When she pulled

it up again she saw in the last of the sun that something sparkled at the bottom of the pail. She put her wet hand to the silver gleam and drew out a little tin cross, set on a pin. It was the cross Corona Cucina had given her to pin her jabot across her chest, the brooch she had cast into the well on the first day on the island. She closed her fist round it, squeezing the metal. Hundreds, thousands of buckets had been drawn from here in the last year, yet the cross had chosen to surface for her, on *this* Sunday.

Feyra opened her hand and looked down at the pathetic shepherd prophet hanging from his tin cross. What good could he do her now? He was just a mortal man who had died like Annibale. Then slowly, slowly she remembered his legend.

He had been dead and risen again. The shepherd had risen.

It was a miracle.

Feyra dropped the bucket, spilling the water and cross over Takat Turan's grave. She began to run, past the alms-houses where she'd birthed the Trianni babies, past the Tezon where Salve had been the last to die, past the gate-house where Bocca had once lived, past the church where the Badessa had given her a Bible and back to Annibale's house. She dashed upstairs, her breath bursting in her chest, and stopped, winded, in the doorway.

He had moved.

Feyra rushed to the bedside and dropped to her knees. The hand that she had held, the hand that wore the ring, that she had placed upon his chest with the other, had now fallen to his side. She took it up again, and held it so hard that the ring of the four horses she'd given him broke cleanly in two.

She climbed on top of him and opened his shirt, pressing her ear to his chest. There below the layers of muscle and bone and sinew, she felt a flutter, a tiny thing, like the first few beats of a new-birthed butterfly's wings.

Somehow those vessels and chambers that Annibale had told her of, those valves and atria had come to life. But there was no science to this; this was a miracle of God. Now the tears came as she pressed her lips to the fluttering place, then moved up to his lips.

And as she kissed him for the first time, pressing her mouth to his, he opened his eyes.

PART VI

The Pale Horse

Chapter 46

Saint Mark's Square had never been so filled with such a press of people, not even at Carnevale. This was the biggest naval muster the city had seen since the days of the Fourth Crusade, when the righteous and the ravenous went to feed on Constantinople. Even the preparations for Lepanto, a mere six years ago, had been nothing to this; but the machineries of war had sprung readily into wakefulness. 'Heigh-ho, poor Venice,' said Palladio aloud. 'Here we go again.'

The Doge's palace formed an apocalyptic background. The beautiful white frontage was now a charred ruin. Last week's fire had turned it from the most beautiful smile of white teeth in the world to the blackened snaggletoothed grin of a pedlar.

Palladio shoved his way through whores taking sailors for a last jump before shipboard and wives pleading with their husbands not to go to war. On makeshift stages the players of the *commedia dell'arte* staged dramas featuring the evil Turk as antagonist, each infidel represented by a walnut-stained actor, with an outsize turban, hideous hooked nose and flowing beard.

Hundreds of citizens queued to go inside the Basilica. The fact that the church and the Saint and his sentinel horses had been untouched by the fire seemed nothing short of miraculous. Inside, in the incensed dark, they would pray to the Madonna of Nicopeia, an icon snatched from the Turks themselves, and ask her to keep the infidel from their door. Venice was a cauldron of gossip at the best of times, but in this past week it had boiled over with seething rumour; word that the Turks were poised to take the city had spread faster than the fire.

Palladio ignored the human drama; he was bound to see the Doge. He turned into the Palazzo Sansoviniano, which was, for the moment, serving as the ruler's headquarters. The great painted chamber hummed like a hive, as powder monkeys and naval cadets with barely a whisker between them ran messages. The frescoed walls were obscured by great maps that had been torn from the *Salle delle Mappa* in the palace, some with pieces missing, some with charred edges, some with great cinder-edged bites taken out of them by the fire. And in the midst of it all, like the long silver needle in a compass, was the Doge.

If it were not for the Doge's commanding tones Palladio would scarcely have recognized him. The long scarlet and white robes and the *corno* hat that he'd worn to the Redentore were gone. He wore the blue cloak and garter of a Sea Lord over silver half-armour; the white hair and beard had been closely trimmed since the consecration and he looked thirty years younger.

Today he was not Sebastiano Venier, ageing Doge of Venice, but Sebastiano Venier, *Capitano Generale da Mar* and Chief Admiral of the Venetian fleet in the new war against the Ottoman Turks.

When he tapped Venier on the arm and the Doge turned,

he stared at Palladio blankly for an instant. Then the moment broke. 'Palladio,' he said. 'What do you here?'

'I would like to buy you a cup of wine, for luck.'

'*Now?*' The admiral opened his arms to indicate the mayhem around him.

'It will take one quarter of the bells,' said Palladio evenly, 'and it may make all the difference to you succeeding in this onward action against the Turk.' Palladio held the blue gaze long enough for the Doge to remember that it was Palladio who had brought Feyra to him. If the architect had something to say, perhaps it had better be listened to.

Sebastiano Venier sighed. 'Very well.'

Outside in the melee, Palladio found the *ombra* cart, the wooden truck that hugged the shadow of the campanile as it moved around the square all day. The cart was doing a roaring trade today as the sailors spent their last few sequins on grog. Palladio exchanged two coins for two brimming cups and joined Venier on the dock. The two men sat on a gun carriage and watched the galleasses gather.

Sebastiano Venier looked out into the infinite blue with his weather-eye, as if he could see what lay ahead for him on those foreign seas. He shook his head a little. 'I had not thought to go back out there,' he said quietly. 'After Lepanto, I thought I had done with the Turks. But, as it turns out, they had not done with me. Plague, Fire and now War and Death.' He took a swallow of his wine. 'What have you to tell me?'

Palladio took out a small quill box. 'Have you parchment?'

Venier unfurled a map of the Straits of Patras and turned it over.

'Good.' The architect drew quickly and fluidly. 'Combat, even at sea, is a matter of geometry. What I am drawing here is the architecture of battle, if you will. Now look. If you entice their galleys into *this* formation –' he drew several small ovals '– then you have the advantage. Your new galleasses have superior firepower but greater bulk and move more slowly. Since they have side-mounted cannon, your best bet is to position *two* of them, in front of each main division –' he drew fast to illustrate his point '– to prevent the Turks from sneaking in small boats and sapping, sabotaging or boarding our vessels. If you let the Ottomans make all the movement, then you are master of the game. Hold the line of the Christian ships at all costs.'

Venier looked hard at the diagram, then at Palladio. 'How do you know this?'

Palladio shrugged. 'I'm working on an illustrated edition of Polybius's *Histories*, an examination of Roman battle formations. Just as classical forms have always informed my buildings, it occurred to me that you would do well to wage your campaign on the models of Hannibal and Scipio.'

Venier nodded, slowly, and blew on the drawing to dry it, his cheeks bulging like one of the four winds. 'Thank you,' he said simply. 'I will heed what you say.' He folded the drawing carefully and then spoke, as if he were trying to articulate something. 'I do not hate them, you know.' It was almost an apology.

For a moment, Palladio was at a loss.

'The Turks. You know now my history from my niece's child. Cecilia Baffo became a *Muselmana* and married Selim II of Constantinople. She changed her name to Nur Banu

Sultan. From her son, this Murad III, who has sent these calamities upon our heads, will descend all succeeding Sultans; men whom, I hope, will foster peace between our nations.' He sighed heavily. 'Five centuries of bloodshed is enough.'

Palladio nodded and rose. '*Varenta vu.*' He blessed the Admiral with a valediction as old as the city. 'And may all the good fortune in the world sail with you.'

The architect began to walk away and then stopped, turned back. The Admiral still sat on the gun carriage, holding Palladio's drawing in his hand and studying it carefully.

'I do not hate the Turk either,' Palladio said, thinking of Feyra. 'But I love Venice more.'

Chapter 47

Feyra saw the architect once more, a month after the consecration of his church.

He came to the island when the doctor was still abed. Feyra greeted him alone but happy for Annibale was recovering day by day.

Until she saw Palladio the outside world had troubled her not at all. She had wondered when the island would be requisitioned once again by the state, but none of that mattered really. She and Annibale could go anywhere, just as she'd once dreamed, to any one of the great medical centres: Bologna, Salerno, Damascus, Ascalon.

During her isolation, Feyra had not concerned herself with the war being waged in distant waters. She had played her part and delivered the warning to the Doge. She had seen the ships sail away, she had seen ships return, but knew nothing of the sequel to the events she had set in train. Venice and Constantinople could blast themselves to hell; none of it mattered now that Annibale would live.

But now, with the architect's visit, she wondered about the outcome of the sea battle, and what had happened to the old man with the horizon in his eyes. It was high summer now, and she led Palladio to the sunken pillar on the green, under the mottled shade of the mulberry trees.

'I am here, dear Feyra,' he said, 'besides my own account, on two commissions from the Doge.'

'He is back then!'

'Yes, and he has commanded me to tell you that the Ottomans have been vanquished once more. Due to your information, they had not even amassed in the straits before the Venetian fleet was upon them. The ships were smashed to tinder and by day's end the sailors had to swim back to Constantinople like so many mackerel.' He stopped himself, remembering to whom he spoke.

Feyra was silent, looking at her hands. Because of her warning, the blood of her people had been spilt. *But you are a Venier*, she thought suddenly. *The Venetians are your people too*. The shadows of the mulberry leaves dappled her palms like bruises.

'I said *two* commissions, Feyra.' The architect spoke to cheer her. 'I mean, the second in a professional capacity. The Doge has granted you the island to run as a hospital.' He smiled at her and spread his hands. 'I am out of contract, you see. He said you might need an architect.' He enjoyed the look of astonishment on her face.

'But . . . but what of rebuilding the city?'

He shook his head. 'I would be rebuilding the city by being here. I have fulfilled my contract with God, now I am anxious to sign one with man.'

As well as an isolation hospital, with Palladio's new buildings and the Doge's assistance, Feyra and Annibale were able to found a research infirmary. From time to time the Doge would summon Palladio's doctor to attend him, always insisting that Annibale bring his female colleague. Annibale never actually saw his exalted patient on these occasions, leaving instead the two Veniers alone to forge the relationship they might once have had. While they talked, Annibale would walk about Giudecca, looking up, always, at Palladio's church as he passed, but never going in.

He had a particular reason.

One day, during his convalesence, when he was well enough to take a turn about the green, Annibale and Feyra had stopped at the well of the stone lion to take a rest. As they leaned there in the summer sun, Feyra had caressed the lion's stone mane. 'Thank you,' she said, quietly.

Annibale studied her. 'You say my recovery was a miracle,' he said. 'But how do you account for the well miracles?'

'The well miracles?'

'Countless pilgrims who take water from holy wells, like the one of the old nunnery of Santa Croce, swear that the water protects them from the Plague. How do you account for it?'

Feyra thought of the well where her father lay, now interred for ever beneath a black star of marble set in the floor of Palladio's church. She felt Annibale's eyes upon her. 'I think,' she said carefully, 'that in the last outbreak the water became infected. A rat, a coney, a cur, something fell into it. Some infected matter.'

'And this time?'

She would not meet his eyes. 'This time, I *know* it to be the case.'

'Then why,' he said, probing, 'do the pilgrims not die from this water?'

She said nothing, and he took her hand. 'So was I really a miracle?'

She smiled into the well. 'Yes.'

'Did you give me any of your linctus, your Teriaca, when I was sick unto death?'

She looked deeper into the depths of the shaft, peering for the circle of light that indicated the water. 'No.' She looked at him. He was stronger by the day, the hollows in his cheeks and beneath his eyes filling out, the sun tanning his sickroom pallor to a healthy hue. 'Do you know why?'

'Let me summarize my findings.' He ticked the points off on his fingers. 'You survived the Plague, but your father did not. You had discovered through your trials that the cases of full-blown Plague in the Tezon still died, but no more *new* cases developed in the families that you had dosed. Thus the Tezon emptied and the families went home. You gave your linctus to the gatekeeper's son but not the gate-keeper. You gave a vial to the architect but not to me, and just now you suggested that there might be infected matter, perhaps even the body of a victim, in Saint Sebastian's well.'

She did not breathe, nor look at him. She must keep looking down the well. 'And what are your findings?'

He turned her to face him. 'You were using variolation. You were inoculating your patients against the disease.'

She held his green gaze. 'And you do not mind? We had an altercation about it, do you recall?'

'A conversation,' corrected Annibale, smiling.

'An altercation,' she said, but she smiled back.

'I assumed that you placed a tiny amount of infected matter in your Teriaca.'

'I did.'

'And the rest of the ingredients?'

'Will neither kill nor cure you.' She quoted one of his favourite phrases back to him.

'For the viable constituent, did you use blood or matter from the buboes?'

'I took the matter, dried and ground.'

'From your father?'

The smile died, and he could see that, for the moment, she was unable to speak.

'*He* was the body in the well.' It was not a question, and he abandoned the subject. 'Your instincts were sound,' he said gently. 'I believe in these cases that to develop an immunity the sample must be taken from a source as close to the primary infection as possible.' He looked out to sea, to the East. 'Your father brought the disease here; perhaps he brought the remedy too.' He looked sidelong at her. 'For did not your Prophet say that God did not create a sickness in this world unless he produced the cure as well?'

Feyra recovered herself. 'You have changed your mind upon the subject?'

Annibale sniffed. 'Perhaps. I will grant that you had great success, but there is a deal more research to be done.' He took her hands. 'But now you have told me, you must tell the *Consiglio della Sanita*. The Doge has granted the island – more on your behalf than mine, I am sure – but we must play the game by the rules. His tenure as Doge will not last for ever, and he has suggested that we act within the con-straints of Venetian law. The time has come to register Teriaca as an official medicine.'

Feyra was taken aback. 'But the *Consiglio* will license it and take tithes from the sale.'

'Let them. They can only make up the linctus to the specifications we give them. You will be called upon to list the ingredients.'

Feyra caught the note of mischief in Annibale's voice. '*All* of them?' she asked.

'*Nearly* all.'

Feyra stood before the Tribunal of the *Consiglio della Sanita*.

Annibale went with her, but sat with the clerks on the long wooden benches at the back of the room. A rogue shaft of light picked Feyra out, vibrant in her green dress, beneath the vastness of the dark and gloomy frescoes. She was young, healthy and stood straight as a willow wand, in contrast to the three ancients sitting in judgement on her.

Annibale was not the only doctor present. Three bodies along from him sat Valnetti, huffing and puffing in his beak, his beady bird-like eye swivelling towards Annibale from time to time. Annibale studiously ignored him.

'You know, I suppose,' the first tribune addressed Feyra creakily, 'that women are not allowed to practise medicine in the Republic of Venice?'

'In that case, your honour,' said Feyra, 'I wonder that you took the trouble to summon me here.'

Annibale smiled behind his new beak mask.

The second ancient spoke. 'You have a sponsor here, with a medical licence ratified by the *Consiglio*?'

Annibale stood.

The third tribune spoke. 'This woman works for you?'

'She works *with* me.'

The first tribune, who had been sharpening his quill,

cleared his throat. 'That is enough of the pleasantries. Let us have it.'

Feyra spoke clearly, 'Registration name: Teriaca.' Her voice rang through the vast chamber, now almost without her native accent, as she listed the ingredients.

'Rosemary and sage, rue, mint, lavender, calamus, nutmeg. Garlic, cinnamon and cloves. White vinegar, camphor. And greater and lesser wormwood.'

Valnetti stood, incensed, his cane dropping to the floor with a penetrating clatter. 'That's Four Thieves Vinegar!' he spluttered. 'There must be somewhat else in there! She has to list *all* the major ingredients. Read the statutes, Tribune!'

Annibale stood too. 'As a matter of fact, *Dottore* Valnetti, there will always be variations in the decoction of medicine. The rules set it down that there may be various or additional ingredients in the amount of one hundredth. Read *that* statute, Tribune.'

'Well,' said the tribune to Feyra, '*is* there somewhat else in that bottle?'

Annibale looked from her to the little bottle on the tribunes' desk, glowing green in the same shaft of light that lit Feyra. At the bottom of the bottle lay a little sediment, not more than a few particles of mortal dust. Annibale held his breath, then let it out in a rush as Feyra said calmly, 'There are of course residual ingredients and impurities that occur in the decoction during the making. But they are certainly in the amount of less than one hundredth.'

Valnetti slammed from the room. The first tribune passed the document to the second, who signed it and passed it to the third, who looked up. 'Have you the necessary ducat to register your medicine in the rolls?'

Annibale patted his robe for his mouseskin purse, but

before he could find it, Feyra had reached in her bodice and pulled out a coin, which she laid down on the table where it winked in the light.

Annibale never knew where she got it, but it was a single gold ducat.

Constantinople

Three Years Later

In the silent precincts of the Topkapi Palace, Doctor Haji Musa regarded the casket that had been sent to him.

He knew it was from Venice because of the seal of the lion and the reek of myrtle smoke. They were most assiduous in the Republic, he knew, about quarantine and the rules about disinfecting packages.

Still, to be on the safe side, the doctor summoned a slave to open the package for him, and instructed the eunuch to carry the package gingerly, well away from the Sultan's quarters. The Venetians had been known to send gunpowder with a clasp that sparked when opened to cause an explosion, or poisonous serpents, or even scorpions to the palace. It was midday and the palace was shimmering with heat, so the eunuch carried the box to the Garden of the Lilies, where fountains played and it was shady and cool.

Once in the gardens the eunuch set down the box on the pavings, opened the clasps and gently eased back the lid. There was a long silence, during which Haji Musa could only hear the plashing of the fountains. 'What is it?' the doctor called from his safe distance.

The eunuch was bewildered. 'It is bones,' he said.

The doctor came closer and peered into the casket. He

dismissed the slave and unwrapped the bones himself, kneeling there in his cinnabar robes. It was the complete skeleton of a young male, each bone painstakingly numbered and catalogued, each wrapped about with a tiny scroll of inscribed vellum. Every bone was there, over two hundred in all, from each phalange of the toes to each vertebra of the spine all the way up to the skull. It must have been done by a medical hand.

Haji Musa laid the skeleton out in the courtyard, piecing it together on the warm pavings while the kites screeched overhead, cheated of their carrion for the fellow was long dead. When he was done the old doctor stood up with difficulty and regarded the man. The skull eyed him back from dark hollows. The doctor, perplexed, looked in the box, and there among sprinklings of Venetian soil was a note, written in Ottoman script.

> *Here are the bones of Takat Turan.*
> *He is to be buried in the garden of the Janissaries,*
> *for he was of their number.*
> *I am well.*
> *Your pupil,*
> *Feyra Adelet bint Timurhan Murad*

Haji Musa crumpled the note to his heart with gladness, and bent again to collect the bones. The skull was full of earth; he knocked it irreverently on the pavings and something fell out with a tinkle. He cleaned it off and held it to the light, for his eyes were not what they used to be. He peered at it, puzzled, not knowing what the meaning might be.

For it was a Christian cross.

Palladio had dozed for most of the afternoon, as he was wont to do these days. He had taken to slumbering on the couch downstairs in his *studiolo*, as he no longer had the wind to manage the stairs. Besides, he liked to lie where he could see his drawings.

Sometimes his gaze would settle on the Leonardo, The Vitruvian Man, and remember when he himself had been in his prime, reaching out with outstretched fingertips to test the very limits of his own geometry. Sometimes he would look at the drawings he had made for the new Rialto, painstakingly set down, every angle beautifully rendered and duly submitted to the Council of Ten. But the bridge was destined to live only in his mind and on his wall, for the contract for the new Rialto had been given to another. His namesake Andrea da Ponte was a younger man than he, and, to add bitterness to the pill, had once been his pupil.

Palladio would comfort himself with the thoughts of his great church. He remembered, dimly, a story he had been told once about a temple in the East, where pilgrims had flocked to worship for hundreds of years at the grave of a prophet's standard bearer. But he could neither remember the name of the temple, nor the teller.

On better days, he would raise himself on his elbow and talk to Zabato Zabatini as he drew, directing him to set down his latest ideas. Sometimes his notions took flight into fancy, fantasies that could never be built, only supported by dreams, not by bricks or mortar. When he babbled out these caprices from his couch he could see that Zabato stopped drawing. The draughtsman would take off his glasses and lay them down, wiping his eyes; and Palladio would wonder why he wept.

Today was not a good day. The architect could barely raise his head. He felt as if a great weight were pressing on his chest. He knew the name of the weight. It was Death, and it got heavier each day.

The low sun had begun to hurt his eyes; so when two figures appeared in front of the window, he felt relief from the glare. They seemed to be dressed exactly the same, turbanned and swathed in robes, but one was a man and one was a woman. He thought he dreamed, so there was no harm in smiling at them both, even if they were infidels. The weight on his chest lightened.

The woman held out her hand to him, as he had once to her. '*Come and see,*' she said.

Once in the boat he could see them more clearly. Neither of them wore a face mask as you might expect of their kind. They were both handsome and dark haired, tanned of skin and exactly the same height. They could almost be brother and sister but for the fact that he could see, even with his old eyes, that they were in love. They never caressed each other, their sleeves did not even touch where they sat, but they were somehow as intimate as when he had seen them once twined together on a bed. He knew them now. They were both of them doctors, and they ran the hospital that he had built.

They neared the Zattere sound and the island of Giudecca.

'See,' said the male doctor. 'They have built a bridge.'

Palladio watched the great procession as the boat drew closer. A bridge of wooden rafts had been lashed together so the citizens of Zattere could walk across the canal to his church.

They were coming in their hundreds.

Every man, woman and child carried a candle, and a serpent of shimmering fire wound across the island, over the canal and up the steps into the church.

Palladio could hear a chant swelling, resolving itself into a word. The word echoed over the waters, but his ears were muffled with age. 'What are they saying?' he asked.

'*Redentore*,' said the male doctor. 'It is what they call the church now. Just plain *Redentore*. The *Redeemer*.' The doctor smiled at his partner, as if the word had a special significance for them. 'They are giving thanks to whichever god it was that saved them from the Plague. They are set to do this every year.'

'*Every* year? For how long?

'For ever.'

Palladio felt his eyes fill with tears.

The three of them disembarked by the great steps and joined the procession. They walked up the fifteen stone stairs together, Palladio in the middle flanked by the doctors, who took one of his arms each to aid him. The architect went unmarked by the crowds. Nor did the two doctors raise comment despite their turbans. Now the Plague had passed, physicians had abandoned their beaks in favour of a *biretta* cloth twisted about their heads. And in a strange caprice of fashion, since the Ottoman conflict Turkish styles had become quite the thing among Venetians.

At the threshold the doctors halted and Palladio turned to them, puzzled.

'Aren't you coming?' he asked.

Feyra smiled. 'Just once was enough.'

Annibale shook his head in turn. 'This is your church, but it is not ours.'

Palladio raised his brows.

In reply Annibale opened his robe. He was wearing a trinket in the shape of a *Muselmano* crescent. Feyra did the same; she was wearing its twin. Palladio peered. On closer inspection the pendants were each half of a ring, a glass ring with some sort of decoration on it. Annibale wore the Eastern semicircle and Feyra the West. Palladio looked back to Annibale.

'You converted?'

'Yes,' he replied. 'I did not love my god, but she loved hers.'

'Be careful.' Palladio did not need to explain what he meant.

'Can you manage?' asked Feyra solicitously, at the threshold of the great door.

'Oh, yes,' the architect said. He took both their hands for a moment in a clasp of valediction, and passed into the church.

HISTORICAL NOTE

As well as building some of the most important edifices of the Renaissance ANDREA PALLADIO gave his name to 'Palladianism', one of the most enduring and ubiquitous architectural styles in the world.

He also had a thorough understanding of the geometry of battle, exemplified in his illustration of POLYBIUS's *Histories*. Palladio corrected the manuscript himself, and among his corrections is the amendment of the copyist's mistake 'Hasdrubal' to read 'Hannibal', as he felt the general should be correctly named.

However, following the great fire of Venice, Palladio was not awarded the tender to rebuild any of the major features of the city, except the REDENTORE, a project which he had already begun.

In the right-hand side aisle of this, Palladio's last church, there is a large nautilus fossil set into the floor.

During the Plague years of the 1570s, the quarantine island known as the VIGNA MURADA became an isolation hospital known as the LAZZARETTO NOVO. Under the Austrian occupation of Venice in the eighteenth century, the island was billeted by soldiers, and, after their departure, fell into ruin.

TERIACA became one of the most popular and profitable medicines in the Renaissance world. It was regulated by the *Consiglio della Sanita*, who taxed it heavily.

The process of VARIOLATION, which later became known as INOCULATION, was common practice in Ottoman medicine well before it was known in the West. In modern times strong evidence has emerged for the efficacy of some Plague vaccines, and research into the production of an effective Plague serum continues to this day.

SEBASTIANO VENIER, Chief Admiral of the Venetian fleet and Doge of Venice, is remembered not just for his naval leadership at the Battle of Lepanto, but for personally helping to fight the fire that damaged his palace. It is said he died of sorrow that the city had burned under his rule.

ANTONIO DA PONTE'S RIALTO BRIDGE became one of the most famous bridges in the world, and perhaps the single piece of architecture that most defines Venice.

At LA CHIESA DEL SANTISSIMI DEL REDENTORE, every year on the third Sunday in July, the people of Venice cross on a raft from Zattere to Giudecca, and give thanks to God at Palladio's church for saving the city from the Plague.

ACKNOWLEDGEMENTS

This book began with a breakfast; not at Tiffany's, but at Claridges.

I was there with film producer Ileen Maisel, who asked me if I'd ever thought of writing about Palladio. I'd like to thank Ileen, first of all, for asking that question. This was back in 2008, the quincentenary of the architect's death, and there happened to be an exhibition of his work at the Royal Academy that very day. I finished my breakfast and walked round the corner to the RA and spent the morning looking at every plan, picture and model. I was hooked. I bought the biggest book I could find in the museum shop and went home to devour it. This comprehensive volume, *Palladio* (2008) edited by Guido Beltramini and Howard Burns, and published in association with the Royal Academy of Arts, was invaluable to me in the writing of this book. Palladio lived in interesting times; in Venice – as in London – plague and fire visited the city close together, and the opportunity to write about this period, with the building of the church of the Redentore as the spine of the story, seemed too good to miss.

Two other volumes, among the many excellent books that I read in the course of research for this book, deserve a full citation. Miri Shefer-Mossensohn's *Ottoman Medicine: Healing and Medical Institutions 1500–1700* (2009) provides an excellent overview of the development of Turkish medical practice. And Philip Ziegler's *The Black Death* (2010) gave me a detailed insight into the more old-fashioned plague cures of earlier outbreaks of the pestilence.

Some of the locations in this book, such as the magnificent Redentore on the island of Giudecca, are easily visited. But the most interesting trip I took in the name of research was to the Lazzaretto Novo itself – the mysterious plague island far out in the Venetian lagoon. Trips are infrequent and access limited, so I would like to thank Giorgia Fazzini for permission to visit such a fascinating place, and for the opportunity to peruse the small but incredibly valuable museum there. I must also acknowledge the voluntary organization Ekos Club, who so carefully maintain the archaeology and ecology of the island.

Thank you also to two fantastic research assistants: Richard Brown who covered the Western aspects of the novel, and Yasemin Uğur who checked the Eastern sphere by verifying Turkish terms and spellings for me. Thanks also to my sister, archaeologist Veronica Fiorato, who gave me the benefit of her expertise on plague graves and skeletal remains.

Thank you to my father Adelin Fiorato who, quite apart from being a fount of Renaissance knowledge, lent a great deal of his character to my portrait of Palladio.

I'm grateful, once again, to costume designer Hayley Nebauer, who tirelessly perused her own archives and Renaissance paintings to check details of Venetian costume.

Thanks to Caroline Westmore and the fantastic team at John Murray for all their dedicated work in the production of this book.

And above all, thanks to my editor Kate Parkin and my agent Teresa Chris, who not only fulfilled their usual roles with their customary excellence, but were also there for me this time in the crucial planning stages of the story; fittingly, over a *very* long lunch at the Royal Institute of British Architects!

Last, but by no means least, I have to thank the central characters in my own story: Sacha, Conrad and Ruby.